EVERYONE L...

Johanna Lindsey

New York Times Bestselling Author of

"Her stories prove that love is timeless. Ms. Lindsey sustains the sensuality of her story from cover to cover. You can almost smell the flowers, feel the wind, and touch the hero."

Romantic Times

"The stories are fast moving and well written, with characters revealing themselves to us through lively dialogue."

Chicago Sun-Times

"Congratulations, Johanna! We look forward to more of the same!"

Affaire de Coeur

Hearts Aflame

Johanna Lindsey

AVON BOOKS ◆ NEW YORK

For Ralph,
because he liked the first one.

HEARTS AFLAME is an original publication of Avon Books. This work has never before appeared in book form. This work is a novel. Any similarity to actual persons or events is purely coincidental.

AVON BOOKS
A division of
The Hearst Corporation
1350 Avenue of the Americas
New York, New York 10019

First Avon Printing: June 1987

AVON TRADEMARK REG. U.S. PAT. OFF. AND IN OTHER COUNTRIES, MARCA REGISTRADA, HECHO EN U.S.A.

Printed in the U.S.A.

RA   15   14   13   12   11

Chapter One

Norway 873 A.D.

*D*irk Gerhardsen dropped to the ground and then elbowed his way closer to the river where the golden-haired girl had stopped. Kristen Haardrad looked once behind her, as if she might have heard him, then tethered her great stallion and walked right to the water's edge. To the left, the Horten Fjord flowed swiftly on its course. But here a spattering of boulders kept the currents at bay, and the water was smooth, calm, like a still pool. Dirk knew from past experience that it would be deliciously warm, too, and much too inviting for the girl to ignore.

He had known Kristen was coming here when he saw her leave her uncle Hugh's house and ride this way. When they were younger, much younger, they used to swim here together with her brothers and cousins. Kristen had a large family: three brothers, an uncle who was Jarl on this side of the fjord, and dozens of distant cousins from her father's side, all of whom thought the sun and moon rose in this one girl.

Dirk had thought so too, until recently. He had taken his heart in hand and asked Kristen to marry him, as so many others had done before him. She had turned him down—gently, he grudgingly admitted—but still the disappointment was nearly devastating. He had watched

1

her grow from a tall, awkward child into a majestic, stunning woman, and there was nothing else he wanted quite so much as he wanted to call Kristen Haardrad his own.

Dirk held his breath as she began to remove her linen gown. He had hoped she would. It was why he had followed her, knowing that she might, hoping, and— Odin help him—she did. The sight was almost more than he could bear—the long, shapely legs . . . the gentle curve of her hips . . . the slim, straight back covered only by a thick tawny braid. Just a fortnight ago, he had held that thick braid in his fist and forced her lips to meet his in a kiss that fired his blood to near madness. She had slapped him soundly for it, a blow that actually staggered him, for Kristen was no small, weak-limbed girl; she was in fact only two inches shorter than he, and he was six feet tall. This did not daunt him, though. At that time, at that moment, he had felt he really would go mad if he couldn't have her.

It was fortunate that Kristen's older brother, Selig, had intruded, but unfortunate that it was precisely when Dirk had reached for her again and was wrestling her to the ground. He and Selig both bore wounds from that encounter, and Dirk had lost a good friend in Selig— not because they fought, for Norsemen were ever ready to fight for any reason, but because of what he had attempted to do to Kristen. And he could not deny he would have taken her, right there on the floor of her father's stable. He would have been dead now if he had succeeded. And it was not her brothers or cousins he would have had to fight, but her father, Garrick, who would have killed Dirk with his bare hands.

Kristen was covered now by the water, but the fact that Dirk could no longer see all of her did not cool the fire running through his veins. He had not thought what torture it would be to him to watch her swimming. He had only reasoned that she would be alone, far from her family, and that this might be the only time he would ever find her alone again. There were rumors she was to wed soon, to Sheldon, the oldest son of Perrin, her father's best friend. Of course there had been rumors before, countless times, for Kristen had seen nineteen winters, and in the last four years nearly every able-bodied man along the fjord had asked for her to wife.

She was floating now on her back, the tips of her toes visible, the creamy tops of her thighs, her upthrust breasts—Loki take her, she was asking to be ravished! Dirk could withstand it no longer. He tore his clothes off in his haste.

Kristen heard the splash and looked in the direction she assumed it came from, but there was nothing there. Rapidly she turned a full circle, but the warm pool was empty except for her, the only ripples in the water those she caused. Nonetheless, she started swimming toward the bank where her gown lay, along with the only weapon she had with her, her jewel-hilted dagger, which was worn more as an ornament than for protection.

She had been a fool to come here by herself, instead of waiting for one of her brothers to join her. But they were busy readying her father's great Viking ship that Selig would be taking east next week, and the day was so beautifully warm after a cool spring and an exceptionally cold winter. She had been unable to resist the temptation.

It had seemed like an adventure to do what she had never done before, and she did so love adventure. But all of her previous adventures had been shared with others. And mayhap it had not been the wisest thing to remove all of her clothes, though at the time it had seemed a deliciously wicked, bold thing to do, and if Kristen was anything, she was bold. It was always after the fact, as now, that she regretted being so bold.

Just as her feet touched bottom, he rose in front of her, big and threatening. Kristen groaned inwardly that it was Dirk instead of someone else, for he had already tried once before to force his will on her, and the look on his face was the same as it had been that day a fortnight ago. He was a brawny man of a score and one years, the same as her older brother, Selig. In fact they had been the best of friends, being the same age. She had thought Dirk was her friend too, until that day he attacked her in the stable.

He was changed from the boy she had grown up with, ridden and hunted with, swam with in this very pool. He was as handsome as ever with his dark-gold hair and gold-brown eyes. But he was not the same Dirk she knew, and she very much feared that what had happened that day in the stable was about to be repeated.

"You should not have come here, Kristen." His voice was low, husky.

His eyes were caught by the beads of water sparkling like diamonds on her long spiky lashes. More dripped over her high cheekbones and the small straight nose. Her tongue came out to lick the moisture from her full lips and he groaned.

Kristen heard him and her eyes widened, not in alarm, but in anger. Those eyes, so like her father's, a cross between the sky and the sea and the land, with a sunburst behind them to make them a clear, light aqua color. Only right now they were more turquoise, turbulent, like the foaming waves of a storm-tossed sea.

"Let me pass, Dirk."

"I think not."

"Think again."

She did not raise her voice; she did not have to. Her fury was evident in every line of her heart-shaped face. But Dirk had a monster riding his back, the monster of lust. Gone were his earlier thoughts of how fortunate he had been not to have ravished her before.

"Ah, Kristen." His hands rose to grip her bare shoulders, holding her firm when she tried to shrug him off. "Do you know what you do to me? Have you any notion of how a man can lose his mind in want of a woman as beautiful as you?"

Dangerous currents glittered in her eyes. "You *have* lost your mind if you think to—"

His mouth came down brutally to silence her. The hands gripping her shoulders pulled her close, crushing her full young breasts to his chest.

Kristen felt suffocated. His mouth was bruising hers painfully and she hated it, hated the feel of his body pressed so close to hers. The fact that they were so similar in height brought his manhood probing directly at the portal he sought, and she hated that most, for she was not ignorant of the ways between a man and a woman and what they did together when they made love. Her mother, Brenna, had long ago explained all aspects of lovemaking to her, but this could not be called that, not when she felt only revulsion.

She damned his brawny strength as she struggled to break his hold on her. She admired strength and courage in a man, but not when it was directed against her will. It would not be difficult for Dirk to find the entry and steal her maidenhood from her. She would kill him if he did, for that was something he had no right to take. It was hers to give, and when she found the man she wanted to give it to, she would do so gladly. But it would never be like this, and Dirk Gerhardsen was not the man.

Catching his full lower lip between her teeth, she bit down hard, her nails digging into his chest at the same time. She increased the pressure on his lip until he took his hands away from her; then she directed him to move sideways until they had changed places. He could have struck her to make her let go, but of course she would have torn his lip wide open if he had and undoubtedly he realized that. But she took no chances, keeping her teeth clamped hard on his lip until she unexpectedly brought her feet up to his belly.

Kristen released his lip at the exact moment she used his stomach for a springboard, thrusting herself toward the bank and Dirk backward into the deeper water. His falling back gave her enough time to exit the water and have her dagger gripped firmly in her fist before he reached her. But he did not try. One look at her weapon gave him ample pause.

"You are as full of tricks as Loki's daughter!" Dirk bit out painfully, wiping the blood from his lip, his brown eyes glaring furiously at her.

"Do not compare me to your gods, Dirk. My mother raised me a Christian."

"I care not what god you believe in," he retorted. "Put the knife down, Kristen."

She shook her head at him. She was calm now, he could see, now that she had a weapon in her hand. And, by Odin, she was magnificent, standing there stark naked with water glistening all over her, her breasts taunting him with their fullness, her soft, flat belly above that thatch of tawny gold hair between her legs. And she was daring him, daring him to make the slightest move toward her, and holding the knife as if she knew exactly how to wield it.

"I think your mother taught you more than to love her God." Bitterness rose in his voice. "Your father and brothers would never have taught you skill with that toy, nor condoned your learning, for it would be a slight to their ability to be able to protect you. The Lady Brenna taught you her Celtic tricks, did she? After all these years she should have learned her Celtic skill is no match for a Viking's. What else did she teach you, Kristen?"

"I know the use of every weapon save the axe, for that is a clumsy instrument of death that requires no skill to wield," she answered proudly.

"Clumsy only because you have not the strength to wield it," he replied sourly. "And what would your father say if he knew? I wager he would take a strap to you and your mother both."

"Will you tell him?" she taunted.

He glowered at her. Of course he wouldn't tell her father, for then he would have to explain how he came to know. And the curving grin on her lips said she understood that. And thinking of Garrick Haardrad, who was half a foot taller than he and still a fine figure of a man even at two score and six years, cooled some of Dirk's ardor—but not all of it.

His brown eyes probed hers. "What is wrong with me, Kristen, that you will not have me?"

This question took her by surprise, coming as it did with a note of confusion and softly uttered. He was as bare to the eye as she was, standing in stiff pride before her, and her eyes hesitantly moved over his long body. She was not unnerved by what she saw, for she had seen grown men naked when she and her best friend, Tyra, had snuck into her uncle's bathhouse and hidden behind the water barrel to watch several of her cousins bathing. Of course, this was more than ten years ago, and there was yet another difference now from then. She had never before seen a man's instrument of pleasure standing so straight and proud as Dirk's was.

Kristen answered him truthfully, for what it was worth. "There is nothing wrong with you, Dirk. You have a very fine body and are pleasing to look upon. Your father has a rich farmstead, and you are his heir. A woman would be pleased to have you for husband."

She didn't add that Tyra would make a pact with the gods to have him and this was why Kristen wouldn't consider him. Tyra had been in love with this man for the last five years, but he didn't know that. And Kristen had sworn never to tell her friend's secret to anyone, least of all to Dirk.

"You are simply not for me, Dirk Gerhardsen," she finished firmly.

"Why?"

"You do not make my heart beat faster."

He stared incredulously at her, demanding, "What has that to do with marriage?"

Everything, she told herself. To him, she said, "I am sorry, Dirk. I do not want you for my husband. I have already told you so."

"Is it true you will marry Sheldon?"

She could lie and use that excuse to get out of this predicament, but she didn't like lying just to make things easy. "Sheldon is like a brother to me. I have considered him, since my parents would like me to wed him, but I will reject his suit, too." *And he will be delighted,* she added to herself, *for he thinks of me as a sister, too, and feels just as uncomfortable with the thought of a marriage between us as I do.*

"You will have to choose someone, Kristen. Every man along the fjord has asked for you at one time or another. You should have been wed long ago."

This was not a pleasant subject for Kristen, since she knew her situation better than anyone, and there was not a single man along the river that she wanted to marry. She wanted a love like her parents had, but knew that eventually she would have to settle for less than that. She had been postponing it for several years now by rejecting all suits, and her parents had let her because they loved her. But she could not continue to do so indefinitely.

She became angry with Dirk for reminding her of her plight, which had been ever present in her mind for the last year. "Whom I choose will not concern you, Dirk, for it will not be you. Turn your mind to finding another, and please do not bother me again."

"I could take you, Kristen, and force you to wed me," he warned her softly. "Because you have turned down so many offers, your father could well give you to me after I ruin you for another. It has been done before this way."

It was a possibility. Of course her father would beat him near to death first. But if Dirk still lived after that, she just might be given to him to wed. The fact that she would no longer be a maiden would have to be considered.

Kristen scowled at him. "If my father did not kill you, then I would. Do not be a fool, Dirk. I would never forgive such a foul trick."

"But you would be mine."

"I tell you I would kill you!"

"I think not," he said with too much confidence for her liking. "I think the risk would be worth it."

His eyes were on her breasts as he said this. Kristen stiffened. She should never have stood here talking to him. She should have leaped on Torden and ridden straight away instead of grabbing her dagger to face him.

"Then try it now, curse your eyes, and I will kill you beforehand!" Kristen hissed.

Dirk eyed her weapon again and saw her raise it in just such a way that it would surely find a mark before he could get it away from her. If only she weren't nearly as tall as he was, and had the strength to go with the height...

His own anger rose again, but it was directed now at her mother for being crazy enough to teach her daughter a warrior's skill. He growled low. "You will not always have that toy in your hand, Kristen."

Her chin rose a notch. "You are a fool to warn me. Now I will be sure never to be caught alone again by you."

He seethed at that. "Then be sure you lock your door while you sleep, too, for somehow, one day soon, I will manage to have you."

Kristen didn't deign to answer that threat, but stooped to pick up the clothes at her feet and toss them over her shoulder. Without taking her eyes from Dirk, she reached behind her for Torden's reins and backed away with her horse. When she was several feet away, she gripped Torden's silky white mane and leaped onto his back, setting him to heel instantly.

Behind her she could hear Dirk's angry curses, but she gave no thought to that, worrying now only about wiggling into her clothes without slowing the steed, before she reached the Haardrad settlement and someone saw her. She would never be able to explain, and the truth would find her with severe restrictions placed on her freedom, and Dirk Gerhardsen in a heap of trouble.

If it weren't for those restrictions she would confess what had happened, but she valued her freedom too much. Her father worried about her enough as it was. Her mother didn't, for Brenna had taught her well to protect herself all those many summers when her father had sailed to trade his goods, taking her brothers with him. Brenna had taught Kristen in secret all that she had learned from her own father: the skill and cunning necessary to wield a weapon against a mightier foe, the cunning because even though Kristen was nearly half a foot taller than her mother, and her strength was greater than that of most women, she still lacked the strength of a man.

Kristen was proud of her ability to protect herself, but

this was the first time she had ever had need to test that ability. She could not openly wear weapons the way a man did, for her father would be furious if he knew what her mother had taught her. She did not want to wear weapons anyway, for she was just as proud of her femininity.

Kristen was loved and cherished and protected by her family. Besides her brother Selig, who was two years older than she, there was Eric, who had seen sixteen winters now, and Thorall, who had seen fourteen, and they were both nearly as big as their formidable father already. She also had her cousin Athol, who was only a few months older than Selig, and dozens of other second and third cousins from her father's side of the family who would fight to the death at even the slightest insult to her. No, she was well protected and did not need to prove herself as her mother had felt the need to do when she was Kristen's age.

Until today. If only she were sailing with Selig and his friends next week to the market towns in the East, then she wouldn't have to worry about Dirk again—at least, not until she returned at the end of the summer. By then he could well have found himself a wife and lost the inclination to bother her again.

Alas, she had already asked to go on this trading voyage and had been refused. She was too old now to sail with so many young men, even if it *was* one of her father's ships, with Selig in charge. If Garrick wasn't going, then she wasn't going and that was that. Even her teasing hint that she might meet another merchant prince like him in Birka or Hedeby and bring home a husband, had not swayed him. If he couldn't be there to look after her as he had done the three times he had let Kristen and her mother sail with him, then, by Odin, she was staying home.

Garrick had not sailed these last eight years, preferring to spend the warm summer months with Brenna, letting his friend Perrin command his ship, or Selig, now that he was old enough. Kristen's parents would ride north, alone, and not return until summer waned. They hunted together, explored, and loved, and Kristen dreamed of a relationship like theirs for herself. But where was there a man like Garrick, who could be gentle with those he loved, but oh so dangerous and threatening to those he did not, who could make her heart beat faster the way Brenna's did when she simply looked at Garrick?

Kristen sighed and rode for home. There wasn't such a man, not here. Oh, there were a few gentle men, but not many, though there were many who could be and were quite dangerous. The northlands raised a hardy lot of men, fine specimens of men, but no one she had met had stirred her young heart yet. If only she could sail east with Selig. Somewhere surely there was a man fated for her, mayhap a merchant or sailor like her father—a Dane, perhaps, or a Swede, or even a Norseman from the South. They all traded in the great market towns of the East. She only had to find him.

Chapter Two

*K*risten waited in the closed-off cooking area for her mother to come downstairs. Selig would be sailing in the morning at what in other parts of the world would be called the dawn, but since the sun only set for a few hours each night in the summer this far north, it could not be called dawn here.

Including Selig, there would be a crew of thirty-four men. A few of them were cousins, but mostly they were friends, younger sons and even older ones, all lovers of the sea. The cargo well would be full of the furs each man had to trade, and other items of value that had been made over the dark winter months. There were fifty-five furs that Kristen's own family had gathered this winter, including two of the prized white polar bear skins that brought such a high price in the East.

It would be a profitable voyage for everyone, and Kristen had to try at least once more to be included. Selig had said he wouldn't mind, but of course he found it difficult to refuse her anything. Since her father had said no three times again this last week, her mother now was her only chance to change his mind.

The servants were preparing the evening meal. Foreigners all, they had been captured on Viking raids to the southern lands and to the East. Those who served the Haardrad family were all bought, though, for Garrick had not raided since he was a youth, nor had Selig since he began sailing in his father's stead. It was a subject that sometimes caused arguments between Kristen's parents, for her mother had been just such a slave, captured by Garrick's father and given to Garrick back in the year 851. Of course, Brenna, with her fierce pride, had never acknowledged that Garrick had owned her, and some of the tales they told of each other were of bitter struggle that was tempered by the love they now shared.

Kristen couldn't imagine her parents at odds with each other as they once were. Oh, there were still occasional fights between them, and Garrick would ride north to cool off sometimes. But when he returned, her parents would lock themselves in their chamber for hours, and when they finally came out, neither could recall what they had fought about. All of their arguments, big and small, ended in their chamber, which was a source of amusement and teasing for the rest of the family.

Bored with waiting, Kristen was pestering Aileen for some of the sweet nuts the cook was adding to the bread she was making. Kristen cajoled her in Aileen's Gaelic tongue, which usually worked to soften the woman. From the servants, who had come from so many different lands, Kristen had learned a variety of languages, and could speak each one like a native. Hers was an active mind, always eager to learn new things.

"Leave Aileen alone, love, before your father's favorite nut bread becomes plain old flat bread."

Guiltily Kristen swallowed the last of the nuts she was chewing before turning to face her mother with a grin. "I thought you would never come down. What did you whisper to Father to make him carry you upstairs like that?"

Brenna blushed prettily and with an arm about her daughter's waist, steered her into the hall, which was empty with all the men down at the fjord loading the cargo on the ship. "Must you say things like that in front of the servants?"

"Say it? They all saw him pick you up and—"

"Never mind." Brenna grinned. "And I did not whisper anything to him."

Kristen was disappointed, having hoped to hear a deliciously wicked confession from her mother, who was always so outspoken on all subjects. Seeing her disappointment, Brenna laughed.

"I did not have to whisper anything to him, love. I simply nuzzled his neck. Garrick has a very sensitive spot on his neck, you see."

"That could make him so lusty?"

"Very lusty."

"Then you provoked him. Shame on you, Mother!" Kristen teased.

"Shame on me? When I have just spent a very pleasant hour with your father in the middle of the day, and with him so eager to get down to the landing? Sometimes a woman has to take matters into her own hands when her husband is so busy."

Kristen made a sound that came out very much like a giggle. "And did he mind it, your taking him away from the fun of seeing the ship loaded?"

"What do you think?"

Kristen smiled, knowing very well he wouldn't have minded at all.

Her mother did not act like other mothers, nor did she look like other mothers. Besides the raven hair from her Celtic heritage, and her warm gray eyes, she looked much too young to have full-grown children. Although she was nearly two score years, she looked much younger than that.

Brenna Haardrad was a very beautiful woman and Kristen was most fortunate to have inherited her mother's features, though her height, tawny-blond hair, and aqua eyes she had solely from her father. She could at least thank God she wasn't as tall as her father and brothers. Brenna had often done so, although here in the North, Kristen's unusual height was not the problem it might have been elsewhere, for the Norsemen were either as tall as or taller than she. In Brenna's own land, though, it would be a definite disadvantage, for Kristen would be as tall as some men, but taller than most.

"Surely you were not waiting on me just to ask me impertinent questions," Brenna said now.

Kristen looked down at her feet. "I was hoping you might have a few words with Father now that he is in such a good mood, and ask him—"

"If you can sail with your brother?" Brenna finished for her, shaking her head. "Why is this voyage so important to you, Kristen?"

"I want to find a husband." There, she had said what she couldn't say earnestly to her father.

"And you do not think you can find one here at home?"

Kristen gazed into the gentle gray eyes. "There is no one I love here, Mother—not the way you love Father."

"And you have considered everyone you know?"

"Yes."

"You are telling me you cannot accept Sheldon?"

Kristen had not meant to let her parents know of her decision so soon, but she nodded her head. "I love him, but in the same way I love my brothers."

"Then what you want is to wed a stranger?"

"*You* wed a stranger, Mother."

"But your father and I knew each other a long while before we finally admitted our love and wed."

"I do not think it will take me so long to know when I am in love."

Brenna sighed. "Aye, I have armed you well with the knowledge I did not have myself when I first met your father. Very well, love, I will speak to Garrick tonight, but do not hope for him to change his mind. I am of a like mind in not wanting you to go off with your brother."

"But, Mother—"

"Let me finish. If Selig returns in time, I believe your father can be persuaded to take you south to look for a husband."

"And if summer is nearly over when he returns?"

"Then it will wait until spring. If I am to lose you to a man farther south, then I would rather it wait until spring . . . unless you are eager to have a man now?"

Kristen shook her head. This was not exactly what she had in mind. She wanted to be away now, away from the threat Dirk posed, but she couldn't tell her mother about that, either, for Brenna was likely to go after Dirk herself.

"But I will be a year older," Kristen pointed out, hoping that would sway her mother.

Brenna smiled at her daughter, for Kristen did not realize how truly desirable she was. "Your age will not matter, love, believe me. They will fight over you when they know you are looking for a husband, just as they have done here. Another year will make no difference."

Kristen said no more about it. They sat down before the open door that let in the warm breeze and the only daylight. The large stone house built by her great-grandfather had no windows, in order to keep out the bitter cold of winter. Kristen was helping Brenna work a large tapestry, for her mother had no patience to do it alone.

Impulsively, Kristen asked, "What would you do, Mother, if you wanted to sail on that ship?"

Brenna laughed, thinking the matter settled. "I would steal away on it and hide in the cargo well for a day or so, until it would be far away from here."

Kristen's eyes rounded incredulously. "Would you really?"

"Nay, love, I am only teasing. Why would I want to sail without your father?"

Chapter Three

*T*he seed had been planted and Kristen couldn't shake it. Her mother had only spoken in jest about stowing away on the ship, but there was that small grain of truth in what she said that couldn't be ignored. Brenna was bold enough to do it, for she had done wilder things before. Hadn't she rounded the fjord in the dead of winter to get back to Garrick after she had been stolen away from him before they were married? Kristen could be that bold, too. She could keep her freedom and avoid Dirk in the same stroke, and it would be an adventure. It was the thought of adventure that really sparked her fancy.

There was only one thing wrong with the idea. She had been forbidden to go, and there would be hell to pay when she returned. But in her excitement, Kristen conveniently refused to think of that, or let Tyra harp on it when she told her friend what she was going to do. Tyra had been amazed, but Tyra had lost her love of adventure when she outgrew childhood. Not so Kristen.

The girls were in Kristen's chamber upstairs, the only place that offered privacy from the farewell feast in progress below. The crew would be sleeping in the hall tonight. Tyra had come with her father to bid her brother Thorolf good-bye, for he had been here the last few days helping with the preparations. Kristen was glad he was sailing, for they were close friends. She had even tried to teach Thorolf some of the languages she had learned when they were younger, though he was not an apt pupil. Thorolf would probably be the only one who would champion Kristen when Selig and her three cousins who were sailing began upbraiding her for her foolishness.

Selig would indeed be angry, as well as her cousins Olaf, Hakon, and Ohthere, the oldest of the three. But as long as they were far enough from land when she was discovered, making it unfeasible to bring her back, then they would all relent after they vented their anger on her. Verbal abuse was all she would receive, for not one of them would lay a hand on her, knowing she was not one to take a beating without fighting back.

"Why, Kristen?" Tyra asked as soon as the plans were revealed to her. "Your mother is going to cry. Your father is going to—" She paused to shiver. "I dread to think what he will do."

Kristen grinned at the smaller girl. "He will not do anything until I get back. And my mother never cries. She will not worry about me as long as you be sure and tell her where I am. She will suspect what I have done when she cannot find me, but she will still worry unless she knows for certain. That is why I have confided in you."

"I wish you had confided in someone else. Your father will be furious."

"But not at you, Tyra. And you must promise me you will tell them tomorrow that I sailed with Selig, before they begin to worry."

"I will do it, Kristen, but I still do not understand why you want to defy them. You have never wanted to sail with your brother before."

"Of course I have wanted to, I just never thought to ask before. And as for why, this will be my last chance to sail with Selig. Next year my father will take me south to find a husband—if I do not find one for myself in Hedeby," she added with a chuckle.

"You were serious about looking for a husband away from here?" Tyra asked in wonder.

"You thought I was jesting?"

"Of course I did. It would mean living away from here, away from your parents."

"Regardless of whom I marry, I would still be moving out of this house."

"But if you married Sheldon, you would still be close to home."

"But not deeply in love, Tyra. I would rather be deeply in love even if I have to live in the Far East. But you forget my father owns two long ships and one smaller one. You think they would not visit me, no matter how far away I move?"

"Nay, of course they will. I did indeed forget about that."

"Good. So stop trying to change my mind about going, for you cannot. I am going to have a wonderful time, Tyra, and not worry about the consequences until we return. You do not know what exciting places the market towns are, for you have never been. I was young when I went before, interested only in the goods for sale, not the men. But men from all over the world go to these towns. I will find me one I can love and bring him home with me, and *that* will temper my father's anger."

"If you say so." Tyra nodded skeptically.

"I do. Now, come along, or all the best parts of the meat will be gone."

They entered the noisy hall and presented a pretty picture for the rowdy men, Tyra small and delicate, standing no higher than Kristen's shoulder, and Kristen looking exceptionally lovely in a blue silk gown that fit snugly to her slim, though generously curved length, with heavy gold bracelets adorning her bare arms.

Sheldon whacked Kristen's behind as she passed him, and she turned around to stick her tongue out at him. He made to chase after her for her pertness, but she scurried away from him. She wished Sheldon were sailing, too, but he and his brothers were helping their father, Perrin, add a few rooms to their house this summer, as well as seeing to their crops.

Her cousin Ohthere detained her next, grabbing her waist to lift her off the ground, then bringing her down for a wet kiss. "That was for luck, child," he told her drunkenly.

Kristen laughed at him. He persisted in calling her *child* even though she no longer was one, just because he was ten years older than she. His father was one of her great-uncles. He and his brothers lived with Kristen's uncle Hugh now. Her first cousin Athol would not be sailing, for he was Hugh's only child, and her uncle persisted in keeping him close to home.

"You need luck just to trade in the East?" she demanded of Ohthere.

"A Viking always needs luck when he sails, no matter the destination." He winked at her after imparting that bit of knowledge.

Kristen shook her head at him. He was already well into his cups and the night was young. He would be bleary-eyed when he set to at the oars in the morning. She would pity him while she was safely tucked into the cargo well.

"Let her go, Ohthere, before she perishes of hunger," someone yelled.

He did, but not before he had whacked her backside too. Kristen made a face at him, then went on her way to the long table where her family was seated. She had never been able to figure out what it was about her rump that invited such ill use, but it seemed she ended up with bruises for a week after every feast. She never minded, though, for it was done in the spirit of fun.

She rounded the table, but got no farther than her

father's chair, for his arm shot out and drew her onto his lap. "Are you angry with me, Kris?"

He was frowning at her, but it was a concerned frown. Her mother had already talked to him, and he had once again said no to her sailing without him. Aqua eyes met those of the same color and she smiled, putting her arms around his neck.

"When have I ever been angry at you?"

"Many's the time I can remember, and all when you did not get your way."

Kristen giggled. "Those times do not count."

"You do understand why you cannot go with Selig?" he asked gently.

"Yea, I know why you do not want me to." She sighed. "Sometimes I wish I were your son." At that he threw back his head with a hearty laugh. She scowled at him. "I do not see what is so funny in that."

"You are more like your mother than you know, Kris," he told her. "For half her life, she tried very hard to be a son. I am just thankful I have a daughter, and one as lovely as you."

"Then you would forgive me if I . . . if I did something you might not approve of?"

He grinned at her. "What kind of question is that? Have you done something?"

"Nay." She could answer truthfully for the moment.

"Ah, this is a 'suppose,' then? Then I suppose I could forgive you for just about anything—within reason," he added with a look that was half stern, half amused.

She leaned forward and kissed him. "I love you," she said softly, and for that she got a tight squeeze that forced the breath from her and prompted her to cry, "Father!"

He pushed her off his lap with a pat and the order, "Get yourself something to eat before there is nothing left." His voice was rough, but his expression was full of love.

Kristen took her place at the bench between her mother and Selig, who promptly filled a tankard of foaming mead for her. "You are not going to sulk, are you, Kris?" he asked her. "I do not need sulking to remember through the whole voyage."

Kristen smiled at the way he set out to then fill a plate for her, for he rarely served her at table. "Feeling sorry for me, are you, Selig?"

Selig grunted at that. "As if you would let anyone feel sorry for you."

"Nay, I would not, so do not do so. And the most I will sulk is to say good-bye to you tonight, so I will not have to watch you sail away without me in the morning."

"Shame on you, Kristen," Brenna chided her. "If you wanted him to feel guilty about leaving you behind, you just succeeded."

"Nonsense." Kristen smiled impishly at Selig, but said to her mother, "I will not even miss him."

Selig gave her a sour look for that unsisterly sentiment and turned to say something to Athol, who sat on his other side. Kristen sighed, for Selig didn't know yet how true her words would be, although he might remember when he found her sailing with him.

Brenna mistook her sigh. "Are you really this unhappy with your father's decision?"

"It would have been an exciting adventure before I marry, Mother," Kristen replied truthfully. "You had adventures before you married, did you not?"

"Aye, and dangerous ones, too."

"But a trading voyage is not dangerous. And Father did say I am very like you."

"Yea, I heard him." Brenna grinned. "And he was right, you know. I did try very hard to be the son my father never had. But your father has three fine sons and delights in his only daughter. Do not wish to be anything but what you are, love."

"It was only the adventure I wished for," Kristen admitted.

"Then wish for it no more, for it does come to you when you want it not at all."

"As yours did?"

"I do not regret the adventure that brought me here, but I did at the time. And you will have your journey south eventually, though your father does not know it yet," Brenna confided in a whisper. "I will tell him you do not want Sheldon after the house is quiet again, for it will be a disappointment to him. He and Perrin were so looking forward to that match."

"I am sorry, Mother."

"Do not be, love. We want you to be happy, and if you cannot be with Sheldon, then that is that. We will find you a man you can love."

If I do not find him first, Kristen thought as she leaned closer to kiss her mother good-bye as she had her father, hoping they would both understand and forgive her for what she was going to do. "I love you, Mother."

Chapter Four

*I*t was the storm that gave Kristen away, and it was not even a bad storm, at least not yet. But as soon as the ship had started riding the bucking waves, she started retching. A fine sailor she made. She had forgotten it had been this way the last time she sailed. The least disturbance to the sea, and she could not hold on to the contents of her stomach.

Someone had heard her retching and had opened the hatch to the cargo well. After one look at her, the sailor had slammed the hatch back down. She did not even see who it was, nor did she care at the moment, for the pitching of the ship grew steadily worse.

She had been so fortunate until now. She had managed to sneak out to her brothers' rooms behind the stable and borrow a set of Thorall's clothes to wear for the voyage, though she brought along some of her own gowns to wear when they reached the trading towns. Getting into the cargo well had been the easiest part, for only one man had been left to watch the ship, and though he sat near the cargo well, he had nodded off to sleep. Kristen, quick and nimble despite her height, had seized the opportunity. And the cargo well had kept her quite comfortable even if it was pitch-dark inside. It was piled high with soft furs to hide behind and make her a nice bed.

So it had done for two days. She could have hoped for at least one more day before revealing herself, for the food she had brought would last that long. It was not to be. The storm had revealed her now. And although no one came yet to confront her, inevitably someone would.

To Kristen, it seemed as if that third day had come and gone by the time the hatch was opened again and the light of day flooded down on her. She stiffened herself to prepare for battle to the extent that her weakened body would allow, which was not much. She still felt miserable, even though the storm was finally over.

It was Selig who dropped down into the well. Kristen lay where she had last been tossed, practically at his feet. The light hurt her eyes, and she couldn't manage to look up and face it. It was his voice, hard with anger, that told her who it was.

"Do you know what you have done, Kristen?"

"I know," she answered weakly.

"Nay, you do not!"

She shielded her eyes in an attempt to see his expression, but still could not. "Selig, please, I cannot look up at the light yet."

He squatted down beside her, grabbing a fistful of the thick fur vest she wore over the tight leather tunic, which managed to flatten her breasts. Darkly his eyes scanned the tightly gartered leggings and the soft-skinned high boots trimmed in fur. Her waist was girded with a wide belt, the large buckle set with tiny emeralds.

"Where did you get these?" he demanded of the clothes.

"They are not yours," she assured him. "I borrowed them from Thorall, since he is still closer to my height and—"

"Shut up, Kristen!" he snapped at her. "Do you know what you look like?"

"Like one of your crew?" she ventured, trying to tease him out of his anger.

It didn't work. His gray eyes were as dark as the

storm that had just passed. He looked as if he longed to hit her and it was taking all his strength not to.

"*Why*, Kristen? Never before have you done anything this foolish!"

"There are several reasons." She could see her brother clearly now that he was down on her level, but she avoided his eyes when she added, "One reason was the adventure."

"Worth Father's fury?"

"That was only one reason. There was also the fact that I want to wed, Selig, but there is no one at home that I want. I hoped to meet many new men at the great market towns."

"Father would have taken you," he stated coldly.

"I know. Mother already told me he might do that when you returned or, if not then, in the spring."

"But you decided not to wait. Just like that!" He snapped his fingers. "You defy—"

"Wait, Selig. There was one other reason. There was someone—and I will not give a name, so do not ask— but someone who meant to force me to wed him by—by taking me."

"Dirk!" he exploded.

"I said no names, Selig. But I could not tell anyone about this man, or I would never have been able to go anywhere or do anything by myself. Father would have dealt with him, but would not have killed him with no harm done yet. And a talking to or a beating—well, I do not think that would have dissuaded this particular man. I would have lost my freedom, so I felt the best thing to do was take myself away for a while, and if I might find myself a husband at the same time, then all the better."

"Odin help me!" he swore. "I should have expected no better reasoning from a woman."

"Unfair, Selig! I told you it was all those reasons combined that decided me," she said defensively.

"More like it was only the excitement of adventure that decided you, for there are ways to deal with a man such as you describe and you know it!"

"Father would not have killed him for simply making threats against me."

"But I would have."

She looked narrowly at him. "You would have killed him just for wanting me? Would you kill every man who wants me?"

"Every one who thinks to have you whether you say yea or nay."

She grinned at him now, knowing it was just the brother in him talking. "Then there is no problem. You will be all the protection I will need in the market towns."

"If you were going, which you are not," he retorted. "You are going home."

"Oh, nay, Selig! The men would never forgive me if so much time was wasted."

"They will every one of them agree to take you home!"

"But why? Where is the harm if I go along? You are only going trading." At his furious look, her eyes widened with a particular thought and lit up with excitement. "You are going Viking!"

At that moment their cousin Hakon appeared at the hatch opening. "You told her, Selig? Thor! That was a fool thing to do," the blond giant grumbled.

"Idiot!" Selig stood up to glare at the younger man. "*You* just told her! She had only guessed before."

Hakon dropped down into the well to stare eye to eye with Selig. "So now what will you do? Take her home so she can tell your father?"

Selig rolled his eyes heavenward. "I swear, Hakon, you are a veritable font of information. How our enemies would love to get their hands on you."

"What did I say?"

Selig did not deign to answer that, but looked down at Kristen, who was smiling widely now. "You would not tell Father, would you?" he asked in the most hopeful tone she had ever heard from him.

"What do you think?"

He groaned at her for such an answer, but he took his anger out on Hakon, pulling his fist back and sending the younger man falling into the pile of furs. He followed the blow by diving on top of Hakon, who retaliated in true Viking fashion.

Kristen let the fight go on for several minutes before she interrupted in a tone just loud enough so they would hear her above their grunts of pain. "If you think to make me feel guilty by having to look at two bruised faces on the morrow, I must disappoint you, for I will not take credit for your sport."

Selig rolled over and sat up to growl at her. "I should throw you into the sea, Kristen. Then I would only have to tell our parents you drowned, instead of having to confess I took you Viking. I think they would rather hear that you drowned."

She crawled over to him on her hands and knees and gave him a kiss on the cheek that was already starting to swell, then sat back on her haunches to grin at him. "Give in gracefully, Brother, and tell me where we are going."

"*That* is something you do not need to know, so do not ask again. You will stay on the ship and out of sight."

"Selig!" But he ignored her plea and pulled himself

out of the well. She turned on Hakon, who was just standing. "Will *you* tell me?"

"And have him mad at me for the rest of the voyage? Have a heart, Kristen."

"Oh, unfair!" she cried at his back as he left her, too.

Chapter Five

*T*hey had sailed south, farther south than Kristen had ever dreamed of going. She knew it was south, for each night the sky stayed darker longer, until finally the darkness was equal to the daylight. For days now they had sailed past a beautiful land whose coastline was kissed by summer's green, but no one would tell her what land it was.

She knew something about the lands to the south; she couldn't help but know with the number of servants that had come and gone from her home through the years, all from different lands. The land they sailed past now could be the large island of the Irish Celts, or the even bigger island that was shared by the Scots, Picts, Angles, Saxons, and the Welsh Celts, her mother's people. Or it could even be the land of the Franks, though she did think that land would be to the left, not on the right as this one was.

If it was one of the large islands, then she had reason to believe they might be raiding the Danes, for those Northmen had set about conquering both islands, and the last she heard, they had nearly succeeded. And if it was the Danes they would raid, well, what an equal match that would be, as opposed to attacking the smaller peoples of those islands.

Selig knew more about it, but he wasn't telling her anything. Although still highly displeased with her, he had finally let her come out of the cargo well. Even Thorolf, Tyra's brother, would tell her nothing. She supposed their logic was that if she didn't know where they were or what they did once they landed, she would have nothing to tell her father when they finally returned home.

As if she would have the nerve to tell her father any of this! He was a successful merchant. He did not condone raiding with his ships. The men of the Haardrad clan had not raided since her grandfather's day. But of course the young men dreamed of the riches that could be had with one successful raid, and these men sailing under Selig were all young, and this was a fine ship for such a venture.

Built of oak, it had a stout pine mast that supported the large square sail of red and white stripes. The long ship sailed swiftly through the waters, helped along by the sixteen pairs of long, narrow-bladed spruce oars, the red and gold dragon's head pointing the way.

Kristen was not sorry she had come, for the excitement of the men became her own. And even though she would not be allowed to leave the ship, God's teeth, she now had a story with which to amaze her children and grandchildren on cold winter nights! And the climax was soon at hand. She could tell by the change in the men, and by the way Selig and Ohthere now watched the coast even more closely.

It was early morning when they turned into the mouth of a wide river, and every man was now needed at the oars. Kristen's excitement built with each passing minute, for this seemed like virgin land to her, even though she could see small settlements and villages from time to time.

The explorer in her was fascinated with everything she saw. The adventurer in her held her breath when they finally dropped anchor and Selig came to her, for she was still hoping she might be allowed to go with them. She had even readied herself for that possibility, tucking her long braid into the back of her tunic to keep it out of the way, and wearing the silver helmet that Ohthere had teasingly tossed to her that morning.

Kristen didn't have a shield, but although she hadn't thought that she would need it, she had brought along the lightweight sword her mother had given her all those years ago when she taught her to use it. However, she wouldn't reveal the sword to Selig unless he did agree to let her go with him, for her possession of such a fine weapon would elicit too many questions from him.

His scowling expression as he looked over her male apparel did not bode well for his changing his mind about where she would stay until he returned. Selig was a very handsome man, but when he scowled he was frightening, except to her, who knew him so well.

"I have been a sore trial to you, Selig, but—"

"Not a word, Kristen." Impatiently he cut her short. "I can see you are still of a mind to do what you want and not what I tell you, but not this time. You will get yourself into the cargo well and stay there until I return."

"But—"

"Do it, Kristen!"

"Oh, very well." She sighed, then gave him a half smile, for she couldn't say good-bye to him with harsh words. "May the gods bring you luck—for whatever it is you are going to do."

He almost laughed, but grinned instead. "That—from you, Christian?"

"Well, I know my god will watch over you without the asking, but I also know you would welcome all the help you can get from Father's gods as well."

"Then spend your time praying for me, Kris."

His eyes softened just before he hugged her to him. But then he nodded toward the cargo well, and Kristen dropped her shoulders in defeat and went.

She did not stay there for long, however. No sooner was the last man over the side and heading for the riverbank than she pulled herself out of the well, gaining a grin from Bjorn, one of the men left behind with the ship, and a scowl from the other guard. But neither of them barked at her to get below, so she was able to watch the crew make their way inland toward a thick forest that blocked the rest of the land from view.

She paced about in her frustration to be stuck here where there would be no action at all. It was only midday and a hot sun beat down on them, hotter than any she had ever known in Norway. How long would the men be gone? God's teeth, it could be days for all she knew.

"Thor!"

Kristen swung around to see the last of the crew entering the dark forest. And then she heard what the man beside her had heard: the clanging of swords and the cries of men engaged in battle.

"They must be a mighty force if they can attack instead of turning tail to run. Get below, Kristen!"

Bjorn shouted this even as he jumped over the side of the ship. Kristen obeyed, but only to collect her sword. When she pulled herself back out of the well, she saw that both of the men who had been left behind were now running toward the forest to help their friends. She did not hesitate to join them, for as Bjorn had said, only a mighty force would attack so many armed Vikings, and she reasoned they would need even her help, little as it might be.

She caught up with the two men just as they reached the forest and charged into it with bloodcurdling yells. She did not follow directly. There was nothing around her but fallen bodies. Oh, God, she had not thought it would be like this. She saw her cousin Olaf lying at an odd angle ... there was so much blood. Selig! Where was Selig?

She forced her gaze away from the ground littered with dead men to look ahead of her, where the fighting was still going on. She took note of the attackers now, and could not believe that these small, wiry men had done so much damage, for there were not so many that she could see—and, she realized, they were not all small, either. There was one even a few inches taller than she, and he was fighting—Selig! And God in heaven, he was not the only one wielding a sword against her brother.

She started forward to help him, but was set upon by a little man with a fierce cry who blocked her way. Instead of facing a sword, she was attacked with a long spear that she quickly cut in two, and the moment she raised her sword against the man, he fled.

Having lost direction, she swung frantically about, searching for Selig again, and then screamed, for just as her eyes found him, he was falling, and the tall one he had been fighting pulled back a bloody sword. She went wild, racing toward him, her eyes fixed on the man who had struck him down.

Kristen struck blindly at a man who appeared on her right to challenge her, leaving him behind. And then she was there, before her brother's killer, and fending off his first thrust. Their eyes met just before her sword entered his flesh. She noted that his blue eyes widened perceptibly as she pulled her sword out, but it was the last thing she saw.

Chapter Six

A single candle cast a subdued light in the small chamber. A narrow bed rested against one wall, with a large coffer at its foot. Covering the opposite wall was a large tapestry of a field of summer flowers with children frolicking. On another hung a highly polished steellike glass, with a narrow shelf below holding an assortment of items from jewel-studded pins and bone comb cases, to tiny colored bottles of floral scents, and a thickly padded bench before it.

A tall carved post stood in a corner of the chamber with wooden pegs running down its length, an ornament in itself, draped as it was with sheer veils and ribbons of different colors. At the only window hung strips of bright-yellow silk, a sheer waste of a most expensive cloth. There were two high-backed chairs set by a small round table with a painted ceramic vase of red roses on it.

The chairs were presently draped with the clothes of the two occupants on the bed. The chamber belonged to the woman, Corliss of Raedwood, a small-boned beauty of a score and one years, who was quite vain of her luxuriant red-gold tresses and eyes the color of rich chocolate.

Corliss was the betrothed of the man lying with her, Royce of Wyndhurst, one of King Alfred's nobles. Four years ago she had been offered to him for wife, but was refused. This past winter she had pestered and coerced her father as only a beloved daughter can, to offer her again, and this time she was accepted. But she knew she was accepted this last time only because she had managed to get Lord Royce to her chamber, where she had thrown herself at him, and he, drunk from her father's feast, had taken her.

Giving herself to Royce that night was no great sacrifice for Corliss, though she hoped he had not realized it, for she had been with one other man before him. Only one, though, for after that first time, she had decided that this part of the man-woman relationship was not to her liking at all. Yet she knew she would have to grit her teeth and bear it often once she was married to Royce.

It was a sign of her determination that in spite of disliking his lovemaking, Corliss still offered herself to Royce each time he came to visit her, which was fortunately not often. She was afraid that if she withheld herself from him now, before the wedding, he would break the betrothal. After all, he did not really want a wife. He was only a score and seven years, and in no great hurry to tie himself down. At least, that was the excuse he had used often enough to the fathers of marriageable daughters. There was another reason known too, though he never used it. He had been betrothed previously, five years ago, to a girl he had loved. He had lost her three days before they were to wed and had loved no other girl since.

Corliss was of the opinion that Royce would never love again. He certainly did not love her, nor did he pretend to. She did not even have an alliance with her father to dangle before him, for Royce and her father were friends. A marriage was not needed to keep them friends. She was as sure now as she had been when she first did it, that the offer of her body had been the only condition that had swayed him.

If Royce were not so desirable as a husband, Corliss would just as soon never marry. But the fact was, every maiden for miles around wanted Royce of Wyndhurst for herself, including Corliss's three sisters. It was understandable, for not only was he rich and favored by the King, he was also a handsome man, even if he was so incredibly big—more than a foot taller than Corliss, in fact. His combination of dark-brown hair and fathomless dark-hued green eyes was striking indeed. As his betrothed, she was the envy of all these women, and that suited her admirably, for Corliss loved being envied. She thrived on jealousy, too, and her sisters were certainly jealous of her now. That was worth whatever she had to put up with from Royce in bed, even his prolonged lovemaking.

The first time had been quick. But the other times, including now, seemed to go on forever, full of kissing and touching. The kissing she didn't mind so much, but the touching . . . ! He touched her everywhere, and she had to lie there in her humiliation and bear it all. She sometimes wondered if he prolonged it intentionally, if he had guessed that she didn't like it. But how could he know? She never protested or offered the least resistance. She lay there perfectly still and let him do what he wanted. What more could she do to let him know that she was willing?

He looked down at her, and there was bemusement in his eyes. She heard him sigh and stiffened, knowing this was the sign that he was ready at long last to mount her. A knock came at her door just as he fit himself between her legs.

"Milord! Milord, you must come now! Your man is below and says 'tis urgent he see you!"

Royce left the bed and reached for his clothes. That he was glad of the interruption did not show in his expression. Making love to Corliss was becoming a tiresome duty, fraught with frustration, that he no longer anticipated with any pleasure. It was confusing, too, for he did not seek her out. She brought him to her chamber each time, leading him to believe it was what she wanted. But once they were abed, Corliss was as passionless as dead meat, and he had done everything he could think of to make her enjoy their encounters.

That she did not wouldn't have mattered to most men, but Royce derived a good deal of his own pleasure from the pleasure that he gave. And if truth be known, he had more fun tumbling a lowly serf than he did this woman who would be his wife, no matter how beautiful she was.

After he strapped on his belt over the leather vest he wore, his only chest covering in the warm weather, he spared Corliss a glance. She had modestly covered herself the moment he left the bed. She begrudged him even the sight of her splendid nakedness. His anger rose for a moment because of that, but he tamped it down. He had to make allowances for Corliss's tender sensibilities. After all, she was a lady of noble birth, and like all such ladies of his acquaintance, she needed to be treated with care, or tearful scenes were likely to be the consequence.

"Milord, how can you leave me now?" Corliss asked plaintively.

Very easily, little one, he thought, but those were not the words he spoke aloud. "You heard your woman summon me. I am needed below."

"But, Royce, it seems so . . . as if you do not care . . . as if you do not want me."

Great tears were spilling from her eyes now, and Royce sighed in disgust. Why did they all have to do that? They cried so easily, for so little reason, clinging, demanding reassurances. His mother had been like that, his aunt, even his cousin Darrelle who lived with him now—how quickly they could burst into tears and make a man wish he were elsewhere. He would be damned if he would have this from his wife, too. Better to break her of the habit now.

"Cease, Corliss. I cannot abide tears."

"You—you do not want me!" she sobbed.

"Did I say so?" he snapped.

"Then stay. Please, Royce!"

He almost hated her at that moment. "You would have me ignore my duty to appease you, lady? Never will I do that. Nor will I coddle you, so do not expect it."

He walked out of the room before she could detain him longer, but the sound of her loud crying followed him down the hall, grating on his nerves. The scene had put him in a foul mood, and seeing the serf Seldon waiting for him below did not help it. A serf would not have been sent to him if the matter were important.

"What is it?" Royce barked at the little man.

"The Vikings, milord. They came this morn."

"What!" Royce picked Seldon up by the front of his tunic and shook him. "Do not say me false, man. The Danes are in the North, dealing with the revolts against their rule in Northumbria, and preparing to attack Mercia."

"'Twas not Danes!" Seldon squawked.

Royce set him down slowly, a cold dread creeping over him. He could deal with the Danes, who now had control of two kingdoms in the country. They had already made their attempt at Wessex, Alfred's kingdom of West Saxons, in what was already called the Year of Battles, 871. The young Alfred had been only a score and two years when he succeeded to the throne that spring when his brother Aethelred died. And in the autumn, after nine battles had been fought with the two great Viking armies for control of Wessex, Alfred negotiated a peace.

It was peace no one expected to last, but Alfred had bought time for his people to regroup and prepare defenses in greater depth. His ealdormen, along with the lords and thanes of all the shires, had been training freemen and improving their own fighting skills as well as fortifying their manors these last two years. Royce had gone one further to even train some of his more able-bodied serfs in the arts of war. He was prepared to ride against the Danish Vikings, who were all intent now on settling the land. It was the Vikings from the sea that were never anticipated, that could take Wyndhurst by surprise and destroy it as they nearly had five years ago.

To have the last Viking raid at Wyndhurst recalled so clearly was anguish for Royce, a rekindling of the hate that had simmered for these five years, hate that had killed many Danes that summer of 871, for it was Danes who had raided Wyndhurst in 868, before going on to sack the monastery of Jurro. He had lost his father in that raid, his older brother, and his beloved Rhona, who was repeatedly raped in front of his eyes before her throat was slit, while he, unable to get to her because of the two spears that had pinned him to the wall, had to endure the agony of listening to her cry and beg and call for him to help her even as his own life's blood poured out of him. He should have died, too, and would have, if the Vikings had stayed for longer than they did.

"Milord, did you hear me? They are Norwegians, these Vikings."

Royce could have shaken the man again. What matter who they were? If they were not part of the two great Viking armies in the North, then they were raiding pirates from the sea, bent only on killing.

"Is there aught left of Wyndhurst?"

"But we beat them!" Seldon said in surprise. "Half are dead; the others, captured and in chains by now."

Royce did pick up the man again this time and shake him once more. "Could you not have told me that first, you fool!"

"I thought I did, milord. We won."

"How?"

"Lord Alden sent out a call to all the men to come for field maneuvers in the east field. But my cousin Arne was south on the river and did not receive the summons. It was he who saw the Viking ship."

"Only one?"

"Yea, milord. Arne ran straightaway toward Wyndhurst, but came upon Lord Alden's men in the east field. 'Twas only that they were armed and ready and so close to the river that prompted Lord Alden to attack. We had time, just enough, to prepare an ambush. The men took to the trees in the forest before the river and fell on the Vikings as they passed under them. So many were killed in the surprise attack that we were able to defeat those remaining."

Royce asked the dreaded question: "How many of our men killed?"

"Only two."

"And wounded?"

"Slightly more . . . eighteen, actually."

"Eighteen!"

"The Vikings fought like demons, milord—giant demons," Seldon said defensively.

Royce's expression grew taut and forbidding. "Let us be on our way, then, and I will see to the rest of those bloodlusting pirates."

"Uh, milord, Lord Alden was . . ."

"Not dead?" Royce groaned.

"Nay," Seldon said quickly, for he knew how close

the cousins were. It was reluctantly that he had to add, "But he is sorely wounded."

"Where?"

"In the belly."

"God's mercy!" Royce groaned even as he ran from the hall at Raedwood.

Chapter Seven

Kristen woke slowly to an awareness of Thor's mighty hammer pounding on her head. God help her, now she was having fanciful imaginings, but this headache was the worst she had ever had in her life. And then other discomforts became known to her and she remembered.

She sat up too quickly and a wave of dizziness washed over her, making her fall to the side with a dazed groan. Two arms caught her, and the attendant rattle of chains brought her eyes wide open with a start. She was looking at Thorolf, who was looking at her, and then she turned her head to see who held her. It was Ivarr, a friend of Selig's.

She sat up, looking all about her frantically. They were grouped around a tall post, all of them sitting on the hard ground. There were seventeen of them, many lying unconscious with untended wounds, all of them chained together at their ankles in such a way that they formed a circle around the post. But she did not see Selig.

Her eyes met Thorolf's blue ones again, and hers were pleading. "Selig?"

He shook his head at her and the scream tore out of her throat. Ivarr instantly put his hand over her mouth, and Thorolf brought his face close to hers.

"They have not noticed yet that you are a woman!" he hissed. "Would you make us sit here and watch while they drag you away and rape you? Have a care, Kristen. Do not give yourself away with screams."

She blinked her eyes that she understood, and Thorolf nodded at Ivarr to release her. She caught her breath, then bent over double, racked with the pain of loss. She wanted to scream, needed to, to let go of the pain that way. Without that release, it built and built until she could not help herself. The anguished moans came out of her until a fist struck her jaw and she fell again into two waiting arms.

When Kristen woke again, the sun was just beginning to set. She started to moan, then caught herself and sat up slowly, looking accusingly at Thorolf.

"You hit me." She did not make it a question.

"I did."

"I suppose I should thank you."

"You should."

"Bastard."

He would have laughed at the mild way she said this, if he felt free to laugh. He didn't. They had been left unguarded earlier while the enemies were busy seeing to their own wounds, but two guards rested near them now.

"There will be time to grieve later, Kristen," Thorolf offered gently.

"I know."

She straightened her ankles with the heavy iron rings about them. Ohthere's borrowed silver helmet was gone, as was her jeweled dagger and belt. Even her fur-trimmed boots had been stripped from her feet.

"They took everything of value?" she asked.

"Aye. They would have taken your vest, too, if it were not such an old shaggy fur."

"And bloodstained," she added, looking down at the dark blotches all over her, for the blood had shot out from the tall man she had killed when she pulled her sword out of him. She felt her head for the bump there that had rendered her unconscious, and then realized. "My hair!"

The braid was still tucked into her tunic, but it would be clearly obvious if she was closely examined. Instantly she began to break the hair from the braid.

"Nay, Kristen." Thorolf grabbed her hands away, realizing what she was trying to do. "It will take you forever to cut it that way."

"You have a knife to offer?" she snapped.

He grunted at such a stupid question, but then began to look her over. With the belt gone, her short tunic lay in straight lines down to just below her hips, effectively hiding the deep curve of her waist. Her dark-brown leggings were bulky beneath the loosened cross-garters, disguising the shapeliness there, too. Her hands and feet, bare now, were not tiny, yet not manly, either. But more dirt would help there, as well as on her bare arms, which were entirely too slim even for a youth.

Thorolf was satisfied. "If not for that glorious hair of yours, it would take only your loud mouth for them to guess that you are anything more than a boy. How did you get your breasts to disappear?"

Kristen blushed scarlet, looking down to avoid his curious eyes. "You should not ask me that."

"But how did you?"

"Thorolf!"

"Keep your voice down! In fact, do not say a word that they can hear. We can tell them you are a mute, and that will solve that problem."

"'But what about my hair?"

He frowned, then suddenly grinned and began to rip away the lower hem of his tunic. He called for Ivarr to block Kristen from the view of the guards, then whipped her braid out and wound it quickly around her head, wrapping the soft leather from his tunic over it and tying it tight at the base of her neck.

"My injury is not there," she started to point out.

"I am not concerned with that puny little bump," he

retorted. "Wait a minute. I have just the finishing touch." And he proceeded to slap at the ugly-looking cut on his arm until he had a good deal of fresh blood on his fingers, which he then smeared on her bandaged head.

"Thorolf!"

"Shut up, Kristen, or that woman's voice of yours will render my clever efforts wasted. What do you think, Ivarr? Will she pass for a boy now?"

"With that swelling jaw, and that big head, no one will look twice at her," Ivarr replied with a grin.

"Thank you so much," Kristen retorted churlishly.

Thorolf ignored her sarcasm. "Aye, it is a little thick around the head, but since they will not be looking for the girl in her, they will only think it is a thick bandage. As dirty and unkempt as she is now, it will do. But keep it tight, Kristen. If it falls off, you are done for."

She gave him a dark look for that unnecessary warning. "I think it is time you told me where we are."

"The kingdom of Wessex."

"The Saxons' Wessex?"

"Aye."

Her eyes rounded in disbelief. "You mean an army of puny Saxons defeated you?"

Thorolf flushed at her aghast tone. "They fell on us from the trees, woman. Half our number were down before the rest of us even knew we were attacked."

"Oh, unfair!" she cried. "They ambushed you?"

"Aye. It was the only way they could have won, for their numbers were not more than ours. And the irony is, that we were not interested in them or what they had to offer. We would have passed by this place that they have brought us to. It was—" He paused, looking suddenly chagrined. "Never mind."

"It was what?" she demanded.

"Nothing."

"Thorolf!"

"Thor's teeth! Will you keep that voice down?" he snapped at her. "It was a monastery we were intent on sacking."

"Oh, nay, Thorolf, tell me not."

"Aye, it was, and this is why Selig did not want you to know, for he understood how you would feel about it. But this was our last chance to share in some of the wealth of this land, Kristen. The Danes will soon have all of it. We thought only to take a little of that wealth first. There would have been little or no killing. It was only the fabled wealth of the Jurro monastery that we wanted."

"How did you know where to find it?"

"Flokki's sister, the one who married a Dane, came home to visit last year. She had much news of what they are doing here, and she told about the failed attempt on Jurro in 871, when the combined armies of Halfdan of the Wide Embrace and King Guthorm first attacked Wessex. They are intent on the kingdom of Mercia right now, even though those fools have paid them Danegeld each year to keep the Vikings at bay. And once they have Mercia under their belt, they will be back here. If not this year or the next, then soon after. You think they can ignore this rich, fertile land? These little Saxons will not keep them out."

"They managed to defeat you," she reminded him.

"Odin's luck was on their side."

"They were not all little, Thorolf. The one I killed was as big as you are."

"Aye, I saw him when they brought the carts to carry all the wounded here. But you did not kill him, Kristen. At least, he is not dead yet."

She groaned, his words filling her with regret. "You mean I could not even avenge my brother?"

His hand went to her cheek in support, then quickly fell away lest one of the guards should see. "He will die soon, I am sure. He was bleeding heavily from his belly when they carried him into that large building over there."

Kristen cringed at the reminder of the scene of carnage she had witnessed in the forest, even though she had added to it. But her part in it was justified. How could she ever face her family if she had not tried to kill her brother's slayer?

She turned to look where Thorolf nodded, not wanting to think of the blood she herself had let. It was a very large building of two floors, built mostly of wood, with large and small windows to let in the daylight, but no doubt they let in the cold of winter, too. There were many other smaller buildings around the place, and a wooden fence that surrounded the area, thick but not very high.

"Aye, you can see how easy it would be to take this place," Thorolf commented.

"But they are preparing well for the Danes. Look there." She pointed to a huge pile of large blocks of stone on the far side of the enclosed yard. "It looks as if they plan to build a more sturdy wall."

"Aye, we saw more stone outside the wooden fence," he agreed, then laughed contemptuously. "The Danes will be here before they can finish it."

Kristen shrugged, for that was nothing to them. They would escape from this place long before then, she had no doubt.

Glancing back at the large building, she frowned a little. "That hall is big enough that it must belong to an important lord. Do you think the tall one might be their lord?"

"Nay. From the little I could understood of what they said, the lord of this place is not here. But I think he was sent for. I really should have given you more attention when you were trying to teach me old Alfreda's tongue."

"Aye, you should have, for you are the only one who can speak for us if I am to be a mute."

He grinned. "Will it be too hard on you, to keep your mouth shut when they are near?"

She made a sound very much like a snort to show what she thought of his teasing. "I will manage somehow."

Chapter Eight

One brave man had walked in among the Vikings to plant a torch in a hole in the post they surrounded. Six guards stood near with swords in hand in case the Saxon was set upon. Kristen hid a grin as the man passed near her. She had heard them arguing about who would carry the torch, for none of them wanted to get this close to the prisoners, even chained as they all were and lying and sitting about in relaxed positions. With so many wounded, they offered no threat, at least not at the moment. But the Saxons weren't taking any chances.

The torch was not for the prisoners, but for the three men who remained to guard them, so they could better see the prisoners now that night had fallen. No food had been brought for them, nor bandages to tend the wounded. This boded ill. They needed food for strength if they were to escape. No food could mean many things, including that they were not to live long.

That possibility was confirmed a while later when the guards began talking among themselves. The Saxon who had walked among them, obviously feeling bold now that he had done so and had come to no harm for it, spoke the loudest, his voice carrying to them all.

"Why does he keep looking at you while he brags?" Kristen asked Thorolf.

"I am the only one who was able to speak for us earlier. They thought we were Danes," he said with a measure of contempt. "I disabused them of that fact.

The Danes are here to steal their land. We only wanted to steal their wealth."

"And you thought that would make them deal more kindly with us?" she scoffed.

Thorolf chuckled. "It did no harm to point it out."

"Nay?" she asked darkly. "Then you are not listening to what they are saying."

"In truth, the little bastard is talking too fast for me to understand more than a few words. What does he say?"

Kristen listened for several moments, then could not stop the look of disgust that came over her features. "They mention someone called Royce. One says he will makes slaves of us. The braggart swears he hates all Vikings too much to keep us alive and will torture us to death as soon as he returns."

She did not add that the little braggart the others called Hunfrith had gone on to describe the torture, suggesting that the one called Royce would make use of the Vikings' own ingenuity, doing to the prisoners what the Danes had done to the King of East Anglia when he was captured. The King had been set against a tree and used for archery practice until he bristled with arrows like a hedgehog. And when he was torn away from the tree, still alive, his back was ripped open, exposing his rib cage. A gruesome torture indeed, but one of the other guards suggested the prisoners would more likely be hacked into small pieces, kept alive as long as possible, and forced to watch as each severed limb was thrown to the dogs to eat.

There was no point in Kristen telling all that to Thorolf. Torture was torture, no matter what form it took. If they were to die when the man called Royce arrived, then they should be making plans for escape immediately.

She turned around to look at the tall post around which they were circled, judging it to be as tall as three men. The chains running from one man's ankle to the next were longer than she could have hoped for, at least two arms' length, a stupid move by the Saxons, for this gave them ample room to maneuver.

"It should take only three men, mayhap four, to climb that post to set us all free from it," Kristen speculated aloud.

"Which is no doubt why they made sure no three of us in a straight line were without serious wounds."

Ivarr said this, and she looked at him to see the open leg wound he pointed to that would make it nearly impossible for him to scale the post. And the man on the other side of Thorolf still had the head of a spear embedded in his shoulder.

"I could carry one man with me," Thorolf said, "but the going would be too slow. We would have arrows in our backs before we got near the top."

"Could you unroot that post?" she ventured.

"We would have to stand to do that, and that would forewarn them what we were about. We could push it over, but it would fall slowly and they would still be warned and be on us instantly with their swords. Even if we should still succeed after that, too many of us would die and be dead weight to hinder the rest of us, chained as we all are. If they are smart, they would not even come close to us so that we could get at their weapons, but pick us off with arrows from afar."

Kristen groaned inwardly. "So with the chains keeping us together, we have no hope?"

"Not until our wounds are healed and we can get our hands on some weapons," Ivarr replied.

"Take heart, Kristen." Thorolf grinned unconcernedly. "They may decide to use us to train them to fight the Danes."

"And then let us go on our merry way, eh?"

"Of course."

She snorted at that possibility, but Thorolf's jesting did make her feel better. If they were to die, then they would die together, and fighting, not calmly accepting the Saxons' torture. That was the Viking way, and though she was a Christian, she was a Norsewoman too.

She would have said as much if the wooden gate had not opened just then to admit two men on horseback.

Only one was worth watching, and watch him she did as he moved his great black steed slowly toward them. When he dismounted only a few feet away, she was amazed to see that he was nearly as tall as her father, which put him at a height above most of the young men with her. He was young himself and not slim for such a height, but powerful across the shoulders and wide chest. His sleeveless leather vest was almost like a short jacket and revealed a bush of dark hair on his chest running nearly to his neck, and arms that were thick and wrapped with steely muscle, the arms of a warrior. The belt wound tight about his waist showed that there was no fat on him.

The long legs were also thick and powerful, and tight within two different types of leggings, instead of the single garment the Vikings wore. The knee-length trousers that the Europeans called braies were tucked into a hoselike covering they called chausses and cross-gartered, his with leather thongs that were decorated with metal studs.

His face was well defined and impossibly handsome, the nose straight, the lips cleanly drawn and firm with a hint of cruelty above a square-cut jaw that was beardless, though dark with bristles. Hair of a rich, gleaming brown fell in waves to his shoulders and formed unruly curls about his wide brow and temples.

But it was his eyes, once seen, that held the viewer riveted. They were such a dark, crystallike green, and so filled with hate and anger as they passed over the chained men, that Kristen caught her breath when his gaze moved briefly over her, and did not release it until he snapped an order at one of the guards, and then walked away toward the large building and was gone from sight.

"I do not like the looks of that one," Ivarr said beside her. "What did he say?"

Many others were asking the same thing, but Kristen shook her head dismally. "You tell them, Thorolf."

"I do not think I have it right," he replied evasively.

Kristen glared at him. The men had a right to know, but either Thorolf didn't have the heart to tell them, or he didn't believe what he had heard.

Kristen glanced at Ivarr, but could not meet his eyes. "His words were 'In the morn, kill them.'"

Royce entered the hall to find the floor littered with his wounded men. He would speak to each one of them later, but right now he mounted the stairs at the end of the hall and went directly to his cousin's chamber.

Alden was stretched out on his bed, covered to his neck with a thick quilt, and so pale that Royce groaned, thinking he was already dead. The crying women in the room confirmed it. Two maids Alden sometimes took to his bed were standing in the corner weeping. Meghan, Royce's only sister, a child of merely eight winters, was sitting at a little table with her face bent over her arms, weeping into them. Darrelle, Alden's sister, was kneeling at the bed, her face buried in the covers, great sobs racking her slim body.

Royce looked to the only woman in the room who wasn't crying, Eartha the Healer. "Did he just die? Am I only a few moments too late?"

The old hag tossed back her stringy brown hair and grinned at him. "Dead? He may yet live. Do not kill him off before his time."

Royce met this news with a mixture of relief and anger. It was the anger to which he reacted. "Out!" he bellowed at the noisy women. "Save your weeping until 'tis needed!"

Darrelle swung around on him, her face as blotchy red as her eyes, her small breasts heaving indignantly at what she considered an outrage. "He is *my* brother!"

"Yea, but what good do you do him with your screaming? How can he sleep to conserve his strength with such noise as you make? He does not need your tears to know you care, Darrelle."

Darrelle scrambled to her feet to face him, the top of her head coming no higher than his chest. She would have pounded on that chest if she had the nerve. Instead she craned her neck to glare up at him.

"You are heartless, Royce! I have always said 'twas so!"

"Have you, lady? Then 'twill come as no surprise to you if your words do not wound me. Go and repair the ravages to your face. You can return and sit with Alden as is your wont—if you can do so quietly."

The two maids had already flown the room. Darrelle stalked out now. Eartha knew she wasn't included in the order to leave, but took herself below with her basket of herbs anyway. Royce was left staring at his sister's frightened little face, and his expression softened.

"I am not angry with you, midget, so do not look at me so," Royce said gently, holding his arm out to her. "Why were you crying? Because you think Alden will die?"

Meghan ran toward him and threw her arms around his hips, for she was no taller than his waist. "Eartha said he might not, so I was only praying, but then Darrelle was crying and—"

"And our cousin is teaching you bad habits at an early

age, midget. You were right to pray, for Alden needs your prayers so he will recover quickly. But do you think he would want you to cry, when you should be happy that he is still alive after facing our worst enemies?" He was loath to talk more of the overuse of tears to her, for she was a timid child who burst into them for the smallest reason. Instead he picked her up and dried the tears from her red cheeks. "'Tis bed for you, Meghan, and your prayers for Alden until you fall asleep. Go on, now." He kissed her brow before he set her down.

"My thanks, Royce." Alden spoke weakly from the bed as soon as Meghan closed the door behind her. "I do not know how much longer I could have pretended to be asleep. But every time I opened my eyes, Darrelle screamed at me to get well."

Royce burst into laughter, pulling a chair up beside the bed. "Seldon, that foul excuse for a man, told me you had a gut wound. God's breath, I did not expect to find you still alive, let alone able to talk!"

Alden tried to grin, but gritted his teeth instead. "A little to the side of my victuals sack, but close enough that the blade might as well have spilled my guts. God, it hurts! And to think that a lad with the prettiest eyes I have ever seen did this to me."

"Describe him, and if he is one of those below, I will see he suffers the most before he dies."

"He was just a smooth-faced boy, Royce, who should not even have been with those others."

"If their children can raid, then they can die," Royce said angrily.

"Then you mean to kill them all?"

"Aye."

"But why?"

Royce glowered. "You know why."

"Aye, I know why you would like to, but why will you, when you can make use of them instead? They are defeated. We have their ship, and Waite tells me it carries a rich cargo, which is yours now. Lyman has been complaining repeatedly that the serfs he has to use are not strong enough to carry the Roman stones to build your wall. Look how many months it has taken just to bring those few piles here. He is already drooling over the strong backs of the prisoners. Admit it, Royce: The Vikings could build your wall in half the time, and think of the irony, that they should be used to keep out their brothers the Danes."

Royce's expression did not change. "I see you and Lyman have already been speaking about this."

"He would not shut up about it all the way he carted me back here. But he has a point, Royce. Why kill them, when keeping them alive would serve you better?"

"You know you are closer to me than my own brother ever was, Alden. How can you ask me to live with the possibility that they could escape and slaughter us all while we sleep?"

"I would not ask that. Precautions can be taken to ensure they cannot escape. Just think about it, before you condemn them."

The door opened then and Darrelle stood there, her eyes dry now but still shooting daggers at Royce. They had grown up together, the three of them, with Alden a year younger than Royce, and Darrelle two years younger than her brother. They were the only family Royce had left, besides Meghan, and he loved them both. But sometimes Darrelle could be wished out of sight when he was so obviously out of patience with her sulks and silly tantrums.

"So, you accuse me of keeping him from sleeping,

but what are you doing, making him talk and answer questions about those loathsome heathens?"

Royce rolled his eyes and grinned at Alden. "I will leave you in your sister's capable care."

Alden shot him a chagrined look as Royce left the room.

Chapter Nine

Royce watched his sister run across the hall and peek out the opened door, then turn around with a frown and run back toward the stairs where she had come from. He called her to him before she reached them. She came, not so quickly now, to the long table where he sat alone breaking the fast. She had already eaten with her maid, Udele.

Darrelle was still annoyed with Royce from last eve and would not sit with him this morn, but she watched from where she bent over one of the wounded men. It was not difficult to perceive Meghan's reluctance to approach her formidable brother.

It was something that tore at Royce's heart, Meghan's reticence toward him, and it was his own fault, caused by his deplorable behavior that first year after he lost so many dear to him in the Viking raid. Meghan was too young to understand what he was feeling, why he was surly with everyone, even her. She began to fear him that year and had never lost that fear, even though he had treated her with the tenderest of care once he realized what was happening.

She had developed many fears from that time—of strangers, of loud voices, of tempers—and he blamed himself for it all. He knew that she loved him. He was the first one she would hide behind when she felt she needed protection. But she was so terribly shy of him, so timid and meek in manner, as if she always expected him to chastise her or worse. She was in fact the same way with all men, but Royce took her behavior to heart.

"Were you afraid to go outside?" Royce asked gently when she finally stood next to him with bowed head.

"Nay, I only wanted to look at the Vikings. Udele said they were all bad men, but they looked like only hurt men to me." She peeked up at him to measure his reaction to this, then relaxed when she saw him smiling at her.

"You do not think they could be hurt bad men?"

"I suppose, but they still did not seem so bad. One even smiled at me, or I think he did. Can such young men be really so bad, Royce? I thought men had to live a long time in wicked sin to be really bad."

"These men have not the benefit of God to temper their wickedness, so it matters not how young they are."

"Udele said that they have many gods and that makes them bad too."

"Nay, that only makes them heathens who sacrifice to pagan gods. Are you afraid of them?"

"Aye," she admitted meekly.

Impulsively he asked, "What do you think I should do with them, Meghan?"

"Make them go away."

"So they can come back and hurt us again at another time? I cannot allow that."

"Then make them Christians."

Royce chuckled at her simple solution. "That is for our good abbot to do, not I."

"Then what will you do with them? Udele thinks you will kill them." Meghan shivered as she said this.

"Udele thinks too much aloud." He frowned.

Meghan lowered her eyes again. "I told her you would not, because they are not fighting anymore, and you would not kill a man unless 'twas in battle."

"Sometimes 'tis necessary—" He stopped himself,

shaking his head. "Never mind, midget. What say you we put them to work building our wall?"

"Would they work for us?"

"Oh, I think they will want to with the right incentive," he replied.

"You mean they will not have a choice?"

"Prisoners rarely do, midget, and do not forget that is what they are. If they had won the battle and taken you back to their land, they would have made a slave of you. They cannot expect less than the same for themselves."

He stood up, for the hour was growing late, and if he had not made up his mind before, he had now after talking with Meghan. "A word of caution," he added, smoothing the hair back from her cheek. "As long as they are here, do not go near them. They are dangerous men, whether they look it or not. I must have your promise, Meghan."

Meghan nodded uneasily, then watched him leave the hall. No sooner was he gone from sight than she ran upstairs to tell the grouchy old woman who was her maid that the Vikings were not to die after all.

The sun was high when he left the hall and walked purposely toward them. Kristen had been waiting for this moment as they all were, pondering her regrets: that she would never see her parents again, that she would never have a husband now, or children, or even see the morrow. She had determined she would not die cowardly, but she did not want to die at all.

Two of the guards stopped him to speak with them, then they both fell into step beside him as he continued crossing the yard. The little Saxon, Hunfrith, had been relieved in the middle of the night, but he had returned early that morn to continue goading them with descriptions of the tortures they could expect. He walked right up to Thorolf now and struck the prisoner's bare foot with the flat side of the sword he had drawn.

"My lord Royce would speak with you, Viking," Hunfrith announced importantly.

Kristen pinched Thorolf to urge him to stand up, but he struck her hand away, refusing. He was in a crouch, ready to charge the Saxons as the others were, if any move was made to single them out for torture. With only three men standing before them, it was not likely that the time was at hand, but he was taking no chances.

The dark-green eyes of the Saxon lord were casually moving over the group, as if seeing them for the first time. His expression, unlike yesterday, was inscrutable. Of course their deplorable condition was more obvious now in the bright light of midday, and he no doubt felt they offered no threat to him, or he would not have stood so close. His unconcern was almost a challenge.

He was not afraid, this Saxon, Kristen was thinking when his eyes slid over her and then came back abruptly. She quickly lowered her own, feeling an uncomfortable leap of her heart at being singled out by those dark eyes, fearing her disguise might have been revealed to him in some way.

She did not look up again until she heard him speak, but then her unease increased. She had not realized that being chained to Thorolf, who was the only one who could speak for them, would place her too close to the object of their attention. She quickly scooted behind him and hunched down, letting his broad back hide her from view.

The Saxon was looking down at Thorolf. "I was told you speak our tongue."

"Some," Thorolf admitted.

"Who is your leader?"

"Dead."

"The ship was his?"

"His father's."

"Your name?"

"Thorolf Eiriksson."

"Then point out to me your new leader, Thorolf, for I know you will have chosen one."

Thorolf said nothing to this, then finally requested: "Say slow."

Royce frowned impatiently. "Your new leader. Who is he?"

Thorolf grinned now and shouted, "Ohthere, stand up and make yourself known to the Saxon."

Kristen watched her cousin stand uneasily, for he had not understood anything that was said until Thorolf called to him. He was on the opposite side of the circle from her, but he had worked his way to her last night, dragging three men with him to do so. Both of his brothers were dead, but he was holding his grief inside, as she was. Being the oldest among them and also Selig's cousin, he was logically looked to as their leader now.

"His name?" Royce asked as he looked Ohthere over.

"Ohthere Haardrad," replied Thorolf.

"Very well. Tell Ohthere Haardrad that I have been persuaded to leniency. I cannot let you go, but I will feed and shelter you if you are willing to serve me. I need a stone wall built around this manor. If you choose not to work, you will not be fed. 'Tis that simple."

Rather than request the Saxon to repeat his words slowly, Thorolf said, "Talk," indicating his comrades.

Royce nodded. "By all means, confer."

Thorolf called the men into a huddle, but only as an excuse to drag Kristen into the center of it, where no one could see her talking. "Thor's teeth! What was all that about, Kristen?"

She was grinning from ear to ear. "He is not going to kill us. He wants us to build his stone wall instead."

"Nay, I will not sweat for the bastard!"

"Then you will starve," Kristen retorted. "His conditions were clear. We work for our food and shelter."

"As slaves!"

"Do not be fools!" she hissed. "This will buy us time to escape."

"Aye, and mend," Ohthere agreed. "Tell him now, Thorolf. No use making him think there are those of us not eager to accept his terms."

Thorolf stood up this time and called Royce back to him. "The chains?" he questioned first.

"They stay. Do not think I am foolish enough to trust any of you."

Thorolf grinned slowly, nodding. The Saxon was wise, but he did not reckon on Vikings well mended and fed and determined to escape.

Chapter Ten

An old woman came among them to tend their wounds. She was dirty and unkempt, wearing the tight, long-sleeved undergown called the chainse, with the shorter sleeveless gown over it unbelted, making it look like a sack. She walked very straight for her age, and said her name was Eartha. Her disposition was that of someone who had lived all the years she wanted to, and so she was bold and saucy and fearless, as if she cared not what consequences her actions might bring her.

Kristen was amused by her and wary of her at the same time. She watched Eartha push and poke the men around, men that were like giants beside her small frame, and laugh at their grumbling or sharp words. She was wary because she knew Eartha would come to her eventually, wanting to see her supposed head wound, which she could not allow.

Kristen was not in the best of moods, either, because of the heat, which none of them were used to. Many of the men had torn away most of their leggings, but much as she wanted to do the same, she knew she dared not. She would have pitied Eartha wearing her two gowns, and no doubt a shift under them, too, except that the heat seemed not to bother her at all. But then, the Saxons would naturally be used to it.

Eartha finished with Ivarr and squatted down next to Kristen, indicating that she should tell her where besides the head wound she was hurt, assuming that she was because of the numerous bloodstains covering her. Kristen simply shook her head. In response, Eartha reached for the head bandage. Kristen slapped her hand away, only to have her own hand slapped in return. When Eartha tried again to remove the bandage, Kristen jumped to her feet, towering over the little woman now, and hoping that her stature would dissuade the nurse. It did not. She had to catch Eartha's wrists and hold them firm to keep the woman's hands away from her head. For this she felt the point of a sword pressed into her side.

Several other Vikings stood, and the Saxon guard who had come to Eartha's defense stepped away. He was intimidated enough to call immediately for help.

Kristen groaned, seeing what she had caused, though it couldn't be helped. Seven Saxons were running toward them with drawn swords. She glared at Eartha for being so stubborn, then released her. It was Thorolf who stopped the old woman now, pulling Kristen behind him.

Fortunately, the Saxons hesitated when they reached the prisoners, seeing that Eartha was no longer threatened. "What is amiss?" Hunfrith demanded.

"The young lad will not let me tend his wound," Eartha complained.

Hunfrith looked for explanation to Thorolf, who stated plainly, "Is mending. Leave alone."

Hunfrith grunted, then glowered at Eartha for causing them all to panic. "Aye, if he can jump up the way he did, he needs not your skills, old woman."

"The covering should be changed," Eartha insisted. "'Tis all bloodied."

"Leave off, I said. Tend those who want it. Leave the rest alone." But to Thorolf he added, "Warn your friend there to keep his hands to himself from now on."

Hunfrith was obviously not willing to make an issue of it when so many Vikings were ready to come to the boy's defense. But Eartha did not like it and moved off grumbling that the lad was too girlish by half. One of the Saxons commented that mayhap that was why the Vikings brought him along, and they left laughing among themselves.

Kristen's cheeks had blushed brightly at the remark. When Thorolf noticed and asked why, she shook her head, blushing more. He meant only to tease her, detaining her to insist she tell him, because it was so rarely that Kristen was ever embarrassed. But she slapped his hand away and angrily sat down, giving him her back.

From that position her eyes wandered over the hall, and she could see that a man stood watching them from an upstairs window. His face was in shadow so she could not guess who he was, but it made her uncomfortable to know that others besides the guards could watch them. She had only been concerned with the guards' positions whenever she had spoken to Thorolf or the others. She would have to be more careful now, knowing that anyone from the hall could also be spying on them.

They were fed after Eartha left, and those of them who had lost their boots because they were new or of a fine quality, got them back, though they couldn't put them on over the chains. This situation was rectified later that afternoon, when the blacksmith came to them.

The iron bands on their ankles were removed and replaced with new ones, these with a short chain permanently welded on each set. The bands snapped on and were held firm, but there was a keyhole on each one to remove them, though there was no sight of the key around. An iron ring at the back of each band allowed for a longer chain to slide through. This chain was only twenty feet long, and once it was threaded through the ring on each man's foot and then the ends locked together, their circle around the tall post became much narrower, making the positions they could assume extremely limited.

Kristen was disgusted with this new precaution taken against them. She supposed the long chain would be removed when they were made to work, but the short chain between her ankles would only allow for short steps, certainly nothing hurried, and she could imagine all of them stumbling and falling as they got used to having to practically hobble as they walked. It would be degrading, but that was probably how the Saxons intended it.

Like the others, Kristen had gotten her boots back, though the fur trimming had been ripped away. But at least they kept the irons from chafing against her bare skin. The bands were tight, however, and would no doubt wear through the soft-skinned boots eventually. Since her ankles were so much slimmer than the others', the blacksmith had had to send for a special pair of irons for her, smaller ones that she could only imagine were made for a boy much shorter than she.

It rained that night, and left out in the open as they were, they were all made miserable by the deluge. Kristen was the most wretched, for she tried futilely to protect her bloodied bandage from being washed clean. Thorolf finally laughed at her efforts and helped by wrapping his own arms about her head and lying partially on top of her. This kept her bandage dry, but made for a very uncomfortable night.

From his window, Royce watched the scene below in the yard. He saw the lad protest being covered and try to throw Thorolf off, saw the larger Viking slap his backside and shout something in his ear and then cover the boy's head with his arms, which forced Thorolf to lie half on top of the boy. They were still after that, as were the others. The guards had erected a shelter from the rain in front of the storehouse. The rest of the yard, growing muddy, was quiet.

"Which is the one Eartha said attacked her?"

Royce glanced down absently at Darrelle. She had come to stand beside him at the window, having put away the ivory pieces of the game they had just finished playing.

"The Viking did not attack her. He simply protested her treating his wound."

"But she said—"

"I saw it all, Darrelle, and the old woman exaggerates in the telling."

"If he were to have laid hands on me, I hope you would not take it so lightly," she grumbled.

"I would not," he said, grinning.

"Which one is he?"

"You cannot see him now."

"Alden said 'twas only a boy who wounded him. Is he the one?"

"Aye, the youngest among them."

"You should have had him whipped, then, if you saw him lay hands on Eartha."

"Too many were ready to fight for him. 'Twould have served no purpose but to have more wounded."

"I suppose," she agreed, though with reluctance. "They cannot build our wall if they are dying. The wall is more important. They are few and can be controlled, but the Danes are many."

Royce chuckled. "I see Alden has convinced you that they are needed."

"You would have killed them all," she reminded him with a haughty look that made him smile. "At least he realized they would better serve you alive."

"Is it not time for you to check on Alden?" Royce threw the hint out deliberately.

Darrelle clucked her tongue indignantly. "You could have just told me to go."

"I would not be so churlish," he replied innocently, pushing her toward the door.

Royce stood at the window often, watching the Vikings labor. It was an indication that he had yet to accept their presence at Wyndhurst that he felt unease except when he had them within his sight. He was not so in favor of using them to build his wall as Alden and Lyman were, for he would be meeting the Danes on the Wessex borders when the time came to fight them again, and he was doubtful they would ever push so far south as to do damage to Wyndhurst.

But since King Alfred wanted his lords to fortify their holdings, and since they had ample stone at the old Roman ruins near here, he had agreed a stone wall should be built, whether it would ever be needed or not. And already the Vikings had set the stones that had taken months for the serfs to bring here, and this done in only a week's time.

"Meghan tells me this has become a new habit of yours, Cousin."

Royce swung around to see Alden in the doorway. "Should you be up so soon?"

Alden groaned. "Not you, too. I get enough coddling from the women."

Royce grinned at the younger man as Alden made his way slowly to the open window to stand next to him. "Your company is welcome, for I find I brood too much on the past in here alone. But, God's truth, I cannot help but feel they will try something now that they are near all mended, so I find myself ever standing here watching them. Only two of them remain unable to carry the stone with ease."

Alden leaned out the window, and then he whistled

softly at what he saw across the yard. "'Tis true, then! We need more stone already."

"Aye," Royce admitted grudgingly. "Only two of them are needed to lift the largest stones that it took five of the serfs to carry. In the same amount of time, the serfs are still not finished with the shelter I set them to build for the Vikings next to the storehouse. It will be another few days before they can be locked in there at night. Then we will not need so many men to guard them, at least at night."

"You worry too much, Royce. What can they do shackled as they are?"

"'Twould take only a strong axe to sever those chains, Cousin. One of them with his bare hands could crush two of my men before a third could draw his sword. And the fools still get close to them, even though I have warned them to keep their distance. If the Vikings are determined on their freedom, and I cannot doubt that they are, then they will make a bid for it eventually, and many will die when they do."

"Burn their ship and let them know the sea is closed to them," Alden suggested.

Royce grunted. "I am surprised no one has told you that has been done already."

"Then what you need is an inducement to keep them tame," Alden replied.

"Yea, but what?"

"You could take their leader away. If they think you will kill him at the first sign of revolt, that should—"

"Nay, Alden. I thought of that, but they say the one who led them here is dead. 'Twas his father's ship I burned. They chose a new leader from among them, and would only do so again if I separate him from them."

"They say he is dead?" Alden was frowning thoughtfully now. "What if he is not?"

"What!" Royce exclaimed.

"If he were down there among them, why should they tell you so and risk losing him for what I suggested."

"God's breath, I did not think of that." But Royce frowned then. "Nay. The only one they rally round is the boy. They protect him as if he were a babe."

At first he had thought that the lad was only Thorolf's brother, and that was why the bigger man cosseted him. But once the prisoners began the wall, they all seemed to look after the lad, stopping the guards from prodding him, taking the heaviest stones from him and pushing him toward the lighter ones, two or more of them moving to help him up every time he fell. But damned if he wasn't the filthiest among them, never making use of the water given them to wash. Still they pampered him.

"Could he be their leader?" Alden ventured, looking at the one in question sitting down on the low wall while the last few stones were moved in place at Lyman's direction.

"Are you daft, Cousin? He is but a smooth-faced boy. Granted, they are all young men, but he is the youngest among them."

"But if his father supplied the ship, then they are bound to follow whom he chooses to sail it."

Royce scowled darkly. Could it be that simple? His own king was younger than he by a few years. But Alfred had been second in command since he was sixteen. This was an untried boy who still needed cosseting. Yet it was that untried boy who had wounded Alden, and Alden was as seasoned a warrior as Royce was. And now that he thought of it, every one of the Vikings stopped whatever he was doing every time attention was drawn to the boy, almost as if they waited, ready to come to his defense if necessary.

"I think 'tis time I had another talk with Thorolf," Royce said tersely.

"Which one is he?"

Royce pointed out the window. "There, the one who just called the lad to him. He is the only one who understands our tongue, though not clearly."

"Lyman is finished with them for this day, it seems," Alden remarked.

"Aye, he will cart them to the ruins for more stone on the morrow. Which means I must waste more of my men guarding them again."

They both watched for a moment as the guards walked beside the Vikings, hurrying them back to the post. Royce turned away from the window, but was stopped short by Alden's cry.

"You have trouble, I think."

Royce turned back around. He could see that one of the Vikings had fallen, and Hunfrith was prodding him with his boot to get up. He did not have to guess which Viking it was, for the whole group had stopped. Thorolf shouted something at Hunfrith, and then Hunfrith's feet came out from under him and he landed hard on his backside. The lad stood up, brushing dust from his hands, and the Vikings roared with laughter as they continued on their way.

"I warned that fool to leave them alone," Royce hissed between clenched teeth. "He is lucky they did not disarm him while he was down."

"God's breath," cried Alden, "he means to attack the boy!"

Royce too had seen Hunfrith rise with his sword drawn, but he was already running out of the room and down the stairs. Nevertheless, when he reached the yard the damage had been done. One of the guards had called for help, and archers surrounded the group at a safe distance. Three of the guards threatened Ohthere, who had Hunfrith gripped in a bear hug that was likely to break his back, though the Viking did not seem to be applying much pressure at the moment.

Thorolf was speaking quietly to Ohthere. Of the lad there seemed to be no sign, until Royce finally noticed him peering above the shoulders of those in front of him. He had been thrust into the very center of the group.

"Tell him to put my man down, Thorolf, or I will have to kill him." Royce said this slowly so the man could understand. He was looking at Ohthere, who was staring back at him without emotion. "Tell him now, Thorolf."

"I told him," the Viking replied and then tried to explain. "Ohthere's cousin. No attack Ohthere's cousin."

Royce's eyes turned on Thorolf now. *"He* is the boy's cousin?"

"Aye."

"Then what are you to the boy?"

"Friend."

"Is the boy your leader, Thorolf?"

Thorolf met this question with surprise, and then he grinned and repeated it to his comrades, many of whom began to laugh. The laughter at least eased the tension. Even Ohthere chuckled and dropped a wheezing Hunfrith at his feet. Royce picked up the little Saxon by the scruff of his tunic and shoved him away from the Vikings.

Hunfrith's sword lay in the dust between Royce and Ohthere. Royce picked that up, too, leaning the point into the ground in a nonthreatening manner.

"We have a problem, Thorolf," he said quietly. "I cannot have my men attacked."

"Hunfrith attack."

"Yea, I know," Royce conceded. "I believe his dignity was suffering."

"Tripped apurpose—kicked—deserved," Thorolf retorted angrily.

Royce took a moment to digest that information. "If

he did kick the lad, then mayhap he did deserve to get laid low. But the boy is becoming more trouble than he is worth."

"Nay."

"Nay? Mayhap if I separate him from the rest of you and give him easier tasks—"

"Nay!"

Royce's dark brows narrowed at this. "Call the boy forward. Let him decide."

"Mute."

"So I have been told. But he understands you well enough, does he not? I have seen you talking to him often. Call him forward, Thorolf."

The fair-haired Thorolf pretended ignorance this time, keeping his mouth shut. Royce decided to take the rest by surprise before Thorolf told them what had been said. He shoved those Vikings in front of him aside, caught the lad by the shoulder, and dragged him out to the edge of the group. Ohthere moved to pull the boy back, but stopped when Royce pressed the tip of the sword against the young one's neck.

Royce looked straight at Thorolf, his eyes narrowed angrily. "I think you have lied to me about this one, Viking. Tell me now who he is!"

Thorolf said nothing. More guards had come forward, and a long spear held him away from Royce. Others held the rest of the group back.

"Do you need an incentive to loosen your tongue?" Royce demanded.

He lost his patience when Thorolf still didn't answer. He began to drag the lad to the prisoners' post. When the boy fell because of his angry stride, Royce yanked him roughly to his feet, barking orders at his men as he went. When they reached the post, he shoved the boy against it, facing it, and caught both wrists together around it, holding them firm until one of his men ran up to him with a short rope, which he quickly used to bind them.

He stepped away from the post then, looking to where he had left Thorolf behind. Other of the Vikings were now shouting at him, but Thorolf kept his mouth firmly closed, though his blue eyes were hostile. Did Thorolf think Royce only meant to keep the lad tied here? He would disabuse him of that notion quickly enough.

Royce stood behind the lad, his own back blocking the post from the prisoners' view. Then, taking the dagger from his belt, he cut away the boy's thick fur vest down its center. The leather tunic he attacked next was so tight that he knew he probably cut the boy's back as he sliced it open from top to bottom, but not a single sound was heard in protest.

Soft white skin met his eyes, making Royce frown. There was no thick muscle to take the sting of the lash. And he had in fact cut the boy's tender skin. A thin streak of crimson ran from the shoulder blades halfway to the waist. This really was just a babe he was about to order whipped—if Thorolf didn't volunteer the truth about him.

Royce stepped to the side again so they could see what he had done. Thorolf cried, "Nay!" and shoved the spear away from him, trying to make his way to Royce. Ohthere pulled a spear from a guard's hands and with it knocked two others away, then dared anyone to take it from him as he too started toward the post in a murderous rage.

Royce called for their attention and they stopped, seeing his dagger pressing against the soft white back. "The truth, Thorolf."

"No one! A boy!" the Viking still insisted.

Waite brought the lash forward. Thorolf shouted, "Nay!" again and started to say something else, but the lad was violently shaking his head back and forth and Thorolf fell silent. Royce was enraged at that. Although he said not a word, the lad's wishes held sway.

"That was stupid of you," Royce snapped as he came around the post so he could see the lad's face, as well as the now-quiet Vikings. "You will suffer, not he. You cannot tell me, but I will have him tell me you lead them. 'Tis obvious. I want it confirmed."

He did not expect an answer from a mute, nor did he think his words were understood. He was angry that they would make him go through with this, and angrier still when those pretty aqua eyes peeked up at him for the briefest second, before the head was bent to where he could not see the face. Damned if that wasn't something a female would do. In fact, too many things about this boy smacked of femininity. If he didn't know it was impossible, he would be tempted to pull down the front of that tunic just to assure himself that his imaginings were groundless. Other lads were known to have long-lashed, pretty eyes and soft skin, until they passed that certain age to become men. This one just hadn't reached that age yet.

Royce nodded at Waite to begin. The lash fell and a soft whistle of expelled breath came from the lad. No other sounds stirred the quiet yard. Thorolf remained silent, though his fists were clenched and every muscle in his body was tensed to prevent him from moving. Royce nodded again.

This time the tall, slim body slammed into the post and then jerked back reflexively to the full stretch of the arms. The opened leather tunic started to slip down over the upper arms. The boy quickly pressed back against the post again without help from the lash, but not before a strip of white linen fell out from under the tunic.

Royce bent to pick up the cloth, which looked very much like a bandage, except there was no blood on it. A knot was on one end, revealing that he had cut through it when he had opened the tunic. Two round indents had somehow worked their way into the cloth, almost as if the strip had been placed over...

"Nay, I will not believe it!"

But his eyes rose to that bent head, and then his hand jerked out and gripped the tunic, yanking it down. He sucked in his breath, then swore violently on seeing the evidence that turned the boy into a woman. His other hand came up and tore the bandage from her head, and he swore again as a long golden braid tumbled down her back.

A collective groan now came from the prisoners, but not a sound had she made, not a tear was in the eyes that looked straight at him now. What in hell kind of woman was she not to prove her sex to save herself a whipping? Or had she not realized that he would not whip a woman?

He cut her wrists loose, and she immediately shoved her tunic back up to cover herself. As soon as she had done that, he grabbed her hand and dragged her back to stand before the subdued Thorolf.

"A boy, is she? No one? And you let me whip her! To hide what? That she is a woman? Why?" Royce demanded furiously.

"To protect me," Kristen answered.

Royce's eyes swung to her, but she did not flinch from the fury in them. "No mute, either, and another one to understand our tongue! By God, you will tell me why you did not open your mouth to stop the whipping!"

"To protect myself from the rape of Saxon men," she said simply.

He laughed cruelly at that. "You are too tall for my men to want, or did you not realize that? Nor are you a temptation in any other way, wench."

It was his anger that brought forth those words, but they stung nonetheless. "What will you do with me now?" she dared to ask.

Royce was chagrined that she ignored his insults. "You will serve in the hall henceforth. How you are dealt with will depend on their behavior. Do you understand?"

"Aye."

"Then make them understand."

Kristen looked at Thorolf and Ohthere, who had moved to stand beside him. "He thinks to hold me as hostage inside his hall to ensure your behavior. You are not to let this affect your decisions. You must promise me that if the opportunity presents itself, you will escape. If just one of you can reach home, then you can send my father to me."

"But he will kill you if we escape."

"He is angry now because he whipped a woman. He will not kill me."

Ohthere nodded sagely. "Then we will make our way to the Danes in the North if the chance comes. They will have ships to sail to the Northlands."

"Good. And I will let you know how I fare if I can, so do not worry over me."

"Enough!" Royce snapped, thrusting her at Waite. "Take her inside and have the women bathe her." As she walked away from him, he was able to see the red welts on her back, one that beaded with drops of blood, and it was all he could do to speak in a controlled tone to Thorolf. "I know she told you more than I bid her. I tell you this now. The first time you try to escape or injure one of my people, I will make her wish she were dead. And I do not make idle threats."

Chapter Eleven

Kristen felt foolish and out of place, walking into the Saxon house. The hall she entered was long and bigger than her father's hall, but she had known it would be in a building this large. At home there was no floor directly above the hall, making it like a huge cavern of stone, so cold in winter that the family preferred evenings spent in the closed-off cooking area. This hall did have a floor above it, but the ceiling was still fairly high.

The cooking area was not closed off, either, as it was at home, something her great-grandfather had insisted on because the smoke bothered him so. Here the cooking was done in a long stone hearth that ran nearly half the length of the back wall on the right side, with stairs on the other side. There was another stone hearth, just as long, in the center of the longest wall on the right, but this one was cold and empty, undoubtedly not used in the summer months. Stone ran to the ceiling above the hearths, and for a few feet at the base of the hall, as well as around the high entrance doors.

The floor was made of wood and sounded hollow as Kristen walked over it, leading her to think there might be some kind of cellar beneath it. A thin square rug of the type Garrick had found in the East covered a small portion of the floor in front of two wide windows, this in the front of the hall and on the right again. Chairs and stools were placed on it, along with sewing looms and a tapestry stand. It was an area obviously reserved for the women, and three were there now working.

All the windows and the doors were open, letting in ample light and warm breezes. Opposite the women's area and in front of windows again, but more toward the center of the hall, there was a large barrel of ale with a spout on it. Benches and chairs surrounded the barrel, as well as several small tables set with gaming pieces. There was a rack of tools and another, longer table covered with weapons, stools, even wooden bowls, all in different states of completion. A man stood at the table working thin leather strips about the handle of a whip. Kristen cringed, the pain on her back suddenly more pronounced.

There were seven women in the hall, and every one of them stopped what she was doing when Waite stepped inside with Kristen. The combination of her male garb, half of it torn open and hanging on her, and her height, which let her tower over every woman there by half a foot or more, made Kristen feel like a freak. All the other women were covered from their necks to their feet by their long-sleeved chainses, a few even wearing veils to hide their hair as well, while her arms were bare and her back was now exposed too. They were clean and tidy, while she was filthy from the dirt and mud she had purposely smeared on herself to disguise her smooth skin.

One woman, garbed more richly than the others, rose from her seat and called Waite to halt. Her light-blue outer gown was embroidered along the edges, even on the wide elbow-length sleeves over the white of her tight-fitted chainse sleeves, and girded about the waist to reveal a tiny frame. Her hair, golden-brown in color, was dressed in a net of woven beads. Her eyes were a light blue, very bright, like those of the man Kristen hoped she had killed.

Kristen thought the woman would be very pretty if she didn't frown so, as she was doing now. She was probably the lady of this hall if she could halt the soldier with such authority in her voice. Kristen was not surprised that the Saxon lord would have a lovely wife. She could almost envy this lady such a fine-looking husband, if she were not the prisoner of that husband.

"How dare you bring him in here?" the woman demanded of Waite after she took a few steps closer, but still left a long distance between them.

"Milady, he is a she and Lord Royce orders the women to bathe her."

"A woman?" the lady gasped, coming closer now, her eyes traveling from the top of Kristen's head to the chain still binding her feet together. She shook her own head. "Nay, 'tis not possible."

Waite grabbed Kristen's long braid and tossed it over her shoulder for the lady to see. "Lord Royce had her whipped, which led to the discovery of her deception." Roughly he turned Kristen around. " 'Tis not the back of a man."

"A smooth back and long hair do not a woman make."

Waite chuckled. "Milord made certain in another way, which you will see for yourself when she is bathed."

The lady made a sound of disgust with her mouth. "And what are we to do with her after she is bathed?"

Waite shrugged. "Put her to work as you see fit, milady. She is to remain in the hall."

"What can Royce be thinking of," the woman wailed, "to keep a heathen in our home?"

"He means to use her—"

"No doubt!" she snorted. "In the same way those Vikings surely used her!"

"Mayhap that, too." Waite grinned. "But used more for a hostage."

"Oh, very well." A long-suffering sigh was forthcoming. "Send someone for the key to those shackles if she is to be washed thoroughly. But take her to the bathing room first and leave two men to watch her until I tell my women what they must do. They will not like this any more than I."

Kristen was left with Uland and Aldous, though she didn't know which was which, for Waite had simply shouted their names as he passed through the hall. The small bathing room was partially under the stairs, with a door leading directly to the back yard, where water could be brought from a well. The other door was under the stairs, near the cooking area. There was a wooden tub inside, not nearly big enough for more than one person as the one in her uncle Hugh's bathhouse was. It seemed the Saxons did not share baths.

The two men Kristen dismissed as servants and ignored as such. They were both small and dark in coloring, one old, the other young, perhaps father and son. They watched her fearfully, as if they knew they would have trouble stopping her if she tried to leave.

Kristen had no thought for leaving. She was very much looking forward to this bath, now that she no longer had to hide her femininity. The filth she had worn on her person until now had been a sore test of her endurance. She would probably have pleaded for this bath if it hadn't been ordered.

The blacksmith came in to remove her shackles, though he did not take them away with him. Kristen immediately sat down on a bench to remove her boots and inspect her ankles. The skin was chafed bright red, but not broken. It would mend soon enough if the foul shackles could be dispensed with.

Kristen stayed where she was, busying herself with

unbraiding her hair, while a line of boys began bringing in buckets of water from outside. It did not look as if they would bother heating any for her, as the tub was nearly full already. She didn't mind, though, accustomed as she was to swimming in cold water.

When five women crowded into the small room, not counting the lady who remained by the door, Kristen finally became annoyed and stood up. "I can wash myself, lady."

"God's mercy, and here I thought I would have much trouble making you understand."

"I understand perfectly. I am to bathe. I will do it gladly, but I do not need assistance."

"Then you do not understand at all. 'Tis Royce's order that the women will wash you, and so they shall."

Kristen was not one to take issue over something so minor. Nor would she give it another thought once she had conceded. She shrugged carelessly, waiting for the men to be sent from the room. When they were not, yet the women all began to crowd about her to remove her clothes, she shoved them back so forcefully that two of them fell, shrieking.

"Listen, lady"—Kristen had to shout over the cries of the fallen two—"I will allow your women to wash me, but not in front of men."

"How dare you tell me what you will allow? They are here to protect my women from you, for you cannot be trusted alone with defenseless women."

Kristen almost laughed at that. Five women, six counting the lady, and they called themselves defenseless against one. Yet they just might be if they insisted on stripping her in front of serfs. And if the women were that afraid of her, it might not hurt to brazen it out.

She pointed a finger at the two men, who were wide-eyed now at the prospect of having to subdue her. "They

are the ones who will need protecting if they do not
leave."

The lady sputtered in anger and began shouting
orders. Kristen picked up the bench she had been sitting
on and threw it at the two men.

Royce could hear the shrieks and screams as he approached the hall. He entered just in time to see Uland
literally tossed out of the bathing room. Aldous stumbled out right after him, and then tripped over the
younger man and went sprawling too. By the time
Royce reached the room it was much quieter, though
Darrelle was still making shrill noises in her anger.

"What the devil is going on here?" Royce bellowed
from the door.

"She would not let us bathe her!"

"Tell him why, lady," Kristen managed to gasp.

She was lying flat on her back on the floor, with four
women sitting on top of her. They had come at her from
behind just as she chased the old man from the room.
Tripping her to the floor, they had pounced on her immediately. She could barely breathe now, with one on
her chest and another on her stomach.

"God's breath, Darrelle!" Royce stormed. "I give you
a simple thing to do, and you make a shambles of it!"

"She started it!" Darrelle protested. "She would not
let them undress her. She lives alone with dozens of men
night and day, yet she is shy now in front of two serfs."

"My order was for the women to bathe her. I said
naught about men."

"But she is a Viking, Royce! You certainly could not
expect us to be alone with her."

"God's breath, she is just a woman!"

"She does not look like a woman. She does not act
like a woman. And she attacked those two cowards with
a bench! And you want to leave her alone with us?"

"Get off her!" he growled at the women as he walked

to Kristen, jerking her to her feet as soon as she was free. "You cause any more trouble, wench, and I will deal with you myself. You will not like it."

"I was ever willing to have the bath, and glad of it."

Royce frowned at her calm reply. "Then have it," he said. To the oldest woman in the room, he instructed, "Eda, bring her to my chamber when you are done with her."

"Royce!" Darrelle protested.

"What?" he snapped at her.

"You cannot mean to—to—"

"What I mean to do is question her, Darrelle, not that it is any of your concern. Now, be about your business. They do not need you to supervise a scrubbing."

Darrelle's cheeks brightened as she stalked out of the room ahead of him. But Royce was in no mood to placate her. Of all the ridiculous things! A simple bath could not even be accomplished without an uproar.

Alden was still waiting for Royce in his chamber upstairs, still standing at the window where his cousin had left him. "You saw it all?" Royce queried.

"Aye, though I could not hear what was said," Alden replied. He added curiously, "Did you see what I think you saw when you pulled that tunic down?"

Royce grunted. "A lovely pair of breasts the lad has."

Alden started to laugh at his expression, but he flushed instead, realizing. "'Twas bad enough when I thought a mere lad had brought me low, but a woman!"

"Be consoled, Alden. She just sent two serfs flying out of the bathing room. She is like no woman we know."

"Mayhap. She is uncommonly tall for a woman, tall enough to have fooled us this long."

"But why would they bring a woman on a raid?" Royce wondered.

Alden shrugged. "Why else? To see to their needs on

the ship. She was late come to the battle. I would guess she was left on the ship, but saw the attack from there and thought to help. After all, if the Vikings were all killed, she would have been left alone. 'Tis no wonder she fought so hard along with them."

"Aye. She would even have taken more of the lash, rather than reveal she was a woman. She said 'twas to protect her from the rape of Saxon men." He laughed harshly at that. "Men are men. What has a whore to fear of a different breed?"

"She would be loyal to her own, and loath to lay with their enemy."

"I suppose. I can see now why *they* went to such pains to hide her sex. They would have been locked up alone with her at night very soon. But, God's breath, what they see in such a big, manly woman is beyond me."

Chapter Twelve

Kristen's whole outlook on her adventure-turned-disaster took an abrupt turn the day she entered Wyndhurst for the first time. No longer did she only have to worry about keeping her mouth shut and her hair hidden. Now she faced the problem that she had only tried to avoid before: How would these Saxons see her as a woman? Would she be an abomination to them because of her height and the fact that she was their enemy? Or would they find her as desirable as the men at home did?

The Saxon lord had said she offered no temptation to his men. If this was his opinion, then she could assume that a man would not want to make love to a woman who was taller than he was, because he might feel inferior and less in control. Very well, that left her safe from all but two men that she had seen in this place. The one she hoped was dead. The other was the lord himself.

Kristen had mixed feelings about Lord Royce. She had seen little of him this past week, and when she did chance to see him, she had avoided looking directly at him. But she could not forget her first sight of him either. He had looked like a young god riding into the yard so straight and proud on that powerful steed, so self-assured, so in command of himself and all those around him. Boldly he had come up to sixteen hostile men who were huge and powerfully built themselves, and let them see his loathing for them.

There was no fear in the man. Again today Lord Royce had shoved his way through the Vikings to snatch

Kristen from their protection. The men did not know what to make of the way he approached them without weapon in hand.

Ohthere thought he was a fool to be so careless. Thorolf thought he tempted them purposely, that he begged for an excuse to slay them. Kristen favored Thorolf's opinion, for she remembered the look in his eyes that first day, and his cold, merciless order to have them killed.

She had feared him because of that. But Kristen couldn't stop herself from admiring him, too. She had always enjoyed watching strong, well-proportioned male bodies. Just that last night of the feast at home, her mother had caught her staring overlong at Dane, Perrin and Janie's younger son, as he arm-wrestled, and Brenna had teased her by asking if she was sure no one there would do for a husband. A strong, handsome body was a feast for the eyes, and her mother had taught her not to be ashamed that she thought so. And the Saxon lord had not only a superb body but a very handsome face as well.

Aye, to be truthful, she enjoyed looking at him. But she did not want him looking at her with the same appreciation. With the hate he bore her and the others, it could not be a pleasant experience, being made love to by him. As long as he did not want her, she would be safe, even though she was now separated from the others. Her goals were still the same. She would work and keep a low profile until the opportunity for escape came. Only now, the question was at hand: How would he see her as a woman?

The women had scrubbed her with a vengeance, no doubt intentionally, rubbing her practically raw. She bore it only because she wanted to cause no more trouble with them that might bring the Saxon back.

The clothes they gave her were laughable. They had

nothing to fit her tall frame, even with hems lowered. She might be slim in proportion to her height, but compared with them, she was large. The sleeves of the white chainse they gave her were too tight to fit over her wrists. An argument ensued on whether to cut the sleeves and lace them for now, or to go ahead and sew in an insert. Kristen solved the problem by ripping the sleeves away. Her own summer gowns at home were sleeveless, and she would have been too hot with the sleeves anyway. No one approved of this, but they were as loath to argue with her as she was with them. They did not want more of the lord's displeasure either.

The chainse, which was supposed to hide a woman's feet, fell far short of Kristen's ankles. And the gray gown they gave her to wear over the chainse came only to her knees. But at least it was sleeveless, too, and was split up the sides so that she could shape it as she liked with the rope girdle they gave her. She chose to wear the rope loosely, even though it let the gown fall away from her sides, revealing the form-fitting chainse, which was much too tight. Since she was not going to be able to hide her figure no matter what she did, this style at least distracted a little from her curves.

They took away her boots, giving her a pair of soft-soled house shoes, which would have been fine, except that they meant to put the shackles back on her, and the shoes did not cover her ankles. She was not going to wear that iron against her bare skin again without a fight, and she told them so. The older one, Eda, chose wisely to let a higher authority decide, and simply carried the shackles with her as she and two others escorted Kristen upstairs.

Though she could not say why exactly, Kristen was nervous now that she knew she would be seeing Lord Royce again. She did not think he would approve of her in any way, yet there was still that tiny possibility that he might, now that she was washed and groomed.

He was seated next to a small table honing a long, double-edged sword when Eda pushed Kristen into the room. Without explaining why Kristen was not wearing the irons, she simply placed them on the table and left, closing the door behind her and leaving Kristen standing in the middle of the room.

It was a large, uncluttered chamber. Besides the low post bed off to the left of the door and the large coffer at the foot of it, there was the small table with four chairs around it in the center of the room. Directly opposite the door, another coffer with a lock on it sat between two opened windows like a bench. There was another, larger window on the other side of the bed that looked out over the front yard. There were no tapestries to brighten the room, or rugs on the floor, but the wall on Kristen's right was hung with an assortment of weapons.

She had yet to look directly at him, though she could feel his eyes on her. She waited for him to speak, but long moments dragged by and he did not. She had perused everything in the room and had nowhere else to look. She was not in the habit of meekly casting her eyes down at the floor. She had only done so outside because Thorolf had warned her that her eyes were too long-lashed for a boy's and she should not draw attention to them.

She started at his boots, moving slowly up his body until their eyes locked. Now she could not look away even if she wanted to. She saw no hate. Surprise was what she found.

"Who are you?"

The question seemed torn from him in bewilderment. What could he have been thinking to be so confused?

"What exactly do you want to know?" she countered.

"My name is Kristen, but I think you would seek more than that."

The way he stood up and moved toward her made her think he hadn't heard a word she said. His expression was still more surprised than anything, though there was something else there now that she couldn't quite define. He didn't stop until mere inches separated them, and then his fingers rose to trace the expanse of one creamy cheek.

"You hid it well, this beauty."

Warily Kristen stepped back. "You said I was no temptation."

"That was before."

She groaned inwardly. Aye, that was desire lighting the green depths of his eyes as they moved over her face and then down the length of her. She didn't fool herself that she might be able to match her strength to his. Not his. He wore a long-sleeved tunic today, and the muscles that she remembered bulged against the thin linen of it. He could crush her with his large hands. He could have her lying beneath him in a matter of moments. And there was no one in this whole land who could stop him from having her, for she was his enemy, defeated, and he could do what he wanted with her.

"You will not find it easy to rape me," Kristen said in a soft, warning tone.

"Rape you?" He changed before her eyes, dark fury etching the lines of his face now. "I would not demean myself to rape a Viking whore!"

Kristen had never in her life been so insulted. It was on the tip of her tongue to tell him so, but she stopped herself as logic began to analyze his words. He had spoken with such disgust. And it was not so farfetched that he should think her a whore. It could be one explanation for her sailing with an all-male crew.

He had returned to his seat and would not look at her

again. He seemed to be grappling with his anger, to bring it under control. She wondered briefly what had caused him to hate Vikings so, for she did not think for a moment that it was herself in particular that he hated, but her people as a whole.

"Would you have such scruples if I were a Viking maid?" She had to know.

" 'Twould be a fitting justice were I to have a Viking maid at my mercy. I would take pleasure in dealing with you as your men deal with Saxon women."

"We have never been to your shores before."

"Others like you have!" he bit out caustically.

So that was it. Vikings had raided this place before. Kristen wondered whom he had lost to make him so bitter that he would not touch a whore used first by those he hated, but would spend his own hate on an innocent virgin simply because she was a Viking woman. God's teeth! That he thought her a whore was going to keep her a maiden!

Kristen nearly laughed aloud as that realization came to her. It was incredible. But if this was the only means she had to protect herself, then she would make use of it. Only how did a whore behave?

"You wanted to question me?" she reminded him, feeling much more herself now that her main worry was put to rest.

"Yea. What do you know of the Danes?"

"They like this land of yours?" she offered, then couldn't help grinning when he frowned at her impertinence at forming the remark as a question.

"You think it amusing?" he demanded sharply.

"Nay, I am sorry," she said contritely, although she was still grinning to belie the point. "It's just that I do not see what you think I might know of them. We come from a different land. The only Danes I have ever met were merchants like—like many of my people are."

She would have to be more careful. If she had told him her father was a merchant, then he would have wondered why she found it necessary to whore. Better he not know her parents lived, or that she had any family at all.

His thoughts were running along the same vein, making her aware that he was still thinking of her personally. "Why would a woman with your looks sell her favors so cheaply?"

"Does it really matter why?"

"I suppose not," he replied rather curtly, then fell silent for the moment.

It was telling, what he thought of her, to keep her standing while he sat, with three empty chairs around him. She had worked all morning, been whipped in the afternoon, undergone a grueling bath that was very much like torture, and now was being made to stand here and go through this interrogation. Mischief-making Loki must be laughing at her troubles. Well, she could still laugh at them, too, and the devil could take standing any longer. She sat down cross-legged on the floor and watched his expression darken again.

"By God, wench, have you no manners at all?"

"Me?" she gasped. "And where are your manners to keep me standing while you sit?"

"Mayhap you do not realize it yet, but your status here is lower than the lowest serf."

"So this lowest serf can sit, but I cannot? Is that what you want me to understand? I am so reviled that I cannot even expect the commonest courtesies?"

"Aye, you have it right!"

Such a stubborn, querulous answer! What had she expected? Apologies to a prisoner?

"Very well, Saxon." She confounded him by laughing and pushing herself back to her feet. "Never let it be said that a Norsewoman cannot endure."

Her acquiescence only seemed to arouse his fury more. He shot to his feet, took a step toward her, then stopped himself, spun back around, and stood there at the table, apparently fighting for control again. What would he have done to her if he had not stopped?

Her brows knitted in confusion. What had she done to make him so angry? She had complied. Wasn't that what he wanted? Or was she supposed to fight instead? Did he not want her subjugation to be so easy? Aye, mayhap he wanted some reason to punish her, to use her as an outlet for his hate, and she was not giving it to him by being so agreeable.

Kristen could not have been more wrong. Royce had been in a quandary ever since she was pushed into his room. He had felt an instant attraction to her, and it was so at odds with what he should have felt that he was totally bemused. She did disgust him. He did hate her and her kind. Yet when he looked at her, his first impulse was to touch her. And when he did, he found her skin as smooth and soft as it looked.

She was too lovely to be real, and Royce was furious with himself that he could desire her, even for a few moments, and worse, that he had let her see that he did. Belittling her was more for his benefit than hers. He had to remind himself what she was. She would sell her body to any man for a price. She had no doubt lain with every man on their ship. She was a Viking whore. No woman could repel him more.

But she didn't repel him, and that was his problem. She should have been meek and frightened. Any other woman would be in her position. She should have been cowering before his anger and crying for mercy. He could have scorned her then. But she baffled him instead, giving him flippant answers and then grinning when it angered him. Laughing when he degraded her.

How could he fight this powerful attraction when she kept surprising him with the unexpected?

"Mayhap I should leave."

Royce swung around, pinning her with an angry glare. "You will not leave this hall, wench."

"I only meant your presence, since mine seems to raise your ire so."

"'Tis not you," he assured her, the lie slipping easily from his tongue. "But, yea, you may go. Only you will put these on first."

He picked up the shackles from the table and tossed them to her. Reflexly, Kristen caught them instead of letting them drop to the floor. The chain wrapped around her wrist, and one iron band slapped against her forearm, causing her to wince. In her hands the iron became a weapon, but she didn't see it thus. She looked at the shackles with loathing.

"You would still make me wear these?"

He nodded curtly. "Aye, so you know your position has only changed, not improved."

She met his gaze levelly as a flicker of contempt crossed her features. "I did not think 'twas otherwise." She lowered her arm to let the chain unwind slowly and fall by her feet. "You will have to put them on me."

"Just snap them on, wench," he ordered impatiently, misunderstanding her refusal.

"Do it yourself, Saxon," she retorted sharply. "I will never willingly restrict my own freedom."

His eyes narrowed at her temerity. His impulse was to crush her defiance immediately, before it broadened. But he suspected it would take more of a beating than he was willing to give to make her back down.

He stalked over to her and swiped up the shackles, then bent down on his knees to carelessly snap them on. Kristen stood motionless and let him, staring down at his bent head, the thick brown hair within a hand's reach of her. It was really too bad they were fated to be enemies. She would have liked meeting this man under different circumstances.

He glanced up at her. Mistaking the cause of the wistfulness reflected in her eyes, he was suddenly mindful of what he had done to her. "Where are the boots you had?"

"The old woman, Eda, said they were inappropriate for inside the hall."

"Then you will have to put cloth beneath these bands to keep the skin from rubbing raw."

"What difference, milord? 'Tis only my skin, and I am lower than the lowest serf."

He frowned as he stood up. "'Tis not my wish to mistreat you, Kristen."

That he remembered her name surprised her. She had thought he hadn't even heard her when she said it, since he had called her "wench" ever since. But his earlier words were riding her hard now that she was shackled again, when she had so hoped he would not actually do it.

"Oh, so I at least merit the same care you would give your animals?"

He understood that she was smarting from his previous remark, but he would not change what he had said, or feel guilty over it. "Aye, the same care. No more, no less."

She nodded curtly, not letting him see how wretched his words made her feel. She turned to go, but he caught her arm, his hand sliding down to her wrist when she did not stop immediately. Crazily, she noted how warm his touch was. And he did not release her wrist until several moments had passed after she looked back at him.

"Since you cannot sleep in the hall with the other servants without a guard to watch you, you will be given a chamber to yourself that can be locked. With the lock, there is no reason—" He paused, frowning, then finished abruptly: "You do not have to sleep with the chain on. I will give the key to Eda to remove it each night."

Kristen did not thank him. She could see he regretted the impulse that had prompted him to concede her that much. She gave him her back instead, leaving the room with as much pride as her slow, hobbling gait would allow.

She deserved this. She deserved all of it for defying her parents and rushing thoughtlessly into this tragic adventure. She felt so helpless of a sudden, so alone, separated from the others. Selig would have known what to do if he were here. He would have given her hope before she was taken into the hall. But Selig was dead. Oh, God, Selig!

She gave into her grief now that she didn't have to hide it any longer. She did it quietly, alone, collapsing where she stood, halfway between Royce's chamber and the stairs. Tears coursed down her cheeks, a luxury her pride would allow only this once. A portion of her grief was for herself.

Chapter Thirteen

*E*ven from her position in the far corner of the hall in the cooking area, Kristen could see the four large carts leaving the yard through the open doors at the other end of the hall. Two of the carts contained the prisoners, another carried their guards, and the last was empty. All four carts would carry back loads of the big stones from the old ruins where they were going. If not for a quirk of fate that had made the Saxon lord think she was their leader, Kristen would be going with them today.

And today might be the day they would escape. There were only nine guards for sixteen men. Something could happen, the chance they needed, and then they would be gone from here. And she would be left behind to suffer the consequences.

She had told them not to worry about her, that the Saxon lord would not kill her. She had said he was angry because he had whipped a woman. But what else could she say to force them to think of themselves first? To say that it was just as likely that he was angry because he had made a fool of himself in thinking she was their leader would make some of them hesitate to leave her behind. And with her separated from them, they would lose their chance if they tried to free her to take with them. They had to go without her.

Kristen was feeling rather sorry for herself as she watched the gates close on her friends. She had spent a wretched night in a dismal little room on a hard pallet. She should have been delighted, since it was such an improvement over the cold ground, but she was miserable instead, and lonely. Hardship was much easier to bear when shared.

Not that she had such hard labor to do now. She had never minded helping to run the household at home. In fact, when the worst storms came in the winter, the servants were not expected to venture from their warm quarters by the stables. Kristen and her mother did the cooking and the cleaning for their family. Well, more Kristen than her mother, because her mother had never liked what she called "women's work." Brenna would laugh and wink, and swear she used to think she was a boy. But Kristen didn't mind "women's work." It was the sharp, terse orders that she minded at Wyndhurst, given by servants who looked down on her.

"Does it hurt very much?"

Kristen glanced to the side to see a little girl now sitting at the end of the long table she had helped to set up for the morning meal. The child was at least six feet away from the table where Kristen was forming pastry crusts for the strawberry tarts to be served later. She had a pretty little face, all clean and pink, and two neat braids of dark brown hanging over small shoulders. Large green eyes met Kristen's, so she assumed the question had been directed at her.

"Does what hurt?"

"Your ankle. 'Tis bleeding."

Kristen looked down at her ankles. Sure enough, blood was dripping into the shoe on her left foot. She was annoyed with herself, for it was a thoroughly stupid thing for her to have done, to stubbornly refuse to put cloth under the iron bands this morn. A childish thing, done with the express hope that she might make a certain Saxon lord feel a small measure of guilt when he saw that her skin was wearing away from his cursed shackles. Whom did she hurt but herself? He certainly wouldn't care, for they were his shackles, after all.

She glanced back at the little girl whose expression was so raptly attentive. "Nay, it does not hurt," Kristen assured her with a smile.

"Truly? Do you not feel pain?"

"Surely I do. But, truth to tell, I have so many other things on my mind, I did not notice a little pain way down there." And she indicated her feet.

The girl giggled at Kristen's reference to her height. "Does it feel strange, to be so tall?"

"Nay."

"But to be taller than a man—"

Kristen's chuckle interrupted her. "In Norway, 'tis very rare for that to happen."

"Oh, aye, the Vikings are all big men."

Kristen grinned at the wonder in the child's voice as she stated that fact. "What is your name, little one?"

"Meghan."

"'Tis such a nice day. Why are you not out chasing butterflies and making flower garlands, or finding birds' nests? 'Tis what I did at your age. Would that not be more fun than staying in the hall?"

"I never leave Wyndhurst."

"Is it not safe?"

The child glanced down at her hands, which were resting on the table. "'Tis safe, but I do not like to go alone."

"But there are other children here."

"They will not play with me."

Kristen was moved by the sad note in the little girl's voice. But it was Eda, coming to stand beside her, who supplied the reason for it.

"The other children are afraid to play with the lord's sister, and you should not be speaking to her, either," Eda hissed in her ear.

Kristen gave the older woman a frigid look. "Until 'tis forbidden, I will speak to whomever I please."

"Will you, wench?" Eda retorted. "Then do not be surprised if 'tis forbidden immediately, for he looks none too pleased."

Kristen had no time to wonder what Eda meant, for her shoulder was pinched in a cruel grip that spun her about to face a very angry Saxon.

Royce had no thought for his sister, for he had not even noticed that she was in the hall. When he entered the long room, his eyes were drawn directly to the tawny head in the cooking area. He had not seen her since she left his chamber yesterday, for he had taken his evening meal with his cousins in Alden's room, deliberately staying away from the hall, where the wench would be.

While she stood at the end of the worktable, with her back to him, his eyes had traveled leisurely down her long frame from top to bottom. It was when they stopped on the iron about her ankles, clearly visible because of the unseemly short length of her chainse, that his ire rose. Even from across the room he could see the blood soaking the side of her cloth shoe.

His countenance was stormy now. "If you think festering wounds about your feet will cause those shackles to be set aside, you are mistaken!"

Kristen relaxed, knowing now what caused him to growl at her so abrasively. "I did not think it."

"Then explain yourself! You were told to pad that iron with cloth."

"I forgot to ask for the cloth," she fibbed. Then she added baldly, "I was shuffled down here before the sun even rose and set immediately to work. I confess I was more asleep than awake and not thinking of something that has become so much a part of me."

Some of the heat left his expression, leaving only a

narrowed frown. She could see that he didn't know whether to believe her or not. This she found so amusing that she laughed, confusing him even more.

"Ah, milord, I see you thought I hoped to stir your sympathy. Be assured I am not so foolish as to think you have such tender sentiments."

He flushed with renewed anger, turning so livid she thought surely he would strike her. She had boldly insulted him, but doing it with humor to make it appear a left-handed compliment instead. Apparently he could not deal with such underhanded tactics from a woman.

He rounded on Eda, terrifying the poor woman with his expression. "Attend to her feet now, and see she does not *forget* to pad the irons again!"

With one last furious look at Kristen, he stalked away. Eda left to fetch the cloth, grumbling that she had enough to do without having to pamper a heathen, one who didn't have enough sense not to anger her lord. Kristen grinned, ignoring the old woman, her eyes following Royce until he left the hall. The Saxon was not so different from the men she knew.

"How did you dare laugh at him when he was so angry?"

Kristen had forgotten about Meghan. She looked over and smiled at her now, seeing those large green eyes filled with amazement and awe.

"His temper was not so terrible."

"You were not frightened even a little?"

"Should I have been?"

"I was, and he was not even shouting at me."

Kristen frowned. "Eda said he is your brother. Surely you are not afraid of him?"

"Nay . . . well, sometimes."

"Sometimes? Does he beat you?"

Meghan seemed surprised by this question. "Nay, he never has."

"Then why would you be afraid of him?"

"He might beat me. He is so big and looks so mean when he is angry."

Kristen laughed now in sympathy. "Oh, little one, most men look mean when they are angry, but that is not a reflection of how they really are. And your brother is big, aye, but my father is even bigger—just a little bit bigger, mind you—and he has a terrible temper, too. Yet there is no kinder man than my father, nor more loving to his family. My brothers have tempers, too, and do you know what I do when they shout at me?"

"What?"

"I shout right back."

"Are they bigger than you?"

"Aye, even the youngest, who has only seen fourteen winters, has passed me in height, though not by much. He still has some growing to do. Do you have no other family yourself, besides your brother?"

"I did have another brother, but I do not remember him. He died with my father when other Vikings raided. 'Twas five years ago."

Kristen grimaced. God's teeth, the Saxon did have reason to hate her and her people. No wonder he had wanted to kill them all at first sight. She was surprised he had changed his mind.

"I am sorry, Meghan," she offered lamely. "Your people have suffered much because of mine."

"They were Danes, those others."

"I do not see much difference. We came here to raid, too, though not your manor, if 'tis any consolation."

Meghan frowned. "You mean your friends would not have attacked Wyndhurst?"

"Nay, 'twas a monastery farther inland they were after, and that only as a lark."

"Jurro?"

"Aye."

"But 'twas destroyed by the Danes five years ago and never rebuilt."

"Oh, God!" Kristen groaned. "Selig dead and half the others, and all for naught!"

"Was Selig a friend?" Meghan asked hesitantly.

"A friend? Aye, a friend—and brother," Kristen replied brokenly.

"You lost a brother in the forest battle?"

"Aye . . . aye . . . aye!"

Kristen's fist smashed a pastry crust with each utterance, and when that did not relieve the anguish, she toppled the table. She was halfway to the entrance of the hall when Eda ran after her, trying to grab hold of her arm to stop her.

"Do not do it, wench," the old woman warned. "You will be punished."

"I do not care!"

"You will. I heard what you told the young one. I wish I had not stopped to listen, but I did. I am sorry for your loss, and I never thought I would be saying that to the likes of you, but I am. Hurting yourself now will not help any. Go back and clean up the mess you made and none need know 'twas done apurpose."

Kristen halted and stared hard at Eda before she finally nodded. She turned back to the cooking area. Seeing the shambles there, she sighed. Meghan was nowhere in sight now. Fortunately, no one else was, either, at this early hour.

"The child?"

Eda snorted. "Took a fright when you got violent. She will think twice ere she speaks to you again."

Kristen let out another sigh.

Chapter Fourteen

*T*wo weeks had come and gone since Kristen was moved into the hall. Thorolf and the others had apparently had no opportunity to escape in this time, for they still labored on the wall. She had not been able to speak to them or even let them see her to know she was faring well. If she got near an open window or door, someone always shouted at her to get back. She seemed to be watched constantly, either by the servants or by Royce's armed retainers, who were often in the hall.

She had made use of her time to learn all she could of the Saxons. She was treated with an unusual combination of fear and contempt by the servants, except for Eda, who offered a grudging sort of respect now, and what might even pass for liking, though this was hard to discern, for the woman had a natural gruffness about her. But Eda was easily maneuvered to volunteer information without being aware that she was being subtly plied for it.

Kristen now knew a good deal about Wyndhurst and its lord. The manor was self-sufficient, a necessity with the nearest town far away. Royce was a thane, one of the king's great nobles, and Wyndhurst comprised miles of land. As in Norway, there were freemen, called churls here, who worked the soil and worked also in the manor, many with specific trades. They could own land, but owed dues to crown and church, as well as military service. Royce trained those in his area for the coming war with the Danes. Many were already his personal retainers. He also trained some of his more able serfs, those people not free but bound to the land, supplying them with arms and the opportunity to buy their freedom. He would have a small army ready to join King Alfred's defense when the time came.

Of Royce in particular, Kristen had learned he was not married yet, but would be later this year. Eda could tell her little about his betrothed, who lived farther north, except that her name was Corliss and she was supposed to be very beautiful. Eda had much more to say about Lord Royce's first betrothed, the Lady Rhona, and Kristen surprised herself by actually feeling sympathy for the Saxon when she learned he had lost more in that other Viking raid than she had first thought. He had loved the Lady Rhona. No one knew what he felt for the Lady Corliss.

Royce's cousin, Darrelle, who ran the domestic side of his household, had ignored Kristen since that first day, leaving her in Eda's charge. She was a fascinating woman to watch, for she was contrary in her behavior, haughty and condescending at one moment, needing praise and reassurance in the next. She was also an emotional woman. Kristen had once seen her complain shrilly to Royce, only to burst into tears when he lost patience with her and replied sharply. She could also cry over something so minor as a few misplaced stitches on the tapestry she was working.

Darrelle was not a problem for Kristen, since she treated the prisoner as if she were not even there. Meghan was no problem, either, though Kristen had worried for a while that she might be. The child's natural curiosity had prompted Kristen to tell her much more about herself than she should have that day they met, things she did not want to reach Royce's ears. If he knew she had a loving family and that her brother was one of those who died in the forest, then he might reevaluate his opinion that she was a whore. But Meghan had obviously not repeated anything she had learned from Kristen, and it was as Eda had guessed: The child did not come near Kristen again.

Royce ignored her also, or pretended to. She saw him every day, for he could not pass through the hall without her seeing him. But he did not look at her at these times. It was when he was at his leisure in the hall that she would find him watching her.

Kristen was amused by his attitude toward her. She knew he held her in contempt for what he thought she was, and also despised her because of her people. Yet aside from that, he was still attracted to her. That he fought so determinedly against the attraction was what was so amusing. She could feel his eyes following her movements, but when she would look up, he would quickly look away.

Once, though, he did not look away. In fact, Royce stared so hard at her that night, the man beside him had to call his name three times before gaining his attention. Kristen had laughed aloud at that, the deep, rich tones carrying across the hall to Royce, infuriating him. He had slammed his tankard of mead down on the table and departed the hall in angry strides, bemusing his men, and delighting Kristen that she had the power to affect him so strongly.

Kristen thought often about that night. In truth, she thought often about Royce. Knowing that he wanted her gave her a heady feeling of pleasure. And, thanks to her mother, she knew why.

Brenna had told her once, "You will know the man for you when you meet him. I knew it and suffered long because I would not admit it, even to myself. Do not be like me, daughter. When you find the man who gives you pleasure in sight, joy of your senses, who makes you feel strange and wonderful inside when he comes near you, this is the man you will be happy with, the one you can love, as I love your father."

Kristen had been fascinated by Royce the first time she saw him. To look at him was immensely pleasurable. And when he was near she did feel different, more alive, more aware of herself. Her humor she attributed to him, for she only felt like laughing when he was around. She was not fool enough to think she loved him, for she would leave this place in a minute if she could. But she was enough in tune with her feelings to realize she wanted Royce of Wyndhurst: to touch him, to feel his arms around her, to know him as a woman knows a man. Love could grow from these feelings, and surely would, if she was here long enough.

It was ironic that the first man she should desire herself, after being desired by so many, should be the one man who resisted her. She was sure she could have him if she set her mind to it. But would he be honorable enough to marry her afterward? There was his betrothed to consider. There was her own position as his prisoner, which in fact made her a slave, as Eda had sharply pointed out one day. There was the hate he harbored for her people, too. Could all of that be overcome with what would begin simply as passion?

The Vikings did not believe in leaving their futures to the fates, but in carving their own fates. It was believed the gods would reward those who went forth valiantly to conquer and to gain. Vikings gave no account to meekness, or suffering patience. They fought for what they wanted. Defeat held no honor.

These sentiments were instilled in Kristen even though she was a Christian. As a Christian she knew she should leave her future in the hands of God, to have patience and depend on him to reward her if it was His will. But as the daughter of a Viking she knew that if she wanted Royce of Wyndhurst for her husband, then she would have to win him, to conquer the fates that opposed them, to fight for what she wanted, in whatever way she could.

Did she want him for her husband? Aye, she did. She had finally found the man she could be happy with. Her enemy. It would be laughable if it weren't so disheartening. Yet she did have faith in her abilities. And the outcome could be more than worth the challenge.

The hour was late. Two of the five women who prepared the meals and served the tables were sick today, leaving more for the remaining three to do, which kept them busy much longer than usual. Since Kristen was one of the three, the other servants who might have helped scorned to do so, the feeling being that if anyone should work longer, she should.

She did not mind. Royce had stayed in the hall longer than usual tonight, and she had enjoyed watching him dice with his men. In fact, she spent more time watching him than she did cleaning up after the final meal. She had missed seeing him leave the hall, though, while Eda was chastising her for not paying attention to what she was doing.

It was quiet now, and dark in the hall except for the two torches still burning by the great hearth. The servants had all spread their pallets about the floor and were quiet for the night. Only Eda and Kristen remained, Eda putting everything in readiness for the morn.

Kristen was not tired, but her feet were sore because she had been standing for most of the day. So it was every day, from the moment she was wakened at first light until she was locked away in her chamber after the last meal of the day. Only today was different.

Kristen had been stretching when she heard the steps crossing the floor, coming from the entrance. She glanced up curiously, her heartbeat quickening when she saw Royce coming out of the shadows, his direction not the stairs, but toward her, straight to her.

She did not move, waiting for him to reach her. His expression was intense, harsh, and her heart beat even faster, not in fear but in expectation. When he stopped, she felt only a moment's surprise when his hand went to the back of her neck, his fingers gripping her hair to yank her head back. She held her breath as his eyes moved angrily over her face.

"Why do you tempt me so?" He asked this not of her, but to himself.

"Do I, milord?"

"You do it apurpose," he accused her. "You knew I stood by the entrance watching you."

"Nay, I thought you had retired."

"Liar!" he hissed before his mouth slashed down over hers.

Kristen had waited for this, to know the feel of his lips, to be able to touch him. She had wanted this to happen, but she had not guessed how devastating the actuality would be. Nothing could have prepared her for such a violent jolt of desire, when she had never felt desire before.

His mouth moved over hers brutally in his anger. He gripped her hair, holding her still for this ravishment, yet he did not touch her otherwise. Kristen was the one to lean into him, until she could feel the full length of his body and know the extent of his desire. This inflamed her more. She didn't care that this was not what he wanted, that he was kissing her against his own will, and probably hating her more because of it. She wrapped her arms around his back, moving her hands up over the hard muscle there until she gripped his shoulders, holding him tight to her.

She heard him groan at her complete acceptance of

him, and his other arm slipped about her waist, crushing her tighter to him. His tongue plunged into her mouth and she drew on it, capturing it like a prize, refusing to let go. God in heaven, this was wonderful, more thrilling than anything she had ever felt before. She would have let him take her there, in the hall, on the table, the floor—she didn't care. She wanted to make love with him now, before he came to his senses and stopped.

He did stop, and Kristen sighed miserably when his lips left hers. He looked down at her, his eyes fierce, filled half with passion, half with fury. She met his look boldly, but this served only to anger him more.

With a snarl, he shoved her away from him. "Bitch! My God, you have no shame, do you?"

Kristen would have laughed at that if she were not so disappointed. He was placing the blame on her, as if she had come to him, not he to her. She did not so much mind that, for she had hoped he would come to her. But how could he now deny them what they both wanted? Where did he get the strength to do so, when she was standing there aching to be back in his arms?

He might not be willing to be honest in what he was feeling now, but she had no such qualms. "I feel no shame in wanting you," she told him softly.

"Or any man!" he sneered cruelly.

"Nay, only you." She smiled then at his snort of disbelief. Deliberately, she added in a teasing tone, "You are my heartmate, Royce. Begin to accept it. You will eventually."

"You will never count me as one of your lovers, wench," he stated emphatically.

She shrugged, the sigh she gave louder than necessary. "Very well, milord, if that is your wish."

"Not my wish, the truth," he insisted. "And you will cease to use your whore's tricks on me."

Kristen could not help but laugh at this order. "What tricks are those, milord? I am only guilty of looking at you, mayhap more than I should, but I cannot seem to help myself. You are, after all, the most splendid man here."

He drew in his breath sharply. "God's mercy, are all Viking whores as brazen as you?"

She had been called whore once too often. She knew she dared not deny it, for she wanted him in passion, not revenge, as he would surely take her if he knew she was a virgin. But his calling her whore now, after he had just ravaged her senses, grated harshly.

Irritation was ripe in her voice. "I know no whores, so I cannot answer that. What you call brazen, I call honesty. Would you rather I lie and say I hate you, that I despise the sight of you?"

"How can you not hate me? I have enslaved you. I keep you shackled and I know you hate the chain."

"Is that why I wear it still, because you know I hate it?" she asked suspiciously.

He didn't bother to answer that. "I think you do hate me, that you tempt me apurpose, hoping to have revenge by bewitching me."

"If you believe that, then you will never accept what I am willing to give, Saxon, and I am sorry for that. I do hate these shackles, but not you. And being enslaved is not new to my family," she added cryptically. "If I thought that I would always be enslaved and shackled, then aye, mayhap I would hate you."

"So you hope to escape?"

Her eyes narrowed at him. "I am through telling you what I hope for, through speaking the truth to you when you will not believe it. Think whatever you like."

She turned her back on him, but was tense, waiting for him to walk away. He did not do so immediately.

She imagined he was fighting to control a new fury that she would dare dismiss him like that. She would have been much appeased if she had seen that his eyes had simply moved over her, revealing for one unguarded moment the yearning in his soul.

Chapter Fifteen

*K*risten was in no fine mood the next morning. She had been open and honest with the Saxon, baring her feelings to him, giving him that advantage over her, and he her enemy, and she got only his hypocrisy in response. He wanted her, yet he was determined to deny it to himself and to her, making them both suffer instead. If that was not enough to unsettle her stomach and make her think herself a worse fool than he was, Eda had witnessed their whole confrontation and was none too pleased.

"Taunt him no more, wench," she had warned Kristen angrily. "You will be sorry if he does take you to bed, for you will never be more than a slave to him."

It might well be true, and it made Kristen furious. Was she prepared to give up her innocence to a man who might never care for her? She had been so sure she could make him care, but now she had doubts, and she did not like being doubtful. It undermined her confidence and depressed her terribly.

They were cleaning the chambers this morning on the front-yard side of the house, as they did every morning. Royce's chamber was one of these. Kristen had looked at his bed before with a feeling of excitement. This morning she felt like ripping it to shreds. She pounded the pillow so hard, in fact, that feathers flew out of the seams.

"From one extreme to the other," Eda remarked, shaking her head at Kristen. "Think no more of him."

"Leave me alone," Kristen warned. "You said your piece last eventide."

"But not enough, I see. If you think to harm him now, you had best think again."

It was the last straw for Kristen, after spending a miserable night confronting the new emotions the Saxon had provoked in her. "Harm him?" Kristen snarled. "If I harm anyone, woman, 'twill be you if you do not cease to nag me!"

Eda backed away warily. She had grown lax around Kristen, who had showed no hostility until now. She had begun to like the girl, forgetting that she was of a race that thrived on death and destruction. She had grown lax enough to be alone with the girl as she was now. And it was made plain to her, looking at the tall young woman seething with emotion, that it would be a simple matter, chained or not, for Kristen to pick her up and throw her out the open window. She was big enough and strong enough to do so. Not that she would be foolish enough to do it. But she *could* do it.

Eda moved swiftly toward the door, grumbling more testily with each step that put her safely out of Kristen's reach. "Threaten an old woman, will you? And after I kept the others from abusing you?" At the door she turned to glower. "Finish here alone. And your attitude had best be improved, wench, ere you come below, or you can spend the rest of the day locked away, and without your supper. See if I care. And do not dawdle, or I will send one of the men up to fetch you down. You will not have such an easy time throwing a man out that window."

Kristen wondered about the woman's last unusual statement for a moment, then dismissed it from her mind. This was the first time she had been left alone in an unlocked room. And it was his room. In no time at all she could destroy its contents. There was no one to stop her until the deed was done. Royce would beat her then, and she would welcome the pain it would bring, the oblivion, the hate afterward, for she still did not hate him. She should, but she did not.

The idea was tempting, but more tempting was the possibility of finding an axe, the one sure weapon that could aid her escape. She had wasted too much time concentrating on the Saxon, when she should have been thinking only of leaving this place. An axe would sever the chain that bound her feet. An axe would open the shutters that were locked in her chamber each night. She had only a thin blanket and a rough sheet on her pallet, but with those and her own clothes tied together, she might have a long enough length to throw out the window and climb down. That same axe would then open the door that locked in Thorolf and the others. If she could find an axe, she could hide it in her chamber now before she went below. Then tonight . . .

There was not a single axe among the assortment of weapons hung on the wall. Kristen quickly bent to the large coffer at the base of Royce's bed and opened it. Carefully she moved the clothes on the top, but only found more clothes underneath. She looked to the smaller coffer between the windows, but the iron lock on it stared back at her.

She turned to the wall of weapons. There were old swords, some richly inlaid with silver, one even sheathed in a pure-gold scabbard. There were spears, a crossbow, a long club that must have been ancient, and dozens of daggers in different lengths and designs. She itched to steal one for herself, but knew the empty space would be noticed immediately. But a dagger might be able to pry open the lock on that coffer in such a way that it would not be noticed, at least for a while.

She took down the smallest dagger, the easiest to work on the lock with, and knelt down in front of the coffer. The lock was not a simple design. In fact, she could find no keyhole on any of its sides.

"'Tis not locked, you know. That is only an ornament you are handling. The chest has no catch. Go on, lift it and see for yourself. My cousin has no need to lock his valuables. He knows no one will steal from him here."

Kristen turned her head slowly with dread, not recognizing that voice. The dread was gone once her eyes touched on the man's face. She knew him. She knew those bright light-blue eyes, that height only a few inches taller than her own. She would never forget the sight of this man with sword in hand, and Selig beside him falling to the ground.

"You!" Kristen hissed, jumping to her feet. "You should be dead!"

He took no note of her words. His eyes moved over her, wide with amazement. "God's breath, Royce's description of you did not do you justice."

Likewise, Kristen was not listening to him, either. She would have flown at him in an instant, but she was not so far gone in the tide of rage that washed over her that she was unmindful of her chain. She moved toward him in her slow tread, the chain scraping against the floor, drawing his eyes to it. He winced, seeing the shackles. His obvious compassion had no effect on her. As long as he did not notice the dagger gripped in her fist, she would have him.

She spoke to draw his eyes back to her face. She would be on him in a moment. "I did not ask after you. I assumed you had died, for no one made mention of you."

"I have been recovering. You very nearly—"

She struck, aiming for his throat. His reflexes were better than she anticipated, however, so she quickly changed direction, slashing beneath the arm he had raised to block her. But he was good, jumping back to avoid the blade. If the dagger were just a little longer, she would have had a clean cut. As it was, she only ripped open his tunic, drawing a thin line of blood. She saw this even as she spun about for momentum to come around for a side attack at his neck.

His left hand caught her wrist, inches away from her target. But he had not so much strength in this hand, and she had thrown her whole body into the slash. The blade continued, drawing blood again, and he could not stop it, only deflect it, bringing her hand down in front of him.

He was a slim man for all his height, nowhere near as strong as Royce. And Kristen had the added strength of revenge goading her. He could not hold on to her wrist with his left hand. She felt his grip slipping, and changed from pulling away to a sharp thrust. The blade half entered his chest, before his right hand came up to help the left, yanking the blade out.

"For God's sake, wench, cease!"

"When you are dead, Saxon dog!"

With her free hand, she gripped a handful of his hair to pull him off balance. But he turned his body into hers, locking her right arm under his so she could no longer maneuver with it and he was free to pry her fingers off the dagger. She screamed in rage when she felt it slip from her grasp. He made the mistake of letting her go then. Before he could turn back to face her, she locked both hands together and clubbed him with them on his back.

The blow sent him staggering into the hall, where he slammed against the opposite wall. The dagger had fallen on the floor, halfway between them. Kristen jumped for it, but the cursed chain tripped up her feet and she lost her balance. Royce's cousin had turned just as she was falling, and he threw himself at her. The momentum carried them both back into the room, where they landed heavily on the floor.

This would have been the end of Kristen's fight, if she were a small woman. As it was, Alden thought she was finished. He had fallen on top of her, then gripped a wrist in each hand, holding them by her head. He looked down at her in confusion, and little patience at this point.

"Why?" he demanded. "Royce said you have not been hostile to anyone. Why me?"

"You killed Selig! He will be avenged, by me!"

She threw him to the side, just as the last word was out. In an instant she was on top of him and had his head between her hands. Twice she slammed his head onto the floor before arms circled her chest and lifted her off.

Kristen struggled until the arms tightened, squeezing out her breath, and a voice hissed in her ear, "Be still!"

Oh, unfair! Not him! She could fight anyone but him.

Kristen obeyed the order, sagging back against Royce but still staring down at the man on the floor. In another moment she would have had him dazed enough so she could have gone for another weapon on the wall. This time she would have gotten one that would have done the deed. Why did the Saxon have to come now?

"What in God's name do you think you were doing, Alden?" Royce demanded.

"Me?" Alden sat up, shaking his head. "Look at me! Does it look as if I was doing aught?"

"Nay, and I will know why! If you tell me a woman has twice bested you, so help me—"

"Have a heart, Royce." Alden winced. "I have been weak as a babe, and she is not exactly a frail woman. You try wrestling with her and see how you fare."

"She is but a woman," Royce muttered contemptuously. So saying, he threw Kristen away from him, a move that was meant to send her flying, but only made her stumble once before she caught herself and tossed her head, glaring at him.

"Just a woman, eh?" Alden shook his head again. "Well, this woman has an uncommon knowledge of weapons, so do not say I did not warn you, though 'twould seem 'tis only me she wants revenge against."

"Why?"

"Ask her."

Royce turned on Kristen. "Why?" he repeated. She crossed her arms over her chest, refusing to speak. Royce was fast losing patience and snapped at Alden, "What did she say to you?"

"That I killed someone she calls Selig. She said she would avenge him."

"A lover, no doubt."

"Not a lover!" Kristen spat now, her eyes dark with fury.

"Then who was he?"

"You will never know that, Saxon."

"By God, you *will* tell me!" he stormed, taking hold of her arm to jerk her back in front of him.

"Will I?" she taunted him with a sneer. "How will you make me? Will you beat me, torture me? You can do that, but I will still only tell you what I want to tell you and no more. Nor will I beg for mercy, Saxon, so you may as well kill me now and have done with it."

"Get below!" Royce growled, shoving her away again.

She walked away slowly, yet her carriage was as erect and proud as a queen's. Royce frowned at the empty doorway even after she was gone. And then he rounded on his cousin just as Alden was standing up.

"Nay, yell at me no more, Royce. God help me, I will hear enough screaming when Darrelle sees all this blood."

"Then tend to your new wounds yourself, and say naught of this. You are not seriously hurt, are you?"

"I was beginning to wonder if you cared." Alden grinned. "Nay, only a few pricks—though, God's truth, I was this close to having my throat slit. She fights like a demon, and she gave me no warning she was about to attack me."

"Go tend your cuts, Alden," Royce said disgustedly.

"I intend to, before Darrelle has a chance to restrict me to my room again. For a loving sister, her concern is stifling."

"Alden?"

"Yea." He turned at the door.

"Stay away from her."

Alden grinned. "That warning was unnecessary. I have had enough dealings with that wench to last me a lifetime."

Chapter Sixteen

Royce leaned back in his chair, waiting for Alden to complete his turn at the dice game they were playing. It was the hottest day yet this summer, and although the small table they were using was drawn directly in front of an open window, little breeze was stirring outside or making its way into the hall.

Most of Royce's men lounged about the large barrel of mead, even though it was only late afternoon. They had spent the morning training the less-skilled churls in the arts of warfare, but the heat had driven them back to the hall early. It was simply not a day for any but the most necessary tasks.

This was the first day Alden had ventured into the hall since the Vikings' arrival. Two days had passed since the mishap that had sent him back to his bed. One of his new wounds was worse than he had at first suspected, and had refused to stop bleeding. He had lost more blood than necessary in waiting too long before he finally called Eartha to tend him. The loss had weakened him to the point where his bed again looked inviting. His only consolation was that Eartha had kept quiet and Darrelle still knew nothing of his second disastrous encounter with the Viking wench.

Royce had been anything but amused when he had seen the nasty chest wound later that same day. He had immediately ordered a new chain for Kristen, a long length that was secured to the wall in the cooking area and also to the chain between her feet, giving her room only to reach the long table there where she did most of her work.

He regretted that order after his anger wore off. He knew she hated her shackles. How much more must she despise this new chain that restricted her. He had not been able to look at her since. He did not want to see misery etched on her lovely face. He did not want to see the hate that she must surely feel for him now.

Royce didn't know what to do about Kristen. He was in the midst of a dilemma that he had never faced before, and he had no one to discuss it with. He had always been able to talk over anything with Alden, but he was loath to let Alden or anyone else know how much the wench troubled him.

No matter how he sought to avoid it, she constantly preyed on his mind. He could not even escape her when he slept, for she invaded his dreams too. She was like no woman he had ever known. Not once had he seen her cry or bewail her plight. Not once had she cowered in fear before him. She hated her shackles, yet she had not begged to have them removed as other women would. She asked for no quarter, no mercy. She had asked for nothing, in fact, nothing except—him. She had said she wanted him.

God, how those words had torn at his vitals and nearly destroyed his resolve when she said them! He had told her he suspected she intentionally meant to bewitch him. Whether it was intentional or not, he was already bewitched, from the day she had been cleaned up to reveal the incredible beauty that had been hidden beneath the grime.

He had never felt such desire as this woman aroused in him. Not even Rhona, whom he had wanted above all women, had ever affected him this strongly. He had only to look at the wench and she destroyed his composure. His blood would run hot. His body would ache with need.

She had driven him past his endurance the other night. He had returned to the hall to retire, but he should never have stopped to look at her, for he was caught, mesmerized by her slow, sensuous movements, watching her hand rise to her face to smooth back a tawny lock of hair, seeing her stretch, her back arch, her breasts thrust forward, more firmly outlined. It was as if an invisible line had been thrown out to lure him in, for he moved toward her without conscious thought, and nothing could have stopped him from tasting those enticing lips when he finally reached her.

He would like to think she was a witch, or mayhap a Viking priestess, with a special magic divined from her many gods. That would certainly explain his dilemma: how he could loathe her and want her at the same time. She stirred emotions in him that he did not understand. It should not bother him if she suffered, but it did. It should not matter to him that she was a whore, but it did. He even became irrational every time he thought of the many men she had lain with, possibly every man from the ship, so he tried not to think of it. But now to know that she had cared for one more than all the others, enough to want revenge for his death, inflamed him even more.

He had asked Thorolf who this Selig was. But the wily Viking had answered with another question, asking who Kristen had said he was. It was obvious he would get no confidences from her companions, so Royce had said no more. It was as Kristen said. He would learn only what she wanted him to know, and she was through telling him anything.

"If you do not want to finish the game, Royce, say so."

"What?"

"I finished my turn hours ago."

Royce sat forward, swiping up the dice. "Do not exaggerate, Cousin. And I have things on my mind."

"You have often of late been deeply thoughtful. Of course, 'tis no wonder with all that has happened this summer. And now we have word that the King is coming for a visit, but he does not say when he will arrive."

"He will come when he comes." Royce grunted. "That does not concern me."

"Nay? Then you must still be worried about the prisoners," Alden speculated. "Or is it only one prisoner who has been on your mind?"

"Who is that?"

"Who, indeed?" Alden laughed. "Come now, Royce. Why did you not tell me she was so incredibly lovely?"

"Tell me something, Alden. She has tried to kill you twice. How can you laugh about her?"

"She has her reasons, I imagine, but even so, who could despise such a beautiful woman?"

"I can."

"Can you? Why? Surely you do not blame her for what the Danes did? She is not a Dane."

"You forget her companions came here to raid and kill, too, and would have laid waste to Wyndhurst if you had not stopped them in the forest."

A small voice intruded on their conversation. "They would have passed by here."

Royce and Alden both glanced toward Meghan, who had come quietly to stand near their table to watch them play. Royce frowned, but quickly smoothed his features out when Meghan lowered her eyes from him.

Gently he asked, "Why do you say that, midget?"

She peeked up at him, then came closer when she saw he was not angry with her for interrupting them.

"Kristen told me so. She said they were after Jurro monastery, and that only as a lark."

"When did you speak to her?"

"The day after she was brought in the hall."

"Did she tell you aught else, Meghan?"

"Many things. She talked about her family. She said her father is even taller than you and he has a terrible temper, too." Meghan stopped, realizing what she had unwittingly stated. "I did not mean to imply—"

"Of course you did," Alden teased her with a grin, pulling her onto his lap. "We all know what a terrible temper your brother has."

Royce smiled at her to show he was not angry. "Go on, midget. What else did the wench tell you?"

"You are not revealing secrets, are you, Meghan?" Alden continued to tease.

"Alden!" Royce snapped impatiently.

"Oh-ho, that interested, are you?"

Meghan surprised them both by asking then, "Why did you order her chained to the wall, Royce?"

He was just annoyed enough with Alden to answer with a sneer, "Because she wants to kill our cousin here, and he has not the strength to protect himself from her, so I must do it for him."

Meghan turned around in his lap to give Alden a wide-eyed look. "Why does she want to kill you?"

"Why, indeed?" he bemoaned mockingly. "I am such a nice fellow."

"Then you must be mistaken," Meghan said.

"Nay, little one, 'tis in fact true," Alden admitted. "I am supposed to have killed someone she calls Selig, and she says she wants revenge for his death."

"*You* killed Selig?" Meghan gasped. "Oh, Alden, why did you have to be the one? She must hate you terribly."

Royce leaned across the table and grasped his sister's

chin to make her look at him. "Do you know who Selig was, Meghan?" he asked softly.

"Yea, she told me who he was. But she got so upset when she mentioned him. 'Twas after I told her Jurro was destroyed by the Danes. She said Selig and half the others died for naught. She frightened me then, for she pounded the table with her fists, then toppled it over. I have not talked to her since, but I suppose now she was only violent because of her grief. She was so friendly to me before that."

"Aye, she can be a very friendly wench when it suits her," Royce murmured to himself, but he was not forgetting what interested him most. "Who was Selig, Meghan?"

"Did Alden not ask her?"

"Meghan!"

She paled at his raised voice and answered quickly, "Her brother, Royce. She said he was her friend, and brother."

Even in his sudden confusion at her revelation, Royce noted her anxiety and cursed himself for causing it with his impatience. "Meghan, sweet, I am not angry with you."

"Not even for speaking to her?"

"Nay, not even for that," he assured her. "Now, why not go and see what treasures Darrelle has found? She has brought in some of the cargo that was taken from the Viking ship. She said something about finding fur trimmings for new gowns for you and her."

Meghan went off happily to the other side of the hall, where the women were gathered. Royce sat back, staring at Alden, seeing that his cousin was as surprised as he was.

"A brother!" Royce said incredulously. "How could she have a brother among those men? 'Twould mean he knew why she was there and countenanced it."

"Mayhap we were wrong in assuming she is a whore?" Alden suggested.

"Nay," Royce replied testily. "She has admitted what she is."

Alden shrugged. "Then they must have a different outlook on such things. What do you really know of their kind? Mayhap they find naught wrong with a woman who gives herself to many. Who is to say all their women are not whores?"

Royce frowned, for he was remembering Kristen telling him she knew no other whores. But he did not mention this to Alden, for he saw that Darrelle was about to interrupt them.

"Royce, look at this," Darrelle cried excitedly, showing him the gown she had found. "Have you ever seen such fine velvet? It must surely come from the Far East."

He merely glanced disinterestedly at the dark-green material she held, until she shook it out and held it up in front of her, so that it lay over her own clothes. The gown was sleeveless, and very rich indeed, with precious pearls forming a thick rope along the deep V of the neckline. Another rope of pearls was tied about the narrow waist, apparently to be used for a girdle. A solid-gold clasp was used for fastening the belt.

"There is another gown of the same design," Darrelle went on to say. "And shoes to match, with armbands of pure gold and a necklace of amber stones. They were all bundled together. Will you give them to Corliss, Royce? She will surely love such rich gifts. If not, I can make use of them myself. But whichever, the gowns will have to be altered. Sleeves have to be added, but the same material can be used, for much of it has to be cut off the bottom. The gowns are much too long, as you can see. I swear the women of Norway must all be giants. To wear such long gowns they would have to be."

Royce was staring at the extra material—a good half foot of it, at least—that lay on the floor at Darrelle's feet. "Have them taken to my chamber, Cousin."

"You do not want me to alter them?" she asked in disappointment.

"Nay, not just yet."

The moment Darrelle walked away, Royce's eyes flew to the cooking area at the far end of the hall, and lit on Kristen. She stood with her head bent over the task she was about, yet she still stood at least half a foot or more above the other women around her. Her long, graceful body was covered in the same clothes she had been given, clothes too tight and confining for her, and much too short.

"What are you thinking, Cousin?" Alden asked suspiciously, seeing where his attention had gone.

"That the clothes belong to my pretty new slave," Royce replied without taking his eyes from Kristen.

"Come now, you cannot really think so!" Alden scoffed. "'Twould mean she is no common wench, to own such rich apparel. Not even Queen Ealhswith has aught so fine as that green velvet. And the pearls alone are worth a fortune."

Royce glanced back at Alden, his expression not as intense, but still thoughtful. "I suppose 'tis unlikely, but I will find out for certain before this day is through."

"How? Asking if the clothes are hers will not suffice. She will tell you aye, whether 'tis true or not, for what woman would not claim such fine garb, when there is no one to deny the claim?"

"We shall see."

Royce said this so ominously that Alden spared a moment's pity for the Viking wench, wondering in what dire manner his cousin was planning to get at the truth. He did not care to know himself.

Chapter Seventeen

*T*he work was done for the day, and Kristen was ready to drop gratefully onto her pallet. The sweltering heat had worn her ragged today, and there had been the added warmth of the hearth, near which she was chained, and no breeze to take some of its heat away.

She could have kissed Eda when she bent down to remove the new chain that Kristen was made to wear now, but she restrained herself. Eda was still sulking over Kristen's sharpness with her the other day. Kristen had apologized later that same day, but it had not gone far toward appeasing the older woman. And her sulking added to Kristen's burden, for Eda was the only one she felt free to talk to. With the old woman's cold silence, Kristen's day was dreary indeed.

Eda led Kristen away, but not to the stairs to retire. She was told curtly that she was to have a bath. As tired as she was, Kristen could not complain about that. It would be only her second bath since she was brought into the hall. She knew Darrelle bathed often through the week, as did Royce, but the servants rarely. As accustomed to cleanliness as she was herself, the small container of water she was given daily to sponge herself with was just not adequate.

Simply the thought of being completely clean again perked up her spirits. Yet she was not to have a leisurely bath, for other servants were waiting to make use of the same water. She was first into the tub, however, which made all the difference. The water was warm this time, and clean, and only Eda remained in the small room with her.

While Kristen bathed and quickly washed her hair, Eda scrubbed her only set of clothes. She was given a tentlike robe of coarse, thin wool to wear for the night, while her clothes dried. It was simply a long rectangle of gray cloth, with a circle cut out in the center for her head to slip through. Wrapped around her sides and belted, it sufficed, though typically it fell short on her. But she was naked underneath, and felt naked underneath. The only reason she didn't balk at wearing a garment without sewn side seams was that she was going straight to her chamber.

But Kristen was not going straight to her chamber as she had supposed. Upstairs, Eda pushed her past her door near the stairs and did not stop until the end of the corridor was reached, where the lord's chamber was. Kristen backed away warily.

"Why?" she demanded as Eda knocked on the door.

Eda did not bother to look at her, but Kristen saw her shrug. "I do what I am told. The reasons are not explained to me."

"He said he wanted to see me?"

"He told me to bring you here. And here you are."

Eda opened the door and waited for Kristen to enter. Kristen hesitated, but only for a moment. She was not afraid, but she couldn't think of a reason why she would be brought here at night. If Royce wanted to question her again, he would have done so during the day, wouldn't he?

She stepped into the room, habit making her take small steps, even though Eda had not put her shackles back on after the bath. As the last time she was brought here after her bath, Eda carried the shackles, and as the last time, she placed them on Royce's table and then left the room, closing the door behind her.

He stood by one of the open windows in front of her, facing her. She was familiar with this room now, so did not glance about it, but looked directly at Royce, waiting to learn what she was doing here. She felt self-conscious in the robe now. She should have balked at wearing it. If the belt loosened, she would be rendered practically naked. That was no way to appear in the presence of this man. A few days ago she might have considered such a tactic to break his control, but now she wasn't sure she still wanted him. No, that wasn't true. She still wanted him. What she wasn't sure of was if it was such a good idea to get what she wanted.

"It has come to my attention that the clothes given to you do not fit you very well."

This was the last thing Kristen expected to hear him say. That he was thinking of her clothes, when she had just been thinking of her clothes, gave her an impulse to giggle. She restrained herself.

"Did you only just notice?"

Royce frowned at her sarcasm. "There is a gown on my bed. See if it fits you."

"You want me to try it on now?"

"Aye."

"Do you leave, or will you stay to watch?"

Royce tensed at her taunting question. Of course she would not care if he watched or not. She was no doubt immune to having men see her naked. He felt his temper rising, and could not seem to stop it.

His tone was caustic when he replied. "I have no wish to see you disrobe, wench. I will give you my back until you have the gown on."

Coward, she said to herself. To him she retorted, "How very noble of you."

Kristen turned toward the bed to get the gown, but took only one step, then stopped abruptly. The green velvet was spread out on the bed so she could see it clearly, including the pearl border. But even if it wasn't, she would have recognized the material of this particular gown. It was her favorite, for her mother had made it for her, and her mother hated to sew, which was why the gown was so special to Kristen. Brenna had spent many long hours on it last year to give it to her daughter for the winter solstice feast.

"What are you waiting for?"

Kristen glanced over her shoulder at him to see that he had not turned his back on her, but had been watching her. She felt a trap as surely as if the hidden door had already sprung open. There could be only one reason he would want to see her in that gown. He thought it was hers. And no gown like that would belong to a whore. He must be thinking just that.

She had every right to be suspicious of his motives. She would be a fool to hide the fact that she knew what he was about. It was too obvious.

She decided to attack. "What does this mean?"

"What does what mean?"

She faced him, her eyes narrowing at his deliberate evasiveness. "Why would you want me to try on such a gown, milord?"

"I told you why."

"Aye, to see if it fits me. And if it does, will you give it to me? I think not. So what is the purpose?"

"'Tis not your place to question my motives, wench."

Irritation bubbled to the surface. "Tell that to your slaves who are born slaves! You forget who I am!"

"Nay!" he shouted at her. "'Tis who you are that is in question!"

"Again?" She feigned surprise now, but was in fact groaning inside to have his suspicions out in the open. "What has a gown to do with who I am?"

"'Tis yours, is it not?"

She wanted to curse him for being so perceptive, but

smiled at him instead. "Is that what you think? Next you will be saying I am a virgin."

"Are you?"

"Would you like to find out firsthand, milord?" she asked provocatively, daringly, playing the part, but praying he would not call her bluff. Her sexual aggression had angered him before, and it did so again now. He glowered at her in answer, and she laughed, pressing her point. "Come now, milord. How can you think that someone like me could own a gown as fine as that one? 'Tis a gown for a princess, or a rich merchant's wife."

"Or a whore with a rich lover who is too generous!" he snapped, not giving up.

Kristen gave him a saucy grin. "You give me more credit than I deserve, Saxon. Truly, you flatter me. But I assure you that if I had ever had a rich lover, I would not have let the fellow get away from me."

"Very well, you have denied the gown is yours. Now appease me and put it on anyway."

Curse him for a stubborn, pigheaded . . . "I will not. 'Tis cruel of you to ask me to."

"Why?"

"'Twould be a luxury beyond measure to feel that velvet against my skin after wearing your coarse slave rags. But for how long can I wear it? Only until your ridiculous notions about me are satisfied," she answered for him. "Then you give me back the rags. Is that not cruel?"

Royce smiled at her. It was the first time she had ever seen him smile. It eased the lean hardness of his face, and made her heart feel as if it had flipped over.

"You have a way with words, wench, and an answer for everything. But you overlook one thing. In your position, you have no decisions or choices to make. You do as you are bid, no matter what is bid, whether it

seems cruel to you or not. Is that simple enough for you
to understand?"

"Aye."

"Then put the gown on."

He had spoken in an agreeably soft tone, but this last
was stated quite firmly. He was determined to see her in
that gown, no matter what she said. And what he would
see if she put it on, was that it fit her like a second skin,
perfectly. He would know it was hers. He would know
she had lied. If he could ask her tonight if she was a
virgin, then something had already made him suspect
that she was not a whore. It was proof he wanted, proof
he was set on having, one way or another, before she
left this chamber.

He was wrong about one thing. She did have a choice
to make. She could put the gown on and watch him turn
cruel and vengeful, and rape her viciously just on princi-
ple, because it was what he said he would do if she was
a virgin. Or she could entice him to make love to her in
passion, because he wanted her, as she wanted him.

Either way, she knew the time had come. She was
going to lose her innocence tonight. And the choice was
simple. She could not bear for her first encounter with a
man to be something she would remember with loathing. Royce desired her even though he was loath to
admit it. She desired him. Their joining could be beautiful. She refused to let it be otherwise, especially for this
first time. If he had to find out she was a virgin, it had
to be after the fact. It would not matter afterward. And
if she were lucky, it would not matter to him then either.
But even if it did, she would have other defenses then,
and the advantage of knowing him intimately.

"How long do you intend to make me wait?" Royce
cut sharply into her thoughts.

"All night, milord," Kristen said softly. "I will not
assist in this foolishness."

He crossed to her with angry strides. When he stopped and she looked up at him, she had the feeling that he wanted to lay hands on her and shake her.

"You dare to defy me?"

She met his furious gaze with an innocent look. "Surely you are not surprised? We Vikings are known to be daring, and bold, and have you not called me brazen too? So I am. If you want to see me in the gown, milord, you will have to put it on me."

"You think I would not?"

"Nay, you will not."

It was a challenge he could not refuse. With a single jerk, Royce opened her belt, then yanked the robe over her head and threw it aside. He would not look down at her, though, at least not below her face. For a long moment, his eyes bored into hers. Then he turned on his heel and stepped to the bed to swipe up the velvet gown in one fist.

It was the full sight of her that met him when he turned around to bring the gown to her. If he could have been spared that, if he could have kept his eyes fixed only on her face, Royce might have succeeded with his purpose. As it was, he couldn't move, he was so entranced.

She stood there proud and unashamed to have him see her thus, with no attempt to cover herself in any way, and he looked long and hard, feasting on the reality of what he had only been able to imagine previously. She was so very beautiful to him, so perfectly formed for all her height.

Royce was unaware that he had walked to her, but he stood next to her now, the velvet gown forgotten, dropping from his fingers to the floor. Everything was forgotten as his hands rose to cup her cheeks, and he lowered his head to taste the nectar of her lips. Slowly he tasted, gently at first to savor, then with the full measure of his need.

In those first moments, he was so consumed with desire that he would not have noticed if Kristen resisted him. But she was not resisting in any way. As before, she was kissing him back with an unrestrained abandon. A part of her was fearful that he would stop as he had before. The rest of her opened up to a wealth of new feeling.

She need not have worried. Royce was incapable of halting what had begun. He did not know it, but he had lost his battle to resist her before she even entered his chamber. He had no control over his actions and for once did not care. Passion alone was ruling him, a fair madness that would not abate without fruition.

Kristen moaned when his mouth left hers, but it was only for a moment as he bent to lift her in his arms. She felt a moment's panic—not for what was to come, but for her new and precarious height. She had not been held like this since she was a child and had grown too big for it to be reasonable for her father to carry her to bed when she had fallen asleep in the hall. But the weight that went with her size seemed not to faze Royce.

His hold on her was firm and he was in no hurry to relinquish it, but stood there for a long moment, resuming his kiss. Kristen's arms went about his neck, keeping his mouth firmly fixed to hers, and the kiss deepened as he carried her to his bed.

Very slowly he laid her down so that their lips would not part. And then he was lying full length at her side, with only his chest leaning half over her as he continued to kiss her. This was not enough for Kristen. She turned toward him so that she could feel all of him, arching her body into his, straining to attain every inch. This was still not enough. His clothes thwarted her, chafing at her skin.

Royce was only barely aware of what she was doing. He had thrilled to the complete contact with her, but had not stopped kissing her when she leaned away from him to work impatiently at his belt. It was when the belt fell away that he was totally aware of what she was about, for she pushed him back and climbed on top of him, sitting up so that she straddled his hips.

He saw her yanking at his tunic to remove it and he raised his back off the bed so she could easier pull it off. He did not think how strange this was to have a woman undress him. He was mesmerized by the sight of her sitting on him, her rounded breasts thrust forward, seeming to demand his touch. He did touch them, capturing a firm mound in each hand.

The sound she made then brought his eyes to hers, and he caught his breath to see heat smoldering in the depths of her aqua gaze. And she kept her eyes locked to his as she worked on the lacings of his braies, not breaking contact until she scooted down to his thighs, and with a suddenness he was not expecting, yanked his braies down over his hips.

She stared now at what she had uncovered, the strong root of him that was already throbbing for her. That she would do so, unabashed, sent new blood pulsing through him. She looked up at him in what seemed like wonder, only to glance down again as her fingers circled the thickness of him.

It was his undoing, more than he could bear. With a groan he sat up swiftly and gripped her shoulders to force her back down on the bed. She was not satisfied to stay down. As he hastily moved to discard the remainder of his clothes, her breasts pressed into his back, her hands coming round to cover his own breasts, kneading the muscle surrounding them.

Royce had never undressed so quickly. The moment he was finished he turned and gripped her hair, his mouth locking with hers in a kiss that was brutal with the passion she had stirred in him.

He pushed her down, and would have ended his torture then, except that the sight of her lying there, his for the taking, reminded him of how often he had ached to know what she would feel like under his hands. He kept her back when she would have pressed to him, and began a slow, leisurely exploration. Lying on his side, braced on an elbow so he could see what he explored, his hands discovered the velvet of her skin.

It was a sensual delight for Royce. It was more so for Kristen, for he brought forth so many wonderful sensations, she felt she couldn't contain them all. She had not thought she could want him any more than before. She was wrong. She burned for him now, her body twisting and undulating of its own accord, her skin seeming to leap up, begging for his touch.

When his fingers slipped between her thighs into the moist haven that ached for him, Kristen thought she would go mad with this shock of pleasure. It stilled her body, brought a cry from deep within. It also stopped Royce, for he did not understand her cry. In no way did he want to hurt her, not now.

Kristen watched his large hand move slowly up her belly, the fingers long, strong, and then she looked up at him, to find him watching her. He bent to kiss her then, a tender kiss, as if to tell her it was all right, he would not hurt her. He was treating her with care, even though he thought her a whore. She was moved by the gesture, more than she could credit. A new warmth of feeling for him filled her.

She spoke to him with her body, her hands reaching for him, encouraging him to come atop her, her legs parting to receive him. She knew what he would do to her, but not how it would feel. She wanted to know now how it would feel.

Royce needed no other encouragement. He gathered her close, amazed that he could, that for once he did not have to hold himself above a woman because he was so much longer than she. This woman conformed to his body perfectly and he did not have to fear that he would crush her with his weight, for she held him tightly to her, wanting his weight, as if reveling in this mark of his possession.

He began to fill her, slowly, marveling that he had the patience to prolong this moment he had dreamed about. He marveled too at the tight sheath she offered him, the searing moist heat. Then the obstacle was met that blocked his easy path, and his whole body rebelled at what this meant.

Kristen was prepared for this moment of truth. Her knees were raised and bent, her feet placed flat on the bed to give her leverage. She was not going to let him stop now, so that he could start again later in a different way. The moment she felt him stiffen and start to raise up on his elbows so he could look down at her, she clasped her hands to his buttocks and pressed down while she thrust her own hips upward.

With his shoulders raised up only partially, Royce was without the leverage himself to stop her, in fact aided her purpose in that position. And having no way of knowing what she intended, there had been no time to even try. He was sheathed completely before his elbows were firmly placed to support him. He was in time only to see her expression, the eyes squeezed shut, the cringe of pain that crossed her features. There was no scream, only a soft gasp.

Her features smoothed out quickly enough and she opened her eyes to look up at him. He could not control the anger that flashed over his own features.

"Will you finish too?"

"Only if you want me to."

He groaned at such an answer, and then he laughed and fell back on her, gathering her tightly to him again, and made love to her as if his life depended on it. This was no time to question why she did the things she did. The fire that raged between them precluded all else.

Chapter Eighteen

A cooling breeze blew in the open window, the first to stir all day. It caused the candles about the room to flicker and sputter out nearly all at once.

Royce got up to fetch a candle from the hall to relight those near the bed, and Kristen shivered at the sudden loss of warmth next to her where the breeze touched her damp skin. She was ready to sleep. He obviously was not.

She turned on her side so she could watch him as he left the room, the dim shaft of moonlight that also came in through the window vaguely lighting his way. What was he thinking and feeling now? She had no way of knowing yet. But she at least had reason to doubt there was anger in his feelings, for he had been holding her close ever since they had made love the second time.

That second time had happened soon after the first, so soon Kristen had barely come back to earth from the wonder of her new experience, only to be caught up again in his passion. She smiled to herself, thinking she knew now why her parents spent so much time in their bedchamber. Brenna had tried to tell her what it was like, but there were no adequate words to describe such incredible bliss.

Royce returned, shielding a candle with the cup of his hand. The hour was late. He had made no effort to cover himself to leave the room. His nakedness apparently didn't bother him, any more than hers unsettled her. His bothered Kristen, though—not in embarrassment, but in the realization that seeing him like this could make her want him again, this soon after her desire had been so thoroughly sated.

His body was a sculpture of firm skin and thick muscle. He was superb in physique, from the long muscular legs to the thick neck rising from those immense shoulders. The bush of dark hair that reached his neck spread out over his upper chest, but tapered to a narrow line over the hard ridges of his stomach. He was not a slim man like his cousin, but a powerful man, and Kristen knew she could never grow bored of looking at him.

The candles on the wall shelf by the bed burned again, and Royce sat down on the bed. When he didn't lie down immediately, Kristen reached out to touch him, her fingers sliding softly up his back, then down again, teasing his hipline. She took her hand away when he turned his head to look down at her, his expression inscrutable.

"Why did you stop?"

"I do not know if you want me to touch you or not," she admitted frankly. "I come from a family used to kissing and hugging and showing love in touching. But if you are not used to it, you will think me bold."

"I already think you bold, wench," he said lightly as he lay down beside her, resting his head on his palm so he could still look down at her. "God's truth, I have never known anyone like you, who could express your love so freely, so unashamed. You make me wish it were possible to love you in return, to give you what you give me."

Kristen closed her eyes, hoping he had not seen the regret those words caused her and, aye, pain too, that he could speak them after they had just shared hours of the most incredible loving. He didn't have to say he couldn't love her. He could have kept that fact to himself and let her go on hoping for a while.

She looked at him again, but her pride was stung now, prompting her to ask, "Why do you mention love?"

She saw him tense and then frown. Good. He could not hide his damaged pride as well as she had.

"I stand corrected," he said tightly. "You have not said you love me, have you?"

"Nay, I have not. I like your body well, milord, but that is all there is between us."

"Very well," he sneered. "For a virgin, you do make an adequate whore."

Kristen sucked in her breath. It was too much, this derision. And she would not accept that insult any longer, not when the reason for it no longer existed.

"Call me whore again, Saxon, and I will scratch your eyes out!" she hissed furiously.

He grinned at her anger. "'Tis a little late to be protesting what you have long admitted to."

"Nay, I never said I was a whore. You did."

"You never denied it."

"You know why."

"I do not," he replied. "But I am most curious to know why now."

"Then recall what you told me in this very room. You said you would rape me if I were a virgin. I wanted you, but not that way."

He smiled at her, then suddenly he was laughing, a deep, hearty sound. "God's breath, wench, you took seriously something I said in anger?"

Kristen glared at him, finding his humor ill-placed. "Are you saying you would not have raped me had you known I was a virgin?"

"Nay, for in truth, had you fought me tonight, I would have taken you anyway and you would have called it rape, while I would call it my right."

"I do not mean that, Saxon," she replied impatiently.

"I know you feel you have the right to use me as you will, and I may contest that another time, but not now. What I—"

"Oh, you will, will you?"

"Let me finish! Would you have taken me apurpose, in revenge?"

"Nay, Kristen, not that," he said softly, and his hand lifted to her face to smooth the frown on her brow. "Is that what you feared?"

"Aye," she muttered.

He smiled at her tone. "We are well met in mistaking each other. I wanted you, but would not touch you because I thought you a whore."

"And a Viking," she reminded him.

"Aye, but that seemed not to matter the more I saw you. 'Twas thinking you were so free with your body that disgusted me."

She giggled then, and caught his hand, pressing it to her cheek. "Do I still disgust you, now that I have been so free with my body?"

He knew she was teasing him, but he was not used to this kind of teasing. He lay down on his back, pulling away from her.

"Who are you, Kristen?"

"That question concerns you overmuch, I think."

"The gown was yours? I was correct in that?"

"Aye, 'tis mine." She sighed.

"Since you cannot have had a husband, I must assume your family is rich."

"My father is. Will you ransom me, then?"

"Nay," he said curtly, drawn to his side to look at her again.

She reacted to his annoyance in kind. "A wise decision, milord, for he would make you marry me."

"The devil, you say! Marry a Viking maid?"

"You need not make it sound a fate worse than death," she retorted.

"For me it would be!"

"Ohh!" she gasped. "For that slur, Saxon, I will see you do marry me!"

"You are mad!"

"Am I? Well, I am also the daughter of the man who will kill you when he comes to find me!"

She regretted saying that the moment it was out, but more so when Royce leaned up to grip her shoulders in anger. God's teeth, how they sliced each other with petty spite. What was wrong with her tonight to make her tongue so wickedly loose?

"Are you saying more Vikings will come here, Kristen?"

She groaned inwardly at the coldness in his tone. She had done that. And he had been in such a pleasant mood only moments ago. So had she, for that matter.

She decided to be truthful. "Nay, Royce, 'tis unlikely. My father would not have approved of the men coming here, so they did not tell him. He is a merchant. He thinks his ship sailed to the market towns, for 'twas a trading voyage. He has no way of knowing they sailed here first."

"Then why did you say what you did?"

She started to smile, but thought better of it. "You should heed your own advice and not take seriously what I say in anger."

He grunted at that, but he latched on to what she had revealed. "You say the ship was his? Then was it your brother Selig who led the men?"

"I did not tell you he was my brother," she said suspiciously. "How did you know?"

"Meghan told me. But why would you not want me to know?"

"I thought you would think it unusual if you knew my

brother had been with me on the ship, when you thought I was the ship's whore."

"I did think it unusual, but I do not know the morals of your people."

Kristen didn't know why she should take offense at that, but she did. "We have very similar morals to your own, milord."

He let her go, but he was still frowning. "Why were you on that ship?"

"Why do you have so many questions about me?" she countered stiffly.

"Is my curiosity so unnatural? Or do you have something more to hide?"

She gave a snort at his reference to the things she had kept from him, for he knew why she had felt forced to deceive him about herself. It was reasonable that he should be curious about her, especially now. But did she want to appease his curiosity? Nay. Why should she? It was not necessary for him to know everything about her, and would only give him an advantage he did not deserve.

But she did not want to appear to be hiding something from him, either. What would he think if he knew that one of the reasons she had sailed with her brother was to find a husband? She had found this man instead, and he would never marry her.

"My reasons for being on the ship are many, but not important," she said quietly. "The truth is, I sailed without permission, hiding myself in the cargo well until the ship was far from home."

"You wanted to go pirating?" he asked incredulously.

"Do not be absurd, milord," she replied with disgust. "I told you no one knew the ship was coming here, least of all myself. My brother was furious when he discovered me. He would have taken me back, except he feared I would tell our father what he and his friends meant to do."

"You were naturally shocked when you learned they would sack a Saxon church."

That was pure sarcasm and it infuriated her. "You are Christian, and to you the sacking of a holy place is an abomination. But do not expect men of different beliefs to hold your holy places sacred. These were men who had never raided before, but their fathers had, and they were raised with stories of the wealth that was there for the taking in foreign lands. They knew the Danes coveted your land, that they mean to have all of this island eventually. They felt this was their only chance at easy wealth before the Danes laid claim to it all."

"If your brother told you all of that, am I to suppose you think that excuses what he planned? Steal from the Christians before the Danes do. The Christians will lose all anyway, so what does it matter who kills and robs them?"

His bitterness stung, for it mirrored her own when she had been told. "My brother would tell me naught of what they planned, because . . . well, it matters not why. 'Twas Thorolf who told me what I told you, and this only after we were chained in the yard below. I am not defending them. I simply understand their motives."

"One small thing was not taken into account," he noted coldly. "We Saxons will not be giving up what is ours to the Danes, or anyone else."

"Aye, so half of these Vikings found out," she agreed just as coldly.

"Your brother died through his own design, Kristen."

"Does that make it easier to bear?" she cried.

"Nay, I suppose not."

They both fell silent, Kristen because she was having trouble coping with her renewed grief in front of Royce. She would have liked comfort from him, and that surprised her. But she knew he would never give her comfort for the death of someone he despised.

She moved to her side of the bed and sat up. His hand shot out and caught her wrist.

"What are you doing?" he asked, not sharply but more than just curiously.

She glanced down at the fingers that held her, then at him. "I would return to my chamber."

"Why?"

"I am done with answering questions, milord." She sighed. "I am tired."

"Then go to sleep."

"You want me to stay here with you?"

He would not speak the words, but pulling her back down on the bed was answer enough. She had not expected it.

She turned her head toward him as his arm slipped across her waist to draw her closer. "You have a wall of weapons here. You do not fear I will kill you while you sleep?"

"Would you?"

"Nay, but I could escape," she said. "You have not locked your door."

He chuckled. "If that were your plan, then you would not bring it to my attention. Rest easy, Kristen. I have not lost my mind. I have a man on guard in the hall."

She gasped. "You knew all along you would make love to me!"

"Nay, but I planned for all the possibilities. Now be quiet if 'tis sleep you want."

She clamped her mouth shut, feeling chagrined. But not for long. He wanted her to spend the night with him. He had used her well, yet still he wanted her near. That thought made her feel very good indeed, so good that she fell asleep with a smile on her lips, and Royce's arm still holding her close.

Chapter Nineteen

Kristen watched Royce while he slept. It was a luxury to lie there and do so, for she should have risen already. Eda usually woke her much earlier than this. The older woman would already be working below. And Kristen was not so naive as to think that just because she had shared the lord's bed, she would not have to work anymore.

She sighed, hating to leave him, but she wanted to fetch her clothes from the bathing room before more than just the servants were about in the hall. She slipped off the bed and quickly put on the coarse gray robe. She picked up the green gown from the floor and held it to her cheek for a moment. Then she sighed again and laid it carefully over Royce's coffer.

She knew he would not let her wear her own gowns. They had made love and likely would again, but it didn't mean the same thing to him that it did to her. To him she was still just a slave, and slaves were not adorned in finery.

"Kristen?"

She turned with her hand on the door to see she had woken him somehow. He was sitting on the edge of his bed, hair tousled, as naked as he had been last night, and looking sleepy. In fact he yawned.

Kristen couldn't help the tender smile that came to her lips. "Aye, milord?"

"You would have left without waking me?"

"I did not think you would want to rise this early," she replied.

"Come here."

She hesitated, but only for a moment. If he wanted to make love again, she could find no objection. She could not think of a more pleasant way to start the day.

When she stood before him, he reached for her hands and held them lightly in his. It was not desire she read in his eyes as he looked up at her.

"Where were you going?"

"Below to work."

"Then you have forgotten something."

"Nay, I—"

She stopped, her eyes widening, for he could mean only one thing. And he saw that she comprehended now.

"Put them on, Kristen."

She tried to pull away from him, but his grip tightened, holding fast to her. She shook her head in disbelief.

"You will still make me wear that chain after . . . How can you be so unfeeling?"

"I know you hate it and I am sorry for that," he replied softly. "If there were another way to ensure you could not escape, then I would use it instead, but there is not. Too many Wessex slaves have escaped, running north to the Danes to join their army. I know that you would do the same, to try to reach your home."

She was not hearing the words of explanation. "The men would, aye, but I would not go without them."

"With your freedom, you could help them to theirs."

"If I told you I would not, that I would not leave your hall?"

"You cannot expect me to believe you."

"Why not?" she demanded angrily. "You would believe me that I would not kill you, but you will not believe that I will not escape?"

"Aye, you have it right!" His voice rose in impatience. "I can stop any attempt you make against me, but I will not take the chance of losing you!"

"You do not take this precaution with your other slaves!" she snapped.

"They are born slaves, descendants of the Britons that we conquered centuries ago. Wyndhurst is their home. But you have been captured, losing the freedom you once knew. You have no reason to want to stay here."

Didn't she? God's teeth, what a fool he was not to see that she did not want to leave him. But he was more of a fool if he thought she would shrug and accept his shackles now, and blithely accept him too.

A coldness entered her eyes, a chill that he had never seen before. "Very well, milord. You can let go of me. I will wear your chain."

He released her, but he frowned as he watched her walk stiffly to the table and pick up the shackles, then bend over to snap them on. "You can forgo the other chain, Kristen, if you will promise not to attack my cousin again."

Was she supposed to be grateful for that? Curse him, he had no idea what his callousness was doing to her.

She stood up to her full height, her voice calm but tinged with bitterness as she said, "I would have promised not to escape, but this I will not promise."

"It matters not to you that he is dear to me?"

"My brother was dear to me."

"Then you will wear the other chain as well until Alden's wounds are healed and his strength fully recovered. If you were not so strong yourself, 'twould be unnecessary."

"I do not regret my own strength. It serves me well when needed," she said cryptically. Then, with stiff pride, she added, "If that is all, milord?"

"Aye, go!" he snapped, her coldness rubbing him raw.

She nodded curtly and departed, leaving Royce with his temper rapidly rising. What in God's name did she expect him to do? Trust her? Surely she could see how unreasonable that would be! He had not only himself to think of, but those for whom he was responsible. She could too easily aid her brother's men to freedom. But how could she stop the slaughter that would follow? She could not.

Having so many Viking captives was the problem. With their size, they could be as effective as a small army. He should have killed them all when he had wanted to. Then there would be no problem now. Nay, for he would have killed Kristen too.

The thought that she could have died by his order, without his even knowing she was a woman, cooled his temper. Her resentment would not last. She was intelligent enough to see that until he could trust her, precaution was mandatory.

Logic held no place in Kristen's mind today. Emotion overruled fairness. She was feeling hurt, betrayed even, and those feelings continued to fester throughout the long day. She said not a word to anyone. She lived in her thoughts, and these grew steadily more acerbated and fraught with resentment. With no outlet for this upheaval of emotions, she was simmering on a dangerous level by the time Eda escorted her upstairs that night.

Eda passed her chamber once again, going on to Royce's. But Kristen went no farther than her own door, and this she slammed shut behind her. Eda opened it within seconds.

"What means this? You saw me go on."

"So?" Kristen said tersely, lying down on her pallet.

"He has bid me bring you to him again, wench."

"So?"

Eda sighed. "Do not be difficult, Kristen. His will cannot be denied."

"So you think. So he thinks, too. You will both learn differently." Kristen turned her back on the old woman. "You need not remove my shackles, Eda. Lock my door and go away."

Kristen did not see Eda shaking her head as she closed the door, nor did she hear it being locked. She drew her knees up to her chest and reached down to grip the chain at her feet, pulling at it so hard the skin scraped on her palm. She let go with a violent sound and turned onto her belly, pounding on her pallet in a feeble effort to rid herself of some of her frustration. It didn't work. She succeeded only in ripping the thin material in several places so that straw spilled out.

She was quiet and still lying on her belly with her head turned away from the door when Royce opened it a few moments later. He moved across the floor until his feet nearly touched the pallet by her hip.

He had not seen this chamber since the servants had readied it for her. Everything had been removed from it except the thin, narrow pallet on which she slept. It was a dismal atmosphere for her to return to each night. Not even a candle had been spared for her.

"Why did you not come to me, Kristen?"

"I am tired."

"And still angry?" She didn't answer that. Royce bent down beside her, touching her shoulder. "Sit up so I can remove your shackles."

She turned over to look at him, but she didn't sit up. "If you will have them taken away, remove them. Otherwise leave them on."

"Do not be stubborn, wench. Take what is offered."

"And be grateful?" she said frostily. "Nay. If you will treat me like an animal, then be consistent."

He ignored her choice of comparisons, reminding her, "You accepted this arrangement before."

"That was before."

"I see. You expected things to change, simply because you shared my bed." He shook his head at her. "Is that right?" She looked away, but he caught her chin, forcing her eyes back to his. "Is that right, Kristen?"

"Aye!" Her cry was thick with bitterness, but hurt also. "I would not treat you so cruelly after what we shared. I do not see how you can me."

"I know you understand why it has to be this way, Kristen; you just do not like it," he said impatiently. "You must know I like it no better."

"Do I?" she retorted. "You are lord here. What is done to me is done by your order, no other's."

He lost patience with her, standing up, his expression stern as he fixed her with his dark eyes. "Very well, I will tell you the alternatives to that chain. You can be locked in a room instead—mine, if you will—but you will not leave it at all. I can spare you little time in the day, so you would be alone mostly, except at night. Would you prefer that?"

"You might as well put me in a cell!"

"We have none here. I offer you my own chamber, rather than this one. I give you the choice."

"There is no choice, milord," she retorted. "You offer me an even worse constriction. You said alternatives. Give me one I can accept."

"There is one other thing I can do that would enable you to have the freedom of Wyndhurst. I can kill your friends."

"What!"

She sat up, staring at him in disbelief, but he went on undaunted: "You can be trusted only if they are no longer here, the threat removed that my people will be slaughtered if they escape. By yourself, you would not get far if you still tried to escape. I would find you."

"You are jesting!" she said half hopefully, half incredulously.

"Nay."

"You know I would not take my freedom at such a price!" she hissed furiously. "Why do you even mention such an alternative? Could you really kill defenseless men?"

"Those men are my enemies, Kristen. They would kill me without a moment's pause, given half a chance. I have never liked having them here, and would just as soon rid myself of them. 'Twas Alden who convinced me they could be useful."

"Then rid yourself of me, too, Saxon!" she seethed. "I am one of them!"

"Aye, you are my enemy, too, wench," he replied softly. "But you I like having around. Now, give me your shackles to remove for the night, or make another choice."

She glared at him, but she stuck her feet out before he decided to take the choice out of her hands. She was still glaring at him when he stood up again, wrapping the chain about his neck to hold one iron band in each hand.

"I want to make love to you, Kristen." His voice turned husky. "I suppose you will deny me because you are angry, but I will ask you anyway. Will you come to my bed?"

"Nay," she muttered stonily, ignoring the responsive chord his tone and words stirred deep within her.

"I could insist."

"Then you will find out what 'tis like to have me fight you, Saxon."

She heard him sigh before he said rather gruffly, "I will hope you get over your anger quickly, wench."

Royce left then, and this time Kristen heard the door being locked.

Chapter Twenty

"What did you do to my cousin, wench, to put him in such a foul mood?"

Kristen gave Alden only a cursory glance. He had come to stand on the opposite side of the worktable from her, the first time he had come near her since she had attacked him. His company was not welcome.

"I am not responsible for his moods," she said surlily.

"Nay?" Alden grinned. "I have seen the way he watches you. You are indeed responsible."

"Go away, Saxon," she retorted, fixing him with a hard look. "You and I have naught to say to each other."

"So you still want to kill me?"

"Want to? 'Tis something I am bound to do."

He gave a mock sigh. "'Tis a shame we cannot be friends. I could give you good advice on how to handle my cousin, for you do not seem to be doing so well on your own."

"I want no advice!" she snapped. "And I do not want to handle him. I want naught to do with him!"

"Mayhap, but I have seen you watching him, too. Such lustful looks that pass between you and—"

"Curse you!" She cut him off furiously. "I swear you must be Loki's kin. Get away from me, before I throw this dough at your head!"

Alden chuckled as he walked away. Kristen pounded angrily at the dough she was making. How dare that man tease her? Did he think she was not serious in wanting his death? She was serious. She did not care if he had such an amiable nature. Nor did it make any difference to her that she had learned he was indirectly responsible for her and the others still being alive. It didn't matter either that he reminded her of her brother Eric with his teasing charm and his boyish smile. She was going to kill him—if she ever got free again.

Her long, thick braid had fallen over her shoulder and she angrily whipped it back behind her. It was the middle of summer now, and the hottest weather Kristen had ever known. At home she would be out swimming with Tyra, or racing across fields on Torden's back, with the breeze whipping through her hair. She certainly wouldn't be stuck near a hearth that burned all day long. She had so many regrets, but the "should have done's" only served to remind her that she was here by her own design.

It had been a little more than a month since the ship had anchored on the river that disastrous morning. Occasionally Kristen saw Thorolf and the others through an open window as they came and went to their labor on the wall. They could not see her, though, in the far corner of the hall where she was.

Kristen knew they probably still worried about her; at least Ohthere and Thorolf would. They should have escaped by now. She hoped the thought of leaving her behind was not preventing them, but it was more likely that Royce and his cursed precautions made it impossible.

She had considered asking Royce if she could speak to them, but Alden was right. Royce's mood had been foul this last week since she had refused to share his bed, and his answer to her, about anything, would undoubtedly be nay. His orders to his men were sharp, his looks dark. His sister and the servants stayed well away from him and were unusually quiet, so as not to draw his attention. Was she responsible for his short temper?

She would like to think so, but did not credit herself with that much sway over him. It was true that he came each night to ask her to share his bed, and each night she held tight to her resentment and refused him. Somehow Alden must have learned about this. Mayhap he had heard Royce's voice raised in anger by her door one of these last few nights, for his patience with her was definitely wearing thin. Or mayhap he was just interpreting the looks Royce gave her, as he said.

It was doubtful that Royce would actually discuss her with his cousin. Why should he? She was just a wench he was attracted to at the moment, enough to want in his bed, but not enough to mention to his family. He would not admit such an attraction to a slave, especially a captive slave of an enemy despised by them all.

Eda knew what was happening, but she was loyal to Royce and not about to tell anyone that Kristen was defying him and he was letting her get away with it. She scolded Kristen daily for her stubbornness, for it was her feeling that if Royce wanted her, he should have her. She was also aware that their one night together had been agreeable to them both, for no screams had come from his chamber that night, no bruises had marred Kristen's smooth skin the next day. She was coldly silent that day, but Eda had guessed the reason why, seeing her glare so often at her chains.

Eda had called her foolish after that for not trying to curry her lord's favor in that age-old way. Kristen had retorted that she could do without such favor that still kept her chained like an animal.

She was puzzled, however, that Royce was conceding to her wishes. He continued to ask her to share his bed, and continued to accept her refusal, though less graciously lately. She had never dreamed he would. In fact, she had expected him to force her instead. That would have been more in keeping with her position that put her utterly at his mercy. But he didn't. And that he didn't was causing Kristen some unanticipated frustration of her own.

She still wanted him. And now that she knew what lovemaking was all about, she wanted him even more than before. But pride, of which she had her fair share, was going to keep her from ever saying so again—to him, anyway.

That night Kristen waited anxiously for Royce to come to her room again, but he did not. She thought of him seeking his pleasure elsewhere and tried to convince herself that she didn't care. She would have been less irritable the next morning had she known where he did spend the night.

As it was, the day proved a long one and she was feeling like the cat that bit off its nose to spite its face. Much of her misery was of her own making. She was sure now that Royce would not come to her chamber again, that he was done with her. Not seeing him the whole day strengthened this conclusion.

Still, Kristen waited a while after Eda removed her shackles and locked the door this night, sitting on her pallet in the dark, plucking at the already frayed ends of her rope girdle, and hoping. She didn't want Royce to just give up on her. She wanted him to force her to give in. Her pride wouldn't let her, so he had to overcome that. Why didn't he?

After waiting more than long enough, Kristen finally sighed and removed her clothes to sleep. That was one thing she had not done this last week, until after Royce had come and gone. Last night she had slept in her clothes, as uncomfortable as they were. But tonight—he wasn't coming.

She was still awake when the door opened. A torch in the hall behind him made his huge frame a black silhouette in the doorway. Her body came instantly alive with tremors of excitement. She was filled with joy that he had come, that he hadn't given up yet. But none of this showed in her expression as she looked toward him, unable to see his own features with the light behind him.

When he just stood there without speaking, she realized he wasn't going to. Well, she supposed he had his pride, too. And words were unnecessary to know why he was here.

She conceded enough to break the silence. "Do you take the chains away for good, milord?"

"Nay."

"Not even if I swear on my mother's life that I will not leave this place?"

"Nay, because for all I know, you could hate your mother, or she could be dead, which would make your vow worthless."

Kristen controlled the pique that pricked her because of that. She rose up on her elbow, letting the thin blanket fall beneath her breasts. This was an unfair tactic on her part, but she was tired of this stalemate.

She put enough anger into her voice to make him think she was unaware of what she had done. "I happen to love my mother very much, and she is most certainly alive, and no doubt worried sick about me. You think because I am a woman that I am without honor? Or is it because I am a Viking woman that you will not trust my word?"

He had taken a step toward her, but he stopped now. "Words, wench, easily said. Actions speak plainer, and yours do not say much for you."

"Why? Because I want to kill your cousin?" she asked, then taunted, "Or because I do not jump when you call?"

His fist slammed into his palm, telling her that her barb had struck home. At least she was inflaming his passion, even if it was the wrong kind of passion.

"God's breath!" he swore in exasperation. "You are the most audacious woman! I see I waste my time here again. You simply refuse to understand."

"I understand, Royce," Kristen replied levelly. "And I was willing to meet you halfway."

"Nay, you want it all your way!"

"Not so," she insisted. "I offered my word, which cost me much, for half of me still wants to leave here and go home."

"And I cannot trust the word of anyone, woman or man, whom I have known so short a time. Nor do I believe part of you can truly want to stay here as you are: without rights, without hope of ever being more than a slave."

"Aye, how right you are, milord," Kristen agreed ironically. "Why indeed would I want to stay here? Surely not because of you."

"Me?" he scoffed. "You want me to believe now that I am the reason, when you turn me away each night? Or do you come with me tonight, Kristen?"

"Do you unchain me for good, milord?" she countered pleasantly.

"By the saints—"

He did not finish, but turned on his heel with a low growl and left the room. Kristen felt like screaming with the closing of the door.

"You accept defeat too easily, Saxon!" she spat in frustration, a little too loudly, for the door reopened, making her gasp with the suddenness of it.

"Did I hear you right, wench?" Royce demanded in a voice too calm for the slamming back of that door.

He left the door open for what light it provided and walked toward her slowly, purposefully. Kristen yanked the blanket back up to her neck. She would have liked to leap to her feet, for she felt vulnerable lying there on the floor with him now standing so far above her, next to her, but she wasn't going to show him that she was concerned at all by his nearness. She turned on her back instead, so she could look up at him.

"What do you think you heard?" she ventured warily.

"A challenge." His voice was still calm, but there was a definite menacing quality in that answer. "And when you issue a challenge, you must abide by the results."

"What results?"

He bent down and swiped her blanket away in answer. In a moment his body lay atop hers, both hands holding her head still so his mouth could descend. But before their lips met, Kristen gave a mighty heave that tossed him off her to the side. She knew it was only the unexpectedness that had allowed her to do that, but she took quick advantage, scrambling over him and to her feet. But his hand caught one foot, tripping her as she took her first step toward the door.

Kristen fell to the floor, twisted over, and kicked at Royce with her other foot, gaining her freedom again. But he was sitting up now, and though she snatched her feet back so he couldn't try to grab them again, she knew she would never make the door in time.

She stood up with him, backing away slowly, her arms out to ward him off. He moved to the side, forcing her to give up the path to the door. He stopped when he effectively blocked that only exit.

"Get back on your pallet, Kristen."

There was ominous warning in that cold order, but she stubbornly shook her head, backing away from him to the side of the room, coming up short against the wall. There was no escape, but she didn't really want to escape. He was finally going to force his will on her, and though she would not give him this victory easily, she wanted the victory to be his—or at least to have him think it was his. Pride would not let her give in, but brute strength would.

Her heart was racing as she watched him strip off his belt and tunic and angrily throw them aside. And he was angry. There was danger in that, for he could very well hurt her. He was such a terribly big man, with immense power in his arms and hands. And he might be feeling at this moment that he needed to beat her into submission. It was what most men would do. But she had known the risk when she goaded him into this.

He did not move until his remaining clothes lay scattered about the floor. He had stood facing her, staring at her the whole while, the light illuminating only one side of him, leaving the other in darkest shadow. If she had not been standing there naked herself, he might have calmed down, or at least reconsidered what he was going to do. But he was too aroused from the sight of her for that.

She did not think he would leave the room to get a candle. She was going to elude him as soon as he closed the door, cutting off the light. That was her plan, as far as it went. Only Royce gave no thought to closing the door, mayhap for the very reason that the dark would hinder him until he laid hands on her. Kristen had to quickly rework her strategy when he started toward her.

She pushed away from the wall, keeping away from the corners of the room that would trap her. She could stay out of his reach only so long, which would not be long at all if he moved more quickly. But he was stalking her now, maneuvering her closer to her pallet, staying in a position where she could not dash around him to run for the door.

Kristen decided on the unexpected again, and with her hands clasped tightly together, she stopped retreating and turned on Royce to swing at him as she had done to Alden. The blow had staggered the slimmer man. But

Royce did not have his back to her, and it was Kristen who was taken by surprise when he caught her locked fists in one hand. And he did not stop the blow, but added his own pull to it so that she was swung nearly full circle, making it possible for his other arm to slip about her waist and heft her off her feet.

He had only two steps to take to reach her pallet, and he tossed her down there. As thin as her pallet was, it was like being dropped on the hard floor.

Kristen was stunned for a moment, the breath knocked out of her. It was all the time Royce needed to position himself between her sprawled legs and enter her before she had a chance to use those strong legs to ward him off.

He heard her gasp of outrage now that she had her breath back, and he chuckled as her hands slipped between them to try to push him back. It was a useless effort. He was firmly planted and prepared for anything she might try.

"Give it up, vixen." He leaned into her to whisper by her ear. "You have lost what you are fighting to deny me."

In answer she bucked her hips to try to unseat him. That was useless, too, and only served to send him deeper into her. She gasped again, but because of the exquisite feeling of capturing all of him. He gasped, too, at the delicious thrill such deep penetration sent through him.

"Ah, woman, I take it back," he breathed huskily. "Fight me all you like."

Kristen very nearly giggled at his impassioned plea, which would have destroyed the impression that she was being forced to submit to his greater strength. But his mouth prevented her, closing over hers in a fervent kiss. She showed him one last bit of resistance by trying to turn her head away, but his mouth only followed hers back and forth and she finally gave up the pretense, accepting his kiss, returning it wholeheartedly.

His humor, although no doubt stemming from his feeling of conquest, had warmed her. She didn't care about its source. As long as he was no longer angry, he would not be brutal—though at the moment she thought she could have withstood that, too, so inflamed were her senses.

Her hands slipped out from between them and gripped his head, keeping his mouth melded to hers as he began to undulate his torso in a most delightful way, not withdrawing completely, but grinding his hips against her instead, his belly, his chest, all combining in an erotic caress.

Kristen reached her climax almost immediately, and unknowingly lifted his entire weight as her pelvis rose off the pallet to beg for all of him. His own thrust as he attained that bit of heaven too, slammed her back down and increased her pleasure, bringing a moan from deep within her throat. She could feel the pulsing of his climax inside her, and this kept her own sweet throbbing alive and lasting much longer than she could have believed possible.

It was with regret that she returned to reality. He was like a dead weight on her, but she did not mind. His head was turned to the side, his breathing still heavy. Her fingers moved dreamily through his hair. She felt she could stay just like this forever. That was too much to hope for, however.

What he thought of her complete submission she couldn't guess. Considering the way a man prided himself on his prowess, he might simply attribute her capitulation to his skill as a lover. Whatever he thought was fine with her, as long as he didn't guess she had maneuvered him into making love to her. She imagined he would be furious if he realized that.

Her hands fell to his shoulders, then on to his chest when he leaned up to gaze down at her. She could feel his heartbeat beneath her palm, steady now, but with a strong beat. She stared at him, trying to divine from his expression what he was thinking, but he revealed nothing. In fact he seemed to be studying her features for the same reason, to see what she was thinking. If only he knew. She smiled at the thought.

"So you are not angry with me?" he said.

"Of course I am."

Royce chuckled delightedly. "Do you always smile when you are angry?"

"Not always, but sometimes."

She said that so seriously. Royce shook his head. To accept everything she said as truth was to be constantly amazed by her. He would rather think she jested.

"I suppose I should apologize," he offered.

"Aye, you should."

He snorted at her ready agreement. He would say no more about it. She had challenged him. Mayhap she did not deserve such a harsh response from him, but she had certainly accepted him in the end and reached her own pleasure too. Why she had stubbornly refused him to begin with . . . He knew why, and there was naught he could do to change it.

He leaned up further to move off her, but for a moment their hips were more tightly pressed together. He was still inside her, and Kristen closed her eyes, savoring the feel of him before he withdrew. Watching her, Royce sucked in his breath.

"God's mercy, wench, do you do it apurpose?"

Her eyes flew open wide. "What?" She truly didn't know what she had done this time.

"When you look like that . . . 'tis how you look when we—"

"How do you know? Do you watch me?"

"Aye."

She was intrigued. "I had not thought of that. I will have to try it when next I make love."

"To stare into those lovely eyes of yours at such a time would drive a man wild," he predicted.

Deliberately, she smiled. "You need not worry, milord. I was not thinking 'twould be you I would watch."

"I hope you jest, wench," he said sternly as he stood, pulling her up with him. "You would not like the consequences if you do not. I will not allow you other lovers. As long as I want you for myself, you will be faithful."

She cocked a brow, feeling a certain satisfaction in being able to tease him. "Will I?"

He did not answer, but pulled her along with him as he swiped up his clothes, her clothes as well, and headed for the door. Kristen felt her cheeks flush with heat as she realized the door had been open all this time, that anyone could have passed by and seen them. Someone could have stood right in the door and watched them the whole time for all she knew, so involved had she been with this lover of hers.

Her lover. How she liked the sound of that. There would be changes now. There had to be. And he would not regret giving in. She would prove to him that he was indeed her heartmate.

As soon as he reached his room and closed the door, Royce dropped the bundle of clothes to the floor and gathered Kristen into his arms. "Now you pay the forfeit for denying me for so long. You will get no sleep tonight."

"Is that a challenge, milord?" Kristen purred, hoping more that it was a promise.

Chapter Twenty-one

*T*he sky was only a blaze of pink when Royce was roused by one of his men. There had been a disturbance among the prisoners. It had been brought under control, but Thorolf wanted to speak to him.

Royce sent the man away. If the disturbance was over, he did not need to rush down to the yard. But he could not dally, either. He sighed, glancing down at his bedmate. The dawn gave only a hazy light to the room, but he could see her clearly from where he sat next to her.

Kristen slept on, having been disturbed not at all by the sound of voices. Royce was not surprised. He had kept her awake most of the night—or, rather, she had kept him awake by her very presence. He simply could not leave her alone. He grinned in remembrance, a little amazed that he was not feeling exhausted himself this morn.

She lay curled on her side with her hands tucked between her legs as if she were cold, a habit no doubt acquired from the frigid winters she was used to. Her tawny hair was loose and tangled, spreading about her head like a pool of gold. The thin sheet that had covered them when they did finally sleep came no higher than her hips now, leaving the creamy-white expanse above her waist exposed to his view.

He felt a peculiar excitement in being able to look at her like this without her knowing. She was the first woman to ever share his bed for a whole night, the first

he had ever watched sleeping. The serfs that he favored
he usually took where he found them. The few he had
brought to his bed left as soon as he was done with
them. Corliss he left himself, having no desire to spend
a whole night in her bed. It was the same with the ladies
of the court whom he had known intimately.

Why didn't he mind sharing his bed with this Viking
wench for other than making love to her? Mind? Nay, he
liked having her next to him in sleep. But why her? He
still despised her for who she was. Or did he? She and
her kind had done him the worst wrong possible. She
was a woman, but she had still been raised with the
same beliefs as the men who had come here to rob and
kill his people. She was a Viking, a heathen, an abomination to all God-fearing Christians.

If he did not still despise her, he should. He should
also have resisted more successfully his attraction to her.
He was disgusted with himself for this weakness she had
made him see in himself, and more so now that she had
proved her will was stronger than his. She wanted him
still. Last eve in this room had proved that. Yet she
denied him all week, and would have continued to do so
if he had not forced her to submit.

Royce made a disgusted sound with his tongue. Cas-
tigating himself now served no purpose. The damage
was done, and he was not ready to put it behind him.
Giving in once to his desire for her had not been
enough. He still wanted her. And to resist her now
would be like cutting off the hand after the fingers had
been severed, causing more pain for no good reason.
Even at this moment he wanted her. The only reason he
did not wake her was the knowledge that he would have
her later.

It was a heady feeling knowing that this particular
woman was in his power. A captured slave had even
fewer rights than those Britons born to slavery, or than

penal slaves, who were free men enslaved as punishment for certain crimes or because they could not pay the fines and compensations they had incurred. The church gave stiff penalties for the mistreatment of these Christian slaves. Those enslaved for crimes could even be redeemed by their kindred after a year. Those born to slavery could buy their freedom. They were also allowed to sell the products of their toil in their free time. But enemy slaves were a different matter. They could be ransomed or not, sold or not, killed or not. The decision belonged solely to their owners.

This made Kristen his for the taking, and only his, as surely as if she belonged to him as wife. He could have her anytime, anyplace, and she had not the right to deny him. But there was an added pleasure in knowing that she did not despise his desire, that she enjoyed his body as much as he did hers.

If he kept pursuing thoughts like these, he would be waking her after all. As it was, he could not resist touching her before he left the bed, inserting his hand between her breasts that were squeezed together to cup one gently in the palm of his hand. Kristen smiled in her sleep. Royce smiled seeing it.

Damned if she couldn't make him feel good inside in so many different ways. He wondered if she knew what a rare woman she was in her joy of the senses. He knew no other who could be aroused to such passion—and so easily, too.

It was going to be a wonderful day, he decided as he dressed and went below. Not even the prospect of trouble with the prisoners could daunt his good mood this morn.

He found them in the yard, herded together in front of the shelter that had been built for them, Waite having held them back from working until Royce came. He dismissed them into Lyman's charge, keeping only Thorolf back. The younger man was definitely disturbed about something, and Royce surmised from the look he received when he nodded Thorolf back into the hut where they could talk in private, that it had something to do with himself.

"I am told you fought amongst yourselves this morn, Thorolf. Do you wish to tell me why?"

Thorolf rattled his chain as he moved about in his agitation. "That?" He dismissed it with a wave of his hand. "'Twas naught. Bjarni anger Ohthere with jesting." Here he became still and met Royce's eyes, his own narrowing. "Concern you and Kristen."

Royce digested that thoughtfully, doubting he would learn exactly what was said. "Do I take it you took exception to Bjarni's jest, too?"

"Aye. Too long Kristen leave us. I need speak to her . . . please."

Royce stiffened, knowing what it must have cost this brawny Viking to say that word. He became suspicious of his motive. This was the man he had watched so often protecting Kristen when she was still thought to be a lad. He claimed to be only a friend. But was that the truth?

"How long have you known Kristen, Thorolf?"

"Always. Neighbors at home. When children, swim, ride, hunt together. My sister Tyra and Kristen close, very close."

"So she is your sister's friend, yet you seem to have made yourself responsible for her. Why is that?" Thorolf remained mute to that question. Royce walked around him until he stood at the Viking's back. "Is it because her brother is dead, or does she mean more to you than just a friend?"

Thorolf turned around to face him. "Speak slower, Saxon. Or, better, bring Kristen speak for you."

"Oh, clever," Royce sneered, "but I think not. She is

well settled in the hall and does not need to be reminded of your plight. She can tell you naught that I cannot tell you. She is well and not overburdened. So you see, you have no reason to worry about her."

"So you say. Need hear her say."

Royce shook his head to that. "If this is all you wanted to speak to me about . . ." He began to walk toward the door.

"Saxon!" Thorolf called angrily. "No touch Kristen."

Royce turned back incredulously. "Are you actually telling me to keep my hands off her?"

"Aye."

He began to laugh. "What arrogance! Mayhap you have not noticed, but you are in no position to make demands."

"Will you marry her?"

"Oh, enough, Viking," Royce said impatiently. "She has been enslaved, not made a guest. What happens to her depends on you and your comrades, as I said before. She has not been harmed, nor forced to do aught she is not willing to do."

"Then you no touch yet?"

This time Royce did not answer. Thorolf drew his own conclusions, which detonated his Norse temper. Royce was not prepared for the attack, but then, he had not thought a smaller, less muscular man would dare. Suddenly he found himself tackled to the floor, his throat enclosed by a pair of hands that were deadly serious. His breath was completely cut off until the point of his dagger slipped an inch into Thorolf's side.

"Ease off, slowly," Royce commanded him.

He did, then stood up and backed away, holding a hand to his bleeding side. He was still angry, more so now because he had failed. Royce was angry now as well.

"What did you hope to accomplish by that bit of fool-ishness?" he demanded.

"So you no touch Kristen again."

"By killing me? Aye, that would have done it, but then you would not be around to gloat over it."

"No kill," Thorolf insisted. "Other ways to make you no touch again, ever."

Royce frowned until Thorolf made a sharp twisting motion with his hand. Then he grunted. "Aye, so there are. I will have to remember to keep you at arm's length from now on, since I like all my parts just the way they are." And then he shook his head as he got to his feet. "Young fool. Did you disbelieve me when I said Kristen had not been forced? She has no complaints residing inside the hall, other than for the chains she wears."

Thorolf glared at him. "You lie! Many want Kristen. *Many,*" he emphasized. "She refuse all."

"Truly? Then I suppose I should count myself lucky," Royce remarked dryly.

"If you say true, Saxon, then must marry."

Royce sighed at such doggedness. "I have a betrothed already, Thorolf, but even if I did not, I would not marry a heathen, nor a Viking, nor a slave, of which Kristen is all three. She already belongs to me. Give me one reason why I would want to marry the wench, and make it a reason that applies to me, not your impartial-ity."

"Bjarni no jest. Kristen like what see in you. So be it. But no marry, no like for long. She choose you, Saxon. Make right or lose."

"I cannot lose what I own," Royce said confidently and left before he became annoyed with the Viking's logic.

Thorolf moved to the doorway to watch the Saxon lord cross the yard back to the hall. Waite stepped up to escort him to the wall, but he didn't spare a glance for the guard. So Bjarni was right after all. He had said he had observed Kristen watching this lord when she was still with them, and had never seen a woman more entranced.

If she had indeed finally made her choice, it was the wrong choice. And kept apart from them as she was, she had no friend to tell her so. The Saxon would never honor her. He was a man of power, she a captured slave. As a free man with several slaves in his own household, Thorolf could understand the lord's reasoning. But then, Kristen was not a slave born. If and when she chose to resist her bondage, she would do so wholeheartedly.

He wondered why he had bothered to warn the Saxon how it would be with her. She was a Christian, though she obviously had not revealed that fact to these people. But she was a Norsewoman, too, with Norse pride and determination instilled in her. It might be better if she were more malleable instead, for Thorolf knew that it would not go easy for her if she did turn against her captor.

Chapter Twenty-two

*K*risten uncoiled her long frame and stretched luxuriously. She grinned at the little bird perched on the window ledge whose song had woken her. It flew away when she sat up.

She was alone. She wondered if the door was locked and got up to test it. It was not. She grinned again, closing it. Aye, the changes had already begun. Royce was going to try trusting her. She would have to be careful not to disappoint him.

Her clothes and his as well still lay where he had dropped them last eve. She dressed quickly, then proceeded to set the room to rights. She felt like singing and did, a simple Celtic verse her mother had taught her as a child.

"So you know another tongue besides ours, do you?"

Kristen glanced up from smoothing the bedcovers to see Eda standing in the doorway. She smiled a greeting. "Aye, many."

"Well, do not let Lord Royce hear you speak that one, for most Celts are enemies of ours."

"Most?"

"Some live in Wessex side by side with Saxon, in Devon, and some even as close as Dorset. But those on the far west coast have always been our enemies, have even sided with the Danes against us."

"What of the Celtic Welsh to the northwest?" Kristen asked, thinking of her mother.

"Enemies also, though they are too far away to cause

178

us grief. It has been many years since they attacked Mercia in force and King Ethelwulf, Alfred's father, was asked for aid against them. He led his army north and wrung promise of tribute from the Welsh. But the western Celts, they raid us still. Just two days ago a small band made off with some of our cattle. Lord Royce retrieved the animals, but though he and his men chased the thieves through the night, they still eluded him. So he would not like hearing that tongue from your lips now, and he knows it well enough to recognize it."

Kristen smiled, then could not stop the giggle that followed. So that was why Royce had not come to her room the other night. She had been miserable thinking he had sought out another woman, while he was actually out chasing thieves.

"Your humor is not meet, wench," the old woman scolded.

"You would not understand, Eda," Kristen said. Then she added, "But I am sorry Royce did not catch the thieves. I had not known the Celts were your enemies."

Eda grunted. "There are others, too, even a few Saxons milord counts as his foes, and one in particular who lives not far from here. Lord Eldred would like naught better than to see milord dead. They have been at odds since they both lived at court."

"Do you know why?"

"Aye. Lord Eldred resented the closeness between Alfred and milord. This was before Alfred became King, when they would all hunt and sport together on the royal manors. Most younger sons live at court. Milord did until his father and brother died. Now he goes only rarely, or when Alfred summons him. 'Tis only the threat of the Danes that has made them put aside their animosity for a time."

"A wise decision. I would not like to think of Royce fighting with an enemy at his back too."

"Do you care so much? Most lords set their slaves free at their death, as encouraged by the church."

"I want my freedom, Eda, but not in that way," Kristen snapped.

Eda snorted half in disbelief, half pleased with that answer. "Well, come along. Milord said to let you sleep, but naught about dallying the whole day away. You have missed one meal already."

Kristen grinned and started for the door. Eda spotted the shackles she had thrown into the corner earlier and started for them. Kristen stopped her.

"Leave it, Eda. I am done with that."

"Did he say so?"

"Nay, but—"

Eda ignored her and picked up the chain. "Until I am told otherwise, you wear this still."

"Nay, I tell you he will not make me wear it now. Go and ask him."

"Are you daft, wench? I would not dare to approach him over something so minor." Kristen's expression turned forbidding, but Eda held up a hand to forestall her tirade. "Give me no trouble on this, Kristen. If he is willing to trust you now, then he will tell me. Can you not wait until then?"

Nay, she wanted to scream, but to what purpose? In a few minutes—or at the most a few hours, if Royce was not in the hall—she would see him and would correct his forgetfulness. She could in fact wait, though she didn't like it at all.

It was more than just a few hours, however, before she saw him, for he was gone the whole day. Eda learned from Meghan's maid, Udele, that he had taken the child riding. Meghan returned to the hall in the early afternoon, full of excitement and rosy cheeked, but Royce was not with her. Eda remarked that it was rare when Royce found the time to amuse his sister. From the look of Meghan, she enjoyed it.

Kristen was subdued for a while, thinking how kind it was of Royce to find time away from his duties for his sister. But impatience was riding her hard, and fast turning to irritation, and hence to the same resentment she had felt the last time he had made love to her, then still insisted she be chained afterward. Was she wrong in her assumption? Could he be so tender with her in bed, then feel no guilt at all in shackling her when she was not with him?

The last meal of the day was in progress when Royce entered the hall. Kristen watched him avidly as he crossed the hall to the long trestle table set up in front of the great hearth. When she caught his eye, he smiled at her and the anger melted away. God above, he was a devastating man. She hoped he would never realize the havoc he could cause her senses. He was powerful enough without arming him with that knowledge, too.

Darrelle claimed his attention, and Kristen went back to filling the platters that would be carried to the table. She had been wrong again. He was not hard-hearted, just forgetful. As soon as he saw that she was still chained, he would be contrite and make amends for his thoughtlessness.

Before the hall was half emptied and settled for the night, Royce approached her. He was well sated with food, had shared a few ales with his men, and water was even now being heated for a leisurely bath. She had filled two of the buckets herself from the vat over the fire.

He stopped beside her, not too close, and did not look at her, but at the mounds of dough set out on the table for the morn. "How fared your day, wench?"

She glanced to the side to see he still was not looking

directly at her, and she realized he would not with so many people still about. "Well, milord."

"Your night will fare even better."

He promised this in a husky whisper, causing quivers to erupt in her belly. But then he walked away toward the bathing room, and she stared after him incredulously. It was not possible that he could not see the iron bands about her ankles when he approached her, for black as they were, they stood out plainly between her skirt and shoes, both of a lighter color. Nor could he have missed the longer chain running across the floor from the wall to where she stood at the table. The women complained at having to step over it so often during the day. It too stood out plainly.

Rage flayed her senses until her hands trembled. God smite his green eyes and black heart! To share his bed without his trust made her no better than a whore! She was done with being used.

"I have said it afore, wench. 'Tis too soon for him to trust you. Bide your time."

Eda stood at her back. Kristen did not turn to answer. She gripped her hands to still the trembling and brought her emotions under control. The rage settled in contempt.

"I will have scars on my ankles if I bide my time. Well and good. 'Tis no more than I deserve for consorting with my enemy. I will take the scars and wear them as penance."

"Penance! God's mercy, you sound almost like a Christian. Do you have priests, then, for your many gods who demand penance?"

Kristen did not answer. Coldly she demanded, "Are we finished, Eda?"

"Aye."

Eda bent at her feet to unlock the wall chain. She removed the shackles while she was at it, to make it easier for Kristen to mount the stairs. She was in fact feeling some of the girl's misery. It could not be easy being favored by the lord, only to a point.

"Come along, then," Eda said gruffly.

She trusted Kristen to follow behind her. She did, but only because bolting for freedom without a weapon or a plan would be foolish indeed. But, as before, she went no farther than her own door, though Eda walked on. This time, though, she stopped short on entering her chamber. It had been barren always, but now it was completely empty.

She felt Eda at her back again. "What means this?" she demanded sharply.

"Milord said naught about your restrictions to me, Kristen, but he did say you would use this chamber no more. The only bed at your disposal now is his."

That brought a harsh laugh. "Truly? Well, I would prefer the hard floor here to what he offers."

"He will be angry, wench."

"Think I care?" Kristen snapped.

Eda left to inform Royce of Kristen's preference. Kristen did not move until she heard the lock turn. It had been too much to hope Eda would forget that, for with Royce below, she could have laids hands on a weapon from his chamber, though what she would do with it she still was not sure.

Kristen stomped over to the far wall and sat down to wait.

Chapter Twenty-three

When Royce unlocked the door, Kristen was sitting with her back against the far wall, her knees bent before her to help her to rise quickly if necessary. She saw that he was not angry, yet. But he was certainly not pleased.

Coming straight from his bath, he wore only a long-sleeved white tunic and, over it, the type of robe that was given Kristen when she bathed, though his was of a fine quality, even to having an inch-deep border of green silk along every edge of the white linen that fell to his feet. The white became him with his dark hair and summer-tanned skin.

If she were not furious with him, she knew she would be waiting breathlessly to see a bare leg when the robe parted as he walked. But she stared only at his face, lit by the tallow candle he held aloft so the light reached across to her.

"Eda has confessed to me why you are here once again instead of where you should be. I want to know why you thought you had gained freedom of the hall, when I said naught of that to you."

Kristen was proud of the way her voice did not falter, sounding calm even to her ears. "'Tis simple, Saxon. You knew *why* I refused to share your bed this week past. Yet you took me to your bed yestereve. I was fool enough to assume that if you would do that, then you must have relented concerning my restraints."

"You are correct," he replied curtly. "'Twas a fool

assumption indeed. I told you why you must be fettered. I also told you the alternatives."

Kristen was no longer so calm, hearing him actually confirm what she had concluded. "I spit on your alternatives! I will wear your cursed fetters, but I want no more of you. I cannot bear your tender care and the chains too."

He walked slowly toward her. Warily she rose to her feet, but he stopped short of her, two arms' lengths away.

"I thought you stronger than this, wench."

She gasped at the deliberate slur. "I am not without mettle, milord. My father was captured and imprisoned in his youth. My mother endured enslavement for a time as well. I am what my parents have made me, and I would not be a credit to them if I could not endure enslavement myself. For me 'tis a fit punishment for defying my parents to sail with my brother. I can endure, Royce. But there is a limit to what I will endure without a fight. Leave me be from now on and you will have no problem with me."

"I cannot," he replied simply. "And you do not really want me to ignore you, Kristen."

"I do. I want you no more."

He did not like what he was hearing at all, and it showed in the tight slant of his lips, the turbulent green of his eyes. "You can say that after last eve?"

"Aye."

"Liar. You want me still and I will prove it."

She snorted contemptuously at the challenge. "Stubbornness is one of my faults, inherited from my mother. She once refused to speak to my father because of an argument they had, and did not say one word to him for an entire month. And they are two people who love each other passionately. Mayhap I do still want you, Royce, because I am attracted to you and that cannot be helped.

But you will never hear me admit it, nor will I accept you willingly again, because when you chain me, you show me that I am nothing to you, that you bear me no feelings at all. I need more than that from the man I give myself to. I need more than just passion."

"So you will deny us both?"

Kristen closed her eyes for a moment as bitter disappointment washed over her. What had she expected him to reply? *I care for you, Kristen. Of course I have feelings for you, strong feelings. How could you doubt it?* Fool! She would never hear such things from him.

She opened her eyes to see that his expression was still tight-lipped. But now a muscle ticked along his jaw. The hand at his hip was clenched into a fist. The dark eyebrows had moved closer together and the eyes were mere slashes of green. He was angry at last. Good. At least he shared something with her.

"Answer me, wench!"

"Aye, milord. I will deny us both."

"The devil you will! You have had your say. Now hear me. Whether I have you or not is my choice, not yours. I let the decision rest with you for a while, but 'twas a mistake, and I learn from my mistakes. Giving you the choice only served to make you think you had a right to choose. You do not, Kristen. I own you. Your life, your body, your mind, all belong to me."

The callousness of that statement enraged her. "Never! You own me, true, for you can kill me, sell me, rape me, whatever pleases you. But 'twill not always be so, for if I am sold, or escape, or am taken from you, then you own me no more. And *belong* to you! Think it if you will, but unless I want it to be so, then the word has no meaning. I would have to love you to truly belong to you. I would have to want to never leave you, to want to return to you if I do."

"I do not ask for your love," he said harshly.

"Good!" she retorted in kind. "Because I will not give it. You speak of choices. Aye, whether you have me or not is your choice. Whether I am willing to have you is *my* choice. I am not willing, Saxon."

"So you will fight me?"

"Aye."

"You have already learned 'tis pointless."

"Nay, what I have learned is how easily you can be manipulated by a mere challenge," she was angry enough to admit now. With a derisive laugh, she went on to taunt: "You have yet to taste the full measure of my resistance, Saxon. You did naught yestereve that I did not want you to do, for I wanted you then. But if you force me now and I fight you true, I promise you will get no pleasure from it."

Her taunting worked to fire his rage. He swore harshly, throwing the candle to the floor in his anger. It seemed his hands were on her even before the flame was extinguished, though she did not see him leap at her.

One hand slid down her arm to fasten on her wrist, and she was pulled after him toward the door. Kristen waited until they were in the narrow corridor to yank her hand away. She succeeded, and had the pleasure of hearing Royce swear again as she ran toward the stairs. He knocked her to the floor before she reached them, his body falling heavily on top of hers.

As soon as he lifted some of his weight to rise, allowing her to do the same, Kristen jabbed backward with her elbow. She connected with his belly and heard him grunt. With enough room between them now, she rolled to the side and would have kicked him even farther away if he hadn't thrown an arm over her legs. In the next moment he caught her hand and she found herself hefted over his shoulder.

Royce had trouble rising with her squirming weight, but rise he did and start toward his room. Kristen, however, was nowise done with him. Hanging halfway down his back, she reached up behind her to grab a handful of his hair. She jerked so hard she would have broken the neck of a less powerful man. As it was, Royce lost his balance and slammed into the wall.

Kristen gasped, feeling herself falling, and landed on her backside this time. But she did not let go of Royce's hair, which brought him to his knees beside her.

Royce growled furiously and knocked her hand away, leaving her with a fistful of his hair. This time when he caught her wrist, he twisted it around behind her back and up, until she thought he meant to break the arm. His intention, however, was to force her to rise—which she did, quickly.

He kept her in front of him now, and if she did not walk forward, the arm bent higher. He got her into his room this way, and once there, he shoved her forcefully away from him.

Kristen stumbled only slightly, but caught herself and swung around to face him. Calmly he locked the door. Just as calmly, he walked over and tossed the key out the open window, the gesture more than intimidating.

She felt a shiver rush down her back. But he did not approach her yet. The room was well lit, and she could see a cold look of determination on his face as he glanced at her. But he did not approach her. Instead he went to the bed. There, taking the cover in hand, he used his dagger to cut thin strips from it.

Kristen's eyes widened on seeing this. It didn't dawn on her yet what he meant to do with those thin strips of cloth. She simply thought him insane, for the cover was a work of beauty, made of soft sheepskin and finely embroidered with half a dozen different colored threads.

Royce stopped when he had four long pieces cut. He moved to tie a strip to one of the low posts on the bed, then moved to the next post. Watching him, Kristen was stunned, but only for a moment. She felt as if her heart had dropped into her belly, for there was only one reason she could think of for what he was doing.

A half yell, half groan ripped from her throat and she ran to the wall of weapons, yanking down a hefty broadsword. He *was* crazy!

"Put it back, Kristen."

His voice sounded so reasonable. How could he sound so reasonable when he meant to torture her?

"Nay!" She turned to glare at him. "You will have to kill me afore I let you practice your cruelties on me!"

He shook his head at her and continued tying a cloth to the third post, then went on to the fourth. He was watching not her, but what he was doing. She did not take her eyes from him, though, and saw a slight smile curling his lips. It turned her blood cold, for there was nothing of humor in it.

The sword was heavy, much heavier than anything she had ever practiced with. But standing there watching him until he was done had cost her the chance to pick another. She was not thinking clearly at all. She realized now, too late, that she should have attacked him instead of waiting until he gave her his full attention.

The small dagger Royce put back in the sheath at his belt. With no weapon in his hand, he walked toward Kristen. There were any number of weapons that he could choose from on the wall, but he would have to get around her first. She was not going to let him.

She hardened her heart to all that she felt for him. Her expression mirrored her deadly intent. She held the sword low, ready to twist sharply up and forward to find target. But Royce stopped just short enough so she would have to step to reach him. His own expression was inscrutable now.

"Tell me something, Kristen. Are all Norsewomen trained so ably to defend themselves?"

"Nay," she replied warily.

"But I know you have been, for you have twice demonstrated your skill for my cousin's benefit. Your father taught you, I suppose? Or was it your brother Selig? Of course, his skill was not as good—"

She cried furiously and swung the sword back to come down in an arc that would have neatly cleaved his shoulder if he had not moved aside. But instead of backing away to escape the blade's next descent, Royce had stepped closer. His fist came down on Kristen's wrist before she could maneuver the heavy sword to attack again.

The sword clattered loudly to the floor, and Kristen was spun about so that her back would face him when his arms circled round her waist. Both of her own arms were captured in the hold. Try as she might, she couldn't pull them loose.

"Foolish girl. Did no one ever teach you to ignore the comments of your adversary?"

She kicked a heel back in answer and struck his shin, but the soft-soled shoe did little damage and she was sure she hurt her foot more than she did him. The blow did succeed in making him hurry with her to the bed. He dropped her there and then fell on her back before she could get both arms out from under her. The one arm she did manage to release he quickly grabbed, and she groaned, feeling the cloth wrapped swiftly about her wrist.

It was the left wrist he had tied to the right post, so she was ready for him, thinking he would have to turn her over now. But her fist struck only air when he rose and she rolled over, for he was after her feet next, instead of her free hand. And he was easily able to secure one leg with his weight while he concentrated on tying the other foot to the post. And her hand stretched just short of him.

Kristen felt like crying, she was so frustrated, but she would not. "You had best kill me when you are done, Saxon, for I will see you in hell for this!"

Royce did not speak. Her legs were spread wide on the bed, her feet tightly secured to the posts. He got up and came to stand near the last post yet to be used.

Kristen glared at him, holding her right arm away from him. When he leaned forward to reach for it, her fist flew at his face, and he did not duck back quick enough this time.

She felt a surge of satisfaction, even though her knuckles throbbed where they scraped against his teeth. But his lip was smeared with blood, and his features were no longer inscrutable. Angrily he caught her last free limb and wrapped the cloth around it, tying an extra-tight knot on this hand. Then he stood back, and those eyes she had thought so beautifully green seemed filled with menace now as they locked with hers. Slowly he wiped the blood from his mouth with the back of his hand.

She closed her eyes against his triumph. It had been too easy for him. And now he would whip her, or whatever it was he had planned, to punish her for resisting his will. What he did next, however, was to strip away her clothes with his dagger.

Kristen groaned inwardly, but kept her features carefully blank and her eyes tightly closed. She was not going to scream when the pain began, nor cry, nor beg for mercy, for if he could do this to her, then he had none.

"Open your eyes, Kristen."

She refused. She felt the bed sag and knew he had sat down beside her. Finally, when he didn't say anything else, or move at all, she became too unnerved not to look. She found his eyes gazing into hers, then deliberately they moved down the length of her. She followed his gaze and felt a swift rush of heat.

Seeing herself like this brought home more clearly her helplessness. She could bend her knees slightly, but not much. Her arms were not stretched out tightly, but were bent at the elbows. They were useless to her, as were her legs, yet surprisingly, she was not uncomfortable in this position. The strips of cloth did not cut into her skin unless she tugged on them. It was her inability to continue fighting that made her miserable, and not knowing the manner of her punishment.

"Your promise held true, until now."

His voice drew her eyes back to his. "What promise?" she demanded.

"That I would get no pleasure from you if you fought me. I assure you 'tis a pleasure seeing you like this."

God help her, he was going to gloat now. "Bring out your whip and have done with it, Saxon!" she hissed.

He smiled. "Ah, you did mention my practicing cruelties on you. Good of you to remind me."

He eased her long braid out from under her as he said this, and devoted entirely too much attention to it. "You mean to whip me with that?" she asked incredulously.

"An interesting idea." He laughed, letting the braid slip through his hand until the tail end was caught by his fingers. "Mayhap—like this?"

The ends of her hair spread out like a fan between his fingers and flicked at the point of one breast. Blood rushed to that area, firming the mound, and turning the tip into a hard little nub.

Goose bumps spread over different parts of Kristen's body. Noticing her body's unwilling response, Royce continued to smile as he trailed the fan down the valley of her breasts to whip with feather softness at the other peak.

Her body told its own story to him, but he could not

know what was happening inside her. What had been a very real, though unacknowledged fear in the pit of her belly, had now burgeoned into excitement. To be completely helpless in the power of a man who knew well how to please her . . . She had not considered that.

"You—you do not mean to beat me?"

"Why do you sound so surprised?" he asked softly, trailing the fan of hair down and across her stomach, making the muscles jerk and contract. "I like your skin as is. Did you truly think I would mar it?"

"You were angry enough—"

"With reason. You made a liar of me this day. I swore to your friend Thorolf that I did not have to force you to my bed, yet here I have had to do just that."

"You told him . . . oh!"

Royce shrugged negligently. "He was concerned and needed reassurance that I was not taking undue advantage of my power over you."

"Are you not?" she snapped, looking meaningfully down at herself.

He chuckled. "Aye, mayhap I am now. But you will agree, by your own admittance, vixen, that yestereve I did not take advantage of you."

"Did you have to tell Thorolf that?"

"You would rather he worry about you?"

"I would rather he not think what he must think now!" she cried furiously.

"That you like me?"

"The devil take you, Saxon, I do not—not anymore," she amended, but then gasped as he leaned over to place a tickling kiss on her belly. "Nay, cease!"

His tongue snaked out to trace a circle round her navel. "Still resisting, vixen? Since you cannot stop me yourself, will you beg me to leave off?"

"Nay!"

He sat up and spread his hands over her stomach,

beginning a slow ascent toward her breasts. "I did not think you would, because you do not really want me to leave off."

His fingers had curled around her breasts. She heard her voice waver as she insisted, "Not so. I—I simply will not beg—for aught."

"Such a proud wench you are."

Between his thumbs and forefingers, he pinched her hardened nipples until she stiffened, then treated them with tender care. He continued applying pleasure-pain to this most sensitive area until she thought she would indeed beg for mercy. She could no longer remain still. She could no longer keep her expression impassive, even though she knew he was watching for her every reaction. Her heart was pounding wildly, her pulses gone mad. Heat seemed to be pouring out of her, though her brow remained dry.

Royce was mesmerized by the seductive slant of those aqua eyes, and the way her teeth kept gnawing on her lower lip. He would not kiss her lips, not yet, for he had little doubt she would sink those teeth into him. But his hands finally moved on, up to cup her face and hold it still while he kissed her everywhere but on her mouth.

At her ear, he beseeched her: "Tell me you want me, Kristen."

"You will never hear me say it."

He leaned back to look at her. A fire seemed to smolder in her eyes. He had never seen a woman more ready to be loved.

He smiled, shaking his head at her. "You are as stubborn as you predicted. But so am I, sweet vixen. And I *will* hear you say it."

He stood up and moved to the end of the bed. There he stopped, and slowly, with his eyes on the whole length of her, he began to remove his robe and tunic.

Watching him gaze at her was nearly the same as feeling his hands on her. It did crazy things to her insides.

Kristen closed her eyes against him. She willed her body to relax, to calm itself. It did no good. The anticipation, the wondering what he would do next kept the excitement building rather than dissipating.

She did not have to wait long. The bed sagged by her feet, then she felt a hand on each ankle. She would not look at him. Slowly the hands moved up the inside of her legs—she was not going to look—past her knees, slower as they inched up her thighs—she wouldn't look —higher, closer...

He stopped, hesitating, while Kristen held her breath, sure her heart was going to explode, it was beating so violently. Then his fingers changed directions, running over the tops of her thighs, then down the outside—but only as far as her knees. Just as she managed to expel her breath in a quiet manner, she caught it again as he started upward once more with those wide-spread fingers.

Again and again he worked his way up her thighs, each time coming closer to the core of her womanhood, but never touching her there, just making her think that he would, hope that he would. She was being flayed with erotic sensations. She was being primed to beg.

"Look at me, Kristen."

She shook her head wildly.

"Kristen."

She tilted her head back, so that if she did open her eyes, she couldn't see him crouched there between her legs. She heard him chuckle at this, and felt the bed move as he lay down at the bottom of it. And then he slipped his arms under her thighs, nearly up to his shoulders. His hands came around to spread over on her stomach, his chin resting on the triangle of curls.

"Do you want me now, Kristen?"

She would not answer. His hands moved up to cup her breasts. He lifted his chin and she could feel his warm breath . . . God help her—oh God!

His tongue touched the tiny muscle that controlled her passion, and that was all it took. Kristen exploded with such a violent shock of pleasure that his name burst from her lips. Her pelvis lifted to him, demanding the pressure of his tongue. She would have held him to her if she could have. But he did not deny her. She experienced her bliss in full measure.

But Royce was not done with her. Reality barely returned before he began a new assault on her senses. And she no longer had the will to resist. She was too sated, and too amazed by what he had done. Just thinking about it sent new excitement pulsing through her.

He lay atop her now, his lips forging paths of heat along her skin. But he would not enter her, would not slake his own raging passion. He was in position to do so, torturing her with anticipation again, but he would not.

He leaned up, and fancifully, she thought of glowing emeralds as she looked into his eyes. "You want me," he breathed against her lips. "Say it."

"I will not say it."

His teeth nibbled at her lips. "You would have me leave you now?"

God help her, she felt she would die if he did. But how could he? Could he? Nay, he could not.

She remained silent, her eyes filling with a mixture of stubborn pride and desire. He groaned, seeing his defeat. But it was only a minor thing in comparison to what he felt as he plunged into her, taking her with him on another wild crescendo of bliss.

When Kristen returned to reality this time, Royce was cutting her loose from her bonds. He wrapped his arms around her when he finished, and lay back with her nestled against his chest. She was done with fighting for now and he knew it, and took advantage of it.

"You knew I would not leave you." There was an accusatory note in his voice.

"Aye, I knew."

He grunted. "Stubborn wench."

Kristen grinned sleepily.

Chapter Twenty-four

The sweetest kiss woke Kristen. She sighed and stretched, but did not open her eyes yet. The dream she had been having of home seemed so real. She hated to give it up, yet the pressure on her lips was a mighty inducement.

"Has the fight gone out of you, vixen?"

Kristen smiled, knowing that Royce sat beside her on the bed. "Nay, milord."

"Then I look forward to another challenge."

"Oh!"

Her eyes flew open and she grabbed her pillow to throw at him. He was already backing away toward the door.

"Nay, Kristen—truce! There is much to do this morn, and little time. I have already sent Eda to fetch you clothes and—" He paused as Eda appeared at the door. "Ah, good. You can explain to her, Eda." And then he was gone.

Kristen sat up to stare at the old woman with a disgusted look. "What was that all about? He said there is much to do this morn."

"Aye, Alfred comes today."

"Your King comes here?" Kristen gasped.

Eda nodded as she came forward. "Advance riders brought the news. We have only a few hours to prepare."

"But why does he come?"

"'Tis an honor."

"If you do not know, just say so."

Eda chuckled. "Aye, you have me. How would I know why he comes? But it has been his habit since the treaty to visit his lords often to inspect their defenses, discern their readiness, and remind them that this time of peace will not last. He also gives praise and encouragement to their men so they will train with more earnestness. This will be the third time he has come to Wyndhurst since the Year of Battles."

"You see. You knew more than you thought you did." Kristen grinned.

"Nay, there are other possible reasons. He has also been known to visit those lords he favors, simply to forget for a few hours or days the menace of the Danes. And Lord Royce is one who has always been in favor."

"How nice," Kristen replied with a degree of sarcasm. She was not so pleased with Royce in the clear light of morning, with him not near to confuse her thoughts and senses. "So what have you for me there? More clothes that do not fit?"

"Nay, these were ordered made for you, so they should be of an agreeable length."

Kristen raised a questioning brow, and then frowned as Eda held the gown and chainse up for her inspection, for they were made of the same coarse materials as those that Royce's dagger had removed from her yestereve.

"Ordered by Royce?"

"Nay, Lady Darrelle," Eda replied. "She thought it indecent, the amount of bare skin that was exposed below your chainse. She was heard to remark that such exposure might prove to be a temptation to the less pious of our men."

Eda's lips twitched as she said this. Kristen grinned, and then they both burst into laughter. Kristen's amusement fled just as suddenly when she found her shackles draped over Eda's arm after the clothes were handed to her. She said nothing, however, and snapped the iron onto her ankles herself. She had accomplished nothing in resisting Royce. She would accomplish nothing in continuing to show her abhorrence to this last part of her apparel. If she would never be free of the fetters, so be it. With them would eventually come the hate she needed to truly resist the Saxon's hold over her.

The hall was nearly empty when Kristen and Eda went below. Most of the women were readying chambers for the King and his party. Royce and his men had gone hunting to supplement the store of meat. The men servants were working outside, moving most of the stabled horses to pasture to make room for those of the guests, bringing in extra hay and fodder, and rolling new barrels of ale into the hall.

The two women who had been working frantically by the cooking hearth left as soon as Kristen and Eda arrived. Kristen was so amazed that she did not even flinch as her other chain was secured.

"Are we expected to prepare food for everyone by ourselves?"

Eda chuckled. "They will return with the others as soon as Lady Darrelle is done with them above. She is always undone by royal visits, and has her women running hither and yon, but getting little accomplished. More would get done, and quicker, if the lady would take herself off to bed."

"Eda!"

"Well, 'tis true," the old woman insisted.

Kristen smiled to herself as they began to work side by side. Eda had revealed a new facet of herself this morn—humor. Other than what Kristen managed to see herself, which was slight, humor had been lacking in her existence since her arrival on these shores. It made her appreciate Eda all the more, and realize just how fond she had become of the old woman. With her gruffness, her ofttimes unwanted advice, and her care, she reminded Kristen of old Alfreda at home, who had been as bossy as a mother—not Brenna, but the mothers of Kristen's friends—but a very dear friend too.

Not a few minutes later, Eda's churlishness returned to the fore. "Would you not know it! Not a wench back yet to serve those three with a smile of welcome. 'Tis left to an old woman to do, as if I do not have enough else."

Kristen followed her frown to the door, where three young men had just entered. "The ones who brought news of the King's arrival?"

"Aye, and young lordlings from the look of them."

The three men were laughing among themselves over some jest the tallest of them had made. They removed their short mantles, but not their weapons, as they made straight for the large barrel of ale across the room. Eda hurriedly swiped up tankards to take to the men, returning with an even deeper frown crossing her brow.

"I thought I had recognized that smooth-faced stripling. 'Tis Lord Eldred. Nay, wench, do not look!" Eda warned sharply. "You do not want *his* attention."

Kristen already had his attention, and that of the other two as well. With the hall so empty, it was only natural that they would glance toward the only two women about. And once she was seen, it was difficult to ignore Kristen. She was just too different from what Saxons were accustomed to: too tall, too striking in appearance, and certainly too noble of bearing for an ordinary serf.

Kristen kept her eyes lowered as warned, but wanted to know "Which is he?"

"The yellow-haired one. 'Twas known he might be with the King's party, but I wonder at his audacity to come here in advance, without the King's protection. I wonder if Lord Royce knows he is here. Nay, he must not," she answered her own question, "for he would not trust that one alone in his hall."

Kristen wondered herself as Eda pushed her to the end of the table so she gave only her back to the hall. It was too soon for her to have forgotten what Eda had told her about Lord Eldred. He was Royce's enemy. Why indeed would he ride into his enemy's stronghold nearly alone? To show he did not fear Royce? Or was he counting on the King's coming to prevent any altercations from arising? Eda had said they were at a truce, these two, because of the Danes' threat. But how secure could that truce be if animosities ran deep?

She pictured Lord Eldred in her mind's eye as she had seen him from across the hall. She imagined that if he came close, she would find him to be as tall as herself. That made him not a small man, except in comparison with Royce.

He was mayhap a year or two older than his adversary, but not nearly as powerful in build. Yet he was still a man in fine condition from the rigorous training for war. And he was by far the most handsome man of face she had ever seen, save for her own brothers. But it was men with bodies like Royce's that pulled the string of attraction in Kristen, so she felt nothing but a mild curiosity toward Eldred and his companions.

"You have lost the wager, Randwulf. 'Tis not a man in woman's garb, but a woman indeed."

Kristen gasped at the first word and swung around. Eda would have warned her of their approach, but she had so hoped the three men would change their minds. They did not.

"'Tis a wager I do not so much mind losing," the dark-haired Randwulf replied.

He flipped a gold piece to Eldred, but did not take his

eyes from Kristen. The coin fell to the floor, for Eldred too was fascinated by their find.

"Tell us, wench, why do they chain you?" Eldred asked her pleasantly enough. "Is your crime so great?"

It was the wrong thing for him to mention, for instead of making Kristen wary of them, it made her ire rise. "I am a dangerous woman. Do I not look it?"

"Oh, aye," one of them replied, then all three began to laugh.

"Tell us true, wench," Eldred persisted.

"I am a Norsewoman," she said stiffly. "What more explanation need there be?"

"God's breath, a Viking!" the third man exclaimed. "I can well see the need for chains."

"Too bad she is not a Dane," Randwulf lamented. "Then I would know how to treat her."

Eldred grinned. "You are a fool, Randwulf. What matters who she was? She is a slave now."

His hand rose to touch Kristen's cheek as he spoke. Kristen turned her face away. She was feeling a definite nervousness now. They were crowded round her, too close, and she had the table at her back, preventing any retreat. But how far could she retreat with the long chain binding her to the wall?

"Have done, milords," she said tersely. "I have work to do."

It was a bold move, turning her back on them and hoping they would accept her dismissal. It was the wrong move. A hard body pressed into her back, and two hands came round to fasten on her breasts.

Kristen's reaction was swift. She only had to turn partially to shove the man away from her. It was Randwulf, and he stumbled back with an expression of amazement that was almost comical.

"You dare, wench?" he blustered once he got his balance. "You truly dare!"

Kristen looked at each one of them. Eldred was amused; the other two were not. God help her, if only she had a weapon to ward them off. But not even a small cutting knife had she ever been allowed to use while she worked. The other women did all the cutting.

"I am not here for your pleasure, milords. I am used as hostage, to assure the behavior of the men I came here with. Royce would not like me to be ill used."

She was bluffing, for she had no way of knowing what Royce would do if these men raped her. He might not care if they did, but he might also use that excuse to challenge Eldred and be glad for it.

Eldred took particular interest in her words. "'Royce'? You call your lord by his name? I wonder why."

"Because she shares his bed, no doubt," Randwulf sneered. "And if he can have her, so then can we."

"Nay!" Kristen shouted, but it was at Eldred she glared. "Do you risk what he will do to you? He will kill you!"

"You think so, wench?" Eldred smiled. "Then let me correct you. Your Royce will do naught, because Alfred does not like his nobles fighting amongst themselves, and Royce never displeases Alfred."

He had moved closer as he spoke, and so did the others. Because she had all three to watch at once, she was caught off guard by Eldred. His hands clamped on her wrists and shoved them both up behind her back, forcing her breasts hard against his chest. He tried to kiss her, but he could not keep her face still when he held both hands. He thought to remedy that by holding both her hands together with only one of his. It was his mistake, her strength underestimated.

It was no measly slap she gave him when she broke one hand loose, but a solid blow with her fist that struck the side of his head and staggered him with dizziness. But the other two immediately laid hands on her to subdue her own. Eldred was now furious, a dark rage contorting his handsome features, turning them ugly.

"You will pay for that, wench," he promised her. "I will demand your life—after I am done with you."

"Enough!"

They all turned to see Alden coming toward them, with Eda close on his heels. Kristen could have kissed the old woman for bringing someone, even him.

"Stay out of this, Alden," Eldred warned. "The wench struck me."

"Did she? Well, 'tis no surprise, for she is no common wench." Alden moved around them to the stake in the wall that held Kristen's long chain, pointing at it with his sword tip. "Why think you she is chained?"

The question was ignored by Eldred. "I warn you, Alden, I mean to have her."

"Aye," Randwulf agreed. "So do I."

"Do you fight us three?" Eldred grinned now.

"Me?" Alden feigned surprise. "I will not have to. The wench fights her own battles, and she does it very well. And in all fairness, she must be allowed to."

Before they knew what he was about, Alden broke the chain from the wall with his sword point. His action brought no concern to the three men. They still watched Alden, sword drawn and only a few feet away, so Randwulf was again taken by surprise as Kristen jerked her arm away from him and bent to pick up the length of chain.

The third man could not release her other arm fast enough, now that she had this weapon in her hands. She twirled the loose end of the chain round her head, forcing the circle of men back. They could not get near her now without gaining some hurt.

Randwulf was bold enough to try, though, thinking that if he could get the chain to wrap about his arm, he could yank her off her feet with it, since it was still connected there. He was prepared to endure the pain, sure the chain would strike on the fleshy part of his arm and be no worse than a stinging blow. He was not prepared to have it slip below his raised arm and strike his rib cage.

One rib cracked. The sound of it was lost to Randwulf in the horrid sting of iron meeting flesh. His skin felt torn away, the pain shooting instantly to his brain. It was so bad he nearly fainted and was unaware he rolled on the floor screaming.

Kristen felt not an ounce of remorse for what she had done. She was fully prepared to do it again. Eldred was the first to realize this and motioned the other man back. But he was not done himself, and turned on Alden.

"Make no mistake, the King will hear of this. He sent us here—"

"To ill use one of my cousin's slaves? I think not. And if I were you, Eldred, I would concern myself with what Royce will do, not what Alfred might do."

"She has injured a man. She must pay for that."

"My cousin will pay the fine."

Eldred snarled at that and stalked away to cool off outside. It was left to the other man to help Randwulf away.

Kristen did not relax until they had all left the hall. Then she turned on Alden. The chain lay at ease in her hand now, but it was still in her hand. He looked into her eyes, divining her thoughts.

"Would you really, wench?" His question was soft. "Even after I just aided you?"

"I did not ask for your help."

"But you needed it."

She fought a battle inside herself, then finally nodded. "Very well. For that—" She dropped the chain to the floor, indicating she would not attack him with it. "But what you did before—I can never forget."

Alden sighed. "I know, and I am sorry for it."

Kristen turned her back on him.

Chapter Twenty-five

*W*hen the women began returning to the hall, no one made mention of Kristen's partial freedom. But then, few had time even to notice, they were kept so busy in preparation for the planned feast. Kristen herself barely had a free moment to think about what had happened. After tucking the long chain through her rope girdle so she wouldn't drag it noisily about, she had resumed her work.

Not more than an hour later, however, she was embraced again, taken completely by surprise when arms slipped around her from behind to lock about her waist, squeezing gently. She felt a moment's panic, but it was nothing compared with the chagrin that followed, that they would dare accost her again. This time all the servants were about, as well as Darrelle, who looked on with a curious frown.

"Are you all right?"

Kristen seemed to turn hot and cold at the same time. And then confusion set in. It was Royce who was holding her, Royce, with unmistakable concern in his voice. The very man who had taken such pains to make it appear he did not notice her, who had even pretended to be doing something else when he spoke to her yestereve in this very spot, now held her close for all to see. She could not fathom it.

"Have you lost your senses, milord?"

She twisted around to see if he was besotted with

drink. He did not appear to be. He was frowning at her, seeming as confused as she was.

"I ask you a perfectly pertinent question, and you reply with a flippant one. Of course I have not lost my senses. Have you?"

"I am beginning to wonder," she replied in annoyance. "You seek me out, here and now, when you have never done so before. Do you not realize everyone is watching you?"

Royce looked over her head to scan the hall. His eyes even locked with Darrelle's for a moment, noting her dismay over his behavior, but not letting it affect him. He looked back at Kristen. His arms remained locked around her.

"I am done with ignoring you for the sake of preventing gossip," he said simply. "If Eda had not been with you this morn . . . No one else would have done as she did. 'Tis time they all know what you mean to me. If I could I would put my seal on you. If Alfred's nobles could read, I would put a sign about your neck. No one else will mistake that you have my protection. If I must show it in actions, so be it."

She could not believe he was saying this. "Why? I am only another of your slaves."

"Do not be coy, wench," he snapped. "You know you are special to me."

"For a time?"

"For a time."

If they were alone, she would have pushed him away from her for answering that without the slightest hesitation. But Kristen was too cognizant of the many eyes on them. It would not do to show such impertinence to a man considered to be her "lord"—not for her sake, but for his. Though why she should consider his pride she did not know.

Stiffly she said, "I am sure you have much to do, milord, as do I."

He recognized the dismissal, but ignored it, though he did drop his hands from her. "I swear I will never understand you. Any other woman would have cried and screamed to me of the indignities visited on her and demanded retribution. You do not even mention the assault. You even accuse me of being daft for asking if you are all right."

Kristen started to smile, but helplessly, it turned into a laugh instead. "Is that what this is about? What happened this morn?"

"You are not even a little upset by it?"

"But why? I was not harmed."

Her attitude was so different from what he had expected, he became irritated with her. He had rushed inside to console her, to swear he would avenge her, only to have her treat the matter with indifference. He had wanted to skewer Eldred to a wall when Alden told him what the cur had attempted to do, and probably would have if Eldred had been within his sight at the telling. But fast on top of his rage had been concern for Kristen, concern she scorned.

"Mayhap you do not realize a crime was committed," he said harshly now.

"Against a slave?" she scoffed, remembering his telling her she had no rights.

"Against the man you injured."

She stiffened, the aqua brightness of her eyes fading to a frigid hue. "What crime? Defending myself? You dare to call that a crime?"

"Not I. 'Tis the law. A slave cannot bear weapons except at his owner's behest, nor attack anyone, especially a noble. To attack a noble carries a high fine even of a freeman, but for a slave . . ."

"Is that why you expected me to be upset?" she sneered. "Am I to be hung for protecting myself?"

"Do not be absurd, wench. As your lord, it falls to me to pay your fine, and there is no question that I will. I just wanted you to see the seriousness of what you have shrugged off as being of no consequence."

"I will not thank you," she replied churlishly. "I do not like the idea that a payment must be made at all to that swine. Were I home, those men would be dead for what they attempted to do to me."

"You cannot expect things here to be as they were for you at home, Kristen." His voice was softer now, his anger having diminished with the reminder that she had not always been a slave, that she was accustomed to more worthy treatment. "I do not like seeing that lout Randwulf rewarded, either, and will ensure that he suffers a bit more for his wergild."

Wergild was the man-price assessed to every free man, the amount of shillings at which each man's value or importance to society in terms of wealth was registered for the purpose of laws. This was the amount payable in compensation for hurt done to a man, or hurt done by him. There were only three levels of distinction in Wessex: twelve hundred shillings, being the King and his family; six hundred shillings, being the King's nobles; and two hundred shillings, the churls. Slaves had no wergild at all, but were valued at eight oxen.

Kristen knew all of this, thanks to Eda. She knew that a man's full wergild was demanded for a death, with lesser amounts required for an injury, even exact amounts for specific injuries according to law. She imagined that a cracked rib, which would limit a man's abilities for a while, would indeed be a high fine, as Royce had said, especially for a noble whose full wergild was six hundred shillings, a staggering amount for most men.

It dawned on Kristen that Royce was not at all annoyed that he would have to pay this fine for her. He had been annoyed that she had scoffed at his concern. And here he was now saying that he would personally see to it that Randwulf was punished even more. He was saying he would avenge her. Whom did she know, even of her own people, who would avenge a slave? God's teeth! Why couldn't this man be consistent? Why did he make her feel like the lowest of the low one moment, then like a cherished loved one the next?

Kristen lowered her eyes, feeling contrite now over her churlishness of the last few minutes. "I appreciate what you would do, milord, but 'tis unnecessary. As I said before, no harm—"

She didn't get to finish. Two of the younger, more exuberant serfs burst into the hall, shouting that the King was here. Royce started away, seeming to have dismissed her completely from his mind with that news. He had not. He turned back, calling Eda to him.

"Remove her fetters, Eda." Then to Kristen, his eyes fixing her with a fierce look, he added softly, "We needs make a bargain, you and I, but I have not the time now to speak of it. For God's mercy, wench, be good."

Kristen watched him move swiftly toward the entrance of the hall. She saw the Lady Darrelle hurry to join him and try to speak to him, but he waved a hand to silence her and did not slow his pace so she could keep up with him. The others in the hall all rushed to crowd about the windows to watch King Alfred's arrival.

Kristen did not move herself, not even when the hated iron slipped off her ankles and Eda tugged the longer chain out of her girdle. Slowly her lips turned up until a brilliant smile sat there. Royce was going to deal with her, to accept her word for whatever the bargain would be. He was finally going to trust her. She felt euphoric. She felt like shouting her joy and would have, if Eda was not still watching her. The old woman had been right all along. She had only needed to bide her time.

"Aye, I can see how pleased you be." Eda did not smile herself. "Just remember his warning, wench. Do naught that will put you back into these." And she tossed the chains into the corner.

Kristen nodded, but absently. Her mind was too full of Royce and what his trust could mean. There was hope again that she had not been wrong after all to choose Royce of Wyndhurst for her man. He still thought of her as his enemy, but Garrick and Brenna had once been enemies, too, and their lives had been joined together despite it.

Strangers began crowding into the hall. In high spirits now, Kristen was open to feeling some of the excitement of the others in being allowed to see this great King of the Saxons. But she was the only one surprised, the others having seen him before. He was so young, surely younger than Royce!

She thought at first she must be mistaken. This could not be the man who had led Saxon against fierce Dane, who had won a temporary peace for his people. After all, there was naught to distinguish him from the nobles who crowded round him. They were all dressed in fine clothes, some more splendid than he. Others there, older men with fiercer looks, might be more readily thought King.

Yet this young man was King. She did not really need Eda to confirm it. There was that certain quality about him the others lacked. It was what she had seen in Royce that first day she met him, when his bearing, not his dress, had told who he was. This was a man used to command. The others, all lords and used to command themselves, deferred to him.

Except for his youth and the power that being King

gave him, at first glance, Alfred of Wessex was not a
remarkable man to speak of. He was tall for a Saxon,
fair in coloring, with blue eyes that were alert, taking in
all about him without appearing to. He had not the look
of a warrior, and Kristen was to learn later that he was
in fact a scholar with gentle qualities. She was also to
find that though he might not be remarkable in appearance, he was remarkable in his drive and energy, and his
single-minded determination to keep his kingdom under
Saxon rule.

At the moment he seemed like any other man, a little
tired from his travels, appreciative of the chalice of wine
Lady Darrelle brought to him, and attentive of the intro-
ductions as Royce reacquainted him with several of his
men before they moved to the tables that were already
set up for the feast. Kristen felt a measure of pride
watching Royce, pride she had no business feeling, for
she had no claim on him, but she felt it just the same.

She could see that Eda had been right again: Royce
was favored by his King. There was no formality between them. They spoke to each other as friends would,
on an equal level. She even saw other men look askance
when Alfred would laugh at something Royce said, and
wondered if Royce knew he was envied by these other
lords.

For the most part, the nobles that made up Alfred's
entourage were men of an age with him, younger sons
who followed the court in hope of currying favor. There
were half a dozen ladies, too, wives and daughters ac-
companying their lords, though the Queen was not
among them.

Only one of these women aroused Kristen's curiosity,
a very pretty lady with flaxen hair bound up under a net
of pearls. She was young, with buxom figure encased in
a lovely fur-trimmed gown that Kristen might have envied, except she thought her own green velvet was much

nicer. But then, she wasn't wearing her green velvet, and she wasn't noticed, and the flaxen-haired lady could not seem to take her eyes from the King and Royce, dividing her attention equally between them.

Kristen looked away from the nobles, experiencing jealousy for the first time in her life. But since she had never known jealousy before, she didn't realize that was what she was feeling. She only knew it disturbed her to watch that lady, so lovely in all her finery, trying to gain Royce's attention. Kristen's only consolation was that he was so occupied with his King he had not noticed.

Chapter Twenty-six

The feast continued throughout the afternoon and on into the evening. Cooking fires had been set up in the yard behind the hall to roast the larger animals, no less than three to offer a variety: the deer the hunters had brought in that morning, a sheep, and a tender young calf. Smaller game was prepared inside over the hearth, as well as fresh vegetables from the manor gardens. Rounds of cheese were brought up from the cellar, along with fruits recently gathered. Tarts were made from these, and sweet pies and sauces.

Kristen ate as she could, whenever she found a few seconds to spare. Feasts like this one were not new to her. She had even helped prepare the food for them before, for in the dead of winter at home it was not unusual for one or more of the servants to be sick and extra help needed for cooking. But there was a major difference: She had never helped with a feast in the summer months at home.

In winter when the closed-off cooking area became too warm, the back door could be opened to let in a cold breath of relief. Here, even with the open window near the hearth, Kristen felt as if she herself were in the oven along with the many loaves of honey bread.

The heat seemed worse than any day previous. It was the overcrowding in the hall, and the fact that it had been overcrowded the whole day. It was also the long sleeves on her new chainse, which were chafing at her arms. Both chainse and gown were plastered to her back and sides. The hair that had worked loose from her braid hung in wet strings about her face.

As strong and healthy as she was, Kristen was drawing on her last reserves today. The other women took every chance they got to rush outside for a respite. She could not. She might not be chained any longer, but she was watched—by Eda, by the other women, and by several of Royce's men—constantly. Gradually she came to realize that the men, even though they sat at their leisure, had been ordered to keep watch on her. So much for Royce's completely trusting her!

This might not have pricked her ire if it were not for the heat. But because of it, Kristen was feeling just as snappish as the other women. Sharp reprimands and slaps were quick to fall, given by the older women to those younger. Even Eda boxed the ears of one girl simply for standing idle for a few moments to fan herself.

Tempers were running high among all the harried servants. At the tables, spirits ran high, for the guests were enjoying themselves. There had been dancing for a while in the center of the room between the tables, and Kristen had looked on wistfully, noting that the Saxon dances were not so different from her own. Bards had told stories of dragons and witches, of giants and elves. A harp-playing minstrel sang of heroes of an older land, but mostly of King Egbert, Alfred's grandfather, who had changed the history of his kingdom from acknowledgment of the supremacy of Mercia as overlord of Wessex, to then twice defeating Mercia and eventually delivering his kingdom from Mercian control.

How much of these tales are true? Kirsten wondered, but she heard as well how this grandfather of Alfred's also defeated the Welsh, the men north of the Humber, and the giant Celts of Cornwall, who had steadily resisted his rule. All delighted in the tales and the minstrel was urged to sing more and more.

So the day progressed, with the nobles being entertained and lavished with good food and drink, while the servants toiled to provide it. At one point Kristen was summoned by two lords who wanted her in particular to serve them. Eda had already told her she was not to serve, even though she had the freedom of movement now. It was just as well. Preparing food in the obscurity of the cooking area was one thing. Actually serving lords and ladies she considered to be no better than herself was quite another. Those two lords she simply ignored until they gave up and called another wench to their needs.

She was not noticed other than that. Or so she thought. She would have felt a degree of embarrassment to know she had in fact engaged the curiosity of everyone there, including the King. Among the nobles, she was pointed out to a neighbor, speculated about, but no one condescended to actually inquire about a slave, as she was assumed to be on the basis of her dress and labors. It was only Alfred who felt no qualms about asking Royce to appease his curiosity.

Kristen would have bristled if she could have heard that conversation. As it was, she bristled at how often she heard the captured Vikings being discussed. Royce was lauded for the feat, and commended for having put the "savages" to work for his defense. Those *savages* were kept to their windowless quarters today because the whole manor was feasting. Those *savages* were her friends and neighbors!

If she was not irritable enough because of the heat, she had heard one too many derogatory remarks about her friends, enough to put her very near an explosive level, whereby the slightest wrong look or word might be her undoing. That wrong look came from Royce himself.

At a lull in activity during the minstrel's song, Kristen deliberately moved to sit on the window ledge and fan herself with both hands. Her guards could not see her there, since the other women around the table blocked her from their line of vision, and that suited her surly mood. But Royce could see her clearly, and she caught his stern look, correctly interpreting it for what it was: a warning to stay away from the window. Did he think she would escape through it? Of course he did. She was to be denied even that little bit of respite from the heat.

It was too much. She stood up. Furiously, slowly, with her eyes never leaving his, she ripped off the long sleeves of her chainse just as she had done once before, and tossed them out the window. She felt the cooling difference immediately. She also heard Royce give a hearty shout of laughter at what she had done.

It was the laughter that saved her from doing anything more extreme, for it enabled her to step outside her discomfort and see the humor of her pique. The irritation she had felt all day drained away. She even grinned as Eda began to scold her and pulled her back to the table.

That had happened less than an hour ago. The hall was quieting down now. Food was being removed from the tables. Preparations were already under way for the morning meal.

Kristen imagined it would be many hours yet before she could find her bed. She was wrong. Royce rose and came to her. Without a word, he took her hand firmly in his and began to lead her to the stairs.

If she were not so exhausted, she might have protested his indelicacy, for she knew exactly what he was doing. He had said that by his actions he would make known to Alfred's nobles that she had his protection. How better to do that than by proclaiming her his bedmate? No one watching could mistake his intention. He even hesitated at the foot of the stairs to briefly kiss her.

Strangely, Kristen was not in the least chagrined by what he was doing. Were she his wife, they would retire of an evening in just such a way. But what really held her silent and acquiescent was that Royce was leaving his King and all his guests to his cousin Alden's care, so that he could retire with her. Her protection meant that much to him.

"'Tis well you did not fight me, Kristen."

He said this as soon as he had closed the door to his chamber and released her hand. By his tone, she knew he was thanking her for allowing his little charade to play. She moved toward the bed, saying nothing until she had sat down to relieve her weariness.

"I would not fight you in front of others, milord."

He came to stand in front of her, a slight frown creasing his brow. "Mayhap you are not aware of what—"

She cut him short with a soft laugh. "Your method was rather crude, but I did not mistake the gesture—nor, I think, did your guests. You have labeled me as you intended."

"And you do not mind?"

"I must not, or I would be angry. Or mayhap I am just too tired to be angry. I do not know. But why are you disturbed? Would it have suited your purpose better to have carried me up here kicking and screaming?"

"'Twas anticipated," he grunted.

She smiled at him, shaking her head. "As I said, I would not fight you in front of others."

"And why is that?" he wanted to know. "You do not hesitate otherwise."

"I have been surrounded by men all my life and know their prideful ways. You would never forgive me were I to best you in front of someone. But here, alone, it would not matter."

He laughed at that. "I think that applies to you as well, vixen."

She shrugged before lying back on the bed to stare up at him with half-closed eyes. Royce sucked in his breath. Her invitation was clear in the way she lay before him, relaxed, waiting. Heat shot through his vitals, yet he did not move, afraid that if he did she would bolt. This was just too much of an about-face after last eve's stormy encounter.

His hesitation brought a laugh from her, a deep, throaty sound. "I understand, milord."

He felt irritation rise and mix with his desire. Dealing with Kristen was a constant drain on his wits. She never once did what was normal or expected.

"What do you understand?" His voice sounded harsh even to his ears.

She leaned up on her elbows. Another woman would have cringed from his tone. Kristen smiled at him.

"I am soaked in my own sweat. 'Tis no wonder you do not find me appealing."

Air caught in his lungs again. "Not appealing?" he fairly shouted.

She still ignored his agitation. "Aye. I would ask to bathe, except I would have to go down to the hall to do it, and 'twould be too obvious to your guests. They would think 'twas your order, that you would not have me as I am. I do have some pride."

He stared at her in amazement for a second's breath, then placed a knee on the bed to bend over her. "Woman—" he began.

She planted her hands in the middle of his chest to stop him. "Nay, I must stink as well. How can you?"

He was chuckling now. "I can, with pleasure. But if 'tis a bath you really want, there is a small lake near here."

Her eyes lit up. "You would take me there?"

"Aye."

He leaned into the pressure of her hands to snatch a

kiss from her, feeling a strange delight in the pleasure of her expression. So he was once again caught by surprise when she groaned.

"Oh, unfair! To tempt me with a swim in cool waters, when I am so tired I can barely lift my hand from this bed!"

"God's mercy!" he growled, leaning back from her. "You will drive me mad, wench!"

"Why?"

He looked at her through narrowed eyes. Then it struck him that she was not teasing him. She was serious. He saw all of her actions since she had come into the room in a different light now. It was true disappointment that made her cry out in dismay.

"Are you really so tired?"

She smiled faintly. "I fear the heat of your hall has drained my strength away. The work I can do, but 'twas so crowded ..." She fell back on the bed again with a sigh. "'Tis well you do not want me now. I do not think we would either of us enjoy the sport."

He started to say, "Speak for yourself," but did not. Weeks ago such a brazen statement from her would have shocked him. Perhaps he was getting used to the way she spoke her mind, if not to her inconsistencies.

"Do you still want that bath?"

She closed her eyes, though her lips still smiled. "'Twould be nice, but I still will not go below. I hope you will not make me stir myself to argue about it."

An annoyed sound came from his throat. She would stir herself to argue, but not to make love. And he did still want her, regardless of her exhaustion and condition. But he had to concede that she was undoubtedly right. He would feel cheated if her response to him was sluggish, when her fiery passion was what he enjoyed most.

Kristen had opened her eyes at the sound he made,

enough to look at him beneath her lashes. Her mind must be as weary as her body. She had made an assumption based on what she was feeling. It was not what he was feeling, as she could see by the way he was looking down at her with an almost pained expression. He did in fact want her now. That knowledge did not fire her blood. She doubted anything could at the moment. But it did make her feel unaccountably good inside.

"If it pleases you, milord."

She saw him tense at her offer, but then he relaxed, his features softening too. "Aye, it pleases me, wench, but I will do what pleases you instead. Come, you will have your bath."

She groaned as he caught her hand to pull her up. "Royce, nay. 'Twould please me more to sleep."

She was tired indeed to let his name slip out, when only *Saxon* or a derogatory *milord* had passed her lips before. He was amused. He had never thought to see her quite this way. Exhaustion had felled her guard completely.

"You need only stand for a few minutes," he told her with a grin. "I will do the rest."

"Stand?"

"Aye, here."

He brought her over to the container of water that had been set on his table. There was a folded cloth there, too, a sponge, and a sliver of soap.

"This is not normal," she said with a frown. "You always wash downstairs."

"The bathing room will be used by my guests. When we have guests, water is always brought here for me. You are not the only one affected by the heat in a crowded hall, though I imagine 'twas worse for you."

"You can imagine," she said. "But the reality is even worse than that."

"Is our clime really so hard on you, vixen?" he asked as he began to undress her. "It has not dampened your spirit until now."

He regretted teasing her as soon as he said it, aware that her pride might reassert itself and she would be chagrined, thinking he made light of her suffering. She surprised him by giggling instead.

"You know, if you had not laughed at me when I tore off my sleeves, I think I would have done something foolish, the heat had me in such ill humor. Why did you find the gesture so amusing?" He would not answer, and she grinned. "Did I remind you of a sulky child? 'Tis how I saw myself after I heard you laugh."

He grunted, for she was too perceptive by far. But he certainly didn't see her as a sulky child now. No child this, and he had made a grave mistake in thinking to wash her himself. The moment she was completely uncovered he knew it. But she would not do it. Her eyes were closed now. She was done with talking. She was practically asleep on her feet.

He hesitated too long, looking at her. "You do not have to do this, milord." Her eyes were still closed.

Royce felt challenged now. "I know."

He reached for the soap, glad that she did not see the way his hands shook. He tried to make quick work of lathering her, and tried to keep his eyes averted from where his hands moved. It was not easy. Nor did it make any difference. What he could not see, he was feeling.

He was mad to put himself through this, when he had no intention of bedding her afterward. And he still would not bed her. The very fact that she would stand there and let him wash her confirmed her exhaustion. And it was his own fault. He had not thought how the extra load today would wear her down. His servants were used to these infrequent burdens. But they were also used to Wessex summers. Kristen was used to neither.

He used the sponge to rinse her, letting the water soak into the discarded clothes at her feet. There was such a look of pleasure on her face as the cool water trickled down her body, that Royce decided his own torment was worth it. He even slowed the rinsing to extend her pleasure.

At last he dried her with the cloth—which, for his own sake, he wrapped around her before leading her back to the bed. He would have carried her there, but that would have been his undoing. As it was, her murmur of contentment as she stretched out on the bed made him groan.

His voice was unintentionally sharp as he threw the thin sheet over her, leaving the cover at the foot of the bed. "You may sleep as long as you want in the morn."

"You pamper me, milord."

"Nay, I am simply selfish."

Her eyes opened partially. "What has that to do with—"

"Go to sleep, wench!"

"You do not come to bed yourself?"

Royce swore violently and turned away from her. He swiped up her clothes from the floor as he left. He would give them to Eda to wash, then he would go to the lake for a cold dunking by himself. But he doubted he would be able to sleep in his own bed tonight at all.

Chapter Twenty-seven

*I*t seemed to Kristen that Lord Eldred had been waiting for her to appear, for no sooner did she reach the cooking area and Eda shoved a bowl of gruel into her hands, than he left his seat across the hall and approached her. She felt no trepidation, seeing him come, and sat down on a stool at the end of the worktable by the window to begin eating.

The hall seemed back to normal, the servants quietly working, several of Royce's men lounging about. It would have been normal, except for the extra women around Lady Darrelle in her portion of the hall. The female guests. She heard snatches of conversation from them about a hunt, and assumed that was where the King and his nobles had gone—all but Lord Eldred.

"You come late to your work, wench."

He had sat down at the end of the long trestle table that would not be taken down until after the guests departed. The end of the table was five or six feet away from Kristen's table. Two other women were working there, but she knew he spoke to her. They looked at him; Kristen did not.

But she did answer. "So I do."

Several long moments of silence followed, then he said, "I see you are no longer being punished."

"'Twas no punishment that had me chained," she replied mildly as she continued to eat.

"Aye, I know you said 'twas because you are dangerous." There was derision in his tone. "I might even have

226

believed that after yestermorn, except that you would not have your freedom now if 'twas true."

She shrugged. "Mayhap Lord Royce feels there is a greater danger here now than myself."

"What danger? Curse you, look at me when I speak to you!"

Her eyes lifted slowly, finally fixing on his angry features. His face was red. There was an ugly slant to his mouth. He was not so handsome in his anger.

Her own look dismissed him, as if he were no more worthy of her attention than a rangy dog. She went back to eating before she gave an answer.

"You were the danger, milord. I have my freedom to protect myself. Lord Royce knows I do that very well."

She was ignoring him again. Eldred had never in his life been treated this way by a woman. Women fawned over him, they loved him, they fought each other for his favor. This one treated him as if he were beneath her notice, and she a slave! He could kill her for that. If they were alone, he would have her beneath him—where she would pay dearly for her contempt.

"Royce chained you," Eldred sneered, "just as he chains those savages in the yard who build his wall. Tell me, wench, does he chain you to his bed as well?"

He heard the women beside her gasp at his crudity, but the one to whom it was directed was not affected by his words at all. She sat there in calm serenity, eating her food, and he wanted to strangle her for it. How had she managed to make him lose control? He had wanted only to taunt and ridicule her, to make her pay for what she had done yestermorn.

There would be gossip if he did not leave go, gossip such as he had heard this morn: that Royce had not even waited until he was alone to summon her to his bed, but had escorted her from the hall. Blatantly he had made known his preference for a slave—a *slave!*—and in front of his King!

Eldred wished he had been present to see that bit of foolishness. But he had been loath to face Royce in Alfred's presence after Alden had made clear to him that this slave was special to Royce. It would be just like Royce to take issue with Eldred for what he had tried to do, and Eldred never won where Royce was concerned. He had worked too hard to gain Alfred's respect to lose it in an altercation with Royce over a slave.

But he still could not leave go. His anger was too great. It could only be appeased by her humiliation.

"Bring me ale, wench," he ordered harshly. When one of the other servants moved to do so, he snapped, "Nay, the Viking wench will do it."

She was looking at him now, by God. But Eldred felt only a moment's satisfaction to have gained her full attention at last, for her eyes were sparkling with humor!

"If you truly want ale, milord, you had best let Edrea fetch it. If she does not, you will have to get it yourself."

"You refuse to serve me?"

Kristen was hard pressed to keep from smiling. "Nay, milord," she said quietly. "I follow Lord Royce's orders —when it pleases me. And it pleases me that he has forbidden me to serve his guests."

She had pushed him too far. It took him only a second to reach her. He yanked her to her feet with one hand, while the other drew back to strike her. She did not give him the chance, shoving him away.

Eldred came at her again, but was stopped this time by a harsh voice behind him. "Do not touch her, milord."

He swung around, staring furiously at Royce's serf Seldon. Another of Royce's retainers was just behind him. Both had their hands resting on their sword hilts.

"Nay, I will not be stopped this time!" Eldred growled. "The wench will be punished."

"Not by you. Lord Royce's orders are that no one touches the woman."

Unexpectedly, Kristen became angry at that. "I need no help with this cur. I would have carved him with his own weapon."

Before they knew what she was about, she snatched Eldred's dagger from his waist. It was pure contempt that made her stab it into the table instead of keeping it to ward him off. For that humiliation, he ignored the warning he had been given and backhanded her. Kristen retaliated by joining her fists and swinging at his jaw. The blow slammed Eldred into the table; he half fell over it. Royce's men helped him up, but did not let go of him, though he was struggling and blustering.

Over the noise Eldred was making, Kristen could hear Darrelle shrieking and looked to see her rushing toward the entrance. Then she groaned inwardly, for Royce stood there—and not alone, but with Alfred beside him. And Royce looked fit to kill. He dismissed Darrelle with a sharp word.

Eldred heard Royce and stopped struggling. The two men saw him now and let Eldred go. Not one of them moved as Royce and the King crossed the hall to them.

Nothing of what she was feeling showed in Kristen's expression. Outwardly she was calm, while inwardly she trembled. This was all her fault. She had deliberately provoked the lordling. She had hoped to make him furious, and had. And now she would pay for that spite. Royce looked furious enough to do worse than merely chain her again.

Eldred saw a chance for revenge and took it, beseeching Alfred before Royce could speak. "Milord, I demand retribution against this slave. Twice she has raised arms against your nobles. Lord Randwulf lies abed with a broken rib from a chain she wielded against him. Now she dares to strike me and—"

Seldon broke into this recital to tell Royce, "He was warned, milord, that 'twas your will no one touch her."

"Is that true, Eldred?" Alfred asked quietly.

"She provoked me!" Eldred insisted.

"It matters not the why," Alfred replied. "She is not yours to chastise, and you were warned against it. This disturbance in the home of your host is transgression enough. You will leave us, and will not return to court until you are summoned."

Eldred paled at that announcement. He seemed about to protest, but must have thought better of it, for he nodded curtly and withdrew.

Royce watched him leave the hall, his fists clenched at his sides. "I would you had not done that, milord."

Alfred was wise enough not to smile. "I know. You would have preferred to draw your sword against him. But have patience, my friend. Wessex needs every man at this time, even those of Eldred's ilk. When we have a true peace, you may settle your quarrel with him."

Royce glanced sharply at his King, and then some of the tension left him and he nodded. He then looked to Kristen. He stepped toward her, putting his large hand over the red mark on her cheek.

"Are you all right?"

Kristen could have crumbled right there at his feet, her relief was so great. That look of black rage had not been for her. Unfortunately, once relief took hold, Kristen's anger shot to the fore. No longer fearing reprisal, she remembered what had made her lose her temper earlier.

She pointed a stiff finger at Royce's two men. "I do not need your watchdogs, milord."

His hand dropped away from her cheek. "So we saw."

They saw? Unease tempered her anger. Very well, they had seen, but they had not heard what happened. She glanced at the two retainers to see if they would say anything more. They were looking at her too. Seldon was grinning at her. They did not speak up now, but they might later. And what they could tell Royce was that she had goaded Eldred with her tongue, that with her insults she had courted the slap he gave her.

More of her anger was tempered. Only resentment remained, and this she voiced quietly. "I know why you set them on me, milord. 'Twas not for my protection, for you know I am my own protector. They replace my fetters, to see I do not escape. Is this how you trust me?"

Royce frowned now. With Alfred privy to the conversation, he would not placate her. He could not. Yet he knew Kristen well enough by now to know that to have her angry with him made all dealings with her most difficult, and he was the only one to suffer for that.

"Until we strike our bargain, vixen, do not question what I do."

His tone was harsh, the dark emerald of his eyes telling. Too late Kristen remembered Alfred's presence. She stole a glance at him, to find that he was amused by this argument between slave and lord. God's teeth! How could she be such a fool as to challenge Royce in front of his King? And she had indeed forgotten about that bargain Royce had mentioned.

She was not too proud to admit her mistakes. She offered Royce a hesitant smile. She offered him more to make amends.

"Forgive me, milord. My tongue ofttimes runs away with me. And I am sorry for the disturbance. Lord Eldred meant to anger me—and I meant to anger him. We both succeeded, but I regret you had to witness such folly."

Royce was stunned more by her apology than by her confession. But it was the confession that made the King of Wessex throw back his leonine head and laugh.

"God's mercy, Royce. Such honesty is frightening. And I thought to envy you your prize. Nay, sir, she is too blunt for a court rife with subtleties and false words of flattery."

Royce snorted. "She was not offered, milord."

Kristen gasped at that bold statement, but Alfred did not take offense. In fact he laughed again.

"I see her bluntness is contagious. I will do well to keep my other nobles away from her, or I will never again hear what an excellent hunter I am."

Now Royce chuckled. "You will not lack such praise today, milord, not when you have yourself supplied our evening fare."

They walked away then, but not before Royce gave Kristen a curious look, then a half smile. She had appeased him as she had intended. Later, he would have to appease her.

Chapter Twenty-eight

Kristen was sent upstairs by Eda. That she was sent alone, unescorted by Eda or her two guards, did much to improve Kristen's disposition. She did not even think to go anywhere but to Royce's chamber.

He was still below. The hour was late. Most of his guests had retired. But the King was still drinking and telling tales to match any minstrel's. It would be unseemly for Royce to retire a second night before his King.

Kristen knew that and had to be patient. Last eve she had been too tired to even remember the bargain they were to speak of. Not so this night. Her load had been minimal today, many of her usual tasks taken over by others. She was allowed to rest often by the window. Eda even took her out of the hot hall for several hours to tend the guests' chambers upstairs.

Kristen remembered last eve and knew her lighter load was by Royce's order. She knew now what he meant by being selfish, but she took no exception to that. She was herself anticipating the pleasure a night spent in his arms would bring. There was no thought now of withholding anything from him. He gave her her freedom. He also gave her many instances that showed he did care for her.

He was coming round, her Saxon. Eventually he would admit he was her heartmate. When he did that, he would marry her. He would also free her friends, and she would get a message to her parents through them. All would work out in the end. It was just a difficult road to that end.

Kristen smiled, seeing that there were two large containers of water on the table tonight, as well as extra cloths for drying and soaking up the water. She made quick use of hers, then slipped naked under the thin sheet on the bed to await her lord. Aye, she could think of him as her lord now, for he would be that in truth once she married him.

Royce came not fifteen minutes later. It would have amused Kristen to know how distracted he had been below after she left, and how Alfred had taken pity on him and retired so that his host could too. As it was, she was warmed by his look of pleased surprise on finding her already abed.

She lay curled on her side, with elbow bent and her head resting in the palm of her hand so she could better watch him as he came forward. God's teeth, but she liked what she saw. His will might be against her at times, but there was not a single thing about his body she could find wanting.

Since the King's party had come, Royce had dressed more impressively than was his custom. He wore a mantle clasped on his right shoulder as the other lords did, his a dark brown with saffron lining of rare silk. The same saffron silk edged his sand-colored tunic at hem and neck, with long sleeves fitted at his wrists. The earthy colors suited him to perfection, making the deep green of his eyes all the more startling. He also wore a wide belt studded round with fat amber stones. Even the dagger in his belt was jewel hilted.

He had not spoken to her since the incident with Eldred. Now he surprised her by saying, "You gave me an apology today that I am not sure I want."

"You have it anyway, milord, to do with as you like," she offered.

"Then I give it back." He sat down beside her on the bed, one knee bent so he could face her. His hand moved toward her hip, hesitated, then drew back. "I have known Eldred long. I know how his mind works to make trouble."

Kristen said quietly, "I did not lie, milord. I did in fact provoke him apurpose."

"But he sought you out, not you him."

She grinned now. "I cannot argue with that."

He moved his hand again toward her, and this time rested it for a moment on her hip. "I did not thank you for your discretion before Alfred."

"Aye, you did," she replied softly.

He had feared she had not understood the smile he gave her when he left with Alfred, but she did. She knew him better than he thought, and that pleased him.

He smiled at her before he stood up to leave the bed. They would get no talking done if he stayed so close to her, and he did want his bargain agreed to. It was not much he would ask of her. As much as she loved her freedom, he did not think she could refuse.

He began to remove his mantle, but his fingers stilled on the gold clasp as Kristen sat up in the center of the bed. The sheet fell about her waist and she did not move to lift it up. She was looking at him expectantly, so at ease with her natural state that she was unaware of how he perceived her. He was in fact mesmerized, his eyes drawn to the soft mounds of her breasts and unable to look away.

"Your bargain, milord?"

"What?"

It was perhaps the hardest thing he had ever done, dragging his eyes up to meet hers. And then to have her expectant gaze jolt him back to his senses. He swung around, feeling heat spread up his neck. This power she had to befuddle his mind and control his body. If she ever knew . . . God help him.

He swallowed with difficulty, keeping his back to her now as he went on to finish disrobing. By the time he was finished, they had best be done with their talk, or it would have to wait again.

He cleared his throat. It sounded like a low growl. "The difficulty you had yestermorn made it obvious to me that you could not effectively defend yourself fettered as you were. I regret that you found it necessary to defend yourself at all."

He glanced over his shoulder to see he had her rapt attention. And she still had not covered herself. He moved to the table to splash cold water over his face and chest. He had to clear his throat again to continue.

"I do not like it that you were helpless, Kristen. I can set men to watch you as I have since, but 'tis not the same as your being able to do for yourself when I am not here to look after you."

"You do not have to explain why you removed the chains, milord."

Without turning to see it, Royce knew she was smiling at him. He sat down at the table to remove his shoes and leather garters.

"Very well. What I need from you is your word that you will leave off your attacks against my cousin until Alfred and his party go."

"You ask for much," she replied softly.

"Think what 'twould mean were you to bring deliberate harm to Alden while Alfred is here. He is a fair man, but you saw for yourself today how he protects his nobles at this time. By rights, I should have been able to challenge Eldred. Alfred knew how dearly I wanted to. Yet he sent the cur home and away from my wrath. Every man he has now, he wants to have when the Danes come again. He deals harshly with any who deplete his army."

"Your point is taken, milord. But why do you ask for my word only until your King leaves?"

He answered easily. "When all his nobles are gone, you will be safe again."

"And after that?"

"The danger will be gone. We go back as before. So will you give your word?"

Kristen continued to sit there for a long stunned moment, staring at his broad back. Then she slipped off the bed, taking the sheet with her. She came up behind him so quietly that he tensed for a second when she wrapped one arm about his neck, for he had not heard her approach.

"Aye, I give you my word I will not touch your precious Alden," she purred into his ear. "But as for you . . ."

She yanked hard with her arm, toppling man and chair over backward. She heard his hiss of pain, then the violent curse he shouted, but she was already running for the unlocked door. Once in the corridor, however, she was faced with the frustrating knowledge that she could not go below as she was. She dashed for the nearest door instead, intending to hide behind it no matter who occupied the chamber.

A fine plan under such short notice, but she had not counted on this particular occupant. A candle still burned by the bed, allowing her to immediately recognize the King of Wessex as he sat up, sword in hand. They were both stunned, but he only for a second. He smiled, taking in her dishabille: the tawny hair cascading over her shoulders, the sheet simply hanging in front of her, for she had had no time to wrap it around.

Unfortunately, Kristen stood there too long in her own surprise. She had closed the door to Royce's chamber, but he threw it open now. She could not close herself into this room. She could not hope to hold the door closed against Royce, nor would his King let her. And she had nowhere else to run now that he couldn't quickly catch her.

She thought of all this before she turned to face Royce, unmindful that she was giving Alfred a trim view of her naked backside. But Kristen did not give the King another thought, not once she saw the look of fury on Royce's face as he stalked toward her.

He said not a word to her, but caught the hand she put out to ward him off. She let go of her sheet to hit him with the other, but he caught that too, bringing both hands up behind her back, which pressed her hard against his chest.

"Your pardon, milord," Royce said to his King.

Alfred chuckled. "Nay, 'twas most entertaining."

Tight-lipped, Royce nodded and closed the door. He then dragged Kristen back to his own chamber. He did not trust himself to speak yet. He felt like throttling her and was very close to giving it serious consideration.

He kicked his own door closed and dragged her with him to the bed. He sat down on it, yanking her across his lap as he did. He held her in such a way that she could not move either hand, and her legs were likewise of little help. For long moments he just held her, trying to bring his fury under control while she jerked and twisted to get loose.

Finally, Kristen's strength was expended and she became still. But her eyes were smoldering with blue-green fire. Royce did not see it. He had closed his own against the sight of her squirming naked on his lap.

"I hate you!"

The words jolted him, they were hissed with such rancor. A tight feeling twisted at his chest, defusing most of his own anger. As unpredictable as Kristen was, he had never thought to hear her say that.

His eyes locked with hers, probing. "Why?" he asked her quietly.

There was more heat to her own voice. "You tricked me! You knew what I thought, and you let me think it!"

"I cannot know your mind, Kristen."

"Liar!" she fumed. "Why else would I come to your

chamber without protest? You take off my chains and you say we will make a bargain. You said naught of it being only a temporary bargain."

He had indeed been surprised by her acquiescence, but had been too pleased to wonder long about it.

"You say me wrong, wench." Royce sighed. "How could I know what you assumed, when a permanent removal of those chains was never my intention? If the notion did not cross my mind, how could I know it did yours?"

"So, I am the fool—again. I see in you what is not there, what will never be there."

He was stung by her bitterness. "What do you see? God's mercy, Kristen, what do you want from me?"

"There is naught that I want—anymore—except to be left alone."

He shook his head, slowly, his eyes almost regretful. "I would if I could."

"If you could?" she sneered. "Have you no stronger will than that, Saxon?"

"Not in dealing with you."

It was something, for him to admit that. But it did not placate the deep resentment she was feeling at the moment.

He spoke again, softly. "You do not hate me, Kristen. You are angry with me, but you do not hate me. Admit it."

It was true. She still didn't hate him. She wished she did, but she didn't. Still, she kept her lips sealed.

"Then if you will not say so, show me," he said in a whisper as he bent to kiss her.

Kristen wished it otherwise, but she did show him.

Chapter Twenty-nine

New guests arrived at Wyndhurst. Lord Averill came to see the King. He brought with him his only son, Wilburt, and his three daughters.

Kristen would have paid scant attention to these newcomers, except that one of them was the Lady Corliss of Raedwood, and Edrea, working beside her, was quick to point it out. Kristen might have guessed for herself from Darrelle's elaborate efforts to make the lady welcome.

So this was Royce's betrothed. Kristen was not surprised that Corliss was incredibly beautiful, but actually seeing that she was made her miserable. Corliss was small, delicate, and graceful, everything that Kristen was not. And she had thought to win Royce away from this tiny woman? God's bones, she was more the fool than she knew!

Kristen could be thankful for only one thing: that Royce was not present to greet his betrothed. It would have been more than she could bear to see him bestow on this woman all the tender care and gallantry she longed for herself, without having time to prepare for it first. As it was, she had to watch the deferential way Corliss was treated by Darrelle, by the servants, and by Alden, who came in later.

It was disgusting, really, but so typical. Even if the lady was not liked, she would be handled with care, for she would soon be Lady of Wyndhurst, supplanting Darrelle, who now enjoyed that position as Royce's only female relative.

There was one among the household, however, who did not try to curry the lady's favor. Meghan. Of course the child could not be expected to understand that the woman would one day have complete charge of her, that it would behoove her to be nice to Corliss now. But Kristen silently applauded when she saw Meghan shake her head at Corliss when the lady bade her come near. And then the child actually made a face at the lady before leaving the women's area.

Kristen nearly laughed aloud, but suppressed the urge, not wanting the servants to wonder what she found amusing. She knew Darrelle would have called Meghan back and chastised her if she had seen what she did. Corliss now wore a tight-lipped look of displeasure, but she did not call Meghan back, either. Kristen would have been unable to stop the laughter, though, if she had noticed that Alden saw the interaction too and turned about to hide his own humor.

Kristen was surprised a few moments later to feel a tug on her skirt. She glanced around to see that Meghan had worked her way around the hall to come up behind her. The child wouldn't look up at her, though.

"Are—are you still angry with me?"

Kristen frowned, wondering what prompted such a question. "Why would I be angry with you, little one?"

"I told my brother what you said to me before, but Alden said 'twas secrets I revealed." Meghan peeked up at her. "I did not know, truly."

"And you thought I would be angry?"

"You were," Meghan said. "I saw you the next day and you were very angry."

Kristen smiled, remembering. "But not at you, sweetling. What you told your brother about me made no difference." That was a lie, for it was what led him to first make love to her, but Kristen could not in truth regret that happening.

Meghan gave a look of self-disgust. "Then I hid from you for naught."

Kristen chuckled, bringing Eda's attention to them. "What do you here, child?" the old woman demanded.

"Talking," Meghan retorted defiantly.

Eda gave Kristen a stern look. "You have work to do, wench."

"And I am doing it."

"Can I help?" Meghan asked.

Hearing that, Eda shook her head and went back to her own tasks. Kristen did not know what to say to Meghan, who was waiting for her reply, and looking hopeful. She glanced at the group of women at the far end of the hall, then back at Meghan. She sighed.

"Should you be here, Meghan?"

Meghan looked toward the ladies, too, then said stubbornly, "I would rather be here than over there."

Kristen repressed another smile. "Why do you dislike the Lady Corliss?"

Meghan looked back in surprise. "How did you know?"

"I saw what you did."

"Oh." The little girl blushed now, lowering her head, and then she said defensively, to explain herself, "She did not really want me to come to her. She does and says things she does not mean. She is full of sweet words now, but she was not before the betrothal."

"I see."

"Do you?" Meghan ventured hopefully. "You do not think I am wrong to not like her?"

"Your feelings are yours alone and cannot be commanded by another. But since your brother likes her, mayhap you should try to."

"I did," Meghan admitted with a touch of rancor. "Until Royce took me with him to Raedwood and she pinched me, so I would go away and leave her alone with him."

"What did he do?"

"He did not see."

Kristen frowned. "You should have told him."

"Nay, he would have been displeased."

And Meghan would never do anything to displease him. Kristen sighed to herself. The poor child really should be made to see that her brother's anger was not such a terrible thing—or, at least, that it wouldn't be to her. Kristen had herself seen the way he treated Meghan with such tender care. She had watched him one evening carry the child upstairs when she had fallen asleep in the hall. How that had reminded her of her own father, and how Garrick used to do the same for her. Royce loved this little girl dearly, yet Meghan was still frightened of him.

Kristen shook her head at the thought. Meghan despaired, watching her. "You want me to go?"

"What? Oh, nay, sweetling, stay if you like." Kristen realized that at the moment she was probably the lesser of two evils in the girl's mind. "But are you sure you will not be scolded if you remain here?"

Meghan quickly shook her head. "There are so many guests, no one will notice where I am."

"Then sit you down on that stool, and I will show you how to make my father's favorite nut bread."

"He likes nuts in his bread?"

"Indeed." Kristen winked as she reached inside her outer gown, where she had made a pouch with the help of her girdle, and pulled out a handful of nuts. "And I swiped these from Eda before she could stuff them into her hens. We will make two special loaves, just for us. Would you like that?"

"Oh, aye, Kristen!" Meghan's face lit up with childish delight. "'Twill be our secret."

* * *

Meghan was incorrect in her prediction that no one would notice where she was. Royce noticed as soon as he entered the hall, for as always his eyes sought out Kristen first. And he could not help but see Meghan sitting next to her, for their heads were bent together, and they were laughing over something, oblivious to everything else around them.

He paused for a moment, feeling a warm rush of pleasure, watching them—his sister and his woman. When everyone else was wary of Kristen, he would have thought Meghan, who feared all strangers, would be even more so. Apparently not. It was obvious that they liked each other, and he was pleased by that.

He would have moved toward them, if Darrelle had not called him. Then he saw Corliss, and he stiffened. How could he have forgotten that she would be here? Lord Averill had come out to the practice field where Alfred had challenged his nobles to some impromptu contests of skill. And whenever Averill came to Wyndhurst, his daughters came too. It had been too much to hope that this time would be different. It was not.

He gritted his teeth and walked forward to greet his betrothed.

Kristen watched Royce and Corliss all evening, where they sat together at the long table. She could not seem to help herself, and simply ignored the painful lump constricting her chest. In spite of telling herself it did not matter, that Royce was not hers anyway, there was still that part of her that felt betrayed, that felt he *was* hers. Only she could not fight for him, could not rail at him, could do nothing to separate him from this other woman.

It hurt, and it made her realize her position here more fully than she had hitherto. She had been blithely getting through this ordeal with the assumption that in the end she would get what she wanted. And so each setback had made her lose patience—and her temper, too—but not complete hope.

She was so naive! Just because her father had fallen in love with and married his slave, did not mean the same thing could happen here in Wessex. At home, her family was a law unto themselves because of their isolation from the rest of the land. Her uncle Hugh was a Jarl, as powerful in authority in Norway as King Alfred was here. But even so, her mother had had to be freed first before Garrick could wed her. Norway had its laws concerning slaves that love could not put aside. And here, there were so many lords, so many laws! And had not Royce called her mad when she mentioned marriage to him?

Seeing him with his betrothed made Kristen realize she had been mad to think she could ever have him for herself. Not once did she see things from Royce's point of view. Once he had called her lower than the lowest serf—said in anger, true—but how close was that to how he really felt about her? She was a slave. He had many. She warmed his bed now, but soon he would have a wife to do so. The concern he showed for Kristen was no more than he would give any of his possessions.

"Woolgathering, are you?"

It took a moment for Kristen's eyes to focus on Eda. "Aye, I suppose I was."

Eda gave her a knowing look, hearing the misery in her tone. "You always did expect too much, wench."

"I know."

Eda shook her head. "You should be thankful for what you have. You are alive, when he could have killed you and those you call friends. He sees to your needs. God's mercy, he even protects you from other men! Half the wenches here will be tumbled by these lordlings tonight, but not you."

"You do not have to tell me how fortunate I am."

"Oh, ho." Eda chuckled, knowing sarcasm when she heard it. "If you do not like the way 'tis, you can always look now for another man. I have eyes and have seen the way these lordlings look at you. Mayhap if you ask milord nicely, he will sell you when he weds."

"Aye, mayhap I will."

"What! Nay, wench, I was but jesting. You do that, and we will all suffer for the storm you will start."

"You make no sense, Eda."

"I tell you true, he will never sell you. You are not stupid," Eda told her impatiently. "You know that what you do has a direct effect on him."

"Not so," Kristen retorted.

"Oh? And that week when naught pleased him, that week you sent him away from your room—what would you call that, wench? Everyone here knew you were the cause of his black mood, though only I knew why." Eda chuckled again. "But as soon as he had you in his bed, his humor returned."

Kristen looked down and away, feeling heat stain her cheeks. "So he wants me now. 'Twill not last."

"That man will want you always, wench. I see it in the way he deals with you. I could tell you other things that would convince you, but I do not want to fill your head with more vain ideas. Nay, he will never sell you, or let you have another. But he will marry his lady."

Kristen stiffened. "Then why do you tell me all this, old woman?"

"Because he will keep you too. Because I do not like to see you so miserable. Because you must begin to accept what you have and cease to reach higher. If you are not happy, then he will be unhappy too, and that affects us all."

"Enough, Eda. I do not believe I wield such power over him. If I did—"

"If you did, what? Aye, I know. You will ignore all I have said. You still reach too high, wench."

"Nay, I understand you well. What you do not understand is that I can never accept things the way they are. My mother was made a slave once, captured same as I. She was the daughter of a great lord in her own land and full of pride. She would never admit that she was a slave to the man who owned her, nor to herself. I am not quite so stubborn. I know my position as 'tis now. Yet I am my mother's daughter. I cannot remain a slave, Eda."

"You have no choice."

Kristen looked away, out over the hall, which was dark now except for a few remaining torches. While she had sat there with her dejected thoughts, nearly everyone had retired. Pallets were spread everywhere, for not only Royce's retainers and servants slept here, but those of the guests as well. She had not seen Royce leave, or his lady.

"Does she stay the night?" Kristen asked Eda.

The old woman grunted, knowing exactly whom she meant. "Aye, they would not ride home in the dark. And I have talked enough to have my words fall on deaf ears. Come, you sleep with me tonight."

A new rush of pain filled Kristen, but she hid behind a stoical expression. "She sleeps with him, then?"

"For shame, such thoughts!" Eda scolded. "You know we have only the six chambers above. The ladies have been put with Lady Darrelle and Meghan. Lord Alden gave up his own room for the King and is crowded in with the lordlings who have the other two chambers."

"Then why—"

"Shush," Eda hissed. "Milord did not like it, but with Lord Averill and his son come today, he could no longer keep his own chamber to himself. There was just no more room above."

Kristen pictured Royce sharing his bed with his future in-laws, and she almost smiled. But not quite.

Chapter Thirty

One torch sputtered out, leaving only the one by the stairs still burning. The noises in the hall were sporadic: loud and soft snoring, a cough, a few grunts and groans. Eda was one of those snoring softly.

She had led Kristen to the spot that was hers by the cold hearth, a coveted place, as it was cool in summer but warm in winter. There was no pallet for Kristen, all the extra ones already in use by the guests. A thin blanket and the hard floor made her bed, the discomfort of it helping to keep her awake. But she would not have fallen asleep tonight anyway.

Kristen sat up slowly and looked around her. Only a few women slept nearby, but not close enough that she might disturb them. She had waited only until Eda fell asleep. She would have liked to wait a little longer on the chance that someone else could still be awake, but she could not afford to waste that much time.

She was leaving. The decision had been easy, for this was the only chance she was likely to have. She had asked Royce last eve how long his King would stay. It was the only thing she said to him after he made love to her, and he had been unable to give her an answer. It could be on the morrow, or a week from now, but when Alfred did leave, Kristen would be fettered again. She was also likely to be ensconced back in Royce's chamber, and it would be harder and much more risky to try to leave his side, if he even left the door unlocked, than it would be to slip out of this crowded hall.

Here, the windows were left open, and there was only a slight jump to reach the ground outside. And she had plenty of time to get far away before the morn when she would be missed.

The decision had indeed been easy. Kristen just hadn't counted on the heavy feeling of gloom that accompanied it. Even though she knew she had no hopes here, she still felt heartsick in thinking she would never see Royce again.

She glanced one last time at Eda, who lay on her back in weary slumber. She would miss this old woman, too, with her crankiness and her gruff concern. And little Meghan, whose curiosity and silent appeal for friendship had managed to make Kristen forget her troubles for a while today.

However, these thoughts did not stop Kristen from making her way toward the window next to the cooking area. No call rang out as she eased her legs over to sit on the ledge. But it was a mark of her dejection that she hesitated for several long moments. And at last it was pride that gave her the final push.

A nearly full moon bathed the yard on this side of the hall. Kristen landed on her feet and jumped back immediately to the shadows by the wall. Cautiously, she worked her way behind the hall and over to the side where the stable was, and the storehouse, and the hut that housed her cousin and the others.

She had not seen their shelter herself since it had been finished, but knew it was only a narrow, windowless room. How miserable it must be to sleep there after the stout door was locked at night. But no more miserable than sleeping out in the rain as they had done before that.

She wished it were raining tonight, to hinder visibility and help conceal the sound of her movements. But there were only a few clouds above, and these were not even near the overly bright moon. This would not deter her, though. Everyone was indoors, sleeping. There was no one to see her.

From the back of the stable, she could hear the soft nicker of one of the horses, reminding her that horses would be needed. But none of these. The large wooden gate was closed and locked at night, and no doubt a guard set to watch. Even if there was no guard, taking any of the stabled horses would make too much noise. This was no problem, though, for she knew that most of Royce's horses had been taken to pasture. She would just have to find the pasture.

The problem she did face was coming around the prisoners hut and seeing a guard sitting in front of the only door. She ducked back behind the side of the building, her heart racing. Had he heard her footsteps? Had he seen her? But she heard no movement from him, and after a short time more she found the courage to peek around the corner.

The man was still sitting there, his back against the door, his head leaning back, too, and bent to the side. She let out the breath she had been holding, realizing he was asleep. This was something she had not counted on, for the door was locked, a guard not needed. But this was minor in comparison to the problem she had known she would face: getting that locked door open. Then again, this would be a blessing if the guard held the key to the heavy lock.

Kristen moved back behind the building to look for a stone large enough to render the fellow unconscious. She could have swiped his dagger while he slept and killed him instead, but couldn't bring herself to do that. Unfortunately, there were no stones about the yard that were big enough, and she finally had to work her way over to where the rock wall was being built. There, it took a while to find a stone that wasn't too big. She did find one eventually, and she did make her way back to the guard without incident.

Her pulse accelerated as she approached him. If he made a sound when she struck, she would be done for. If she struck too hard . . . God help her, she didn't want to really hurt him, just put him into a deeper sleep.

The stone hit near his temple and the man sagged to the side. He breathed. That was enough to satisfy Kristen's conscience for now, and she made fast work of searching his body for the key. Her luck did not extend that far. She would have to waste more time trying to pry the lock loose. But at least this unexpected guard provided the dagger to work with.

She went quickly to the task, calling in an urgent voice that did not carry far, "Ohthere. Thor —"

A large hand clamped over her mouth, silencing her, while another gripped the wrist that held the dagger. "Drop it. Do it now."

She did, feeling a strange mixture of dread and joy as she recognized that voice. He let go of her wrist as soon as the dagger clattered to the ground, his hand then going round her waist. It was not a tight hold he had on her, but she knew it could be if she struggled.

And then she felt nothing but regret, hearing Thorolf on the other side of the still-locked door. He had heard her soft call. He thought she was there to help them escape.

"Kristen? Kristen, answer. Tell me I was not dreaming."

"What does he say?" Royce whispered by her ear.

"He knows 'tis me."

"Then tell him what has happened."

She swallowed hard. What *had* happened? How? She had got this far. No cry of alarm was raised. Yet she was stopped, and by the one man here whom she would not turn around and fight in earnest. If it were anyone else . . .

"Thorolf, I am sorry. I nearly succeeded, but the Saxon lord has found me out. He is here."

There was a long silence from behind the door, and then: "You should not have come for us, Kristen. You should have flown while you were able."

"That matters not now."

"What will he do to you?"

How could she answer that? She said to Royce, "He wants to know what you will do to me."

"What would have happened if you had succeeded in opening that door?"

His voice was so frightfully calm. God's teeth! Why wasn't he shouting at her? He had to be furious. She hadn't looked at him yet to see for herself, but he must be. But if he could hide his fury, then she could hide her fear.

With equal calm, she said, "If I had opened the door, we would have run for yonder fence and been gone from here."

"After the slaughter?"

"You jest, milord. They are sixteen men. You have a like number of warlords in your hall at the moment, and your retainers, and their retainers as well. You have a well-trained army. Vikings are bold, milord, but not stupid."

"Then tell him naught will be done to you, because all you did was render punishment of a guard who was deserving of it for sleeping at his duty."

She could not believe he said that. More to the point, she could not believe he meant it. He would do something. He had to. She was a slave who had tried to escape and had tried to help others escape as well. But she did not want Thorolf to know that, any more than Royce did.

She explained quickly, but Thorolf was as doubtful as she. "He does not believe you, milord."

"Then tell him you will bring their food to them on the morrow, and at that time you can report to him exactly what I have done to you."

A shiver passed down her spine. She repeated his words to Thorolf, and that seemed to satisfy him, which was well, for Royce was done with talking. He led her away, his arm still firm about her waist. Her fear was increasing. How ominous that had sounded: *exactly what I have done to you*. She was about to reconsider her option of fighting him when he stopped.

They were before the stable. He brought her around until she stood in front of him, facing him. Both arms were about her waist now, but he did not press her close. His head tilted back, his gaze taking in the clear, bright sky, the glory of the near-full moon. She heard him sigh.

"I offered the other night to take you to the lake where you can bathe," he said quietly. "Would you like to go there now?"

"So you can drown me?"

He glanced back down at her, the barest trace of a smile forming on his lips. "You did not believe what I said back there?"

"I tried to escape. You stopped me, but I still tried. What does your law demand of that?"

"You are an enslaved prisoner, not a Briton. The laws have more leeway concerning prisoners. But the law is not involved here, for no one knows what you did but I."

"And the guard."

"The man will think he dreamed that bump on his head. Mayhap he will not sleep again on duty."

Her eyes widened. "You are sincere. You really will do naught to me?"

"The wolf will chew off his paw to be released from the trap. He escapes, but at great cost. Had you escaped with the others, make no mistake, I would have found you. Your friends would have fought and there would have been bloodshed. That would be punishment enough for you. But you did not succeed. And as I can understand the wolf, I can understand also the will that drives you. You want your freedom. I cannot punish you for that. But I cannot let you go, either."

"You could," she said stonily. "The others build your wall. What they do is necessary to Wyndhurst. But what I do in the hall is of little import. You have no reason to keep me here."

"You are necessary to *me*, Kristen!"

The force of those words silenced her. He meant it, and it thrilled her to know it. But she was a fool no more. She would not take those words to heart. He was simply obsessed with her, for he had never known anyone like her. But in time the obsession would wear thin and he would need her no more—probably when he had his lady to wife. Mayhap then she could convince him to let her go.

In the meantime, God help her, she would have to go on suffering and wanting and praying she could retain a measure of her pride. It would not be easy.

Royce pulled her closer and felt her stiffen. "You still doubt me?"

"Nay, but for you to take me to the lake, after what I did . . . 'tis like you reward me for defying you. You confuse me, Saxon."

He laughed, and did draw her closer. "I am glad to hear it. I have been alone in confusion so long, 'tis a pleasure to have company now. Nay, do not be piqued with me," he said as she tried to pull back. "I will appease your confusion, which is more than you do for me."

"Well?" she prompted when she saw his humor leave, his expression turning serious again.

"I simply choose to forget what you did. I came down to the hall to take you to the lake. When I found you gone—" He would not tell her what he had felt. He never wanted to feel that way again.

He gathered her tight against him, pressing his cheek against hers before he continued. "No harm was done, Kristen. I can overlook the intention and hope that you now see 'tis useless for you to try to leave here. I will always second-guess you."

She gasped. "You knew! That is why there was a guard."

"And a wrong choice of guards," he grunted. "But I did not know. I just do not take chances where you are concerned."

Intuition told her he wouldn't, either, that he would be this cautious of her as long as he still wanted her. She really did have no hope of escaping this place, not until he found his pleasure elsewhere.

"When do you marry, milord?"

She knew the question surprised him. She felt him tense. He would not be able to reason what this had to do with what they were discussing.

"What are you thinking, wench?"

"Does it not concern me?"

"Nay, it does not."

"But I am curious, milord."

"I think you are more cunning than curious. Do you try to anger me?"

Now Kristen was surprised. "Why would you think so? 'Twas a very simple question, milord, that does in fact concern me. When your lady wife lives here, there will be changes. She will share your chamber, not I."

If she thought to appease him, she failed. "And you look forward to that!" he stormed. "Well, I must disappoint you, for 'twill not be soon. The time for the wedding has yet to be discussed."

Without thinking, Kristen replied from the heart, "In truth, that does not disappoint me."

Those few words did manage to appease Royce, completely. Kristen wished she could take them back when she heard him chuckle. She had not meant to let him know she still desired him. Now she was annoyed, by her loose tongue, and how it had returned him to good humor.

And she blundered further by letting him hear her annoyance when she snapped, "Your amusement is misplaced. Your betrothed can have—"

"Shush. Say no more of her," he warned. Then, softly: "I still do not wish to return to my chamber, where Averill makes noises in his sleep like a lion. Do you come with me to the lake?"

Oh, unfair, to use that against her now! But she was not so angry that she would spite herself.

She made her tone conciliatory. "Aye, I would like to come with you."

His own voice deepened to a husky pitch. "And will you let me make love to you there?"

Kristen gasped. "You said naught of conditions!"

Royce chuckled. "Then I will just have to take my chances."

Chapter Thirty-one

Royce and Kristen did make love that night. They also slept the night through on the grassy banks of the lake. At least, Kristen did.

In her enjoyment of the cool water, she was so relaxed and at peace for a while, she even forgot for a time that Royce watched her from the bank. He did not swim himself. He confessed to not knowing how. But Kristen frolicked to her heart's content. It was like being free again, like being at home, except the water was not quite as cold. And at home, she would not have a lover waiting for her on the shore.

When she did finally emerge from the water, Royce did not even give her time to dry off. He gathered her immediately into his arms and proceeded to kiss the water from her lips, her cheeks, her breasts. She had no will to deny him there in the moonlight. She could not even summon a token resistance. She wanted him, wanted too to give him back some of the pleasure he had given her in bringing her to the lake.

He could not know how much it had meant to her. But perhaps he knew now, for she had loved him thoroughly, releasing her passion until it surpassed even his own. He would not soon forget this interlude at the lake.

But he did not fall blissfully to sleep afterward as she did. She saw now, as she woke with the first stirrings of the birds in the trees that announced the dawn, that Royce was wide awake. She also saw how tired he looked.

He still held her close. She had slept wrapped against him for warmth, for neither of them had dressed and the night air was cool there by the lake. They were covered only by her thin gown.

Kristen sat up, stretching widely, then glanced behind her and shook her head at Royce, who was watching her. "You should have slept, milord."

"With my horse at your convenience?"

"Unfair. You will not blame me for your lack of sleep. You could have taken me back and set your men to watch me."

"Ah, but you object most strenuously to having guards watch you, as I recall."

"And what have you been all this night?" she retorted indignantly.

He sat up, grinning at her. "But I got to hold you, wench. 'Twas a duty I did not mind."

"You are impossible." She laughed, leaning forward to kiss him lightly on the lips. "But I am grateful. 'Twas much more comfortable here, on the soft grass, than on the hard floor in your hall."

"And I make a nice pillow?"

"That too."

His finger traced along her collarbone, then playfully detoured down the valley of her breasts. "I will have you back in my bed this eventide."

"And what has made you think I want to be there?" she said primly.

"You do."

She shook her head. "We have had a truce here, but when we return—"

"Shush." He leaned forward, his lips brushing softly against her neck. And then abruptly, making her squeal in surprise, Royce had her stretched out under him. "Now admit it. You like my bed."

He was incorrigible this morn. And she was in no mood to be serious either.

Wicked laughter danced in her eyes. "I like your bed fine, Saxon. 'Tis a most comfortable bed."

Her tone left little doubt that she was talking only about the bed. "I will not let you up"—he began nibbling at her lips—"until you admit"—his tongue teased her now—"that you want me."

"Then, milord . . ." Her arms curled around his neck, her fingers sliding up into the soft waves of his hair. "We will be here for a very long time."

It was late morning when they returned to the hall. They did not spend the whole morning at the lake, though Kristen did swim once more before finally dressing. But when Royce set her up on his horse, where she rode in front of him, it was not toward the hall that he headed.

He took her through forests, through grain fields, through meadows of wildflowers, and through pastures. He showed her his land, his people, the villages. She saw that those who worked at the manor were only a handful in actuality. There were so many more people who worked the land, who tended the herds of cattle and horses, who hunted in the forests. And she sensed Royce's pride in what he was showing her.

The morning became an enchanted time. The warm feeling of contentment with which Kristen had awoken continued, as did Royce's good humor. Most men became cranky when they were overtired. Royce was teasing and playful, almost ridiculously so. He took exception to nothing she did or said. He would drop the reins to make her grab for them, while he grabbed for her breasts. His hands would constantly stray to her legs, for she sat astride the horse, her chainse hiked up to her thighs. He would not leave her bare skin alone, no matter how many times she slapped away his hands. He would tickle her until she begged mercy, then nuzzle and kiss her neck. He laughed at her and with her. He simply would not leave her alone.

And Kristen enjoyed all of it. For a while she felt free. And she felt loved, even if his feelings did not run that deep. So it was natural that she should regret returning to the hall and reality. She would go to her work in the hall. He would no doubt go straight to bed, since Alden had taken the King and his party hunting in Royce's absence. They had even heard them in the forest, though Royce did not ride toward them. And the lack of horses in the stable said they had not returned.

He lifted her down from the horse, but his hands did not leave her waist immediately. His expression was subdued now. Perhaps he too was regretting the end of their idyll. She would like to think so.

"Your cheeks are blooming with color."

Kristen smiled slightly, offering, "The fresh air."

"Mayhap, but that has naught to do with the sparkle in your eyes. I would like to hear that you enjoyed yourself."

"Would you?" His horse had been taken away, there were at least three other men near, and he was still holding her. "Will you keep me here until I admit it?"

He grinned at the reminder, and then he laughed, lifting her up for a hard kiss before setting her down with a whack to her backside. "Vixen. I would not be so boorish as to keep you in the stable. But later . . ."

"Threats!" she cried playfully. "I suppose I will have to admit it, then. I did in fact enjoy myself."

"Then as long as you are in an admitting mood . . ."

"Nay, Saxon, I make only one confession a day."

He swallowed a laugh, trying to look disappointed. "You have no mercy, wench," he said as he led her out of the stable into the yard.

"I suppose your persistence should be commended."
She sighed.

He did laugh this time. "I retreat, for now." His hand
rested on her back as he walked her to the hall. And
then he added hesitantly, "It cannot be often, but when I
can, do you come with me to the lake again?"

Kristen looked sideways at him. This she had not expected at all. He was giving her something to look forward to, whether he knew it or not. And that was
something she desperately needed at this time.

"I would like that, milord. But can I have a horse to
myself next time?"

"Nay."

Her brow rose. "I know how to ride."

"So Thorolf told me."

"Then you say nay because you do not trust me."

"Of course I do not trust you." He grinned at the face
she made to that. "But more than that, I liked having
you on my lap where I could—"

"Royce!"

"Do you blush, wench? God's breath, you do!"

"Cease, Saxon, or I will—"

He was not to hear what she would do. He followed
her gaze to see what had subdued her, and saw Corliss
standing in the doorway to the hall, one of her sisters
beside her. They were not there to greet him, surely, for
neither lady looked in the least bit welcoming.

"You must have disremembered she was here, milord," Kristen whispered aside to him.

He had certainly tried to, but he did not say that
aloud. One glance at Kristen told him she did not pity
him this confrontation. Her eyes brimmed with secret
humor. Merciless wench, she wanted to see him taken to
task for his neglect of his betrothed.

"Milady," Royce said stiffly in greeting.

"Milord," Corliss replied just as stiffly. She did not

move aside to let Kristen go on into the hall. In fact, she looked directly at Kristen as she inquired, "Who is this freakish giant?"

Royce's chin went hard. The muscles in his neck moved alarmingly. Kristen would have been amazed had she seen this, though she would have assumed his anger stemmed from the jealous bite of the lady's attitude. But Kristen wasn't looking at Royce just now. She was looking down at the lady, and she did have to look down, for the top of Corliss's head came no higher than her chin.

If Kristen were not so comfortable with her size, she might have been hurt by the lady's deliberate slur. She was amused instead, recognizing the jealousy, delighting in its implications.

And as was her nature, she did not mince words or appear subservient in any way. Brazenly she said, "If your question is asked of me, lady, I must tell you that where I come from, babies of puny size are more times than not left to die, because they cannot survive our harsh clime."

"Barbaric!" Corliss gasped.

"Aye, I can see why you would think so," Kristen replied, her eyes saying much more as they traveled down the lady's tiny length.

"Milord . . ." Corliss began to whine, bright-red spots staining her cheeks.

Kristen was quick to interrupt, lips twitching. "Forgive me, milady. I see your question was not asked of me after all. But then, Lord Royce can only tell you that I am his prisoner, enslaved by his will. About me he knows only what I have told him, which is very little. Is that not so, milord?"

She caught only the tail end of Royce's anger when she glanced at him. His expression was nearly bland, but she did not mistake that he was displeased, for his hand at her back pushed her past Corliss, and his order to be about her labors was decisively curt.

So, she surmised, she had overstepped herself in his opinion. But she did not care, and the look she tossed at him over her shoulder as she sauntered away told him so.

Royce had to glance away from Kristen quickly before he burst out laughing, but in doing so his eyes fell on Corliss. He sobered instantly and issued a harsh curse in irritation. It was enough to send Corliss's sister scurrying away, and Corliss backed away herself.

His hand shot out to stop her. "Nay, lady, you will explain yourself."

"Royce, you hurt me!"

He swore again as tears brimmed instantly in her eyes. Immediately he released his hold on her wrist. She was like a child in her frailty. He had not realized that until now. But after knowing Kristen, who gave as good as she got, who thought nothing of physically fighting him, and who never once cried that he had hurt her, Corliss only fueled his disgust of all women with her tears.

"Dry your eyes," he said brusquely. "I know my strength, and I know I hurt you not. So why do you cry?"

Her tears dried at will, though her expression was still suffering. "You are abusive!"

"Me! What do you call that petty insult you dealt the Viking wench?"

"What insult?" she countered defensively. "I stated the truth. Her height does make her a freak."

"She is not as tall as I am, Corliss, so what does that make me?"

"You? But you are a man," she pointed out needlessly. "'Tis natural you be as you are. But she is taller than most men. And that is unnatural."

"Not most men," he said tightly. "Most Saxons, true, but there are sixteen Vikings here that sailed with her, and every one is taller than she. Would you like to see them?"

"You jest!" she gasped.

"Aye, I jest." He sighed. "I am sorry, Corliss. I am churlish when I am tired, and I am overtired."

She ignored the hint. "But what were you doing with her, Royce?"

He gritted his teeth to hold back another curse. "You are not my wife yet, to concern yourself in my affairs."

"And when I am your wife?"

His conscience pricked him, making him snap, "You will learn not to question me."

Corliss did not take offense at this attitude, for it was no different from most men's attitude toward women. But she disliked his tone and brought tears to her eyes again to make her complaint known to him. Royce, who hated tears and never let them affect him except with anger, walked away in disgust at the guilt her fresh tears made him feel.

Chapter Thirty-two

*F*ood for the prisoners was late in being delivered that eventide. Eda, who cooked it, and Edrea, who usually carried it with Uland's help, both disbelieved Kristen when she told them she was to be allowed to take it to them today. But Eda was cautious enough to hold off the delivery of the food until confirmation from Royce could be obtained.

So they waited until Royce came down from his chamber, and he was late in doing so. He had spent the whole afternoon there, after leaving Corliss by the door. Kristen had watched from her corner as he spoke with his betrothed. He was angry. Corliss cried. He left angry. Corliss's tears dried as soon as Royce turned his back on her, and her expression denoted chagrin, not misery.

Kristen had shaken her head in disgust when the drama was over. She had too much pride to ever use such ploys herself, but knew some women found pleasure in the power of their tears. Darrelle was one. Corliss was obviously another, and Kristen could almost pity Royce, for he would never have an easy time with such a woman for wife.

Kristen did not spend the afternoon with gloomy thoughts as she had the day before. Her earlier contentment remained, and she tried not to wonder why. She succeeded, for she was kept busy making more nut bread.

Eda had tasted a chunk of the bread Kristen had made for herself and Meghan and liked it so well she had struck a bargain with Kristen. She would supply the nuts and Kristen could make half a dozen loaves for the prisoners, if she would make a like number for Royce's guests. Kristen could not refuse, and even had Meghan's company again to help her.

So the rest of her day was spent pleasantly. But she could not help fretting when Eda began to grumble as the hour grew late and Royce still did not come down. The prisoners' stew thickened. Edrea now had other duties to attend to, as the guests were already being fed, so she could no longer take the prisoners food. And Kristen knew what Thorolf would think if she did not make an appearance today.

Kristen finally said to Eda, "Go wake him and ask him. He will not want to sleep this long anyway."

"You keep saying he sleeps, wench. Why would he sleep the day away?"

Kristen looked away, shrugging. "Just do it, Eda. He will not be angry if you disturb him."

Eda did, and came back a few minutes later, shaking her head. "Aye, he was asleep, and shouting why no one had roused him sooner." Kristen grinned at this, and Eda gave her a sharp look, seeing it. "You spoke true, after all, but I cannot think why milord would let you . . . You can take the food, but you take two guards with you. And Uland will help you to carry it."

Eda called the men over to instruct them. Kristen could not object. She was so looking forward to talking to Thorolf and the others that she could not stop smiling all the way to the prisoners' quarters.

They were all inside the long hut. The door was open. The two guards in front, carelessly involved in a knife-tossing contest, barely gave her a glance as she approached with Uland and her own guards.

The reason for this laxity was made known to her as she heard the many rattlings of chains. It dampened her spirits somewhat to know that, unlike herself, they still were made to wear their chains constantly. But the moment she stood in the doorway, her spirits soared again.

Her eyes lit on her cousin first, and she dropped her basket of bread and fruit on the floor and flew into Ohthere's startled arms. So many surprised shouts of her name met her ears that she knew Thorolf had told no one what had happened last eve, probably on the suspicion that she would not appear. Ohthere quickly lost his hold on her as she was grabbed by one and then another and another of her longtime friends. Squealing and laughing, she received bone-crushing hugs and greetings and teasings.

Uland, standing in the doorway watching this cheerful welcoming, could hardly believe his eyes. Edrea had professed that at least one of the Vikings, the one who always came forward to take the food from her, could not possibly be as savage as the others, for he frequently smiled at her. Foolish talk from a girl fascinated by a handsome man, Uland had reasoned. But this show of warmth and affection for the giant wench...God's bones, it made them seem almost human, not the heathen monsters everyone thought them to be. In amazement, Uland set down the large cauldron of stew in the doorway and hurried back to the hall to regale his friends with what he had seen.

Inside the hut, Kristen at last came to Thorolf. Upon seeing him, her bubbling joy faded, for his expression was nearly solemn as he looked her over, and she remembered suddenly what Royce had admitted to telling him. A shyness came over her that was particularly uncomfortable inasmuch as she was so rarely shy about anything.

Her reticence hit Thorolf like a blow, and he flushed, knowing he had caused the smile to vanish from her lips. He had spent the day in an agony worrying about her and had been so relieved to see that she had actually come, and that there was nothing wrong with her, that he was slow in bringing his anxiety under control. He was still looking for bruises where there were none, when he should have been expressing his joy in seeing her, as the others had.

A hand came up, fingers gently lifting her chin. "Forgive me, Kristen. The Saxon whipped you once. I was sure —"

"He would again?" she interrupted with a half smile. "I thought so, too, but he did not."

"Might he still?" he had to ask.

She thought for a moment about last eve. Royce had taken her swimming, a joy to her. He had let her come here to see her friends, another joy. And he had made love to her under the stars . . .

It was with complete confidence that she shook her head to Thorolf's question. "Nay, it is already forgotten by him."

The Viking laughed then, throwing back his head and jerking her forward for one more bone-crushing hug. "Thor's teeth, that is good to hear!"

"What is, and what has been forgotten?" Ohthere wanted to know.

He and half the others were standing around Kristen. She thought briefly of giving some lie, for they could not know what she and Thorolf spoke of. But she couldn't lie to them. The explanation she gave of her attempted escape and why she was not punished for it was not easy, though, for it required skimming over so many parts and jumping ahead before questions were asked. But then she went on to tell them what she knew of Wyndhurst and Wessex, which was not much, but more than they knew till now. She told them where the horses could be found, where the Danish army was likely to be, which was, unfortunately, a far ways north. She also told them of the giant Celts she had heard of who were hostile to the Saxons and how they might help if the Vikings decided to escape to the west instead of north. It at least gave them an option in their planning.

Escape was never far from their minds. She heard grumble after grumble about how cautious the Saxons were. When she remarked how strong and able they all looked now, grinning as she ran her fingers over the increased biceps on several arms, Bjarni laughed and demonstrated his new strength by lifting her up over his head. She glared at him when he set her down, but he did not look at all contrite.

"You are at least ready for escape," she remarked.

"Aye, so much stone lifting has done us no harm," Odell replied. "When I return home, plowing my fields will be child's play."

"These walls cannot contain us, Kristen," Ohthere said seriously. "But it would do no good to break them down, without an axe to sever these chains first."

"I have not seen one in all these weeks," she said thoughtfully. "Every other kind of weapon is at hand in the hall, but not a single axe. It would not surprise me if they are locked away somewhere, Ohthere, for the Saxon is overly cautious in that way."

"Then we need the key for the door and these chains."

"Do you know who keeps it?" she asked.

"The wall builder, the one called Lyman."

She remembered him, but had not seen him since her separation from the men. "He does not come in the hall. He must live outside the manor."

She could see how that news was met. Their disappointment became her own. God's teeth, none of this was fair!

Ohthere chucked her under the chin. "Come now, Cousin, do not fret yourself about it. We will find a way somehow. They grow used to us. Someone will make a mistake sooner or later, and we will have our chance."

"They grow used to me, too, but they still do not trust me." She frowned. "Today is only the first time I have been let out of the hall."

"There is the wench Edrea that Bjarni is wooing. Do you think she could be persuaded to help if he succeeds in winning her affections?"

Kristen's eyes widened and then she laughed. "God's teeth, you think of everything. But now you mention it, she did seem disappointed that she would not bring your food this time." She looked pointedly at Bjarni. "How do you woo a wench when you cannot speak her tongue?"

He grinned roguishly. "Thorolf is teaching me the words I need to know."

"Ah, *those* words." She grinned too.

"Does the wench have freedom to come and go?" Ohthere asked now.

"Aye, as far as I know. But of Edrea I know very little, so I cannot say if she would help—even for Bjarni's sake. The servants all fear me still and barely speak to me, except for the old woman Eda, but she is very loyal to her lord. I will try to speak to Edrea, though, and see if she does have some feeling for Bjarni. I can at least tell her what a fine, loyal, and faithful man he is."

Kristen said this with another grin, for everyone knew what a womanizer the young Viking was, including herself. Yet he was in fact the most handsome among them. If any of them could win a young girl's heart and make her betray her own people, Bjarni was the one.

They continued to ply her with questions, wanting to know who the young lords were who had come to look them over the other day. They were surprised to learn that one was the King of these Saxons and that he was staying at Wyndhurst for a time. She had to describe him down to a hair, for he would make the perfect hostage if he ever got near enough to them again so they could grab him. With Alfred of Wessex in their hands and threatened, they could demand their freedom, and hers as well. It would be the easy way.

But although Kristen obliged them in telling all she could, she doubted her Saxon would ever let his King that close to the prisoners for just that reason. He was careless with his own person, but he would not be with Alfred.

She finally chided them all for letting their food get cold, and they went for the poorly carved wooden bowls they had for their use, bowls that gave up as much splinters as food—except Thorolf. He pulled Kristen down beside him to sit against the wall, twining his fingers with hers, which he rested on his bent knee.

He did not look at her, but out at the room. Ohthere had made a point of not asking her how she fared, for he could see with his eyes that she was well in mind and body. Thorolf had no such reluctance in addressing a delicate subject.

He came right to the point. "It is true, then, what the Saxon told me? You like him?"

Royce was their enemy. He had enslaved them all. She knew what Thorolf was thinking. How could he understand, when she did not?

Kristen did not hedge words either, saying plainly, "When I look at him, I feel wonderful inside. That has never happened to me before, Thorolf."

"You would have him for your husband?"

She grinned ruefully, though he did not see it. "I would, but he would not."

His fingers gently squeezed hers. "I feared you did not know it, that you expected him to honor you."

"I did not lose my mind or reason along with my . . . I know exactly what to expect. He likes me well enough now, but—"

"Now?"

"He thought I was a whore at first. Nay, Thorolf." She smiled as his eyes swung to her angrily. "You are supposed to laugh. I did. And I let him think it. He was disgusted and it kept him from me for a while. But I came to regret that he did leave me alone. I was most willing when he finally . . . As I said, he likes me well enough now, but he will not trust me farther than he can see me. And yet he keeps other men from me. He even had my chains removed while these young lordlings are staying here at Wyndhurst, so I could protect myself when he is not near."

"So you have him, or half of him?"

"Aye, half of him, and I will lose that half when he weds. And yet . . ."

She sighed instead of finishing. Thorolf squeezed her fingers again to let her know he understood. He would not be a hypocrite and tell her she was wrong to want the Saxon. He knew he would do exactly as she if their positions were reversed and he found himself desiring his foe. He would take his pleasure, too, while he could, even of an enemy. That she was a woman and not expected to feel that way about it would make little difference to her. She was her mother's daughter, and Brenna Haardrad was a bold one who thought of herself before she thought of what was proper for a woman.

"Do not fret over it, Kristen."

"Not fret?" Her tone was soft, traced with bewilderment. "Logic tells me I should hate him already. I did have hope," she admitted grudgingly. "But that has been crushed now that I have seen his betrothed. And yet, God help me, Thorolf, he took me swimming after he caught me attempting to escape. Why would he do that?"

"I suppose he had no pleasure in it?"

"He could have had his pleasure anywhere. He did not have to take me to the lake."

"Well, there you are. The man is bewitched by you, and that is not likely to change."

"Bewitched? Nay, I am the one who is bewitched. I know I will hate him eventually, but I would rather it be now than later. I wish he would marry soon and have done with me."

Thorolf grinned at the sullen tone, then burst into laughter when she scowled at him for it. "I pity your Saxon, wench, I really do. Done with you? Odin be praised, it is the other way around. When you are done with him, let us hope he is not too heart-stricken."

Kristen giggled at the unlikely notion of Royce being heart-stricken, and then she laughed heartily too. It was too absurd, really, but she appreciated Thorolf's trying to bolster her self-esteem.

That was how Royce saw her when he stepped into the open doorway: sitting practically in the Viking's lap, their hands entwined and laughing together. His first urge was to tear them apart and thrash the young Viking to a pulp, but he tamped it down. He had forgotten how these Vikings felt about her.

The room grown quiet made Kristen look to see why, and then she groaned inwardly. "I think I have stayed too long."

Thorolf's hand tightened on hers when she started to rise. "Will he come in here and get you, Kristen?"

His question appalled her. "Look at him. That is not his pleasant look, I can assure you. You want him to drag me out of here?"

"I wonder what would happen if he tried."

In that moment her thoughts apprehended his and she cried, "Thorolf!"

"We can take him, Kristen," he said quietly, his eyes locked with those of the Saxon as he spoke. "He will do as well as his King as a hostage. In here they cannot fire arrows at us from afar to force us to release him."

Her mind and body screamed nay, but her voice spoke reason. "I know him, Thorolf. Listen to me well. His people and his duty come first with him. He has it set in his mind that slaughter will be done if you are freed. He cannot be convinced otherwise. He will sacrifice himself before he will give the order for your release."

Thorolf had reasoning of his own. "His guards will not listen if his life is threatened."

"It will not work, I tell you!"

"Your cousin disagrees. Look at him, Kristen. Oh-there has already reached the same conclusion as I. If your Saxon is foolhardy enough to come in here to get you, then he deserves what happens."

God help her, she could almost hate Thorolf for forcing her to choose between them. If she ran out of here now, no one would stop her, but she would be denying her friends their chance for freedom, and there was no guarantee they would ever have another chance. But if she stayed . . . if she stayed, Royce could very well die.

Thorolf divined some of her thoughts, probably from her anguished expression. He loosened the grip on her hand which had kept her by his side. He was making her choose, leaving the decision wholly with her. But softly he said, "We will not kill him, Kristen. That would serve no purpose."

His words made no difference. The choice was no longer hers, for Royce's patience had run out. Instead of closing the door and forcing her out in some other way, his arrogance—his cursed, foolish arrogance—brought him forward. It was as if he walked in his own hall, with only his trusted servants surrounding him. That was how relaxed and at ease he was as he closed the distance between them.

Ohthere obviously did not believe this could happen. He had waited to see what Royce would do, but now that he had done the unlikely, Ohthere stood there doubting his own eyes. Thorolf must also have doubts now, for he rose, pulling Kristen up with him, his expression much less confident. Yet she felt the tension in his hand, still holding hers. He was still going to go through with it and try to overpower Royce. And she could not warn Royce, for that would only make it happen sooner, now that he was in the midst of them.

Vikings were by nature a superstitious lot. For men who would not step foot on a ship that they knew inside and out without making a sacrifice to their gods first, Royce's boldness, which bordered on sheer madness, had to unnerve them. It allowed him to walk through them without a single man moving to stop him. He had done it before and they had not believed it then, even with his guards standing about with arrows at the ready. But now, alone, with his sword still in his scabbard, with his hands empty...

He reached Kristen and Thorolf, stopping to stand in front of them. Thorolf released her hand. She expected to feel Royce's hand next, his long fingers curling about her wrist to drag her outside. His expression was nearly bland, yet she knew he had to be in the grips of a terrible rage to do what he had done.

She was past revealing emotion herself, her stomach tied up in knots, her nerves gone dead, numb, waiting ... waiting.

Royce's hand shot out, but it was Thorolf he grabbed. In a move that was so swift it was almost a blur before her eyes, Royce was behind Thorolf and had the prisoner's neck twisted at an odd angle inside the arm he had circled round it, his other hand braced against the Viking's head. It would take no more than a second to give the twist that would break Thorolf's neck.

"Royce—" she began.

He cut her short, without looking at her, his tone, to her astonishment, dry. "Mayhap now you will leave, wench?"

Thorolf made a sound in his throat that drew her eyes

worriedly to him, but what she saw made her emotions come back to life with a vengeance. He was choking on his own laughter! God's teeth! If he could think it was funny that his own plan had been turned around and used against him . . .

She gave the two men her back and stomped over to Ohthere. "Do you let him go, or do you let him kill Thorolf? Thorolf might think it amusing to find himself outwitted, but the Saxon does not share his humor. He *will* kill him."

"So I see," Ohthere replied, and then he too somehow found it amusing. With a grin he added, "The Saxon will leave, with no help from us, I think. Thor's teeth, he is ever a source of entertainment, that one. Let us be amused a bit more to see how he does it. Go on, child, take yourself out of here. I am sure he will follow after you."

He gave her a hug before he let her go, for it was unlikely she would be allowed to see them again after this incident, and they both knew it. Then he pushed her toward the door. She went, getting farewells and whacks on her bottom as she passed the others, just as she used to at home. Were they all mad to see the humor in what had happened, instead of nurturing the disappointment?

Well, while they were all laughing about this later, she would be dealing with Royce, and she had every reason to believe it would not be pleasant. She wasn't going to stand around and wait for his anger to wash over her. He had told her to leave. She did, making her own way back to the hall.

Chapter Thirty-three

"*I* wonder, if I hide under this table, will he notice me?"

Eda gave Kristen a sharp look. "What kind of question is that, wench?"

"A whimsical one," Kristen retorted as she plopped down on a stool.

After such heart-stopping suspense, she had a right to be irritable now, but that was not why she was. She did not like being blamed for something that was not of her doing, so in defense she was in the proper mood to face Royce's fury. She would rather avoid it. She did in fact wish there were someplace she could hide for a while, just until he calmed down. But there was not, not in his hall.

"You came back alone?" Eda broke into her thoughts. "Where is Lord Royce?"

Kristen waved a hand dismissively. "There was some minor trouble with his prisoners. He will be along directly."

He was, just then, and his eyes lit on her from across the hall. But apparently he was not ready to deal with her, for his look was only brief, and he crossed to his empty chair at the long table, not to her.

So, he would return to his drinking and entertainments, as if he had not just come close to losing his life. Why did that irritate her even more?

"Do I sleep with you again, Eda?"

277

"You know you do not. You saw Lord Averill and his family leave today."

"Aye, but I would prefer to sleep with you."

"Do you? When yestereve you grumbled because you had lost your soft bed?"

"I did not grumble!" Kristen snapped.

"Oh, ho, what has you in such a grouch?"

That did not deserve an answer. "Why did he come after me, Eda? I was not gone so long."

To that Eda shrugged. "He saw Uland come in and make his rounds with some story that had him excited. Milord sent Edrea to find out what. The fool boy thought it amazing that you should be greeted by those Vikings of yours like a long-lost sister, and that you would probably not have a bone uncrushed after being passed around and hugged by all those giants."

"*That* made him come after me?"

"Nay, he went on to eat. But I watched him." Eda chuckled here. "And he watched the door, waiting for your return. I suppose at last he decided you *were* gone too long."

And Kristen supposed that at that moment, Royce was not willing to let the King see his anger. But she had little doubt that she would feel it later. He would not let this incident pass unpunished, as he had her attempted escape.

She glanced his way, but could not see him, with Alden sitting this side of him and blocking him from her view. Alfred was on Royce's other side, and she could not see the King, either, from where she sat.

Edrea came next to Kristen, setting down a wooden tray on the table. All that remained on it were a few bread crumbs.

"They liked it, you know, your bread," Edrea said to her. "Milord even made comment on it, asking who had made it."

"Did you tell him?"

"Nay, I feared half the lords would spit it out, fearing you might be poisoning them."

Edrea's dark-brown eyes were twinkling. She had made a joke. Kristen could hardly believe it, let alone that the girl was actually talking to her of her own accord.

"The time to have told them would have been after they had eaten it," Kristen rejoined.

Edrea laughed outright now. "Uland was right. You are not so strange. Eda had said so, too, but then, Eda had taken a liking to you. *That* was strange."

Kristen grinned despite her bad humor. "'Tis hard to know it, when the old woman is such a harridan." Her voice rose at the end so Eda would hear.

This got a snort from Eda, and an answering grin from Edrea. "Aye, Eda can be deceptive in her moods. Mayhap the Vikings are not so fearsome, either."

"His name is Bjarni," Kristen offered.

"Who?"

"The one who likes you."

The poor girl did not know how to hide her pleasure. Her pretty face lit up in wonder. "Did he say so?"

Kristen was not exactly in the mood to further Bjarni's and the others' cause at the moment, but at least talking to the girl was distracting. "He frets because he cannot tell you so himself. He is having Thorolf teach him your words, but do not be surprised when you hear them if you cannot understand, for Thorolf does not know your tongue too well himself."

For the next hour Edrea would not stop asking questions about the young Viking, and Kristen painted a glowing picture that would no doubt lead to disappointment in the end, for Bjarni was not the paragon of virtue she made him out to be. He was a man to be enjoyed, not taken seriously. But if Edrea was foolish enough to believe anything he would tell her in order to enlist her aid in an escape, then Kristen could not pity her.

Her friends and their freedom came before the feelings of one Saxon girl. If Kristen could get to Lyman and that key, she would do it herself. But already she was to be installed back in the lord's chamber.

"You sit there doing nary a bit of work," Eda came over to grumble at Kristen when Edrea was called away to refill some ale horns. "You might as well go on to bed, so you can have an early start on the morrow. Lady Darrelle has herself requested more of your nut bread. She thinks 'tis a recipe I have kept to myself all these years."

"And of course you let her think so."

"Of course." Eda chuckled. "And what were you and Edrea bending heads about?"

"She likes one of the prisoners."

This brought a sharply raised brow. "I hope you told her naught could come of that."

"And why not? They are men, just as Royce is. Surely he is not so cruel that he will not eventually supply them with women to satisfy their natural needs. Otherwise frustrations will ferment. Trouble will follow. 'Tis only sensible—"

"God save us!" Eda cut her short in amazement. "First you bring them food. Now you want to bring them whores. Get you to bed, wench, before you get the idea next that they should be allowed to marry and settle here."

"Now that you mention it . . ."

Kristen rushed away before Eda could have the last word. She carried a grin on her lips until she reached the top of the stairs. Then teasing Eda was forgotten as she spied the door down at the end of the corridor. She sighed, making her way slowly toward it, wondering how long she would have before Royce came up to join her.

She had not even half a minute. He must have left the hall the moment she did. She was standing by the table, her back to the door. She had meant to strip off her clothes and make use of the water there. She had not even untied her girdle when the door opened.

"What happened with the prisoners, Kristen?"

She swung around, aqua eyes wide as she looked at Alden, not Royce. It took her a moment to adjust to this surprise; then she glanced toward the weapons on the wall.

"Nay," he said, reading her mind. "Hear what I have to say first before you try to slit my throat again. I know my cousin. When he is angry, he shouts, he blusters, he knocks heads together. When he is furious, he is deadly calm, and God help the unfortunate soul who shatters that calm. He is furious now. What happened to cause it?"

"Why do you not ask *him?*"

"Ask him?" Alden shuddered, and Kristen wondered whether it was feigned or real. "When he is like this, I do not want to be anywhere near him."

"And I do not want to be near you, Saxon. You need not fear I will attack you. I gave my word to your cousin that as long as your King is here, I will stay away from you."

A half smile formed on his lips. "You mean 'tis actually safe for me to get close to you?"

"I would not suggest it," she returned darkly.

"Will you at least tell me what happened? Mayhap I can then know how to temper some of his fury."

She shrugged offhandedly, yet her words belied her indifference. "He behaved like a brainless fool. He came in among the prisoners to take me from their quarters." Her voice began to rise, her irritation returning. "Thorolf detained me, but instead of Royce seeing the wisdom of leaving then, for I would have too if he did, he came in to get me. 'Twas the most stupid, arrogant thing he could have done. 'Twas just what they hoped he would do!"

"And yet naught happened."

Kristen's expression mirrored her disgust. "That is not the point. He turned it around so he had the upper hand. He could just as easily have found himself at *their* mercy."

"And that displeases you?"

She glared at him. "I told you what you wanted to know. Now leave me."

He nodded, but before he turned to go, he added, "A word of warning, wench. Do not say to him what you have said to me. I do not think he will tolerate being called a brainless fool at this time."

He opened the door to leave, and there stood Royce. Alden groaned inwardly, offering a silent prayer that Royce had not heard anything that was said. Kristen schooled her own features, seeing that Alden had been right. Royce looked calm enough on the outside, but that was only at first glance. A closer look revealed the tight set of his lips, the dangerous gleam in his eyes.

"What do you here, Cousin?"

Alden said in jest, "Helping the wench prepare for the siege."

Royce was not amused. "'Tis an unwise habit you have developed, helping her. 'Twill eventually get you a blade in your back. Leave us."

It was said most softly, but Kristen recognized the underlying menace. She turned her back with the closing of the door, worrying at her lower lip. Only once had she seen Royce like this before: the first time she saw him. He had spoken cold-bloodedly then of killing them all. This time? She was not so much afraid, sure that he would not kill her. What she felt was the apprehension of facing the unknown.

"I am forced to wonder now, if everything you say and do is not a lie."

Kristen stiffened. God help her, she certainly could not help herself if she could not understand him. What had that casually uttered remark to do with what had happened?

"I must assume you have a reason for saying that, milord. Do you tell me, or do I guess?"

He came up behind her while she spoke, which was why she did not hear him, and why she gasped when his fingers bit into her shoulder to turn her around. But her expression was stony now that she looked into his dark eyes. She would not be played with, like cat and mouse.

"Make your accusation and have done with it!" Kristen snapped.

"He is more than a friend to you, your Thorolf."

"You say that because I let him detain me?" she asked incredulously. "Aye, I let him, because I did not think you could be so foolish as to fall for his ploy."

"Who was the fool?"

Her eyes flew open. "You knew! You knew what he would do and yet you still came in! You *are* mad!"

He held both shoulders now and shook her. "What I am is without patience. Do you love him?"

That she could knock his hands away, as tight as they held her, attested to her own loss of patience. "Another question that has naught to do with what happened! Of course I love him. He is like a brother to me. Now you tell me what that has to do with aught! You put yourself at their mercy. Thorolf said they would not kill you, but you could not know that. You had only to return to the hall, Saxon, and I would have followed on my own."

"Did *I* know *that*?"

It dawned on her that he was shouting now, that he

was no longer furious—just angry, if Alden could be believed. Which statement of hers had appeased him enough to bring about the change? she wondered.

She lowered her own voice. "Common sense would have told you. Outside that room, you held control. You could have forced me out in any number of ways. I knew that. 'Twas not my intention to stay," she even admitted. "I did not mean to stay as long as I did, but it had been so long since I had talked to them."

"Or touched them—him! I have eyes, wench. You were practically on top of him!"

"Oh, unfair!" she cried. "I sat next to him. He held my hand. How could you read more into that than there was? I told you long ago I was raised to be unafraid to show my affections. 'Tis natural for me to touch someone I love."

"Then touch me, Kristen."

Those words hit her like thunder, slamming through her with an electrical charge. Of a sudden, his expression was fraught with desire, not anger, and it touched a like response in Kristen. She was already emotionally stimulated. His look simply redirected that emotion, focused it on her senses, which were screaming to throw herself into his arms.

She almost did. She almost took the step that would meld their bodies together. It took every last bit of will she possessed not to. God help her, if he had only said it differently, if love were not the issue . . .

"Kristen?"

"Nay!" The word tore out of her, as much for herself as for him. "I do *not* love you!"

The denial was too emphatic, she knew. It was no wonder he ignored it, taking the step she wanted to take, bringing her up hard against his body. Another thunderclap, pelvis to pelvis, chest to chest, and lips that were a balm for the fever spreading through her. Scorching, insistent, he forced his mouth over hers, drawing passion from her soul.

He bent forward, holding her so that her body curved into his, tightly, while his lips burned toward her ear. "I concede, Kristen. Touch me not because you love me, but because I need you. Touch me!"

It was the groan that did it, coming from deep within him as if he were in mortal pain. Her heart could not resist that entreaty. Her body had already lost the battle. Her hands cupped his face, forcing him to look at her, and his look was more potent than any caress.

Aye, my Saxon, I will touch you. I will touch you until I reach your heart. She did not say it aloud, but it was in her eyes for him to see: her own need, her desire —her love. But she kissed his eyes closed, not wanting him to discern too much. And then she brought his lips back to hers and proceeded to drive him wild with what he had asked for. She touched him to her heart's content.

Chapter Thirty-four

Six hot loaves of nut bread were put in a basket and taken outside to the waiting baggage carts. Eda had woken Kristen early to come down and make them for the King's departure. He and his party were finally leaving.

Servants again gathered at the windows to watch as the many nobles mounted their fine horses. The sky was thick with angry clouds. They were likely to be drenched in rain before the morning was through. Yet no order was given to delay. Alfred did not await the weather.

Unlike the arrival of these nobles, Kristen was able to watch their leaving along with the others. She saw the King embrace Royce. She saw them laugh together over something Alfred said. And then she watched this young King of the Saxons ride out of Wyndhurst.

She was not sorry to see him go, disliking the upheaval his visit had caused. And yet she knew what his going meant to her: The bargain she had made with Royce was at an end.

She walked slowly back to the cooking area, Eda by her side. "Did Royce say aught to you this morn?" she ventured.

"Aye, he did."

"Oh."

" 'Oh'? 'Tis not like you to hedge, wench," Eda said testily. "If you want to know about the chains, ask me.

Nay, do not ask. I have his order, no more than you expected."

"Aye, I expected no more."

"If 'tis any consolation, he was no more happy about it than you are."

"'Tis not."

Eda glowered at her apathy. "You made one bargain with him. Make another. You have sense, wench. Use what you have to get what you want."

The old woman finally managed to spark her ire, which came out in sarcastic scorn. "You go against your lord to suggest it. You forget how little I can be trusted. I am likely to escape in the bright light of day."

"Aye, do not listen to me. You never listen to me. What do I know? I have only known the man since he was a babe. I have—"

"God help me!" Kristen's annoyance snapped. "If you do not cease to nag me, old woman, I will—"

"God help you?" Royce queried from behind her. "Which god is that?"

She swung around, too heated to notice his surprise. "What do you want, Saxon? Have you not hunting or training or some such to do? I hate it when you sneak up behind me!"

He knew what had set her off. He had anticipated it would not be easy to get the chains back on her. It was why he was here, to see that nothing untoward happened. But she had thrown him off guard by using an imprecation that only a Christian would use.

"Which god do you entreat?" he repeated.

Her mouth set mulishly. She was not going to answer. He gripped her arms and shook her until, in a burst of fury, she shoved him away from her.

"Rattle my teeth again, Saxon, and I swear I will lay your cheek open with my fist!"

He should have exploded into fury himself. Instead

he laughed. "'Twas only a simple question, Kristen. Why are you so defensive?"

His laughter worked on her like magic, soothing the edges of her pique. Why *was* she still keeping this secret? There had been reason to in the beginning, but not anymore.

Kristen smiled at her own foul temper. Eda turned away, shaking her head at such quick changes of mood. Royce was just as confounded. The way she could master turbulent emotions so easily was uncanny.

"Forgive me, milord," Kristen said, though she did not look at all contrite. "I did not mean to push you . . . well, I did, but I am sorry for it."

"Which does not mean 'twill not happen again."

"True." Her eyes laughed at him.

Royce grinned, shaking his head. "Do you answer my question now?"

She shrugged. "I pray to my mother's God."

"Then why not call him by name?"

"I did." At his raised brow, she explained, "My mother's God is your God."

He stiffened, humor flown. "How is that possible?"

"Very easily, milord. Vikings have raided other lands for many, many years. Raids bring home Christian captives. My mother was one. My father's mother was also Christian. My father and brothers"—she smiled here—"they do not take chances and worship all gods."

"And you?"

"I believe in the one true God."

He frowned, reminding her sharply, "You defended your friends' intent to sack a monastery!"

She frowned back at him. "I did not defend. I understood, which is more than you are willing to do. I told you my brother would not tell me their intent. I did not tell you why, but the why is that he knew I would fight with all my heart to change his course. So he did not tell me. So he came here and he died! I know in my mind 'twas God's will, but half my blood is Viking blood and my heart cries for revenge. Do you tell me Saxon Christians do not avenge a loved one's death?"

He could not tell her that. The church abhorred blood feuds, but could not prevent them.

"Why did you never tell me you are Christian?" he demanded.

"What difference would it have made? Your other slaves are Christian and yet they are still slaves."

"It makes a difference, Kristen. It gives us a common bond, and gives me the leverage I have lacked to deal with you. It gives me something to trust in."

Her eyes slanted suspiciously. "What are you saying, Saxon?"

"I can accept your word if you will swear in God's name. Swear you will never try to escape from here, and you will have the same freedom afforded the other servants."

"No more chains?" she asked incredulously.

"None."

"Then I swear—"

She stopped herself. This was too fast. She was committing herself without thinking about it first.

"Kristen?"

"God's teeth!" she snapped. "Give me a moment."

Never, he had said. Never was forever. What would happen when he no longer wanted her, when he had a wife to see to his needs? She would hate it here then, and no doubt come to hate him, too. And yet by her word she would have to stay here, to go on serving in this hall—forever.

She gave him a level look. He would like that. What did he care for her feelings? But then, he must care something, or he would not be willing to make this bargain with her.

"Very well, milord. I swear in God's name that I will not try to escape from Wyndhurst—until such time as you marry." His eyes narrowed, and she added reasonably, "I am sorry to say it, but I do not like your betrothed. I do not think I will be able to tolerate this place once she rules the hall."

"Done," he snapped.

"You mean it?" she asked in surprise. "You accept those terms?"

"Aye. 'Twill just mean you will be back in chains at that time."

She gritted her teeth, chagrined. "So be it. But that is all I will swear to."

"Nay, you will also swear you will not aid your friends in escape." He touched a finger to her lips to still her angry cry. "Until such time as I wed."

"Done!" she retorted bitterly. "But I will *not* swear off my vengeance!"

"Nay, I know you will not," he said regretfully. "Alden is sufficiently recovered to protect himself against you. I will trust in his ability, as long as you do not attack him in his sleep."

"I seek revenge, not murder," she replied with contempt.

"Very well. Then I only need warn you that if you do kill Alden, I will be forced to take your life in payment."

Those were his last words. He walked away, leaving her simmering in exasperation. Somehow she did not feel she had come out the winner in this bargain, either.

Chapter Thirty-five

Royce returned to the hall in the late afternoon after putting his men through strenuous practice on the training field, something they had lacked in the last five days. The hall was back to rights. Tables had been put away during the day, and Darrelle was back to holding court in her sewing area. Darrelle. She had barely spoken to him since it became clear to her that he was sleeping with Kristen.

She was expressing her disapproval in a sulk, which ordinarily would not bother him in the least. But Royce found himself again comparing her with Kristen, who did not sulk, who did not keep her displeasure to herself but voiced it most bluntly. Strange, but the bluntness was not as irritating as getting countless sullen looks over a matter of weeks.

Mayhap he should find Darrelle a husband, despite her adamant insistence that she did not want one.

"Did your sister give particular attention to any of our departed guests?" Royce put the question to Alden.

They sat at the game table, the game in progress one of war strategy. Alden paid scant attention to the question, as it was his turn to deploy his army.

"I have not given it much thought."

"Do."

Alden looked up then, a grin coming slowly to his lips. "I swear you have the strangest things on your mind of late. Now that you mention it, she did seem more lively while Wilburt was here."

"Corliss's brother?" Royce was surprised, but after he digested that, he ventured, "Think you she would like him for husband?"

Alden whistled softly. "Does she know you are thinking along these lines?"

"How can she know what I am thinking when she will not talk to me?"

"Aye, she is not happy with you, but for that you would give her in marriage?"

"I cannot say I would not rather someone else be the recipient of her sulks, but do you not think 'tis time she wed?"

"Aye, long since time. But she will not, not until you do."

"What has that to do with aught?" Royce demanded.

"Come now, Cousin. Why do you think she has refused all these years to let you arrange her a marriage? She is afraid that with no lady in this hall, 'twill fall into slovenly neglect, which is no doubt true."

Royce grunted. "If you knew that was her reason, Cousin, as her brother, you should have told me ere now."

"And have to deal with her sulks for revealing a confidence?" Alden looked appalled. "You jest, Cousin. But speaking of marriage, when do you commit to yours?"

"When I have the time," Royce said tersely. "And do not say I have the time now, for I will tell you I do not."

Alden shook his head. "If you do not want to marry her—"

"I never wanted to marry her, Alden. It just seemed the appropriate thing to do after . . . well, it seemed appropriate."

"Then break it off."

"Aye, easy words from a man not involved," Royce said sourly.

Alden chuckled knowingly. "Life was certainly simpler here before the Vikings came." For that he got a dark look and he laughed the harder.

The attention of both men was drawn abruptly to the front of the hall, where two of Royce's men came in escorting a stranger. He was an extremely tall man, and a Celt by the look of him. Both factors made him of interest, especially the latter, after the recent trouble they had had with the Cornish Celts.

He was brought to stand before Royce as the report was given of how he was found west of here on Wyndhurst land. A search had been made far and wide to determine if he in truth traveled alone, as he claimed, and no one else had been found. He rode a broken-down nag that should have been kindly disposed of long ago. He carried no possessions save an old rusted sword, the hilt in an ancient Celtic design.

Royce accepted all that for what it was worth as he gazed thoughtfully at the man. He had never seen another man quite this handsome, for all his bedraggled appearance. His hair was overly long and tied back with a strip of leather. And he was dressed no better than the poorest serf, with loose long-sleeved tunic belted with a frayed rope, and threadbare chausses with ragged holes in them. Yet there was nothing subservient about his bearing. Dark-gray eyes met Royce's boldly. There was no belligerence, no wariness, no slyness, nor even tension. It was a look Royce was more accustomed to from an equal, and it pricked his curiosity.

"Who are you?"

"I do not understand."

Royce tensed, hearing the Celtic tongue. Most Celts west of here spoke the Saxon tongue, as they lived side by side with Saxon. Not so the Cornish Celts who so often raided his land.

He repeated the question in the stranger's tongue.

"I am called Gaelan."

"Of Cornwall?"

"Devon."

"A freeman?"

"Yea."

Royce frowned. He did not say much, this freeman of Devon. "How do I know what you say is true?"

"Why would I lie?"

"Why, indeed," Royce grunted. "You are a long way from your home. Where do you go that takes you across my land?"

"I search for a lord to serve who will fight the Danes. Have I found him?"

Alden laughed at Royce's surprise. "'Twas the last thing you expected to hear, eh, Cousin?"

Royce gave him a quelling look, then eyed the Celt narrowly. "There are many lords 'tween here and Devon who will fight the Danes. Why come so far east?"

"There are none who prepare in earnest. I want assurance I will see true fighting."

"Why?"

"'Tis not enough the Danes have wrested land in the north to settle on, they still raid by sea. I lived in a fishing village on the southern coast. 'Twas destroyed in a Viking raid. I lost my wife, my two sons, my family, and my friends. No one was left alive."

"Save you. Why is that?"

"I was hunting inland. I returned in time only to see the ship sail away."

It was a story Gaelan had told again and again in his search. It served him well with these Saxon lords. And these two before him were disturbed more than most. Was his search at last over?

"When was this?" Royce demanded.

"At the start of summer."

"Why do you say 'twas Danes who attacked your village?"

"Who else has plagued this land for so long?"

A look passed between Royce and Alden, before Royce glanced down at his fist, clenched on the table. The question was not answered.

It was Alden who told Gaelan, "If the Danes cross into Wessex again, we will be there to stop them. You have the will to fight, but can you?"

"I—I will need training."

"And if my cousin agrees to train you, how do you serve him in return?"

"I offer to serve as personal guard—because of my size."

"Even if you could fight, look at me," Royce interjected. "Do I look as if I need protection?"

The gray eyes crinkled as a slight grin formed on Gaelan's lips. "The other lords I petitioned were not as well set as you, milord. I am willing to serve in any way you request, if you will accept me."

Alden switched to their own tongue to ask Royce, "Well, Cousin? We can always use another man, and one this size, with the right training, will be a valuable man."

"I do not like it," Royce replied.

"You think he will end his quest for revenge when he sees your prisoners?"

"There is that."

"But you have them so well guarded he could not get near them."

"Kristen is not so well guarded," Royce said shortly.

Alden rolled his eyes heavenward. "Of course, now she has the freedom of Wyndhurst, she is not guarded at all. You could always confine her freedom to the hall, and restrict the Celt from it."

"I made a bargain with her. I cannot change it now."

"And I was but jesting, Royce. By all reason, he would not harm her. He wants the blood of Vikings, not a woman's. If you doubt that, test him. But do not send him away for such a weak possibility. That would be taking your caution of the wench too far, especially when there cannot be any woman alive who sees to her own protection as that one does. And if that is not enough, your quest is the same as his, yet you did not harm her."

Royce's lips turned down in disgust. All true. He glanced again at the Celt, who stood there a model of patience.

"We were likewise raided by Vikings this summer," Royce said, watching closely the man's eyes. "We were more fortunate than your village in defeating them."

"You killed them all?"

Even Alden raised a brow at the force of those words, and he offered, "'Tis unlikely they were the same Vikings. These were Norwegians, after riches. 'Tis doubtful they would raid a fishing village that would offer little plunder."

"But you killed them?"

"Not all. Those captured are prisoners here. They are forced to work toward our defenses."

"They are also under my protection," Royce added, not liking at all the way the man relaxed as soon as Alden mentioned they had prisoners.

Gaelan heard the threat and replied accordingly. "If you have enslaved these Vikings, then justice is met. They will raid no more. I want those still running free in the north, for 'tis likely that is where the ship sailed that raided my village."

"If I accept you, Gaelan of Devon, will you work toward building my defenses, along with the prisoners?"

The man tensed. "I will not seek my vengeance of them, milord, but do not ask me to work beside them."

"I do ask it. 'Tis the only work I have at this time for a man of your size. You did say you were willing to do aught that was requested of you."

"So I did." There was a long silence, then: "So be it."

"You can resist the temptation?" Royce persisted.

"I have said I do not want the blood of enslaved men."

"Then you are welcome. You will begin work in the morn. In the afternoon you will train with my men. Seldon, see to the man's comfort."

Alden leaned close to Royce as Seldon took the Celt to the barrel for a horn of mead. "You are sure?"

Royce raised a brow. "You ask that after you spoke for the man? Aye, I am sure." But he added darkly, "Sure enough to have him watched until I am even more sure."

Chapter Thirty-six

*L*ate in the afternoon, when Kristen returned to the hall with Eda after putting the guest chambers to rights, she was still wondering how she could have her revenge against Alden, without forfeiting her own life. She had wondered about it all day. She had listed in her mind the many ways she could wound him—or, rather, permanently maim him, so that he might succumb to depression and take his own life. The only problem with that was, what if being a cripple did not do it? How would a man who was otherwise so carefree and cheerful react to depression?

She did not consider giving up and letting Alden live. Quite the contrary. Fretting about it all day had made her think more and more of her brother, and that only strengthened her resolve.

But it was perhaps having Selig on her mind so strongly that caused her to have such a bad reaction on her first sight of the stranger in the hall. He sat with his back to her, and yet she turned deathly white, lost her breath, lost the use of her legs, even lost her sight for that one heart-stopping moment when she thought her brother had come back from the dead.

Eda plowing into her brought Kristen back to life, too much life, for she reacted badly to her momentary madness. "God's teeth, woman! Watch where you are going!"

"Me!" Eda was taken aback. "Me? Who stopped dead? I ask you."

Kristen merely glowered at her and stalked on toward the cooking area. Once there, her eyes were drawn back to the stranger again and again. It was the cursed hair, blackest black. It was the cursed breadth of shoulder, just the exact width. It was the cursed long-muscled back, just like the one she used to ride on when she was so much younger. No wonder she had thought she looked at Selig, despite every sense that told her it was impossible. From behind, the stranger was his double.

She could not stop watching him. She could not stop the need that built to see his face. Yet he did not once turn around. He sat with Seldon and Hunfrith swilling mead, an occasional laugh coming from one or more of them as they talked quietly together, too far away for her to hear their voices.

When Royce came into the hall, some of Kristen's agitation calmed. He had that power over her. Yet she was still annoyed with him for his threat and gave him only a cursory glance. Alden was with him, and to Royce's cousin she cast a murderous look that made him chuckle. No more than ten seconds later her eyes were back on the stranger. Who *was* he?

"His name is Gaelan."

"What?" Kristen turned to see Edrea grinning at her.

"Gaelan," Edrea repeated. "A Celt from Devon. I noticed you watched him too."

" 'Too'?"

Edrea giggled now. "Look around you." She indicated in particular the sewing area. "Even Lady Darrelle stares at the man."

"Why?"

"Why? You jest, Kristen. He has a face made in heaven. Why else do you stare?"

"I only wondered who he was and what he does here," Kristen said testily. "I thought we were done with strangers coming here."

"As to why he is here, milord has retained him. He will work on the wall with the others."

"Aye, he has the body for such work."

"Indeed." Edrea sighed.

"I thought you held a tender for Bjarni."

"I do." Edrea smiled blushingly. "But if the Celt would notice me . . ." She sighed again. "But then, I have the same problem. He does not speak our tongue, and though many here can speak his, I am not one of them."

Eda came over to scold: "Edrea, make haste and help Aethel set up the tables. Gossiping does not get work done. And you, Kristen, finish shelling those peas."

Kristen grabbed the old woman's arm before she could turn away again. "Eda, did you notice the Celt?"

Eda looked across the hall to where Gaelan sat. "Aye. You cannot help but notice him, as big as he is."

"But I thought only the Cornish Celts were giants, and you said Royce is enemies with them."

"True, but this one is not from the Cornish coast. And there are exceptions everywhere as to the size of a people. Look at Lord Royce in comparison with other Saxons, but he is a Saxon true."

"I suppose."

Eda's eyes narrowed. "I see you are interested, but you would do well to quell that interest immediately. Milord would not like it at all."

"Royce does not—"

Kristen grinned, the words *own me* dying in her throat. Royce *did* own her and she should worry about his likes and dislikes—as long as it suited her. But she was not really interested in the Celt, not as Eda meant. She just wanted to see his face.

"Your warning is taken, Eda."

"Good. And now the peas, ere they have not the time needed to cook."

But not five seconds after Eda turned back to the hearth, Kristen deliberately moved the heavy cauldron of shelled peas to the edge of the table, where it balanced precariously for half a second. When it crashed loudly to the floor, peas rolling out like a green carpet toward the hearth, her eyes flew not to the mishap she had caused, but remained fixed on the Celt.

His was not the only head that turned at the sound of the crash. But his was the only one Kristen saw.

"God's mercy, wench!" Eda exclaimed behind her. "What ails you to be so clumsy today?"

Kristen did not even hear. Her eyes were locked with gray eyes she had never thought to see again. A strangled sound came from her throat, escaping through the hand that covered her mouth. Her other hand pressed against her breasts, for her heart pounded so it hurt. It could not be true! God help her! *Selig! Alive!*

She rose from her stool to go to him. He rose from his chair to meet her halfway. At the exact same moment they both came to their senses and stopped.

Kristen swung around, her hands now gripping the table behind her to keep her there. Alive! Her eyes closed tightly. Really alive! She breathed deeply, fast and hard, to try to stop the urge she had to scream, to laugh, to cry.

She couldn't go to him. God help her, she couldn't hold him in her arms. To do so would have him locked away with the others. Yet joy washed over her in rapid degrees and she thought she would burst from it.

She finally noticed Eda staring at her in bewilderment. On an impulse she leaped forward, grabbing the old woman off her feet and swinging her round and round, laughing at her shrieks. She could laugh at that. She had to have this excuse to laugh. Oh, God, her brother was alive!

"You are mad, wench! Put me down!"

"I am apologizing!" Kristen's smile was brilliant. "For all your advice I did not heed. I concede you are wise beyond your years, Eda. Oh, Eda, I love you!"

Kristen twirled the old woman once more before she set her down to commence the worst grumbling and scolding Kristen had ever heard before. She smiled through it all as she hurried to collect all the scattered peas, not daring to look again across the hall.

But across the hall, Selig was also smiling. His search was indeed at an end. He had found Kristen, and she was hail and hearty and making a fool of herself to keep from racing to him. He knew her exuberance. She had knocked him flat on his back more than once when he returned from a sailing trip and she threw herself into his arms in greeting. How she contained herself now was a wonder, but it was a warning, too, of which he was already aware. He could not go to her, could not acknowledge her in any way. Throughout his search he had been tormented with the thought of her death. But she was alive. Alive!

"What do you make of that, Royce?" Alden wanted to know.

They had both watched Kristen behaving most bizarrely. "What can I say? She ceases to surprise me with the strange things she does. Nay, she still surprises me, but I am more used to it now."

"Well, 'tis strange indeed that she should find such humor in spilling peas."

Royce laughed at Alden's disgruntled tone. Several feet away, Selig tensed, seeing the lords watching Kristen.

He nudged Seldon beside him. "What do they say?"

"They are speaking of the Viking wench."

"She is a prisoner here, too?"

"Aye, but 'twould be more meet to call her Lord

Royce's personal slave, if you know what I mean." Seldon chuckled. "That is one Viking he has tamed."

Selig closed his eyes. Beneath the table his hands clenched into fists. He had only feared for her death. Not once had he thought of her ravishment at the hands of these Saxons.

His eyes opened slowly, a dark and violent storm gathering there. He was going to have to kill this Saxon lord.

Chapter Thirty-seven

———

*K*risten came to Royce as soon as he stepped into his chamber, her arms going around his neck to drape loosely there, while her fingers played with the hair at his nape. His brow rose questioningly at this unusual display of welcome.

"Alden tells me you gave him a look earlier that could have smote a man to his knees, and not two hours later, you smiled at him."

"Ah, well, milord, I let my hate pour out of me, the last of it, ere I put it to rest." She laughed at his doubtful frown. "I took your warning to heart. Is that so strange?"

"From you, aye."

"Time will tell."

One finger traced circles about his ear. Her eyes were soft, inviting, yet her mind was not in tune with what she was doing. She thought if she did not show some curiosity about his new retainer, he would think that strange too.

Casually she said, "I noticed you have a new man. Is that normal, for you to retain strangers?"

Her question had the opposite effect from what she sought, arousing his suspicion instead. "You show not one whit of interest in the King of all Wessex, nor his nobles, yet you ask about this Celt. Why is that?"

"I was no more than curious, milord. All the women talk of him."

"They can talk," he said roughly. "'But you will stay away from him. He hates all Vikings as much as I do.'"

It was time to redirect his thoughts. Her eyes half closed. Her finger came down along the edge of his jaw, then moved up to slide across his lower lip.

"Do you, Saxon?" she murmured huskily. "Do you still hate *all* Vikings?"

His answer was to crush her to him with a groan. And Kristen no longer had other things on her mind. But her joy in her brother's return from the dead was prevalent in all she did. Just as she had grabbed Eda earlier because she had to share her joy with someone or burst, she shared it tonight with Royce.

She was playful and passionate, shy and aggressive. By turns she was the seductress, the virgin, the wild vixen. She was everything to him, until Royce ceased to marvel at the changes. Her throaty laughter, never before heard in his bed, fired his blood to boiling. He took her again and again, and was only vaguely amazed that he could. But when she whispered that she wanted more of him, she tempted his soul. She wrung him dry, and when he finally slept, it was the sleep of the dead.

Kristen slept too. But with her emotions still so charged, for her it was a fitful sleep, from which she was able to awaken early, long before dawn.

She spared only a moment to savor the feeling of being held in Royce's arms. Then she carefully worked herself loose from his hold and quietly dressed in the dark.

Intuition told her she would find Selig waiting for her. He was, at the bottom of the stairs. He had waited through the night, sitting with his back to the wall and facing the stairs, sleeping in only short bouts, waking with each little sound he heard. So he had heard her soft tread and was standing when she reached the bottom of the stairs. And he was braced to take the weight of her body, which she did indeed throw at him.

They held each other fiercely for long golden moments. And then Kristen leaned back to run her hands over his beloved face. She could not see him. All the torches had ceased to burn, and only vague moonlight came in through the open windows. She did not have to see him.

"I thought you were dead, Selig." The tears in her eyes were heard in her voice.

"I thought you were." His hand caressed her hair, and then he pulled her close again, pressing her head to his shoulder. "It is not manly to cry."

"I know." She sniffed, thinking he spoke of her tears, until she felt one of his own fall on her cheek. She smiled, leaning up to kiss his cheek. "Come. We cannot talk safely here."

Kristen took his hand in hers and led him around the stairs and to the back door. Like the windows, the door was not locked. Selig hesitated as he stepped outside, expecting to find a sentry on guard.

Kristen recognized his caution. "I do not think guards patrol. I have been out once before at night and saw no one about the yard. But it is not like these Saxons to be so careless. Mayhap there are patrols outside the walls."

"Then we will deal with them when we come to them. Let us be gone, Kristen."

She jerked him back when he started to pull her away from the shadows of the hall. "Selig, I cannot leave."

"Cannot?"

"I gave my word I would not."

"By Odin! Why?"

She flinched at his tone. "To keep from being chained again."

There was silence, and then softly: "Again?"

"I had been chained like the others since our capture. My—"

"Who is left, Kristen?" he interrupted.

She gave him every name, and then waited while he thought of those who had died. She noticed the breeze while she waited, teasing at her hair. She heard the sound of night insects chirping. She felt his pain, but knew it could not be as bad as it could have been, for he had thought them all dead.

At last he said, "Go on."

"My own chains were only removed earlier this week when the Saxon's King and his nobles came here. I was harassed by some of the lords, and Royce had my chains taken off so I could look to my own protection while they were here. But they left this morn—or, rather, yestermorn—and my freedom would have been lost again if I did not swear not to try to escape from here."

Frustration marked his words. "You condemned yourself willingly to never leave here?"

"Nay, I compromised. When Royce weds, I am freed from my word."

"When will that be?"

"Soon."

He relaxed some, digesting that. She felt it in the easing of his grip on her hand.

She said, "Now tell me, before I burst. How did you escape? I saw you wounded."

"You saw?"

"Shush!" she hissed at his raised voice. "Of course I saw. I could not stay on the ship after I heard the sounds of battle. I had to help."

"You, help?"

She ignored the scorn of that. "So I did not help much. But at least I took down the Saxon who wounded you."

"You did!"

"Selig!"

"Odin's teeth! You could have been killed!"

"But I was not. Alas, he was not, either. I only wounded him. He recovered and has since done me a good turn, though I would have still tried to kill him. I am glad now I do not have to." Selig was shaking his head at her, and she added impatiently, "Well, tell me. The last I saw of you, you were lying unmoving on the ground, covered in your own blood."

"Aye, my wound was bad. I came to my senses as the carts left, taking the captured away. I had been left with the dead, and as we were all thought dead, no one was left behind to watch. But I did not know if they would return or not for the burials, so I managed to drag myself away from the carnage in case they did come back. I meant to stay hidden in the forest for only a few hours, then to follow and see where you were taken. But as I said, my wound was bad.

"I lost consciousness again and did not wake until that night. I found myself too weak to even rise at that point. I do not know how long I stayed there. The cursed wound festered. A fever raged, but I recall little of it. I know I left my hiding place at some point. I remember wandering, searching for the Saxons."

"As if you could have done much good if you found them," she chided.

"My mind did not grasp such logic." He smiled at her. "I only know I kept moving, kept trying to find you and the others before it was too late."

"Too late?"

"I did not think any of you would be allowed to live. I thought you would be taken to the lord of those Saxons who ambushed us, so that he could dispose of you."

"He very nearly did," Kristen admitted softly. "This place, Wyndhurst, has been raided before by Vikings.

He lost most of his family in that raid, and has hated Vikings ever since."

Selig chuckled. "No wonder he let me stay. I told him the same had happened to me. He must have commiserated."

"How could you tell such a story?" she demanded sharply. "God's teeth! He will tear you apart if he finds out who you really are. And to think I only worried that you would be chained and confined with the others if he knew!"

He grinned at her surliness. "He will not find out. Ohthere and the others have enough sense not to hail me when they see me."

"If they do not faint dead away, as I nearly did," she retorted.

"I noticed your quick recovery." He laughed.

Kristen hit his chest in exasperation. "Will you just finish your tale!"

Selig choked back another chortle. "You have lost your sense of humor, Kris." He gave in when she hit him again. "Very well. I have said I wandered. Even now I do not know for how long, nor how long I lay near death the last time my senses left me. I woke up in the hut of an old Celtic woman. It was she and her daughter who found me on their way back from market at Wimborne. It was a day's ride from where they found me to their home farther north."

"Where is that?"

He shrugged. "I do not think I could find them again. Loki has had a fine time with me. You would not believe how lost I have been."

"You had only to find the river," she pointed out.

"Aye, so I thought," he said with a measure of disgust. "I was with the old woman for nearly two weeks. She was suspicious of me because of the way I was dressed, and I mumbled in a foreign tongue when I was delirious. But because I also spoke Mother's tongue, which was hers too, she nursed me back to health and even led me to a trader, who took my belt and gold armbands in exchange for these clothes you see and a broken-down horse. She even directed me to the nearest river."

"So?"

"So *that* river was so far west of here that I had nearly reached land's end. The problem was that I did not know in which direction I had wandered, or whether I had managed to cross the river somehow in my delirium. I had no way of knowing if the Saxons I sought were east or west of me. And when she directed me west, I assumed I had wandered east. So I went west, to the waste of good time."

"And when you found that river, you knew you had gone the wrong way?"

"Aye. But then I did not know how far from the river I sought, where you and the others would have been taken, so I was forced to stop at every fortified hall as I progressed back this way. I gave the same story to each lord, which stood me well. But I moved on as soon as I ascertained they had no knowledge of Vikings come from the sea. I did not know when I came here that I had found the right place, until the lord admitted they had also been raided this summer."

"And your wound is completely healed?"

"Aye, it bothers me no more."

"Well, it is fortunate you said you were from Devon and not Cornwall, or you would not have been welcomed here."

He chuckled. "I learned of the hostility between the Cornish Celts and the Saxons at the first hall I approached. I nearly found myself in chains there, but you know what a golden tongue I have."

"Aye, I know it. Oh, Selig, I am so happy now—"

His fingers at her lips stopped the rush of her exuberance. "Make me as happy, Kris. Tell me you suffered no ravishment by these Saxons."

"Ravishment? Nay, I have not been ravished." She did not give him a chance to feel relief. "But I have been well and truly bedded by Lord Royce." Air hissed through his teeth, but she quickly put her fingers to his lips, as he had to hers. "Do not say something that will make me sorry for speaking plainly to you, Selig. I think I love the Saxon. I am more sure about wanting him. I have wanted him from the first . . . well, mayhap not that soon. But I was fascinated by him from the first, when he rode into the yard where we were all chained, and looked at us with such loathing. He gave the order we should all die. But he had changed his mind by the next day and came out to tell us we would be put to work building his stone wall."

"We? He put you to such work?"

She laughed. "Aye. Thorolf and the others helped to disguise me. I was thought a boy, and that lasted for about a week. But the men could not keep it straight that I was supposed to be a boy. They kept helping me, and I think that is what gave me away, or at least it drew too much attention to me. The Saxon concluded that they protected me because I must be their leader. Anyway, that is what led to his finding out I was a woman, and I was moved into the hall then."

"And into the Saxon's bed?"

She hit him solidly in the belly for that. He bent over double with a loud *whoosh*.

"Thor's bones, Kristen! Have a care!"

"Then you have a care what tone you use," she warned angrily. "I am a woman full grown. I am not answerable to you for what I do. And I did not go right to his bed." She was not going to tell him everything she had told Thorolf. She ended more quietly, "The truth is, he resisted me."

"What?"

His amazement made her grin despite her annoyance with him. "God's truth. I knew he wanted me, but he fought it. No man has ever resisted me before."

"Well I know it, for how many heads have I clobbered for their lack of resistance?"

She couldn't help but giggle at that. "But the Saxon did fight his attraction to me, and the more he did, the more I came to want him. I deliberately tempted him, Selig." That was hard to admit to one's brother, but she wasn't going to have him blaming Royce for seducing her, when it was in fact the other way around. "Two weeks ago the victory was mine—he took me to his bed. I have slept in his chamber ever since. I just came from there now."

"You really love him, Kris?"

"I must. I do not agree with everything he does. I have been furious with him many times. But I could not hate him, not even for chaining me, when I hated those chains more than anything."

"And what does he feel for you?"

"I do not know. I have his protection. He has shown some concern for me. But that is no more than he would give any possession of his. Yet he did naught to me when I tried to escape. And I know he did not really like chaining me. I just do not know," she finished.

"Does he still want you?"

"Aye, that has not changed."

"Then—"

"He will still marry someone else."

"Aye, you did mention that," he said, then suddenly exploded. "By Odin, nay! He *will* marry you."

She shook her head at him. "Selig, I am his slave. To

his thinking, why should he marry me when he already has me in his possession?"

He grunted. "Father could tell him a thing or two about that."

Laughter glittered in her eyes. "Aye, he could, but he is not here to."

"Then I could—"

"But you will not, for Royce is not to know you are my brother, at any cost."

"Then what do you do, Kris?"

Her chin hardened. "I will enjoy this man while I can. When he weds, I will leave here."

"Just like that? Even though you love him?"

"What else can I do? At least you are here now to help me escape when I am ready. And if you can help the others to get away any sooner, do so. You can come back for me."

"So be it."

She clasped his face in her hands and kissed him. "Thank you, Selig, for not scolding."

He squeezed her tight. "As you said, you are not answerable to me. But Odin help you when you try to explain all this to Father."

"Oh, unfair, to remind me of that!" she cried.

He whacked her bottom playfully. "Come, we have been out here too long."

The sky had begun to lighten, too much. "Aye." She stepped back to the door, but hesitated there, touching his cheek once more. "I will not speak to you again for a while. And do not be surprised if I ignore you completely in the hall. He has already warned me to stay away from you."

He chuckled. "He probably thinks I will harm you if I know you are a bloodthirsty Viking."

"Whatever his reason, his anger is not pleasant, so do be careful, Brother."

They were extremely quiet in entering the hall, to no purpose. Royce was there, angrily kicking several of his men awake. He stopped when he saw her. And then his eyes narrowed dangerously when he saw Selig beside her.

"We were outside for the air," she whispered quickly to Selig as Royce approached them. "We only met on coming in."

"Is he going to believe that?"

"He will have to."

But Royce did not ask any questions at all when he reached them. He simply grabbed Kristen's wrist and began to pull her toward the stairs, shouting over his shoulder at Selig: "Wait where you are."

Kristen tried to yank her hand loose from his grip, succeeding once halfway up the stairs, but he caught her again and continued to drag her after him. "Curse you, Saxon, you had better have a good reason for handling me so!"

He did not answer. He tossed her into his chamber and locked the door. She stared at it in amazement, tested it to be sure it was locked, then banged once on it in anger.

"Oh!"

In the hall below, Royce nodded to Selig to follow him, and he led him out to the front of the hall, shutting the door behind them. Selig turned, and Royce's fist slammed into his jaw, knocking him flat on his backside.

Royce stood over him, his face set in hard, angry lines. "I will not forbid you the hall, Gaelan, but I forbid you to go anywhere near that woman again. She belongs to me and I am careful of what is mine."

With that Royce reentered the hall. He left the doors open. Selig could have followed him back inside. He did not. He sat there on the ground fingering his jaw, a slow grin turning his lips, then finishing in a chuckle.

Upstairs, from the window that overlooked the front yard, Kristen had watched the whole exchange. Her hands had gripped the window ledge, until she heard that chuckle. She turned away, shaking her head, disgusted with all men in general.

Chapter Thirty-eight

A polished hand mirror sailed at his head when Royce opened the door to his chamber. A silver plate followed. He spotted Kristen across the room, digging through his coffer for something else to throw.

"You must not be angry, or you would be throwing weapons instead."

"Do not tempt me, Saxon!"

He had kept her locked in his chamber the whole day. She had not eaten. She had spoken to no one. She had lost her temper long ago.

"Why have you confined me?" she demanded.

"I woke this morn to find you gone. I went below to look for you and you were not there, either. I thought you had broken your word."

"You lock me in here for what you *thought* I did?" she stormed. "But you know I did not break my word, nor will I! So why?"

"What you were doing with the Celt is another matter," he said harshly.

"Is it?" she sneered. "And what am I supposed to have done with him?"

"'Tis what I want to know, Kristen."

"Then you had best ask him, for I am too furious with you to tell you aught!"

He closed the space between them in a few angry strides. Kristen joined her fists and raised them, daring him to take the last step. He stopped, glowering at her.

"Tell me you have no interest in the man."

"The devil take you!"

"Tell me!"

"I have no interest in him!"

"Then what were you doing outside with him?"

Kristen lowered her fists, her eyes widening. Incredulously, she asked, "Are you jealous, Saxon? Is that why you struck him?"

He glanced at the window, realizing how she would know that. But she could not have understood what he told the Celt. He looked back at her, frowning still.

"What I am is possessive, Kristen. No other man will touch you while you belong to me."

"And when you wed and I am gone from here, I will belong to you no more."

He grabbed her arms and gave her a rough shaking. "You will not leave me, vixen, ever. Now tell me what you were doing with the Celt!"

The anger had gone out of her with the realization that he really was jealous. Jealous of her. What an extraordinary concept that was.

She launched into a few white lies she hoped would appease him. "I did naught, Royce. I could not sleep, so I went for a walk and waited to watch the sunrise. When I noticed I was not alone in the yard, I came back inside. The man followed behind me. He said a few words to me at the door, but I did not understand him. I do not know what he was doing outside. You will have to ask him that. 'Twas probably no more than he was seeking fresh air, as I was."

Less harshly, more as a grumble, he ordered, "I do not want you outside at night, Kristen."

"You had not forbidden it, milord."

"I do now."

"Then the next time I cannot sleep, I will be sure to walk only in the hall so that I wake everyone," she replied sarcastically.

He smiled at last. "You can wake me instead, and I will see you have something to do other than walking."

She would have given him a wicked reply if a timid knock had not sounded on the door just then. Meghan peeked around the door after Royce's terse command to enter.

"Alden said I should tell you anger breeds anger, and violence breeds misery. What does he mean by that, Royce?"

Kristen burst into laughter, seeing Royce's look of surprise. "Oh, clever, that cousin of yours, milord. Did he think you meant to beat me, or that I would have clobbered you?" She laughed even harder when his green eyes stabbed her. "And he sends your sister... aye, he is very clever. Come in, sweetling. Your cousin Alden was just playing a silly prank to send you up here, but you are welcome."

Meghan moved to Kristen's side, whispering, "I thought Royce was angry."

"And you came anyway to deliver your message? How brave you really are."

Royce made a snarling noise deep in his throat as he looked away from them. Meghan's eyes rounded alarmingly. Kristen could have kicked him for frightening the child.

"Pay no attention to him, Meghan. He growls like most men growl. It means naught."

"Kristen..." Royce began warningly, glancing sharply back at her.

"Shush," she retorted. "I am giving your sister a valuable lesson. You see, sweetling, you do not have to be afraid of men when they are angry. What are they but a little bigger than you?" Meghan's eyes traveled up the length of Royce, and Kristen grinned. "Well, there are a few exceptions. But you take your brother here for an example. He was angry, and so was I. He shouted at me. I shouted back at him. And we both feel better for it now."

"But he is still angry." Meghan hid her face in Kristen's side.

"He is just being churlish, as men are wont to be. Of course, some anger runs much deeper and 'tis best to just stay out of the way of a man who is in a real rage. You will learn in time to judge the difference. But your brother . . . Have you ever seen him hurt a woman?" She gave a silent prayer the answer would be the correct one. It was not.

"He had you whipped."

"He did not know I was a woman then."

"He had you chained and your feet bled."

Kristen sighed. "Did I not tell you that was no more than a scratch, that I did not even feel it? And that was not his fault, sweetling. He had warned me to bind my ankles under the iron bands. 'Twas I who forgot to do it."

"Then, nay," Meghan conceded. "He has hurt no woman."

"Because he is a good, kind man beneath all his bluster. And if he would not hurt a woman, even in his anger, then he certainly would not hurt a child. And you can be even more certain he would not hurt his own sister. You, sweetling, could even get away with this." Kristen stepped over to Royce and kicked him solidly in the shin. "And he would do naught to you."

Royce stood still because Meghan had begun to giggle. He even wiped all emotion from his features while she still looked at him.

"You really would not hurt me, Royce?"

He smiled at her. "Nay, midget, never."

She ran forward to hug his waist. Then she did the same to Kristen.

With a grin, Meghan said, "Thank you, Kristen," before she ran out of the room.

"I thank you, too," Royce said from behind her. "I could never make her understand she should not fear me. But as for that kick, vixen . . ."

His arm went around her waist to lift her off her feet. He carried her to the bed, where he maneuvered her face-down across his lap.

"Royce, nay!" She could not believe he would. "I was only proving a point!"

"You could have proved it another way, wench. And until the pain goes away on my shin, you will feel some yourself on your backside."

Kristen ate her meal that night standing up. But she carried a secret smile on her lips. She might have gotten herself spanked for daring too much, but her Saxon had also made up for it afterward.

Chapter Thirty-nine

Kristen bemoaned the irony that Royce should offer to take her riding the next morning, when her backside was not up to it. She went anyway. How could she refuse when he gave her a horse to herself, when he suggested a race? Would she ever understand the man?

She lost the race, but enjoyed it anyway. It brought back carefree memories of racing Torden through field and forest. The horse she rode now was not as fine, but her companion made up for that.

Late in the morning, they stopped to water the horses from a rain-fed brook. The area was vibrant with summer colors, darkest greens and yellows and reds. The sky was clear for a change, the sun hot beyond the shade of the tree where Royce led her.

He sat down, leaning his back against the trunk and motioning her to come to him. Kristen ignored him and sat down by his feet instead. She plucked a blade of grass to worry between her teeth. Her eyes were soft as she looked at him.

Royce sighed. She might have given him her all the other night, but she was back to denying her willingness again. If he did not force her into his arms, she would not come.

"I thank you for the ride, milord."

He shrugged off his generosity. "Thorolf was right. You are used to riding. You do it well."

"I do many things well, but Thorolf would not know all of them."

"Such as?"

She stretched out her legs and put her hands back to lean on. Her thick tawny braid lay over her shoulder, the tail end fanned out on her lap. He watched the way the breeze stirred the ends.

She was looking up at the sky when she replied. "Thorolf does not know I have skill with weapons. None of them know. But you do."

"'Tis something I wish I did not know," he grunted.

Kristen grinned. "That is the attitude that has kept my secret, until I needed to use it."

"Who among them taught you, then?" he ventured. "Surely not your father?"

She shook her head. "Nay, most surely not him. My mother taught me."

"Your—" He could not finish for the laughter.

Kristen smiled tolerantly. "Laugh all you like, milord, but 'tis true."

"Oh, I have no doubt." He chuckled still. "And what else would this warlike mother teach you?"

Now Kristen laughed. She pictured her beautiful, delicate mother in her mind. Warlike? God's teeth! There was no one who looked less warlike.

"My mother might turn her nose at cooking and sewing, for she never acquired an enjoyment for such. But she is not warlike, milord. And she did teach me another valuable lesson. She taught me to feel no shame in wanting a man."

Royce sobered instantly. She might as well have run her hands over his body. Those words had the same effect.

"And you feel no shame?"

"Nay."

"And you want me, Kristen?"

"Nay."

His grin matched her own. "Liar. You admitted it once before. Why will you not do so again?"

"I told you I would not and I will not."

"You told me that in argument over your restrictions. You are no longer chained."

"I beg to differ," she replied quietly, her humor gone. "You have me chained by my word now, which is just as effective. You could have simply asked me to stay. Instead you had to bargain again."

"God's breath! Do not try to tell me you would stay simply because I ask it."

"You will never know, will you, Royce?"

"Kristen—"

He had started to lean forward, but the arrow, entering his shoulder, threw him back against the tree trunk. And it had enough force to exit his back and embed in the trunk. He tried to pull away. When he could not, a vision of the Danes' attack flashed through his mind, Rhona screaming for his help, and he unable to aid her because he was impaled to the wall.

His blood turned cold as he looked at Kristen jumping to her feet. "Take my horse and ride! Quickly!"

She straddled his hips instead as another arrow struck the tree above their heads. Swiftly she broke off the end of the arrow close to his skin.

"I will pull you loose, but you must help," she told him urgently.

"Kristen, just go." His voice was urgent. "Please. You must get away from here."

"Push!"

She yanked so hard he did not have to help. He fell forward onto his knees. Blood began spreading on both sides of his tunic. She bit her lip, thinking she would have to get him to his feet now. He rose on his own. There was no weakening yet. And he was furious with her.

"If you do not get on that horse, woman, and ride for safety now—"

"Only if you ride with me," she cut in, her tone more adamant than it had ever been.

The opportunity was lost. Well-armed men began emerging from behind trees and shrubs. Kristen counted five that she could see.

"Get behind me, Kristen," Royce ordered as he drew his sword.

She gasped. "You cannot mean to fight them all, not with your wound!"

"They will not take you, not while I live."

"Very commendable," the voice sneered behind them, and Lord Eldred stepped out from behind the tree under which they stood. He had two more men with him. "But we will take her, and you too, I think."

Eldred made a grab for Kristen. She twisted her way loose from him, but his two men were swift to help subdue her. A blade materialized at her throat and she stopped struggling.

Eldred's smile was loathsome in its humor. "Now your sword, Royce, or you know what I will order done to her."

The sword dropped to the ground. Eldred gave sharp orders then to his men. Kristen flinched as her hands were gripped together in front of her and a rope was wrapped about them. She watched helplessly as the same was done to Royce.

Eldred gloated as they were dragged to their horses. "I must thank you for coming my way, Royce, and for bringing her along. This is an unexpected pleasure, after I thought I would have to waste my time in your forest, waiting to find you alone. And now I have a double prize."

They rode north for the rest of the day. By eventide

they came to their destination: a hall, much smaller than Wyndhurst, but well fortified.

Royce was still able to dismount by himself, but his legs were not so steady now. Kristen bit her lip to keep from crying, seeing the extent of the blood soaking his tunic. She assumed this was Eldred's manor, but she did not guess he was not lord here until Royce tried to reason with Eldred.

"Your father—"

"Will not help you." Eldred cut him short with a tinge of bitterness now in his tone. "He has gone to beg Alfred to reconsider and let me return to court. My father does not like me at home, you see. He says I impregnate all his slaves, and nine months after my coming, he has no one to serve him." And then he added with anger to his men, "Take him to the storeroom and chain him to the wall."

"His wound—" Kristen began, but Eldred cut her off, too.

"Will bleed, just as you will bleed when I am finished with you."

Royce began to fight, hearing that, but one of the men rendered him unconscious with the hilt of his sword. Kristen had to watch as he was dragged away. And then she was prodded with the tip of a sword into the hall.

It was a slovenly place, built all of wood, and all on the one floor. The rushes she walked over were filthy. The servants she saw were frightened creatures, not even daring to look at her or the men who pushed her to the back of the hall.

There she was shoved into a tiny, windowless chamber. The door was slammed shut behind her, leaving her in darkness. She did not bother to see if it was locked, hearing the wooden bar falling into place.

Laughter was also heard, from the other side as the men walked away.

She had seen a bed before the door closed off the light. She made her way slowly toward it and sat down. She was not going to become hysterical. She had been through this before: captured, not knowing what would happen next. Only she had an idea what would happen next this time.

A shiver passed through her, thinking of Eldred. He hated Royce. He wanted to hurt him, to make him suffer, mayhap even . . . Oh, God, why else would he bring him here except to kill him, probably slowly?

Hysteria began to rise.

Chapter Forty

Kristen was able to hear Lord Eldred out in his hall. He was eating, drinking; he was celebrating. But as long as she could hear him, she could hope that nothing had been done to Royce yet, telling herself that Eldred, in his hate, would want to be there for whatever he ordered done to Royce, or want to do it himself.

Thinking that, she was able to calm herself, to plan. She had to get out of this room as soon as the door opened. She had to make her way to the storeroom where she had seen them taking Royce. She had to get him loose, then get their horses . . . God help her, *how*, with so many people about?

She made a search of the room with her hands, cursing the dark which made it take so long. But she had the time. No one came to interrupt her. But the room yielded nothing that she could use as a weapon. She had not really thought it would, but she had to be sure.

That left only herself and her wits. She doubted Eldred would be easy to dupe, but he might be overcome, if he had imbibed too much, and if he were alone. When he did finally come, he was alone and had been drinking, but he did not seem drunk, not at all.

He carried a candle, which he set on an empty wall shelf after he closed the door. Kristen saw now that the room was completely empty, except for the bed, but she saw it in the briefest glance, not daring to take her eyes from Eldred for too long.

He had a look of anticipation about him. He even

smiled at her as he faced her. His sword still hung from his belt. But now there was a short whip there also, made of numerous thin leather strips.

"What have you done to Royce?" It came out in a whisper, full of hope.

"I have not seen him yet," Eldred told her casually. "I decided I would deal with you first, so I could then tell him all about it. Lord Alden seemed to think Royce has a care for you. We will see."

"You mistake," she hastened to assure him. "He has a betrothed."

"What has that to do with the wench he beds?"

Kristen flinched at the insult. What, indeed? "Why do you hate him so?"

"He is blessed. He can do no wrong—or so Alfred thinks, has always thought."

"Envy?" Her eyes moved over him with contempt. "For petty envy you do this?"

"What do you know of it?" he snapped. "You do not know what 'tis like to compete, to always be found lacking."

"Nay, I do not. But I do know you cannot get away with this. Too many people saw that you brought us here."

He laughed. "My people would not dare say aught against me. Unlike you, wench, they know their place."

"They are your father's people," she taunted him. "He will find out."

He leaped at her, slapping her hard. Her face turned; her body did not budge. This gave Eldred a momentary surprise. He was used to women falling down from his powerful blows, and then cowering in fear. But this woman was of a size with him. And she did not cower. Blood trickled from the corner of her mouth, but her eyes flashed with fury as she looked back at him.

Eldred stepped back, somewhat unnerved. And this

made him angry, that he should be leery of a woman. He pulled loose the whip from his belt. She would cower before he was done with her, by God—cower and beg.

He drew back the whip and put all his strength into the first blow. She tried to step aside, but it caught her on her bare arm and half her back. Satisfaction surged through him, hearing her gasp. He drew the whip back again. That was when she threw herself at him, knocking him to the floor.

He lost his breath, taking her full weight upon him. But he kept a firm grip on the whip, thinking she would try to wrest it from him. That was his mistake. She went for and came away with his sword, and he was thrown half into shock, feeling the tip of it press into his throat.

"Move even a little, milord, and I will skewer you to the floor." Her warning was all the more frightening for the quiet way she said it. "I might anyway, for what you have done."

It was the last Eldred heard, for she slammed the hilt of his sword against his temple.

Kristen quickly cut her bonds, careful to do so near the knot so she could use the rope on Eldred. This she did just as quickly, turning him over and tying his hands behind him. That had been his mistake: tying her hands in front of her, which still gave her some use of them. But his main mistake had been in thinking she would stand there and let him whip her.

He wasn't dead. *More's the pity,* she thought. *I should have killed him.* She still gave it some thought as she sliced strips from the bedding to bind his feet too and gag his mouth. But in the end she couldn't bring herself to kill a helpless man.

Now she waited for no more sounds to be heard out in the hall. Eldred regained consciousness, and she clobbered him again. She could have taken pleasure in doing that all night, but did not have all night. She left the tiny chamber as soon as all was quiet without.

A single torch burned on the other side of the hall. The servants were all sleeping, their pallets lining the walls. Kristen walked straight to the entrance door without pause, her breath held, her heart pounding. No alarm was sounded. But there was a guard outside the door, one of those men who had captured them.

The man was as surprised to see her as she was to see him. She was too accustomed to a lack of sentries at Wyndhurst. Eldred must have more to fear, or he expected trouble after what he had done.

The man was even more surprised when he saw the sword she carried. He made to draw his own, but she had the advantage of having hers in hand already. She pierced him before he could defend himself.

There was no time to waste now. She ran toward the storeroom and threw the door open. There was another guard inside, who woke and started to rise. She gave him a taste of the sword hilt, too, and he slumped back down.

Royce was indeed chained to the wall, both hands stretched out a little above his head, supporting his full weight. His wound had bled more. The red stain ran in a path clear down one leg. His head was bent over on his shoulder. She could not even be sure he still lived.

She found out, running to him, taking his head in her hands. She patted his cheek, harder, harder still until his eyes opened. Relief paralyzed her.

"How?"

It was his only question. It brought her back to her senses. She ran back to the guard, searching for the key to his shackles.

Over her shoulder she said, "I wounded a man, mayhap even killed him. Will your Saxon law punish me for it?"

Her fingers finally closed over the key and she hurried back to Royce. He was shaking his head at her.

"Is that all you are worried about?"

"I do not know how your law works," she replied tersely. "I only know that by your law I was wrong the last time I defended myself. Am I wrong this time, to try to leave this place any way I can?"

He started to laugh, but choked it off when it hurt. "Nay, you have done more than I could have hoped for."

"Good." She smiled at him, unlocking his wrist manacles. "Now let us be gone from here, milord."

But Royce sagged to his knees when he was completely freed. Seeing how weak he was, Kristen quickly ripped off the hem of her gown. Dividing it in two, she stuffed it inside his tunic, front and back. They would have to ride hard, and he could not afford to lose any more blood. But she could not bandage him properly now, either. She could only pray that he could ride.

It was slow going to the stable, with her having to support Royce. As heavy as he was, it was not easy even for her. And then she had to let go of him to take care of the guard in the stable.

Royce was stretched out on the ground when she came back to him. She felt like crying then, but forced him back to consciousness, forced him back to his feet, and forced him to garner the last of his strength to mount his horse.

"How do you propose—to get through the gate?"

"Let me worry about it," she answered.

Worried she was. She led his horse and her own, walking the distance across the quiet yard. The gate was high and wooden, with a long, heavy bar across it. There was a narrow platform above, off to the side, with a guard there, sitting with his back to the wall. He was asleep. Kristen carefully mounted the ladder to him and saw that he remained asleep, then hurried down and threw her weight into lifting off the heavy bar.

It was indeed heavy. She could not manage to lower it gently to the ground, but had to drop it. The noise slammed through her.

She looked about, expecting to see a legion of armed men running toward them. Her heart nearly stopped when she did see one man, a serf, step out from the stable. He yawned and went back inside. There was another, in the doorway of another building. He just stood there watching them.

Relief soared as she realized they were not going to sound any alarm. They were apathetic, uncaring, and not willing to stir themselves for their lord. It was fortuitous for her and Royce that Lord Eldred had such loyalty in his household.

Kristen nearly laughed at the thought as she pushed the gate open and then grabbed up the reins of Royce's horse before she leaped onto her own. They rode swiftly through what remained of the night.

Chapter Forty-one

Kristen was exhausted and beside herself with worry. Royce was using the last of his strength just to stay on his horse. She had stopped once to pad his shoulder again, but he had lost so much blood, too much. He slumped over his horse now, barely conscious.

Not even sight of the walls of Wyndhurst could abate her worry. Dawn streaked the sky and they had been seen approaching. The gate was being opened; men were rushing out. Another group on horseback had spotted them and came from the woods. Soon Royce could rest and be tended properly. Yet the nagging fear would not let go that it might not do any good, that she had helped him so inadequately that he was going to die anyway.

She cried out when he fell from his horse. She leaped from her own mount and ran to him, lifting his head from the ground. His eyes were open, but he seemed dazed.

"Must have—fallen asleep."

Oh, God, he did not even know what he was saying. Her heart cried, seeing him this weak and helpless. She was not aware that tears streamed from her eyes.

"Be quiet, Royce. Be still. They will be here in a moment to help you."

His eyes found her face. "Will you at last admit you want me, Kristen?"

God's teeth! How could he think of that now, when his life's blood was draining out of him?

"Kristen?"

"Aye, I want you. I swear I do."

"Have you come to love me—a little?"

She did not hesitate. "Aye, that too."

One hand rose to slip behind her neck and pull her face down to his. His lips were warm and dry on hers, gentle, but only at first. Out of her misery came the realization that there was too much strength in the hand holding her, too much passion in this kiss.

She pulled back, her eyes narrowing as she saw him grin at her. "You are not dying!"

"Did you think I was?"

"Oh, unfair!"

She nearly hit him, especially when he began to chuckle. Instead she got up and stalked away.

It had taken more than a paltry wound to weaken Royce. He stayed to his bed no more than four days. In a week he was about his full duties again. And after two weeks, his wound gave him only an occasional twinge.

He had dealt with Eldred not as he wanted, but as Alfred's current policies dictated. He had simply informed the King of Eldred's perfidy. It was nearing the end of summer when he learned that Eldred had panicked, fearing retribution, and flown north, seeking refuge with the Danes. His body had been sent home to his father.

When Royce told Kristen this, she had simply shrugged, remarking that such a petty lordling was like to come to a bad end. She brought very little emotion to bear on the matter.

She had been angry with Royce, the more so when she realized he had deliberately refrained from helping in their escape. In no uncertain terms she told him what she thought of his deception, yet he could not be sorry he had taken that opportunity to test her. She could have left him at any point on their journey home. Instead she led him to safety. That meant more to him than he could say.

And Kristen did not stay angry. She was gentle and teasing with him while he regained his strength, keeping him from fretting over his weakened state. She almost made him wish for more wounds that she could fuss over. It was the exact opposite of what he would have felt if Darrelle had nursed him.

It was with the waning of summer that Kristen grew melancholy, and no matter how often Royce asked her, she would not admit anything was wrong. He took her swimming often, he took her riding, and she would smile for him, laugh with him. But he would still see sadness in her eyes when she was not aware he watched her.

He cut her labors in the hall down to half. When that did not make her happy, he doubled them. That did not work, either. He even gave her her own clothes to wear, but she refused to put them on, in fact seemed more depressed after seeing the dark-green velvet gown.

Royce didn't know what else to do. But the day Kristen asked him again when he would marry, he was afraid he had the answer to what was wrong. She still wanted to leave him. That was why she was miserable. She was counting the days till he wed and she was released from her word. But he was not going to let her go, so there was only one other thing to do.

He would have been amazed had he known what really bothered Kristen. It was the time, summer's end, when she and Selig and the others would have returned home from the market towns—if that was where they had gone. The whole summer long, her parents would have worried about her, but it would have been with the certainty that she would return. Only now, at summer's end, the real anxiety would begin, with the daily waiting for the ship. And with each day the ship did not come, the anxiety would increase. How could she find happiness here, knowing what her parents must be going through now?

She had managed to speak to Selig again. She had begged him to leave, to find his way home somehow, so at least their parents would know she was safe. He refused, not only because he could not leave her, but because he was sure Garrick would tear him apart if he came home without her.

Royce tried hard to cheer her. She loved him more for that. But she could not tell him what was wrong, for the only thing he could do for her would be to let her go, and she had a deep fear that he would even do that. She was damned either way. It would destroy her to leave Royce now, yet she ached with wanting her parents to know she was all right. And she couldn't stop thinking about them.

For the first time that whole summer, Royce left Wyndhurst. He was gone for two days. No one knew where he went, but when he came back, he informed Darrelle that he had arranged her marriage. And she burst into tears because he would not tell her who her husband was to be, promising only that she would approve his choice.

Kristen for once could not blame Darrelle for crying. She knew she would not have stood for such secretiveness about so important a matter. Yet all Royce would do was insist Darrelle needed the time to get used to the idea of being wed, before she learned to whom.

That night in bed, she told Royce plainly, "'Tis unfair, you know, to keep your cousin in such suspense."

He chuckled, disagreeing. "You do not know Darrelle. At this moment, she will be making a list with her maid of all the men she knows and wondering which one will be her husband. Instead of worrying about leaving here, she will become excited in wondering where she will be leaving to."

"You do not think she fears your choice?"

"I told her she would approve him, and she knows she can trust in that. She is simply impatient. Will you be impatient, too, when I tell you I have a surprise for you as well?"

Kristen raised a brow. "A surprise you do not intend to tell me about, either?" He only grinned in answer. "I can be patient, I suppose, if you tell me when you will tell me about it."

"All in good time."

Kristen went to sleep that night in a much lighter mood than she had felt for some time. If Royce had done anything with his secrets, he had managed to distract her from her woes.

Chapter Forty-two

It was a nasty sting, sharp enough to wake Royce from his slumber. His hand came up to swipe the offending insect away from his neck. Fingers encountered cold metal instead, and the sharp point of the dagger pressed more firmly into the side of his neck, warning his hand away.

He was not dreaming. He could feel Kristen snuggled close to his left side, one hand resting slack against his chest. And on his right the sting of pain was too real. He could not see his assailant in the dark, but the man had managed to come stealthily into his chamber to threaten his life. And since no one of Wyndhurst would do so, he came to the most likely conclusion: The Vikings had escaped. And if they could get to his chamber, were all dead below?

Kristen had sworn there would be no slaughter, that they would simply leave if they could. Had they merely come for her, then? He was not going to let them take her with them. They would have to kill him first. And he realized that would not be so difficult, as the situation stood.

"Can you understand what I say?"

The muscles in his chest tightened. The husky whisper was indeed clear to him. No Viking tongue, but a Celtic one. Gaelan? Nay, the voice was not deep enough. The Vikings had not escaped, then, but just as bad, the Celts were raiding again. And they dared come into his hall this time.

"Answer, Saxon!" Still a whisper, but angry now.

"Aye, I understand you."

"Good."

The pressure of the dagger slackened and then the blade was lying across his neck, where it would only take the slightest jerk to sever his jugular. He could not move yet. He had to lie there and accept what came next. Anger rose from such impotence.

"State your demands!" he hissed.

"Easy, Saxon," the whisper warned. "I come for answers while they still fight amongst themselves. I am not so quick to judge until I know all the facts."

Royce frowned into the dark. He could make no sense out of what had just been said. He could hear no fighting. In fact, he heard nothing but their own breathing. The hall was as quiet as it should be in the middle of the night. All either still slept, or were dead.

"Who—"

The blade drew blood, silencing him. Kristen stirred at his side. He tried to relax the arm she lay on. He did not want her waking to this.

"I will ask the questions, Saxon. You will answer truthfully if you value your life."

This made less and less sense. What knowledge could he have that would interest a Celt? And who was fighting amongst themselves?

Royce said quietly, "I will tell you whatever you want, if you let the woman go."

"Let her go?" It was said in surprise, but he was not prepared for what the Celt said next. " 'Tis my daughter you sleep with. Has your Saxon church given you this right?"

Royce closed his eyes. He had not heard right. He couldn't have. Kristen's father was no Celt.

Impatiently the voice continued: " 'Tis no question

that requires thought, Saxon. Either you have the right from your church, or you do not."

"I do not."

"Then has my daughter given you the right?"

Royce felt like laughing suddenly, this was so unbelievable. "I think you have made a mistake. 'Tis no Celtic wench I sleep with."

The blade pressed again against his neck. "I have not much time to learn the truth, so do not waste it with evasions. Kristen is my daughter, and I make no mistake in who you are."

The whisper was gone. She spoke in a clear, husky voice—a woman.

Royce said incredulously, "You are her *mother?*"

"God save me, who the devil did you think I was?"

"Not a woman!" he growled.

Kristen could not sleep through that. "Royce, what—"

"Be still, love, or this blade I hold to his neck is going to slip deeper."

"Mother! Oh, God, it is really you? How—"

"Kristen, be still!" Royce added his warning as she sat up, shaking the bed, and more blood trickled down his neck.

"What blade?" Kristen asked, and then cried in alarm: "Oh, nay, Mother, do not hurt him!"

"Do not?" Brenna removed the dagger, throwing her arms up in exasperation. "Do not hurt him, after all Ohthere has told us he has done to you? He *whipped* you!"

"That was a mistake," Kristen said, pushing Royce back down as he started to sit up. "Did Thorolf not tell you so?"

Brenna paused. "Mayhap he would have, but your uncle Hugh gave him one of his fists when he started to speak in the Saxon's behalf. I think he still sleeps."

"Uncle Hugh is here too?"

Royce caught Kristen's arms and sat up despite her effort to keep him down. "You lied to me," he said coldly. "You said you could not understand Gaelan, and yet you speak to your mother in the same Celtic tongue."

"Of course I do. We both learned it from her. Gaelan is my brother."

"Selig?"

"Aye."

"Then you lied about his death!"

"Nay! I thought he was dead. It took him a long while to recover from his wound and find me. But I could not tell you who he was. You would have put him in chains with the others if you knew he was a Viking."

His hold on her relaxed as he remembered her strange behavior the day Gaelan—or, rather, Selig—showed up. He brought one hand to her cheek, the fingers gentle there as he leaned close to brush his lips against hers.

"I am sorry," he said simply.

"How sweet," Brenna sneered. "If you two are done fighting and making up, there is still a serious matter to be faced. Your father wants your Saxon's blood, Kristen."

"Nay!"

"'Tis not as simple as that," Brenna said sternly. "I was only able to slip away and come in here because they argue among themselves—Garrick, Hugh, and your brother—not about *whether* to kill him but about who will have the pleasure of it."

"Not Selig," Kristen insisted. "He knows how I feel."

"Mayhap. But once he heard of the whipping—"

"That again!" Kristen cried impatiently. "'Twas naught—two minor lashes. 'Twas ordered done when he thought I was a lad and he was after the truth. He stopped it as soon as he saw I was a woman."

"Then you should have explained that to Selig, instead of letting him hear about it from Ohthere—who, I am sure, understood naught of it but what he saw."

"*I* never blamed Royce for it. How can they? Thorolf knows. Oh, curse Uncle Hugh for being so quick-tempered and striking him down."

"They are all angry, love. Did you think it would be otherwise when we come here and find you enslaved and forced to share the bed of your captor?"

"I will kill Selig!" Kristen stormed. "He knows I am not forced. Why did he not tell you so?"

Brenna laughed at her daughter's vehemence. "Mayhap he lost sight of that in his anger. But I am glad to hear it. Now calm down, love. Getting angry yourself is not going to solve aught."

Royce asked with forced evenness, "Am I to assume you have freed my prisoners?"

"Aye," Brenna replied. "That was the easy part. Your yard is not well guarded, Saxon."

"The patrol in the woods?"

"Taken."

"You mean killed!"

"A few were. It could not be helped. Your guard on the gate also. The only reason we withdrew outside your walls without taking your hall is that you have Kristen inside it. You have the upper hand as long as you hold her. But they will not go away, Saxon."

"My name is Royce," he said curtly.

"And mine is Brenna. And if we have come to first names, then let me tell you: I could have killed you while you still slept and taken my daughter out of here to safety."

"Your men apparently want my blood," he returned angrily. "Why not you as well?"

"I did think of it."

"Mother!" Kristen protested.

"'Tis true, love. As God is my witness, I wanted to see him and all his people dead. I finally understood, after all these years, how your grandfather felt, and why he sought revenge against my people for what had been done to your father when he was captured in a raid. I came here for revenge myself, just as Anselm did when he captured me."

"But how did you know where to find us?"

"Ivarr's wife. You know what a worrier she is. Ivarr had told her what they planned, and long before the ship could be expected back, she came to Garrick and confessed all. But we thought we came for naught when we found Jurro monastery only a ruin. We thought the men had succeeded in the raid and we had left home too soon, that you were probably there now. We were making our way back to the ships—"

"More than one ship?" Royce interrupted.

"Three," Brenna replied. "So if you were thinking about fighting us, do not. We came prepared to fight, with over a hundred men."

Kristen found his hand. "You would not fight my father, would you?"

He only grunted in answer. Brenna made a sound very like it. "He may not have a choice, Kristen."

"Nay, there will be no fighting," Kristen insisted stubbornly. She scrambled out of bed, pulling the sheet with her. "Mother, I—Oh, God's teeth! I want to see you, Mother. Stay where you are." She swiped up a candle and left the chamber to find a torch to light it.

Royce reached for his clothes, then proceeded to calmly put them on. "You said why you wanted to kill me, Brenna. Now tell me why you did not."

"Because I was captured and enslaved once myself, yet I came to love the man I was given to. Garrick is my husband. He has come here not as a Viking, but as a father. And 'tis the father you will have to deal with."

"I could take you now," he speculated, strapping on his sword. "I would then have two hostages to bargain with."

There was soft laughter from across the room. "I would not try it."

He said nothing as light moved toward the door. A moment later, Kristen appeared, shielding the candle with her hand, with the sheet drawn over her shoulders and around her.

"Oh, Mother, put that down," Kristen chided. "He is not going to attack you."

With light now, Royce was staring at an evil-looking crossbow trained on his chest, and it was not even one of his own. Brenna had brought it with her.

He began to laugh at his own foolishness in underestimating the woman. He would have been in for quite a surprise if he had tried to disarm her in the dark.

Kristen scowled at him, seeing his hand on his sword hilt. He grinned at her, putting both hands up in surrender. And then he watched as mother and daughter were reunited, Kristen running into Brenna's outstretched arms. But it was Kristen who towered over her mother.

Royce shook his head, amazed. How could this woman be Kristen's mother? She was so small, so petite, her slender form molded snugly in a black velvet gown. Long raven hair was braided down her back, and tender gray eyes moved over Kristen's face as she held it cupped in her hands. Her coloring was that of the brother's, which could only make him assume Kristen took after her father. And yet her face was so like Kristen's. But, God's breath, she did not look old enough to be a mother. The woman was beautiful.

"You did not explain how you found us here," Kristen was saying.

"'Twas Perrin, making a wide circle of this area, who

found this place today, and saw the men working in the yard. We withdrew to the forest, to await night."

"Oh, Mother, you cannot know how glad I am to see you!" Kristen said, still hugging her tight. "I have been so miserable of late, knowing you would be waiting for our ship to come home, now that winter grows near, and knowing how upset you would be when it did not."

"*That* is why you have been depressed?" Royce said incredulously.

Kristen glanced toward the bed, looking rather shamefaced. "Aye. I am sorry I did not tell you, Royce, but there was naught you could do about it."

"I thought . . . Never mind," he said testily. "Next time tell me and let me judge whether I can help or not."

"There is no more time to waste with questions of your own, children," Brenna said matter-of-factly. "You must answer mine, and quickly: Will you marry my daughter, Royce?"

"Mother!" Kristen cried. "You cannot ask him that!"

"I must," Brenna insisted. "I must have something to appease your father with, although it may be too late to matter."

"I will not have a forced marriage," Kristen said stiffly. "And he has a betrothed. He cannot marry me."

Brenna looked to Royce with raised brow. He smiled at her. "The betrothal she mentions has been broken."

"What!" Kristen gasped. "When?"

"When I was gone those two days, I went to Raedwood to speak to Corliss's father. He was not too disappointed that I did not want his daughter, when I offered Darrelle for his son, Wilburt, instead."

"This was the surprise you said you had for me?"

"Nay, your own wedding was the surprise, though I was not sure you would agree. You were tricked into admitting you love me, and I have not heard you say it since."

"You really meant to marry *me?*"

"Aye."

"Oh, Royce!" She threw herself at him, knocking him back onto the bed.

"Then you do love my daughter?" Brenna interrupted their kiss.

"Mother!" Kristen rolled over. "God's teeth! I have heard none of this before, and now I must hear it in front of you, and by coercion? Is that any way—"

"Be quiet, love. I have no time to cater to your sensibilities. 'Tis no fault of mine if he has not told you until now, but I will hear him say it."

Royce said it. "I love her."

"It means naught when you are forced to say it," Kristen grumbled.

He caught her chin, bringing her eyes to his. "Do you really think I could be forced to say it, vixen? I love you."

Behind them, Brenna chuckled. "Your father came just as late to admitting it, Kristen."

Kristen was smiling quite bemusedly. She did not even hear her mother. But Royce could not ignore Brenna's presence, no matter how much he wished her gone at the moment.

Soberly he said, "And now what?"

"Now I have my answers I will leave as I came, and hope I can talk some sense—"

"Brenna!"

Royce saw both women cringe at the sound of that booming voice outside the window. It raised the hairs on his own neck.

"God save us, I knew it was too much to hope he would not find me gone."

"Brenna, answer!" Garrick bellowed again.

"Your father?" Royce ventured.

"Aye."

"And he speaks the Celtic tongue, too?"

"I told you his mother was Christian. She was a Celt—"

Brenna cut in sharply. "You had best make haste below, Royce. Garrick has no doubt awakened your men. See they do not leave the hall armed, or they will be cut down." She did not wait to see if he obeyed, but rushed to the window, calling down, "God's teeth, Viking, you do not have to shout down the hall. I am here, safe, and Kristen is with me. Nay! Do not come inside, Garrick. I will come to you."

Kristen had moved to the window beside her mother the moment Royce left the chamber. Torchlight illuminated the whole yard below, and what she saw were more than a hundred Vikings—helmeted, armed with sword and axe, and ready to storm the hall. She could only pray Royce would not call his men to arm. They would not stand a chance.

Chapter Forty-three

"Nay! Nay, Thorolf, you cannot mean it! Let me speak to him."

It was morning, but the hall was still quiet. Women cried silently and prayed. The men solemnly sharped their weapons.

Brenna had gone back to Garrick, but he had not allowed her to return. Thorolf had been sent instead to tell them what had been decided. The Vikings had withdrawn outside the walls again. Kristen had waited with Royce throughout the rest of the night. They had waited for an attack, an ultimatum, but not for what Thorolf had been instructed to say.

She stood with Royce by the entrance, where they had met Thorolf. He had come unarmed at first light. His jaw was twice its size, testimony to her uncle Hugh's hot temper. He had spoken only to her, leaving it to her to interpret his words for Royce. She had not done that yet.

"You can come with me now to see him," Thorolf told her plainly. "But if you leave this hall, your Saxon loses his only bargaining power. I do not think you want that."

"Then bring him here to me."

Thorolf shook his head. "He will not come. He trusts no Saxon."

"You came!"

"Aye." He grinned. "But I trust in your ability to

keep your man from slitting my throat. Your father has not witnessed the power you have over him, as I have."

She was angry enough to say, "For minor things, mayhap, but not over something that pertains to the safety of his people!"

Thorolf was not daunted. If he was going to be cut down, it would have been done already. But the Saxon just stood beside them, his face inscrutable. He did not even seem impatient to learn what they were arguing about.

"Do you tell him?" he asked. "If I have to, he may not understand clearly."

"Thorolf, please! This cannot happen. I love them both. There can be no winner for me!"

"I do not think that has been taken into account. Sixteen of us have been enslaved, forced to labor for these Saxons. Not all want revenge for that. A few would even like to stay and settle here, if they could do so as free men. But those who do not want revenge have brothers and fathers here now who do."

"Oh, unfair!" she cried. " 'Tis the risk they took when they raided here!"

"They do not see it so."

"God's teeth! Did my mother not speak to my father at all?"

"They spoke long—or, more like, argued. It was afterward the decision was made."

"Did my mother approve this?"

"Nay, she did not, but like yourself, she had no say in it. As Jarl, your uncle is in command. He has the final say, and he agreed. And your father was chosen unanimously, the feeling being he bears the most enmity against the Saxon because of your involvement. Now tell him, Kristen. The hour grows near."

She looked at Royce. Her face was stark, bloodless. Abject misery poured from her eyes. How could she tell him? She had to tell him. God help her, she was going to be destroyed this day.

Her voice was hollow. "You are challenged, milord. They have chosen their champion and you will fight only him. Do you defeat him, they will leave."

Royce trampled on her heart by smiling at her. "This is better than I could have hoped for, Kristen. Why do you look so? Do you fear I cannot win?"

"There is that," she said wretchedly.

"Very well. What will happen if I am defeated?"

He exuded confidence. She could not meet his eyes. "Alden will still have me to bargain with. 'Tis my uncle Hugh who is in command. He does not think you will kill me, but he is not so sure about another Saxon. Hugh will not risk my life. They will leave if I am given to them. Your people will be safe either way."

"So 'tis only me they bear malice against?"

"Aye. A Viking would rather die in battle than be enslaved, for there is no honor in capture. You forced on them what they hate the most."

"And yet they will be satisfied if I win?"

"They are fighting men, Royce. They fight for sport or the slightest insult; it matters not why. Men die at our feasts from what could begin as a simple argument. Friends fight friends—'tis the challenge they thrive on. But the victor is always revered as the better man. They send you their best. They do not think you can defeat him, but if you do, you will have proved your strength and be respected for it."

He tilted her chin up, forcing her to look at him. "Yet this still distresses you? Do you want me to refuse this challenge?"

She groaned. "You cannot. My mother must have told them you will not harm me no matter what. As I said, my uncle is sure of it. They will attack your hall if you do not fight, Royce. You have no choice if you want to spare your people."

"Then they could attack even now, yet they challenge me instead. 'Tis fair, Kristen. So do not fret so. I cannot lose."

She choked, then turned and ran toward the stairs. Royce frowned after her until she disappeared above. Then he glanced sharply at Thorolf.

"What did you tell Kristen that has upset her so?" Royce demanded.

Thorolf's head hurt from trying to follow their rapid conversation. He had given up after he was certain the Saxon knew he was challenged. But he must know why Kristen would naturally be upset. He must mean something else.

Thorolf shrugged. "Garrick furious with Selig . . . lose ship . . . bring Kristen here. Will likely thrash."

Royce continued to frown. Could worry for her brother make her look so stricken? Mayhap so, when combined with worry over the outcome of this fight.

"When does your man come?" he questioned.

"Have time only to prepare."

"Does he come fully armed?"

"Aye."

Royce dismissed Thorolf with a nod. He sent a man to his chamber to get his armor while he told Alden what was to happen, and gave him instructions on the unlikely chance he was defeated. A short time later he was helmeted and weighted down with chainmail. Alden was sharpening his sword when the call came from outside.

Royce stepped outside, his sword in one hand, his shield in the other. The Vikings had all come inside the yard, yet they had spread out along the outer walls, their shields and swords lying at their feet as a sign they were only there to watch. Seeing this, Royce's own men began to come outside the hall, and he gave the order that they were likewise to put down their weapons. He saw Kristen's mother, gripping the arm of the huge, barrel-chested man beside her. Kristen's father?

Royce did not wonder long, his attention drawn to his opponent, standing only a few feet away. He was a big man, mayhap even an inch or two taller than Royce. Powerful legs were spread apart and thickly gartered with leather, his only covering besides the conical helmet with its long noseguard that concealed most of his face. Muscles bulged across the wide chest and were tight across the flat stomach. The arms were like meaty clubs. Wide golden armbands circled his wrists, etched with dragon serpents. His large shield was covered with leather, with a two-inch spike in its center. And his double-edged sword was one of the finest-wrought weapons Royce had ever seen, the hilt richly engraved and inlaid with silver and gold.

Royce saw all this at a glance. That the man was bare-chested was a sign of contempt he could not ignore. He called Alden over to help him off with his own mail.

"Are you mad?" Alden wanted to know.

"Nay, he has the advantage if I am weighted down and he is not. I do not think this will be over with quickly, Cousin. I do not intend to give him any advantage."

A cheer went up from the Vikings when Royce bared his own chest. His opponent had stood there and let him. Alden handed him back his sword and shield, and Royce approached the man he must kill. And then he froze, seeing the aqua eyes staring out at him from beneath the eyeguards of the helmet. He swore violently, stepping back. He swore again, throwing his sword down on the ground between them.

Garrick lowered his own sword. "By Thor, she did not tell you, did she?"

"I cannot fight you!" Royce snarled angrily. "'Twould destroy her!"

"Is that the only reason you will not fight?"

The tone was insulting enough that Royce could not mistake the slur of cowardice. He nearly retrieved his sword. But Kristen's stricken face appeared in his mind and he clenched his fists tight against the impulse.

"Send me another to fight," Royce gritted low. "Send me that bear who stands next to your wife."

"Nay, my brother is in no condition to meet a man of your size and youth, though he would not admit it. You fight me or no one. Or did my daughter also neglect to tell you what would happen if you refuse to fight me?"

"She told me!"

"Then pick up your sword, Saxon. You know you have no choice."

"Are you sure you are not too old for this yourself, Viking?" Royce sneered. "I train in warfare daily, in preparation to meet your brethren the Danes. Yet I understand you are no more than a merchant."

"Oh, ho!" Garrick guffawed. "Now I have been well and truly challenged. You have one second before I start hacking you to bits, child."

Royce dove for his sword, rolling with it, and coming up on Garrick's left side. He had only that promised second before the first blow landed on his shield. Another followed before he found solid footing.

Brenna had been right. Kristen's father did want his blood. He did not let up once in his attack, raining blow after blow, driving Royce back across the yard. No Dane Royce had ever drawn his sword against had been this merciless. But then, no Dane had had such motivation. He was fighting an enraged father first, a Viking second. He was being made to pay for every time he had taken Kristen to his bed.

In the upstairs window of Royce's chamber, Kristen stood like a statue, watching the combat below. It was torture to watch, yet she could not pull her eyes away. Half a dozen times her heart had already dropped to her feet, when it looked as if Royce could not raise his shield in time, when he slipped and her father's blade had come within inches of him, when he finally began denting her father's shield.

They stood like bulwarks now, hammering away at each other, blow for blow. Kristen's lips bled where she bit them to keep from screaming. How long could they last like this? How long before . . .

Royce was knocked to the ground with the force of the last blow. Garrick swung at his right side, but Royce's feet tangled in his and Garrick went down as well. Royce was quicker to rise, and he had a clear opening to the Viking's midsection. He did not take it. He stuck his sword in the ground instead and threw off his helmet.

"I am done!" he snarled. "I could have killed you then!"

Garrick was slower to rise. He put his swordpoint to Royce's chest and held it there for an agonizing moment, then stuck it in the ground, too. He also tossed his helmet aside, shaking loose his thick mane of golden hair.

"Aye, we would both be fools to continue, for I cannot kill you, either. But I feel no such qualms about this."

The fist caught under Royce's jaw, putting him flat on his back again. But he rolled over quickly and, with a mighty thrust, plowed his shoulder into Garrick's belly. The fight was still in earnest, but with fists now instead of swords.

Upstairs, Kristen began to cry in relief. Across the yard, Brenna turned away to hide her own tears. Both women smiled, sure now that their men would live. The Vikings did not so much care that the thrust of the fight had changed. They still cheered on their man, as did the Saxons across from them.

When it was finished a long while later, Royce could not raise his head to save his soul. Garrick, still on his knees, was hailed the victor just before he keeled over on top of Royce. The yard was quiet then. The possibility that both men would still live had not been considered.

Kristen allowed no time for them to consider it at all. She ran toward the fallen combatants and gave orders they should both be taken into the hall. When no Saxon moved to obey her, she pierced Alden with a furious glare.

"Do not make me regret forgiving you, Saxon. Get them moving!"

He did, and Kristen quickly picked up one of the discarded swords as her uncle and most of the others approached. She faced Hugh with it, brandishing it before her.

"It is done, Uncle Hugh," she warned him angrily. "I am going to marry that Saxon now, and woe betide anyone who dares to stop me. He has fought for the right to demand peace. Give it to him."

Hugh threw back his head and laughed mightily. He slapped Brenna on the back, which sent her stumbling ahead. "Like mother, like daughter, eh, Brenna? Odin help us all if this is the new breed of women we are raising on our shores."

Brenna turned around to glare at her brother-in-law. "Oaf! And how would she have survived here if I had not taught her how? Give her the answer she awaits, Hugh."

He smiled at his niece. "Aye, your man fought well. He can have his peace."

"And you will all leave?"

"Not until we see you properly wed."

Kristen grinned, and then she burst into joyous laughter and threw herself into her uncle's mighty arms.

Chapter Forty-four

Royce was not so stiff and sore today, but he still did not think he was ready to crawl from his bed. He was improving after three days, but he had never felt so wretched in his life. For a while it had seemed as if every bone in his body had been broken. Some were, and Kristen had bound his chest tightly to set the cracked ribs.

But he did not need to leave his bed to know what was going on in his hall. It seemed as if everyone in Wyndhurst had traipsed through his chamber at one time or another. His people to see how he fared, Kristen's people to meet the man who would marry their fair flower of Norway.

Darrelle came the most, for she was in a state bordering on hysteria with so many Vikings in her hall. Alden was amused by it all. And Meghan, that amazing child, was awed and delighted with their visitors, and had even come to tell him excitedly that Kristen's uncle Hugh had promised to show her his Viking ship. The change wrought in his sister, thanks to Kristen, was truly a wonder. But then, the vixen had changed him, too.

He wondered sometimes if the fates hadn't corrected the err in taking his first love in a Viking raid, by sending him Kristen in another raid. She had certainly healed the emptiness he had lived with all these years. He rarely thought of Rhona anymore. When he tried to picture her in his mind, it was aqua eyes he saw, and flowing tawny hair. And Kristen loved him. After all he had put her through, she actually loved him. This would never cease to amaze him.

The only one who had not come to his chamber to see him was Kristen's father. Brenna had told him with a half smile that Garrick was not up to leaving his bed, either. That confession had made Royce's day, for he dearly hoped the older man was suffering just as much as he was. The man had wanted his blood, and Royce had spit mouthfuls of it. He could wait until doomsday before he had to come face to face with that merciless Viking again.

Doomsday arrived three days later, or so Royce felt. Kristen rushed in to warn him, only seconds beforehand, that her father was coming. Royce buried his head under his pillow. She giggled and swiped it away from him. And then Garrick Haardrad appeared in the doorway, filling it with his large frame.

He had seen the superb body in action, but this was the first opportunity Royce had to really look the man over. He did not look old enough to have a son only five or six years younger than Royce.

It did not sit well with Royce at all, knowing that he had been trounced soundly by a man nearly two score years his senior, and a merchant, a man who by rights should have grown soft with his advancing years. And worse, he was up and about first. Royce knew the power of his own strength. A man Garrick's age should have been bedridden for a fortnight at the very least.

Yet here he stood, straight and tall, with only a few remaining signs giving testimony to their battle: a scab on his lip, a bruise still on one cheek, a slight discoloration beneath one eye. Royce wished he could have seen the eye when it was at its blackest and still swollen. God's breath, he resented the Viking's ability to heal so quickly.

Garrick wore a sleeveless leather tunic with his long,

tight-fitted leggings. His soft-skinned boots were studded with gold and came to his knees. Golden links also trimmed the tunic. In fact, he was a walking fortune, with a gold buckle the size of a fist on his belt, gold with precious jewels winking from his fingers, a solid-gold medallion on his chest, and more gold clasped to his wrists.

Royce found to his consternation that he was intimidated, not by the wealth and strength that exuded from every inch of the man, but by Garrick's grim visage. This was Kristen's father. One word from him and Royce could lose her.

It might be true that the wedding feast had begun, flaunting tradition, before the wedding, and without the happy couple in attendance. In fact it began on the very day of the battle, because Hugh Haardrad had claimed they would have to sail for home before winter made the voyage too difficult, that they could not afford to wait until Royce recovered. So they began the celebrating before the fact, as Viking celebrations had to be long, drawn-out affairs or Kristen would not feel she had been properly wed. So Hugh claimed.

This had made Royce feel the matter was settled. And yet, looking at Kristen's father, he knew it was not. He still had to have this man's approval, and at the moment Garrick did not look as if he would give it.

The fact that Kristen was smiling softened the edges of Royce's rising panic. If she did not see anything amiss in her father's stern countenance, mayhap Royce was overreacting. After all, he did not know the man. It was possible he always looked so forbidding.

Brenna came up behind Garrick and pushed him gently into the room. She came around the side of the bed and sat down next to Kristen. She also had a stern look about her as her gray eyes traveled down Royce, stretched out stiffly in the bed.

"I realize you must enjoy my daughter's pampering, Royce, but enough is enough," Brenna told him with marked disapproval. "If my husband can manage to be up and about, so can you. I will see Kristen wed today."

Emerald eyes flew to the Viking to see if he would disclaim that statement. When he did not, Royce relaxed. In fact his earlier resentment toward the man returned.

He managed to sit up without flinching once. "'Twas no more than a courtesy, madam. I did not want to force your husband out of his bed to attend the wedding, before he was able."

"Royce!" Kristen gasped.

Brenna grinned, forming a retort that was cut short by her husband.

Garrick threw back his head and laughed. "Is that so, Saxon? If I had known that was your only excuse, I would not have let my wife coddle me for so long."

Now Brenna gasped, and Kristen giggled. "Such baldfaced lies, from the both of you. What do we do with them, Mother?"

"I do not know what you will do," Brenna retorted, "but if your father does not mind his tongue, he will find himself back in bed."

"We just left there, mistress," Garrick replied with a wolfish grin. "But if you wish to return . . ."

Kristen watched her mother blush and chided Garrick. "Father, please. Royce does not realize you tease. You shock him."

"If I do, then I must needs apologize for the beating I gave him. But I could have sworn I was told you shared his bed this whole summer long."

If Royce had not been shocked before, he was now. He noticed Kristen blushing and felt heat in his own cheeks. Garrick's humor was flown. The man had become too serious of a sudden. And now he knew from where Kristen got her mercurial changes in emotion.

"You tried your best to kill me for that," Royce reminded Garrick sharply. "If you still want to—"

"Do not be a fool," Garrick cut him short. "I could not kill you after Brenna told me how our daughter feels about you."

"You could have had Thorolf tell *me* that!" Kristen cried.

"So you could tell him?" Garrick shook his head. "Nay, Kris, it had to be the way it was, to satisfy everyone. But he deserved the beating."

Brenna sighed. "Your father forgets his own youth, love." She gave Garrick a meaningful look before she smiled at Kristen. "But then, he is unreasonable where you are concerned." Although she moved to stand by Garrick's side, taking his hand in hers, Brenna still addressed Kristen. "'Tis not so much that you were bedded, but that you were not wedded first. We both object to that, and so we will see the matter corrected."

Royce had yet to hear a confirmation from Kristen's father. He demanded it now. "Do I have your blessing, then?"

Brenna jabbed Garrick in the side when he did not answer immediately. "Aye!" he exploded.

Royce began to laugh, having seen the flinch of pain cross Garrick's features. But then he groaned, feeling his own, and it was Garrick's turn to laugh.

"At least I do not have to prove myself this eventide," Garrick could not resist saying. And for that he got a scowl that made him laugh the harder, which brought another jab in his ribs from his wife.

Brenna told her daughter, "His cousins have made all the arrangements, so I will take your father below if you will see Royce prepared." Then she pushed Garrick, who was still chuckling, out of the room.

Kristen closed the door after them, then turned with a half smile toward Royce. "They take getting used to," she offered.

He could see she was trying hard not to laugh. She had been bubbling with good humor ever since her parents had moved into the hall. Surrounded by her family and friends, she could not have been happier, and he was loath to spoil it by complaining about her father.

Hesitantly he asked, "You will miss them, when they sail?"

She smiled in earnest now, coming toward him. She moved between his legs, draping her arms loosely about his neck.

"Aye, but Father has promised to visit us. 'Tis not such a long voyage, to sail here for the summer."

Royce groaned inwardly. "I suppose 'twill not be often?" he asked hopefully.

"Mayhap every other summer."

He hid his cringe in her breast. And then the scent of her assailed him and he forgot about her parents.

His arms wrapped about her waist and he looked up at her, his chin resting in the deep V of her green velvet gown. She had worn her own clothes ever since he had admitted to her that he loved her. There had never been any mention of her previous status. She had simply shed the mantle of slavery as easily as she had worn it, making him realize that she had never really worn it at all.

The dark green of the gown added a darker hue to her eyes, making them more turquoise. A wealth of love and tenderness filled his own eyes.

"They have waited nigh a week for this wedding." His lips pressed forward against her skin before he added, "Dare we make them wait a while longer?"

"You jest, milord." Her palms cupped his cheeks, before she bent to run her tongue slowly, sensually over his lips. "Surely you are not suggesting . . ."

She giggled as he pulled her down onto his lap. "Aye, I jest, vixen. But you could change my mind."

"Can I?" Her hand on the back on his neck drew his lips back to hers. "Then mayhap I will, milord. Aye, mayhap . . ."